FIRST WE TAKE MANHATTAN

First We Take Manhattan

Colette Caddle

ISIS

LARGE PRINT

Oxford

First published in Great Britain 2014
by
Simon & Schuster UK Ltd.
A CBS COMPANY

Published in Large Print 2014 by ISIS Publishing Ltd.,
7 Centremead, Osney Mead, Oxford OX2 0ES
by arrangement with
Simon & Schuster UK Ltd.
A CBS COMPANY

CIP data is available for this title from the British Library

ISBN 978–1–4450–9900–2 (hb)
ISBN 978–1–4450–9901–9 (pb)

Printed and bound in Great Britain by
T. J. International Ltd., Padstow, Cornwall

Dedication

Producing a novel each year is a team effort and there are two lovely ladies who are always a part of my team.

Sheila Crowley is an agent extraordinaire, who is at the end of the phone whenever I need an ear or just want to shoot the breeze.

Suzanne Baboneau is the perfect editor with that rare talent of editing by osmosis! She makes me think and brings out the best in me in the gentlest possible way and each book is one hundred per cent better as a result of her input.

So, Sheila, Suzanne, this one is for you with my humble thanks. Next, we take Berlin!

Acknowledgements

This book required a little knowledge of the world of fashion and millinery and I knew nothing of either so I turned to Bríd O'Driscoll Millinery in Galway and spent a fascinating and fun-filled morning in her wonderful studio. Thank you for giving me your time and sharing your knowledge, Bríd. Watching you work and seeing my beautiful headpiece take shape before my eyes was a wonderful experience!

Thanks too to Gwen Owen and Tom Baldwin, who are always there to answer my legal queries, and to Sergeant Tara Sharpe for her advice on missing person cases. Any mistakes are entirely mine!

My profound gratitude, as always, to the people who get me through each year and each book:

Suzanne Baboneau, Clare Hey and all the team at Simon & Schuster; my agent, Sheila Crowley, and her very capable and obliging assistant, Rebecca Ritchie; Simon, Declan and Helen of Gill Hess, who do all the leg work in Ireland; the booksellers who, despite difficult times, are always unfailingly generous and supportive

And my thanks to you, friends, for picking up this book. I hope you enjoy it.

CHAPTER
ONE

Sinéad stared into the grey-green eyes of her dead sister and shivered. She'd watched the clip from *The Late Late Show* so many times, but she still drank in every detail. To the audience, Sheila had probably appeared cool and relaxed. They didn't know she'd thrown up before the interview and that her high-heeled foot bobbing up and down meant she was as nervous as hell.

Sinéad pressed pause and studied her own image. In the funky hippie dress she looked younger than her identical twin. Sheila oozed class and sophistication. Sinéad wore an elaborate hairband, her dark auburn hair free around her bare shoulders while Sheila's was gathered into a neat coil on one side of her neck and covered with a delicate web of netting that matched her dress. Their smiles, laughs and voices were identical, but, while Sinéad's eyes were wide and open, Sheila's were more reserved.

It had always been that way. Sinéad had lived life as if it were a roller coaster. It scared the hell out of her, but she couldn't resist the thrill. Her big sister — by nine minutes — hung back and observed and spent her life trying to stop Sinéad from rushing headlong into trouble. Most of the time she was successful, but when she wasn't she'd been there to pick up the pieces.

Sinéad choked up as she pressed play and the camera zoomed in on Sheila. She had planned on wearing a dreary black tunic that night, but Sinéad had talked her out of it. Black so close to the face didn't suit either of them: their hair was too dark and complexion too fair. The knee-length royal-blue dress she'd worn instead complemented the rich tones of her hair and creaminess of her skin. It was in no way revealing — that wasn't Sheila's style — yet it clung sexily to every single curve.

"You're stunning," Sinéad whispered to the TV screen.

"Cooee, only me!"

Sinéad groaned. Why had she ever given her neighbours a spare key? Ellen was in and out every day, wearing that anxious expression.

"So this is where you're hiding —" Ellen stopped when she saw what Sinéad was watching, put down the coffees and tried to prise the control from her hand. Sinéad clung on to it.

"You've watched this a hundred times," Ellen complained, flopping down on the sofa beside her.

Sinéad hushed her. This was the best bit. She turned up the volume as Sheila started to talk.

"This beautiful girl came into the shop just as we were closing and bought two hats and a headpiece, just like that!"

"And you didn't recognise her?" The presenter smiled.

2

Sheila pulled a face and blushed. "I'm embarrassed to say that I didn't."

The audience laughed appreciatively.

"Isn't it incredible?" Sinéad took up the story. "She's only the most famous actress around and the newspapers have been full of gossip about the filming of her new movie down in Wicklow."

"When you saw her on the red carpet wearing your . . . What are those things called again?" He frowned.

"We call them headpieces but they're also known as fascinators," Sheila told him with a smile.

The presenter pulled a face at the audience. "Sorry, I'm not really up on these things. But she did look stunning." An image of the actress, the delicate creation of silk and veiling on her shiny blonde bob, flashed up on the large screen behind him. "That must have been an incredible moment, Sinéad, seeing one of your designs on the head of a famous actress at the BAFTAs. Describe for me how you felt."

"I honestly can't, it was amazing, I was in shock. I couldn't believe it."

"And the best part was that she gave us a really great plug when she was interviewed. The phone hasn't stopped ringing since," Sheila chipped in.

"You must have had some celebration that night!"

Sheila laughed. "We were working flat out on a wedding order so we had pizza and sparkling wine in paper cups and then got back to work!"

Sinéad scrolled down the menu to the next recording and pressed play.

Ellen nudged her. "I brought coffee."

"Great. Thanks. Shouldn't you be working?" She fast-forwarded, wishing Ellen would just leave her to be miserable in peace.

"The search was called off today for the milliner, Sheila Healy, wife of independent politician and member of Dáil Éireann, Philip Healy, who disappeared eight days ago. Her car was found on the coast road in Sandycove. Her mother, Margaret Fields, died twenty years ago when swimming on the family holiday in Kilmucridge. Mr Healy thanked the Gardaí, the services and the volunteers for their efforts to trace his wife and said he is still hopeful that they will find her. He, Sinéad's father, Kieran Fields, brother, businessman Max Fields, and twin sister and business partner, Sinéad, are being comforted by friends."

Ellen wrenched the remote away from Sinéad and switched off the TV. "Enough! You've got to stop watching this stuff. It's been nearly a year."

"Only eight months," Sinéad snapped. "She disappeared on March the first."

"But she's gone, sweetie, and you're not."

Sinéad swallowed back the tears that were never far away. "I'm not sure I can go on without her."

"Course you can." Ellen rubbed her back as if she were a child. "You're not alone. You've got me and Rory and Max and Dylan and your dad."

"Yeah, right," Sinéad grunted. Dad had retreated into his own little world. Her brother meant well but he wasn't the sort that you ever had a heart-to-heart with. Dylan . . . She sighed. Well, her boyfriend had turned out to be a total asshole. He had been sympathetic for

4

the first couple of months after Sheila disappeared but he'd grown tired of her moping around and spent more time out wandering the hills and beaches with his bloody camera than he did with her.

"Yeah, well, you've got me and Rory, anyway, and your work. Throw yourself into that — it's what you love — and blot out everything else. Whenever Rory's worried about the business, I send him into the kitchen to bake, and within a few hours he's calmed down."

Sinéad pulled away and dragged her sleeve across her eyes. "Sheila was the brains of the business. I don't have a clue to be honest. When I try to sew, my fingers feel clumsy, as if I'm wearing rubber gloves. I can't even sketch —" She broke off as the familiar feeling of panic overwhelmed her, and she reached with shaking fingers for her coffee. Caffeine, alcohol and sleeping tablets were all that got her through lately. But, although they numbed the pain, she couldn't forget.

"You're trying to do too much too soon. You should hire someone to take care of all the paperwork and sales and concentrate on what you're good at: making hats. And leave the bloody shop to Karen to run. Where is she, anyway?"

Sinéad looked at her. "Downstairs . . . isn't she?"

"Nope. Did she come in this morning?"

"I'm not sure," Sinéad admitted. "I opened up and came back upstairs to work."

"She's a lazy cow. It's a good job you have to buzz to get in, isn't it? Call her. I'll keep an eye on the place till you're ready to come down. You might want to tidy

5

yourself," she added gently. "Slap on some makeup, sweetie, it'll make you feel better."

"Aren't you needed next door?" Sinéad said, thinking she'd much prefer to close up and crawl back into bed. Ellen and her husband Rory ran Café Crème and were good friends, salt of the earth, but sometimes she just wanted to be left alone.

"No, there'll be a lull until twelve, and it won't do Rory a bit of harm to manage without me for a while."

"You two aren't fighting again, are you?"

"He's just grumpy because I was out with the girls last night and got back a bit late."

Sinéad raised an eyebrow. "How late?"

"Around three." Ellen grinned.

"No wonder you're in the doghouse."

"It's not like I go out without him often," Ellen protested. "He should trust me. We've been together nine years now. Does he think I'm going to jump on the first man I meet?"

"If the shoe was on the other foot you wouldn't talk to him for a week," Sinéad retorted.

"Two," Ellen laughed. She was halfway out of the door but stopped to look back at Sinéad. "You know, spending your nights holed up here isn't going to help. You need to get some proper rest and you need Dylan. Let him mind you, Sinéad, I know he wants to."

Sinéad wasn't sure at all. Dylan had enjoyed being with her when she was fun but he wasn't as keen now he was faced with her other side. Ellen stood waiting for a response. "I just need a little time alone."

6

Ellen nodded in understanding and disappeared downstairs.

Sinéad forced herself up off the sofa and went into the adjoining room. In the past it had been a storeroom, but after a particularly bad blow-up with Dylan, Sinéad had unearthed an old fold-up bed and started to camp out here. Her clothes were tossed carelessly over the chair in the corner. She wrinkled her nose in disgust — the air was stale with the stench of wine and cigarettes. "You're turning into a pig, Fields," she muttered and pulled up the blind. She winced as sunlight flooded the room, making her head pound even harder. She threw open the window and gasped as the cold air hit her. She took a deep breath, hunted for her mobile and called Karen. All she got was the woman's voicemail. She left a clipped message and tossed the phone onto the bed.

Turning to the mirror, she saw only too clearly why Ellen had suggested makeup. Her skin was the colour of putty and there were enormous dark circles under her eyes, though she had no idea why, given that all she did was sleep these days. The wonderful little white tablets the doctor had prescribed brought total oblivion, which was infinitely preferable to reality. She patted on some moisturiser and foundation, mascara and a lick of red lipstick before tugging a brush through her thick hair. As long and wavy as Sheila's, it was currently black, too black for her colouring and so darker foundation was required. The look aged her. She stared into her eyes, frightened by what she saw there. How many people really looked into someone's eyes?

Really looked. They said more than words ever could. They couldn't lie. If anyone took the time to look properly, they would see a lonely frightened woman. I'm not waving, I'm drowning, she thought and shuddered at the sad irony.

It would be easier — at least she thought it would — if they talked about Sheila, but her brother and father never mentioned her, and if Sinéad did there was an awkward silence or Max would change the subject. It was driving her insane. They were behaving as if Sheila hadn't existed. Dad and Aunty Bridie had been the same when Mum had died, but at least back then she'd had Sheila to talk to.

Sinéad went back to the window and stared out to sea. She couldn't accept that Sheila was dead, or, if she was, that it had been suicide. This thought led her, as always, to wonder about Philip. Her supposedly devastated brother-in-law seemed to be getting on just fine.

"What do you expect?" Dylan had said, looking exasperated. Philip had popped up on the evening news complaining about a social-housing scheme the government had reneged on and she'd made a snide comment about how you would never think he was a widower. "Not everyone wears their heart on their sleeve. The man has a job to do and he's trying to do it. You could take a leaf out of his book."

His words had stung. How could he talk to her like that? How could he be so cruel and hard? Dylan didn't understand her, but then no one did. Sinéad didn't have the courage to leave him, but neither could she forgive him. And so she had taken refuge in the shop, either sleeping on the narrow bed or conking out in front of the TV after too much wine.

She heard Ellen moving around below and realised that she was keeping the woman from her own work. She turned back to the mirror, smoothed down her black dress and fastened a wide red belt around her waist. After tying her long hair back with a matching silk ribbon, she added large silver hoop earrings and hurried downstairs.

"Much better." Ellen beamed with approval when she saw her. "Now you look like a successful designer."

"Ha!"

"Did you call Karen?"

"I just got her voicemail."

"Get rid of her," Ellen said, heading for the door.

"How would I manage alone?" Sinéad retorted.

"Darling, there will be kids just out of college queuing up to work for you. Hell, they'd probably do it for nothing just so they could add your name to their CV. Get onto an agency and give that bitch the push."

"Maybe. I'll talk to Max about it."

"Good girl. I'd better go before I'm divorced."

"Thanks, Ellen."

"Any time, sweetheart."

Left alone, Sinéad half-heartedly tidied the shop, rearranged the window display and then, perching on the stool behind the counter, started to sew a trim onto a hat. Thanks to some painkillers and the coffee, her headache had settled down to a dull throbbing. The phone rang every so often, but she let the machine pick up the calls. They would mainly be queries or complaints and she just couldn't deal with that right now. She would check them later.

A group of excitable women arrived with wedding outfits looking for matching hats. Relieved by the distraction, although the high-pitched squeals weren't helping her headache, Sinéad abandoned her sewing to give them her full attention.

After she had spent hours with them, they left without placing an order, and Sinéad's feelings of doubt and insecurity escalated. She was tempted to pick up the phone and call Dylan. God, she missed him so much, and it had been days since they'd talked. But no. Feck it. He had been in the wrong. Why should she go crawling to him? He wasn't exactly being supportive. He wanted her to pull herself together and stop feeling sorry for herself. As if she should just take losing her twin sister in her stride.

And Dad was no better. She knew he was hurting, but why wouldn't he let her comfort him and comfort her in return? Why was he shutting her out? Sinéad felt the familiar taste of resentment in her mouth, the same resentment she'd felt when Aunty Bridie had moved in to look after them after Mum had died, and it felt as if he'd abandoned them. He was selfish then and he was being just as selfish now. At least Max kept in touch regularly, but, if she stopped phoning or dropping in to see her father, she doubted he'd notice.

There were only a couple of other customers that afternoon and Sinéad was just about to close up early when there was a rap on the door. She looked up to see her brother-in-law smiling in at her. Great, this was all she needed. Sinéad had always got on well with Philip, although she had been stunned when Sheila announced they were getting married. The couple behaved more like best mates than boyfriend and girlfriend. Still, she'd had to admit they seemed to make a great team. Sheila seemed content with Philip and he obviously adored her. Sinéad had thought he was going to fall apart when the search had been called off, but he'd coped quite well. Too well? That was the thought that constantly played on her mind. Something about him bothered her, but she couldn't figure out what that was.

As the weeks rolled into months she found it harder and harder to be around him. Right now, as she looked at him through the glass, she longed to scream at him to go away, but she didn't have the guts. She forced a smile to her lips, though it probably looked more like a grimace, and went to the door to let him in. "Hi, Philip, you just caught me. I'm on my way to a meeting."

"Oh, good. I'm glad I didn't miss you."

He embraced her and kissed her cheek, either oblivious to the hint or simply ignoring it. Bloody politicians. They were all the same. She steeled herself not to shudder or pull away. When he released her she went behind the counter to put some distance between them. He was looking as dapper as ever. The beautifully tailored taupe suit and shirt a shade darker were set off perfectly by the flamboyant silk tie. His brown brogues shone almost as much as his manicured nails and his hair was slicked forward to disguise his receding hairline. She had always assumed that Sheila was the

11

one who'd selected his wardrobe, but he seemed to be doing just fine on his own. Her doubt and suspicion bubbled up again and she dug her nails into her palms that itched to slap him.

"How's business?"

"Just fine," she lied.

"Great."

"You seem pretty busy these days, Philip. Every time I pick up the paper you're attending some opening or other." It sounded like an accusation, she knew, but she was past caring.

"Yes, it's all go," he said equably.

"Was there something in particular you wanted to see me about?" She glanced pointedly at her watch.

"Oh, yes, of course, sorry. It's about your birthday. I was thinking of booking a room in the Four Seasons, or would you prefer somewhere more low-key?"

She stared at him in horror. Their twenty-ninth birthday was at the end of November and he wanted to celebrate it? "A birthday party without Sheila?"

He flushed. "Well, no, not a party, of course not. It just feels wrong not to acknowledge it and it seems the perfect time to remember her and celebrate her life."

"Celebrate what? That it's over?" she retorted, making no attempt to hide her anger and contempt. "What's the problem, Philip? Are you down in the polls and in need of some good publicity? Going to invite along a couple of hacks and play the part of the grieving husband?"

Philip recoiled from the attack. "I don't have to play the part, Sinéad. I miss Sheila just as much as you do. Not a day goes by that I don't think of her."

He looked so sincere, Sinéad thought, so why didn't she trust him? Why did she feel he had something to hide? Sometimes it felt as if she was losing her mind. And, the way Dylan looked at her lately, it was obvious he thought so too.

She met Philip's eyes and was filled with doubt at the hurt that she saw there. "I'm sorry. I'm just having a bad day."

He accepted the apology with a brief nod. "I understand. I have days like that too, believe me."

"I suppose getting everyone together is a nice idea," she relented, "but you'd better clear it with Dad first."

Immediately Philip's expression relaxed. "I did talk to Kieran, but whether he heard me or not is another thing. You know what he's like. Max was there and he said to go ahead once you were happy about it."

Happy? Sinéad thought. Yeah, feckin' delirious. But she nodded and squeezed his arm. "Why not?"

He hugged her and she tried to relax in his embrace. Max and Dylan were right. This wasn't any easier on him. She should cut him some slack.

"Great, I'll be in touch. Enjoy your evening, Sinéad. Give Dylan my best."

"Will do," she said and stood in the doorway, watching him stride down the town nodding and greeting people, and immediately her doubts and suspicion returned. If only he knew the thoughts that raced round her head and the dreadful dreams she had. They all involved Sheila and death, and in each and every one her dear devoted husband was standing over her, smiling broadly.

CHAPTER
TWO

Max Fields sat in his family home in Monkstown and looked from his vacant father to his fidgeting sister. He was finding it hard to feel any sympathy for either of them any more. They were so bloody self-absorbed. Sinéad, who had always been the more emotional twin, had become more moody and hypersensitive than ever — he wondered if she was on something. His father was even harder to fathom. He had never been a "hands-on" Dad. Sure, he loved and was proud of them but always from a distance. It had been hard on the girls. They'd seemed to need that attention, whereas he'd always been quite happy in his own company and that hadn't changed.

Despite having dated some gorgeous women, Max felt no inclination to settle down. A few hours in the company of any of them and he was ready for some space. He was obviously a chip off the old block. Dad had been without a long-term partner since Mum had died almost twenty years ago and seemed perfectly content. But Sheila's death had turned him into a shell of his former self and Max couldn't understand why. Sheila had been his pet, presumably, because she was very like their mother.

"It's like he's lost his wife again," Max's latest girlfriend, Natalie, had told him with a wise nod. "Sheila's been the key maternal figure in your lives."

"No, my aunt was," he'd replied.

"But you said that none of you were that close to her."

And it was true. Bridie had been a steady, reliable figure in their lives but there had been no cuddles, and he couldn't remember any of them ever confiding in her. He'd come to believe that she had moved in to look after them out of a sense of family duty. And then, poor woman, when they no longer needed her, dementia had set in and robbed her of her freedom for a second time.

"Well, there you are, then. Sheila was the surrogate mother. Oh, and she drowned, too!"

"We don't know that," he'd said automatically, though he did think that his sister had killed herself.

A few times after she'd been drinking, Sinéad had suggested foul play and even said Philip might have murdered her. It was laughable. Max worried about his sister and her business. She was an easy target in her vulnerable condition. Sheila had protected and pampered her twin far too much. He'd like to see Sinéad finally stand on her own two feet.

Max had considered talking to Dylan about it, but quickly dismissed the idea. What was the point? The man seemed fed up with the whole situation and it probably wouldn't be long before he left for pastures new. Fresh fields. Max snorted at his own joke. God, he wouldn't mind escaping himself sometimes, so who could blame Dylan? Granted, Sinéad was gorgeous but she was definitely high-maintenance at the moment.

Max wasn't equipped to deal with it. His was a world of figures and spreadsheets. You knew where you were with numbers: they were so much more reliable than people. It was a pity Aunty Bridie was in a home for the bewildered. She'd have been the perfect woman to get Sinéad back on the straight and narrow. She wouldn't tolerate this self-obsessive rubbish from either her brother-in-law or her niece.

Just as Sheila and Sinéad had completely different personalities, Bridie was nothing like his mother. While Maggie had lost herself in her needlework and had seen herself as a free spirit, Bridie had been a pragmatic woman with her feet firmly on the ground. It was hard to see someone so intelligent slip into dementia. Not that he did. Dad and Sinéad visited occasionally but Sheila had been the dutiful one who'd accompanied her on her doctor and hospital visits. She'd been the one to arrange the home help and, when it was clear that Bridie could no longer be left alone, organise the admission to the nursing home. It was Sheila who had arranged the house sale and dealt with the solicitors and it was Sheila who had continued to visit Bridie in the nursing home and take her out occasionally, for a treat. She had insisted on bringing her home for the day last Christmas, though no one else had been all that keen on the idea. But Sheila had bullied them into submission. They always spent holidays together. It was the Fields tradition and one that Bridie had kept going. They owed it to her, Sheila had argued. It was the least they could do. It had been a difficult day. Philip had been full of bonhomie and Sheila had cooked up a storm, but they were all in shock at how much Bridie had deteriorated. They had always gathered at Sheila's on these occasions and, now Christmas was looming, he wondered what would happen.

His eyes drifted back to his father slumped in the chair. The temptation to book a flight on Christmas Eve was immense. He could go somewhere hot with Natalie and lose himself in her body and drink himself into oblivion, but how could he desert them? He resigned himself to the fact that they would all have to be miserable together.

"Do you think Philip will still have us all for Christmas?" he asked.

His father gave him a blank stare while Sinéad's eyes flashed angrily. "How can you even think about celebrating Christmas without Sheila?"

He shrugged. "Just wondering what will happen. We can't leave the man to face it alone, and what about Bridie?"

"As if Philip would ever be alone," his sister said, her voice bitter.

"Oh, give it a rest, Sinéad," Max said, weary of her insinuations. How she could think Philip would have had anything to do with their sister's death was beyond him. They had been a very close couple. Philip had always been proud of Sheila and her achievements. And, quite apart from being a successful entrepreneur, she'd been an excellent hostess. The guy must feel lost without her. The job was probably the only thing keeping him going.

He looked over at his father. "What do you think, Dad?"

"About what?"

"Christmas."

"It won't be the same, will it? Not without Sheila."

"No, of course it won't." Max struggled to keep his patience. "But shouldn't we spend it together the way we always do?"

"I suppose."

"Then we should just have a quiet day here," Sinéad insisted.

Max glared at her. "Fine, let's do that but *with* Philip."

She shrugged. "I'm sure he'll have other plans."

"Dad?"

"Whatever you think. I need to sleep." He stood up and shuffled towards the door.

Max glanced at his watch. It wasn't even eight o'clock, but this was the norm now. Dad spent most of his time either in bed or walking.

Sinéad hurried after him and kissed his cheek. "Will I bring you up a cup of tea, Dad?"

"No, love, I'm grand." He patted her hand. "You get on home."

Max stood up. "I'll give you a lift."

"Are you sure, Dad? I can stay if you want."

Max sighed at the almost desperate note in Sinéad's voice. He put an arm around her shoulders and gave her a gentle squeeze as their father waved away the offer. "Come on, Sinéad. Let him rest."

Outside, Sinéad hesitated by the car door. "You know, I think I'll head into the shop for a while. There's some work I'd like to finish off."

"At this hour?"

"Yeah, well, it's easier to work when there are no interruptions."

"Hop in, I'll drop you down."

"It's only a ten-minute walk."

"I need to take a look at the books, so now is as good a time as any."

"Oh, not tonight, Max," she groaned.

"Don't worry, I'll take them home with me and leave you to create." He grinned, happy that she was at least working. In the early days he'd had serious doubts that the business would survive without Sheila at the helm. Sinéad had no understanding of how to balance the books and showed no interest in learning. "I think you need to hire someone to help you out," he said as he reversed out of the driveway.

"Ellen said the same. She thinks I should get rid of Karen."

"What do *you* think?" he asked, feeling exasperated. Though he agreed with Ellen, he wished his sister would start thinking for herself.

"I could do with help, but where am I going to find a good designer who's also willing to serve in the shop and be capable of doing the books?" She sighed. "We're looking for another Sheila."

"Or a couple of people."

She turned to look at him. "We couldn't afford that, could we?"

"Part-time, possibly. I'll tell you after I look at the figures. You just concentrate on doing what you do best," he said as he pulled into a parking spot near the shop.

After he'd collected the folder that Sinéad had stuffed her paperwork into and said goodnight, Max stopped off on his way home to his apartment in Donnybrook to pick up a curry. He ate it in front of the TV. Channel hopping but finding nothing that interested him, he decided to get stuck into Sinéad's accounts. He figured she could probably afford to hire a part-time secretary and that would leave her free to devote her time and effort to her designs.

It was a pity Dad hadn't something to distract him. Giving up his job in the council had been a huge mistake. It would have given some purpose to his day and forced him to talk to people. He needed something to pull him out of this stupor. Yes, life sucked sometimes, but you just had to deal with it and move on.

He contemplated having another beer before getting down to work, but decided to put on a pot of coffee instead. With a bit of luck he could get through it all tonight and he would be able to spend Sunday in bed with Naughty Natalie enjoying every inch of that glorious body.

It was almost midnight, papers were scattered across the opaque glass dining-room table and he was pacing the room, a tumbler of whiskey in his hand, which was shaking from a mixture of panic and anger. How could she have been so fucking stupid? After all Sheila's hard work, after they had finally found success, Sinéad was letting it all slip away. He was filled with a sense of impotent rage and had a sudden flashback to an argument between his mother and father.

Max had been tucking into his boiled egg and soldiers when the kitchen door had flown open and Dad had stormed in, shouting at his mother. It was years later that Sheila had told him the whole story. The electricity had been cut off and Dad had discovered, that instead of paying the weekly instalment into the account at the post office, Maggie had been spending the money on material and wool. He was furious. Max had sat in terrified shock until Sheila rescued him from his high chair and hurried him and Sinéad upstairs. The three of them had huddled together and listened as their parents rowed and then a door banged and there was silence. Mother had carried on as if nothing had happened, but, for days after, silence descended on the household once Dad got in from work.

For the first time, Max could understand exactly how his father had felt. If he hadn't had a couple of drinks he would be tempted to jump in the car and drive straight over to Mount Merrion and let Sinéad have it. He could phone but perhaps he should calm down a bit. Sinéad was so damn fragile at the moment. Who knew how she'd react? He was pouring himself another drink when the intercom buzzed.

"Hello?"

"Room service."

He smiled at the giggly voice of his girlfriend and pressed the button to admit her before going to meet her.

"Surprise!" She smiled at him when the lift door opened.

"I thought you were on a night out with the girls," he said, pulling her inside and kissing her.

"I was nearby and I thought I'd come by and tuck you in."

Max felt his anger abate as she stepped back and began to unbutton her shirt, her eyes teasing. She was just the right side of tipsy to be randy as hell and he felt his body react as she let the shirt slip from her shoulders and pulled him close, kissing him hungrily. Her body melted into his as her tongue invaded his mouth.

"Come to bed, darling." She smiled up at him. "Your Natalie is in a very, very, naughty mood."

He groaned at the desire in her eyes and the beautiful, full breasts barely covered by the peach gauzy bra, and kissed her gently. "Sorry, sweetheart, I have some stuff I really need to do."

"You know, they say that you're much more productive if you take breaks," she said, rubbing her body against his. "And I bet one of my special massages would help you concentrate better."

He grinned as her hands moved to open his belt. "How special?"

Her eyes twinkled and she licked her lips. "Very," she promised and led him towards the bedroom.

*   *   *

After closing the door gently on his sleeping girlfriend, Max went to get some coffee before returning to his sister's accounts. Natalie had calmed him and he was able to think of Sinéad as just another client — a very dumb one. Tomorrow he would pay his sister a visit. He only hoped he'd be able to control his temper and not throttle her.

CHAPTER
THREE

It was lunchtime before Max arrived at his sister's apartment. Dylan opened the door, obviously not long out of bed.

"Sorry for dropping in unannounced but I really need to talk to Sinéad."

Dylan looked surprised, puzzled even. "She's not here."

"Damn. Will she be long, do you think? This is important." He wanted to talk to her today. He wanted to have his facts completely straight so he could take immediate action in the morning.

"Max, she's not coming back, at least, not today."

"What? But where is she?"

"Camping out at the shop. She sneaks back here every so often to shower and change when she knows I'll be out."

"But why? What's going on?" Max started and then held up a hand. "Sorry, none of my business."

"It's okay. Coffee?"

"Please." Max dropped his computer bag at his feet and slid onto a stool.

"I got fed up of her living like a hermit and pointed out that Sheila was the one who'd died. Sorry."

"Hey, I've been saying the same thing." Max sighed. Was there any hope at all for his sister? She seemed completely unreachable. "I know Sheila's death probably hit her harder because they were twins, but the way things are going she may as well hop into the grave after her."

"If only there *was* a grave," Dylan groaned. "Shit, you know what I mean."

Max grinned. "Yes, I know what you mean."

Dylan handed him a mug. "She's either clinging to the idea that Sheila's still alive or, if she's dead, she seems convinced Philip murdered her."

"Yeah, poor Philip," Max said. "I suppose she needs to blame someone."

"What do you think happened?" Dylan asked.

"To Sheila? I'm not sure. Perhaps it was just an accident, perhaps not. She's always been the strong one of the family and spent all her time worrying about us, looking after us." He thought how he had always taken Sheila's dependability for granted. Throughout school and university, she was always there to help or just listen. Had he ever listened to her? He looked at Dylan and shrugged. "Maybe she needed looking after too and we just never noticed."

"Surely Philip would have known if anything was troubling her."

"He's a nice guy, Dylan, but let's face it: he's a politician and the most important person in his own life. I'm not sure he'd have noticed and Sheila never complained or moaned; she just wasn't the type."

"Do you think she was happy with him?"

"Who knows?" Max finished his coffee and glanced at his watch. "I'd better go out to the shop and talk to her."

"Can I ask why you need to see her so urgently?"

Max met his eyes and was glad to see the concern there. Dylan was a good bloke. He hoped he would stick around. Sinéad needed a strong dependable man in her life. "She's running the business into the ground."

Dylan looked stunned. "But how can that be? Even before we had the row she spent more time there than she did here."

"Maybe, but she certainly hasn't been working. I've found letter after letter complaining that orders were late and several just cancelling. She'd be out of business already if it weren't for the goodwill as a result of Sheila's death and the fact that, though she hasn't been designing, she's continued to make some hats based on old designs. Unfortunately, she seems obsessed with making Sheila's, and they were never the big earners. Sheila's strengths were in running the business. Sinéad was the creative one." Max walked to the door and Dylan followed him.

"Perhaps I should come with you."

Max thought about it for a second and then shook his head. "No, I need her full attention. I have to make her see that she's in serious shit. Why don't you drop over and check on her later, though, just to make sure that she's okay?"

"Sure."

* * *

Sinéad was sitting on the sofa staring into space when her mobile rang. She reached for it and her eyes filled up when she saw it was Dylan. She clutched it to her ear. "Hi."

"I'm outside the shop, Sinéad. Are you in there?"

"Yes, sorry, I'll buzz you in." She hung up, went to press the button and then sat back down, hugging her arms around her chest self-consciously. She must look a right mess. She heard Dylan come up the stairs and gave him a wary smile when he appeared in the doorway. "Hi."

"Hi." She shifted uncomfortably as his eyes wandered from her pyjamas to the cold mug of tea and piece of half-eaten toast sitting on the table in front of her. He crossed to the other side of the room and perched on a small stool, and she cringed as he sniffed the air and wrinkled his nose.

"You're smoking?"

"What if I am?" she retorted, feeling defensive.

He shrugged. "You talked to Max?"

So he knew. Max had told him. In a way it was a relief. No more pretence. "He did most of the talking," she said, trying to smile.

"He's looking out for you."

"I know that," Sinéad said. Though Max was furious with her but he had been very businesslike and not given her the earful that she deserved.

"So, what's the plan?" he asked, clapping his hands together and looking at her expectantly.

Sinéad nodded towards the file on the table. "Help yourself." She watched as he leafed through it and then paused on the final page, a summary of Max's proposals to save the business. It all revolved around the premise that Sinéad needed to get out and sell both the product and herself. He also wanted to engage a PR firm on a short-term contract to arrange some interviews where she would talk about her struggle to carry on without Sheila. The final proposal was the one that had shocked her, and she could see it surprised him, too.

Dylan looked up. "He wants to close the shop?"

"Yes. He says it'll cut our overheads and leave me free to concentrate on the design and sales. It would also mean I could hire another milliner, which would speed up productivity, and if business improved then I could take on an administration assistant part-time."

"Sounds reasonable."

"Yes. It's all fine except for the PR bit. I'm really not sure I could pull that off, Dylan. I'm a mess. How can I go on the TV or radio and talk about Sheila?"

"You'll be fine."

"If you tell me one more time to pull myself together —" she started.

"I'm not saying that." He came to join her on the sofa and took her hands in his. "I'm sorry if you feel I've been tough on you, but it's been hard watching you so miserable and to feel so helpless. Nothing I do or say seems right. When you left I thought you were throwing yourself into designing and I was happy to leave you to it. I could relate to that. When I've a camera in my hands I can forget everything, and life seems more manageable. I thought that working round the clock would help you through this, but Max tells me you haven't been working at all."

"I was, well, a little, But —" she felt a catch in her throat — "I just can't seem to design any more. The well's dried up." She looked up at him. "I'm scared, Dylan."

He cupped her face in his hands and ran his thumbs under her eyes, catching the drops. "No, sweetheart, it hasn't. This is a temporary glitch and it's completely understandable. You are so talented and you could be a huge success."

"I don't care about success," she protested.

"No, but Sheila did. She put her heart and soul into this business. So why not do it for her, in memory of her?"

Sinéad stared at him and felt a flicker of guilt at his words.

"What if she's not dead?" he continued. "Say she hit her head and lost her memory and one day she comes rushing home to find that you've gone bust. How do you think she would feel?"

"She'd kill me," Sinéad said, laughing and crying at the same time. "She'd be furious."

He smiled into her eyes. "So, let's pretend that's the way things are, Sinéad. If she's coming home someday let her come home to something that she can be proud of."

She searched his dark eyes. "Do you think she killed herself?"

"She didn't strike me as someone ready to give up on life, not at all."

She threw her arms around his neck. "Thank you."

He held her tight and then pulled back and looked into her eyes. "But after all this time it seems unlikely she's still alive."

Her momentary happiness dissipated. "Which means that she either had an accident or . . . someone killed her."

Dylan gave a weary sigh. "You mean Philip? Why on earth would he want to?"

"What if she'd found out something about him that would ruin his career? That he was taking bribes, on drugs, having an affair, oh, I don't know." She shook her head, feeling frustrated. "Something."

"Look, Sinéad, we've been through this. You talked to the detectives. There's no evidence of foul play and there are a dozen people who can guarantee Philip was in Brussels when Sheila disappeared. She never touched her bank accounts and she didn't have her passport. The police chased up every possible lead. She's gone, sweetheart. I'm sorry but she's gone." He gripped her hands and stared into her eyes. "It's lousy, Sinéad, really lousy, and I know how much you miss her, but you can carry on. You are so much stronger than you realise, and talented, clever and beautiful. You can make a go of this."

"Do you really think so, Dylan?" She raised her eyes to meet his.

"I do, but guess what."

"What?"

"If you don't want to, that's okay, too. You're a designer, not a businesswoman. If you can't handle being weighed down by all of that bureaucratic nonsense, then pack in the business and go work for someone else."

She stared at him, taken aback at the suggestion. "You think I should close the business?"

He smiled and shook his head. "No, I'm saying that you are the boss and you can do what you want, and I will support you, whatever you decide. There's only one condition."

"What's that?"

"You have to come home."

She looked around the grim, untidy room. "And drag myself away from all this?"

"I realise it's a tough call." He smirked.

She closed her eyes tight as he enveloped her in a hug and clung to him for dear life.

Gently he disentangled her. "Get dressed, sweetheart, and let's get the hell out of here."

As they emerged onto the street, Ellen was just pulling down the shutters of the café. She smiled broadly when she saw them. "Well, about bloody time that you two got yourselves sorted out. Howaya, Dylan?"

"Fine, thanks, Ellen."

He bent to hug her and she winked at Sinéad over his shoulder. "Got time for a coffee? There's some apple-and-rhubarb crumble left."

"Sounds good," Dylan said.

Sinéad reluctantly followed them inside. She was still trying to take in her brother's proposals but she wasn't

31

ready to share with her friends the news that she was closing the shop just yet.

Rory looked up and smiled when he saw them. "Hello, Sinéad, darling. Who's this, then? Introduce me."

Dylan rolled his eyes. "It hasn't been that long."

"It's been too long," Rory retorted. "Still, nice to see you two lovebirds together again."

"Cappuccino, Americano, and two crumbles?" Ellen asked as they sat down.

"Just the coffee for me," Sinéad said. "I don't fancy cake."

"Then I'll make you a wrap."

"There's no need," she protested.

"There's every need. There's more flesh on a greyhound," Ellen retorted, and hurried back to the counter.

Dylan chuckled. "She's like a mother hen the way she fusses over you."

"Yeah. I'm going to miss her so much; Rory, too." Sinéad hadn't always appreciated their attentions in the last few months, but the thought of not seeing them every day made her sad.

"You don't necessarily have to leave Blackrock," Dylan pointed out. "Will you get it into your head. You're the boss. Yes, Max will advise you on the financial stuff and what cuts you should make, but that's all it is, advice. You. Are. The. Boss."

She stared at him in silence for a moment. He was right. She felt a flutter of excitement and panic inside her. "What if I'm not up to it?" she whispered.

He gave a casual shrug. "As I said, you close the business and go work for someone else. Somehow I don't think it would take you too long to pick up a job. It's your decision, sweetheart. It's all up to you."

Rory arrived with their coffees and food. "Now, folks. Enjoy."

"Thanks, Rory," Dylan said.

"I can do anything I want," she murmured, her eyes returning to meet his.

"You can," he agreed, tucking into the delicious buttery concoction.

"I don't have to leave Blackrock at all."

He shrugged. "Maybe not, though there are probably cheaper places to rent space. Remember, once you don't have the shop to worry about the location doesn't matter."

"No, I just need a decent-sized space with good light." She started to smile as an idea began to take hold. It was the perfect solution.

"That's all," he agreed. "Eat your food. Ellen's right: you're far too skinny."

Sinéad picked up the wrap and took a large bite. God, it was delicious, and she was starving.

"That's more like it. I miss those curves." Dylan's eyes twinkled at her.

She finished her wrap and eyed the last of his crumble. "That looks really good."

"It is." He grinned and called to Ellen to bring another portion.

CHAPTER
FOUR

Krystie dawdled along Fifth Avenue studying the window displays with a critical eye. It was one of her favourite pastimes, looking at clothes and figuring out what change she'd make to turn a piece of clothing into something that wouldn't look out of place on the world's most famous catwalks. But, every so often, she came across something that made her gasp because it was just so incredibly perfect. She would stand and study it until she figured out what it was that made it special, then she would jot it down in the precious ideas notebook she carried everywhere. Her cell phone rang — ha, she even thought like a Yank now — and she rummaged in her bag. "Hi, Sandy, what's up?"

"What's up is you're late and the boss is going to bust a blood vessel if you don't get your ass back here."

"Ah, now, don't get my hopes up."

"I'm not kidding, Krystie, she's, like, seriously pissed at you."

"I'll be there in five." Krystie tossed the phone back into her bag along with the notebook and hurried through the crowds to the laneway off 37th Street and the building where she had worked for a year. It wasn't the sort of place she'd expected to end up when she came to Manhattan convinced she'd become rich and famous overnight, but then nothing had feckin' turned out quite as she'd expected since she left Ireland.

Sew Splendid was a small business that specialised in altering gowns and suits, but the only splendid part of it was the reception area with its fancy fitting rooms. Behind the curtain the workshop was drab and basic with two rows of tables and eight sewing machines at which she and seven other drones worked. There was no air-conditioning and the heating was unreliable, so in summer they sweltered and in winter usually sewed muffled under layers of clothing and wearing fingerless gloves.

Climbing the stairs to the fourth floor — the elevator was reserved for customers — meant Krystie arrived back to work red-faced and breathless. On the plus side, it meant it would probably be an hour or so before her teeth started to chatter again.

Sandy's dark eyes peeked out from the scarf wound round her face and neck. "Get your head down — she's out for blood."

Krystie slid in behind her machine and got to work on the hem of the second petticoat of the dress that looked more like a panto dame's costume than a wedding gown. She shot a quick glance towards the office where Phyllis Miller was pacing and yelling down the phone at someone. "What's up with her this time?"

"She lost the Levi order."

Krystie stared at her in dismay. "No way!"

"Way," Sandy assured her, looking grim.

Krystie thought of the eight morning suits, seven bridesmaids' dresses and the outfits for the four flower girls, not to mention the bride's and groom's mothers, and groaned. "Ah, crap, that's not good."

"Tell me about it. She'll cut our pay or our hours for sure this time."

Phyllis had been threatening pay cuts since the day Krystie had started work here, but it was all talk. Despite the fact the woman constantly moaned and complained about how tough it was to make money, business was steady and Krystie had felt pretty secure. But losing the Levi order was a serious blow.

"Kelliher, get your butt in here!"

They all jumped at the bawl and Krystie was conscious of everyone's eyes on her as she made her way slowly towards the office. Phyllis had gone behind the desk and was flicking through a file, not a good sign.

"Sorry I was a bit late back from lunch, Phyllis, but I'll work late —"

"That dress was supposed to be finished by two. Mrs Waldron will be in to pick it up in an hour."

"Shit."

The other woman glared at her over the rim of her specs. "Exactly, and you're in it."

"Phyllis —"

"No more excuses, Krystie, I've heard 'em all and I'm sick of it. You're my best tailor, but you spend more time daydreaming than you do working."

Krystie gaped at Phyllis. The fact that she wasn't shouting and had even paid her a compliment — sort of — was worrying. "What are you saying?"

"Sorry, kid, but I've got to let you go."

"But you can't! If you're letting anyone go it should be Jenny," she said, ignoring the guilt of betraying a mate. She needed this job. "Last one in, first one out, apart from the fact that she can't sew half as fast as me."

"At least she's here when she's supposed to be and can keep her mind on the job instead of having her head in the clouds," her boss retorted.

"Aw, come on, Phyllis, I know you lost the Levi order and I'm sorry, that's tough. But, cheer up, there will be lots of other weddings." She tried a playful grin. "You need me, Phyllis. Like you said, I'm the best. Where are you going to find someone half as good?"

"Already have," Phyllis said, writing a cheque, "and hopefully she'll be a bit more dependable than you."

Krystie felt queasy as she realised she may not be able to talk her way out of trouble this time. "You're kidding, I know that. I'm sorry, Phyllis. I promise I will be employee of the year from now on."

"You're fired, Kelliher." Phyllis put the cheque in an envelope and tossed it across the desk. "Your papers are in there along with a letter of recommendation — not that you deserve it."

"You want me to go now, this minute?" Krystie stared at her.

For the first time Phyllis's expression softened. "Look, kid, we both know you don't belong here. Get out there and do what you really want to do. You have the talent. You just need a break and you're not going to find it working for an alterations company. Trust me. One day you'll thank me for this."

The others watched in shocked silence as Krystie packed up her few meagre bits and pieces, pulled her hat on over her dark curly hair and raised a small smile for a tearful Sandy. "See you at home," she said and, slinging her bag across her shoulder, she tramped down the four flights for the last time.

Wandering the streets in the general direction of the apartment she shared with Sandy and two other girls, she grew even more miserable as she realised that she would have to move out. It was a struggle each month to make the rent and they couldn't afford to carry her. She found herself outside Saks and stared longingly in the window at a bolero that cost more than she earned in a week — *had* earned, she corrected herself. It was a good design, intricate, yet simple, but in her heart she knew she could do better. If only someone would give her a chance.

She had left Dublin so full of hope seven years ago, convinced that she could make it really big in the fashion industry, but she'd been kidding herself. Not that she intended to give up on her dream, no way. She'd just been thrown off course a bit. Maybe coming to New York hadn't been her smartest idea. She probably should be grateful to Phyllis. She'd got too settled and lazy in Sew Splendid and it was a dead-end job. She had to stay positive and look on this as an opportunity to get back on track. But how? She needed to think outside the box, as Sandy would say. She went into a coffee shop and ordered a small hot chocolate —

not that she should be spending money on such little luxuries, but she needed cheering up. After taking a sip, she tugged off her gloves, unwound her scarf and pulled out the reference Phyllis had given her. She felt a little tearful as she read. It was more than generous and not at all what she would have expected from the tough broad from Brooklyn: "Krystie is an excellent seamstress and has an eye for style and a natural flair for design. She would be an asset to any fashion house. I wish her well."

She refolded it carefully and put it back in the envelope. The cheque she would lodge after she'd finished her drink. Not that it would last long now she was unemployed — again. On her visits home, she'd always made her jobs sound a lot more important than they were; well, she had her pride and was damned if she'd admit to her family that she was a failure. But, while they all accepted whatever she said, her nasty little sister would wait until the entire extended Kelliher clan was assembled before asking pointed, direct questions. Was she operating alone? Did she have her own line now? Who stocked her clothes? Bloomingdale's? Saks? Wal-Mart? Of course, the snide comments would always be accompanied by a laugh, and everyone would treat it as a joke, but as time went on Krystie found it harder to laugh, and she started to find excuses not to travel back to Dublin. The thought that she might have to go home for good was very depressing.

Of course her ma and da would be thrilled. They'd gone mad when she'd told them her plans. Had she lost her reason? How could she up and go to a strange country where she knew no one and had no job waiting for her? But Krystie was determined. She'd read the fashion magazines. She knew that New York was the place to be, and she'd been planning her escape for months.

"I do know people and I do have a job and a visa," she'd told them triumphantly. Her best friend Jenny had emigrated with her family last year and her dad had agreed to employ Krystie so that she would be able to get a visa. They were also going to let her stay with them until she found her feet.

"You'll be back with your tail between your legs in a few months," her dad predicted, while Mum just cried.

"Be happy for me, Ma," Krystie begged her. Her mother's sadness was making her feel guilty as hell.

"I am, love, but you know that I'll worry myself sick about you."

She laughed. "I'm a big girl, Ma, I can look after myself."

"But what if you get sick?" her mother said.

"It's been two years since I had a fit," Krystie reminded her, "and they have doctors and chemists in America."

She had completely dismissed her mother's worries, but it was the one area she hadn't thought through properly. Living at home in Ireland, she'd never had to think of the cost of medical care, but it was a whole different matter in New York when you had a condition like epilepsy and no health insurance. She had had only a couple of seizures but they had been costly ones.

"So, Krystie, baby, think outside the box," she muttered now, staring out at the people purposefully striding past the window all with someplace to go. Why the hell didn't she have some rich maiden aunt somewhere who would kick the bucket and leave her enough cash to open her own little shop? Why didn't she know anyone with contacts in the business who could get her in the door of one of the design houses? But she didn't, and, despite Phyllis's opinion and kind words, Krystie admitted to herself that there wasn't a hope in hell of her making a name for herself as a famous fashion designer in Manhattan. She thought of her paltry savings and the money she owed Sandy for her meds and she knew it was time to leave.

"No way!" Sandy screeched, looking fierce — well as fierce as it was possible for her short, skinny friend to look. "You're not going home," she said, taking a beer from the fridge.

Krystie gave her a sad smile. "It's not like I want to go but I've no choice, Sandy."

"Are you shittin' me? You got plenty of choices, girl. Hell, you haven't even checked out the vacancies and you're buying your plane ticket?"

"I've lost my job, I can't pay my rent and I've no health insurance. Tell me, Sandy, exactly what are my options?" Krystie helped herself to a beer. She didn't really drink much but she needed something to numb the pain. She was barely holding it together and Sandy wasn't helping. As if she wanted to leave.

"We'll talk to Laura and Jess. Maybe they could get you some work at the bar." Sandy was not ready to accept defeat.

Waitressing was all very well for their flatmates, two young girls working their way through college. But a twenty-seven-year-old graduate scraping a living working in a bar was not how Krystie saw her life panning out. There had to be some way of digging herself out of this hole, but she didn't see how she could do it and stay in New York. Perhaps if she went home she could save face by telling the family that she was on a sabbatical. Everyone knew that creative types often needed a change of scene when they were looking for inspiration. She brightened at the thought. If she was "on holiday" at her folks' she would be able to live very cheaply and, on the quiet, check out the job market. She put down her beer and smiled at her friend. "Good idea. It'll pay for my ticket. I'm going home, Sandy, but with a bit of luck I'll be back before you've even had a chance to notice I'm gone."

Sandy's sigh was resigned. "I'll keep your room for you."

"No way, hon. Rent it out. You need the cash."

"What will you do in Dublin?" Sandy asked.

Krystie swallowed back her tears and smiled. "Start over."

She felt better once the decision was made. She checked all the flights to Dublin and finally found a relatively cheap one that would mean she'd be home in a couple of weeks. Laura had indeed got her a job at the bar in the evenings and she'd done pretty well on tips so far. With most of her things packed, Krystie spent her last few days walking the streets of Manhattan, drinking in the noise and the smells, and wallowing in the atmosphere. She survived on coffee and bagels in the cheapest coffee shops, sitting in the warmth and sketching. She didn't know what it was about this city that she loved so much and why it felt like she belonged here, but it did, and she was heartbroken to be leaving. It was as if she was admitting defeat and giving up on her dreams. Had she been kidding herself? Was it really her destiny to spend the rest of her life behind a sewing machine, taking up hems and letting out waistlines? Was she going to end up like the rest of her family, working to live as opposed to living to work? The thought really depressed her. So many people like her had started out with nothing and now their designs were showcased in the windows of these fancy posh shops. Why not her?

With a heavy heart she turned away from a particularly stunning display of colourful, chic berets in her favourite millinery to see another woman gazing in the window with the same intensity. I'm not the only one with dreams, she thought with a sigh. Krystie stared in surprise when the woman turned. She'd guessed the lady to be in her forties, given the drab clothes and sensible shoes, but her face was young, her skin smooth and pale and the blonde strands that escaped her bobble hat framed startling grey eyes and high cheekbones. Krystie smiled at her in solidarity but, looking slightly alarmed, the woman turned away and disappeared into the crowds. Krystie chuckled. She'd forgotten that you didn't look at strangers in this city, let alone smile at them.

That was one huge difference between New York and Dublin. Back home it was commonplace to chat to someone while waiting for a bus or help someone who'd dropped their shopping or was having trouble getting a buggy through a doorway. The thought cheered her and for the first time she felt excited at the thought of returning to Ireland. It might be nice to spend a while in her hometown and catch up with old friends.

Sandy sat cross-legged on the bed watching Krystie pack the last of her stuff. "I still think this is a seriously bad move."

Krystie shrugged and smiled. "I told you, Sandy, it's the only way I can get back on my feet. I can stay with my folks rent-free and sign on the dole and get some money while I figure out what I'm going to do next."

"Have you told Jacob?"

Krystie froze for a second, and then continued to fold her clothes. "We're finished, Sandy, I told you that. What's going on in my life is none of his business."

"Oh, *pur-leeease*, don't give me that! As for being finished, ha! I've lost count of the times it's been over." She made dramatic quote marks in the air and rolled her eyes. "But you always get back together in the end."

Krystie thought of the last time she'd seen Jacob, and shivered. "Not this time."

"What the hell happened between you two? You never told me? He wasn't fooling around with someone else, was he? Hell, he's not the real reason you're leaving, is he?"

Krystie sank onto the bed. "No, I'm going home because I can't afford to stay. And, no, Jacob wasn't fooling around. Everything was going great. I know we had rows but they were almost worth it because making up afterwards was always so wonderful."

Sandy shook her head, confused. "So what went wrong?"

Krystie had to swallow back her tears before she could continue. "Do you remember the night that I ended up in the hospital?"

"How could I forget it? You scared the hell out of us."

"I certainly scared the hell out of Jacob. It completely freaked him out. That's why he broke up with me."

"The asshole!" Sandy was incensed.

Krystie shrugged. "Some people just can't handle sickness."

"But you're not sick. You've got a condition and you've only had, what, two or three seizures since you got here?"

"Maybe it was just an excuse — who knows? It doesn't really matter, Sandy, does it? He dumped me."

"You're better off without the sonofabitch."

Krystie laughed. "I am. Now, do me a favour and see if you can find my red bag. I've looked everywhere. Oh, and my blue scarf, too."

"Did you check the girls' room?"

Krystie grinned. "No."

Sandy stood up. "I'll go have a look. They're just like magpies and they so love your style." She paused and looked at Krystie. "I'm going to miss you, Irish."

Krystie enveloped her in a big hug, smiling at the pet name. "Gonna miss you too, hon."

CHAPTER
FIVE

Sheila stared at herself in the mirror. You're not Sheila Healy, she told herself. You're Donna Cassidy. She now wore her hair in a short blonde bob. Who would have possibly recognised her as Sheila Healy, especially dressed like this? She barely recognised herself. She hadn't possessed a pair of trainers since she was a teenager. As for the sweat pants she lived in these days, she wouldn't have been seen dead in them in Dublin. "Seen dead." The unfortunate phrase brought a wry smile to her face.

Karl Fitzsimons came to stand behind her and massaged her shoulders. "Will you stop worrying? Even if she did recognise your face, out of context it would mean nothing. How long is it since you've met?"

"Maybe eight years? We went to the same college."

"Did you have anything to do with each other?"

"No."

"Did Sinéad?"

Sheila didn't have to think twice. If Sinéad and Krystie Kelliher were friends, she'd have known about it. She met his eyes in the mirror. "No."

"Then this girl, if it is her, may not even know what's happened," he said, his voice soothing and sensible.

It was her. Sheila was sure of it. The girl had always worn very eye-catching clothes and still did. She may have only seen her for a few moments but she remembered the colourful jacket and jaunty hat. But there was no reason why she would recognise Sheila, who looked nothing like she had in her college days. "You're right," she said, smiling at Karl. "She could be anywhere in the world now. I must ask Sinéad . . ." She broke off. When would she get used to not being able to talk to her sister any more?

He squeezed her shoulders. "Come on. Let's go eat."

"No," she said, suddenly nervous at the idea of going out. "I'll make us something."

He snorted. "You are not going into hiding because you saw a woman on the other side of town who you *might* know and who *might* have recognised you."

"Perhaps it was a mistake to come to New York. There are too many people."

"Rubbish." He grinned. "Haven't you heard? The best place to get lost is in a crowd."

In the restaurant she tried to relax but she still had an uneasy feeling. She had deliberately dressed down in a black sweater, slacks and flat pumps and had pulled her hair back into a knot.

"What's the worst that could happen?" Karl asked, as usual reading her mood.

She looked at him, so calm, so self-assured and so unflappable. She considered his question. "I suppose the worst is that the truth is splashed across the front of the Irish newspapers."

"The truth?" He raised an eyebrow.

"The fact that I'm alive and well and living here," she amended.

He nodded. "Would it matter that much?"

She took a sip of her Martini. "Maybe not, but I don't want to think about the past. I want to get on with my new life." She had adapted so easily to New York, to being with Karl. It was as if she belonged. She didn't want to leave or look over her shoulder wherever she went.

"You could always lie low for a while, spend some time in Minnesota." He helped himself to more noodles. "The light down there in winter is amazing, inspirational."

Sheila thought of his beautiful and very large ranch that had literally taken her breath away the first time she'd seen it. Looking at him now, sitting in the chic Chinese restaurant in the best part of town, it was hard to believe he had come from such humble beginnings. With his blond hair, blue eyes, perfect smile and fine clothes, he reeked of wealth and breeding. She still couldn't quite take in the extent of his success or his affluence, not that he flaunted it. He was as unassuming as he'd been the day she'd met him. He had developed a gaming website that had become hugely popular in a matter of months and was bought out a couple of years ago for almost a billion dollars. He could easily retire and live comfortably for the rest of his life on his ranch, but he'd be horrified at the very idea. He lived for his work and continued to develop gaming software, but now for smartphones.

"What do you think?" he asked.

She smiled as she gazed around her at the busy restaurant buzzing with conversation and full of dramatic, beautiful and confident people. "I find New York pretty inspirational."

He laughed. "I'd noticed. You have worked so hard these last few months, as if you're possessed. The floodgates have opened."

"I know, I can't quite believe it. I get so lost in what I'm doing the day flies by."

"Because you're finally doing something you love. When are you going to go public?"

She nibbled on the skewer of chicken. This was a regular topic of conversation. Karl was a man of action and he was eager to see her shine. "It's too soon. I'm still finding my way. And I don't want to draw attention to myself, certainly not after what happened today."

"You're Donna Cassidy now," he reminded her. "Forget that woman. There's no way she would have recognised you. You're safe, darling, stop worrying."

"Unless of course I'm an overnight success and become famous. And the hacks start to dig into my mysterious *Oirish* roots." She grinned. "Seriously, though, I'm in no rush to go public, Karl. I'm having fun developing my style."

He smiled. "Then that's all that matters. I suppose I'm just dying to see what reaction you get. It's tough being your only audience."

"I wonder what your friends think I do all day," she mused.

"They think you shop, hang out in expensive spas and do lunch, what else?"

"What else indeed?" She laughed. There had been some women who had invited her out when Karl first introduced her to some of his friends, but she had been afraid that she would say something to give away her identity and so always declined. It hadn't bothered her. She was enjoying the solitude. It had never occurred to her in the past, but she had spent little time alone. She was also quite enjoying being spoiled. Karl was so obviously thrilled to have her here that it bowled her over.

Of course, she thought about her family and Philip, especially with Christmas looming. Would he be able to cope without her? He certainly wouldn't cancel. This was the time of year when Philip thanked staff, party members and his most loyal constituents. And would the family still congregate in her house now she was gone? And what about Aunty Bridie? Would she be left in the home, out of sight, out of mind? She felt guilty at the thought. Poor Bridie. For all her faults she didn't deserve to be abandoned.

How different her life was now, she thought, as they strolled back, arm in arm, through the streets to his penthouse in Gramercy Park. No more worrying about Philip's schedule or schmoozing retailers, or trying to balance the books. Now each day was her own and she lived it at a gentle pace, working when she felt like it, taking long walks and cooking for Karl.

"Are you okay?" Karl looked down at her.

"Fine," she assured him and they continued on their way in comfortable silence. It was one of the things she liked most about Karl. He was quite content to be silent and he didn't plague her with questions.

They had exchanged life stories and knew everything there was to know, the good and the bad. It had been a wonderful release and brought them incredibly close very quickly. She felt happy with him. She still had to pinch herself sometimes, unable to believe she was here. She never thought she would have the opportunity or the strength to change her life so radically, but she'd done it.

Kieran Fields puffed a little as he reached the top of the hill. Pulling out his cigarettes, he sat down on a bench to get his breath back. Of course he probably wouldn't need to sit down if he gave the bloody things up and took some exercise. Sinéad and Max were always on at him to socialise more, to join a club or take up golf or bridge, anything rather than sit at home all day. But there was nowhere Kieran wanted to go and no one he wanted to talk to. And whenever he put his nose outside the door there was some bloody do-gooder giving him pitying looks and asking him if he was okay. What kind of a question was that? How the hell could he be okay? He would be sorely tempted to jump into the sea himself if it weren't for Sinéad. If he went he knew that she wouldn't be far behind.

He took a last long drag on the cigarette and started up the narrow path, his head bent against the biting wind. He was grateful for the miserable weather lately that kept most indoors by the fire. There wasn't a soul in sight. He laughed out loud at the phrase that had come to mind. He stepped between the headstones to reach his wife's grave. "The Dead Centre of Dublin" was Glasnevin Cemetery's nickname. Every landmark in the city had a nickname. The statue of Molly Malone was "the Tart with the Cart" while the Anna Livia sculpture was quickly dubbed "the Floozie in the Jacuzzi".

Kieran didn't like graveyards.

"Who does?" Bridie had snapped when the maintenance of her sister's grave was left to her. He'd only started to visit after Sheila died. Not that she was here, but it was where he felt drawn to, probably because it was the resting place of her mother. He couldn't bear being near the sea, and you certainly wouldn't catch him in Sandycove. He knew every inch of that piece of coastline since they'd joined the rescue services and volunteers in the search for Sheila.

"It's your bloody fault, Maggie," he said aloud at his wife's graveside. "If you hadn't died things would be very different."

He patted the stone. "Sorry, love, sorry." He knelt down and tugged up some weeds. "I didn't bring you any flowers but that's nothing new, is it? Women and flowers — what's that all about, anyway?" He tossed a weed aside, sat back on his heels and dusted off his hands.

"Why did Sheila do it, Maggie? She was the sensible one. You and Sinéad were away with the fairies but Sheila was our rock. She always had such an old head on young shoulders, didn't she? Even as babies, remember, Maggie? Sinéad would be gurgling and smiling all the time but Sheila would be watching, taking everything in, always so serious, so wise.

"I'd like to think she took after me but there was some of Bridie in her." He sighed. "Ah, your poor sister, she's not good, Maggie. And I know I should be looking after her, the way she looked after me and the kids, I know that. But I'm no good at that sort of thing — you know that better than anyone." He sat down heavily on the edge of the surround. "It's so hard to see her like that. God forgive me but she'd be better off dead and you know she'd prefer it. Sheila was great of course; went to see her nearly every week. Took her out from time to time, brought her home for the holidays. She was like a daughter to her." He pulled out a hankie, dabbed his eyes and blew his nose. "I'll never understand why Sheila did it, Maggie, I won't.

"You know, I used to be able to tell the girls apart by their eyes, but now that Sinéad is so broken-hearted she's never looked more like Sheila. I can't bear to look at her. It's a mess, Maggie. It's all a bloody mess. If it wasn't for Max . . ." He smiled. "Ah, love, he's nothing like you or the girls but you'd be proud of the way he's turned out. Sharp as a tack, he is, and doing so well for himself. A fancy car and a posh apartment in Donnybrook and a steady flow of girlfriends. I'd like to see him settled. Still, I suppose there's plenty of time. Sure he's only, what, twenty-six?" He scratched his head as he tried to remember. "I'm lousy when it comes to remembering stuff like that. Sheila always used to remind me." He sighed again. "Ah, Maggie, this is all your fault." He scowled. "I don't know why Sheila did it, but I know she would still be here if you were. And poor Sinéad wouldn't be in the state she's in.

"She's always been so bubbly, talking nineteen to the dozen, on her way to or from somewhere, never sitting still unless she was working, though according to Sheila she usually did that standing up or sprawled on the floor. She's a very different girl now. You should be here. Sheila should be here!" He pulled himself to his feet and paused to lay his hand on the headstone. "See you next week, Maggie."

As usual after he left the graveyard, Kieran bought a newspaper, went into the pub across the road and ordered a pint and a sandwich. As he waited for his food, he spread the paper out and bent over it. He had no real interest in reading, but it stopped people bothering him. He didn't know anyone in the area, but if there was a funeral the pub was usually packed afterwards and you just never knew who you'd bump into. He kept his eyes fixed on the page but his thoughts were of Sheila. She had seemed content to him. Always busy, she was a great woman for planning. She left nothing to chance. She had bossed them all about, taken control of everything, and they were all only too happy to let her.

Kieran could understand why Sinéad was suspicious of Philip. She couldn't accept that Sheila had taken her own life and he was the only other person she was close to. They had seemed happy, but who really knew what went on behind closed doors? Much as he'd like to be able to blame his son-in-law, much as he'd love to think that Sheila hadn't taken her own life, he couldn't believe that Philip would hurt her, or anyone for that matter. Behind all the bluster and posturing, Philip was a gentle person.

The man had lost more than any of them, really. The saying that behind every good man there's a good woman was never as true as it was for Philip and Sheila. He had taken a risk going into politics, but she had backed him every step of the way and, despite running her own business, had still made herself available to go to functions with him and help him on the campaign trail. She'd also brought an element of glamour to politics when she acquired some degree of notoriety for being one of the designer twins, the latest Irish success story. There was no doubt that Philip was photographed more than most politicians and that was because his beautiful and successful wife was on his arm. But quite apart from Philip appreciating Sheila being so supportive, Kieran had always got the impression that they were an excellent team because they were happy together. He couldn't remember them ever having a cross word, and even in a crowd they were never too far away from each other. No, he was sure that Philip was innocent and in as much of a turmoil as they were.

"Kieran Fields, is it you?"

He jerked his head back, startled, and saw a woman standing over him. Her face was vaguely familiar. "It is."

She sat down opposite, not at all put off by the newspaper or the fact that he hadn't asked after her health. Some women couldn't take a hint.

56

"Good to see you again, although not eating alone like this. You need your friends around you, dear. I'd never have coped after Gerry died if it wasn't for them."

Gerry McKenna's widow, that was it, though he couldn't remember her name. "I've got my son and daughter and plenty of friends," he said curtly.

"That's good, I'm glad to hear it," she said, not seeming to notice. On a cloud of perfume, she made herself more comfortable in her seat, and smiled.

Oh, not again. Kieran was used to single women of a certain age chatting him up. They saw a widower with a good pension and a nice house as prospective husband material, insurance for when they got old or sick. In the good old days women came after him for other reasons.

"So, how are you keeping? How are the family?"

"We're okay, thanks." She was still a good-looking woman considering she was in her sixties. She'd looked after herself, but her heavy makeup and even heavier perfume didn't do her any favours. He'd always leaned towards the natural look. He had a sudden flashback of Maggie playing in a paddling pool in the garden with the children wearing a light summer dress, her skin pale, her hair held back in a colourful scarf. She had never looked more beautiful.

"You must come over for dinner."

He looked at her in alarm. She was more forward than most. "I wouldn't want to put you to any trouble —"

"Cooking for two is as easy as cooking for one, and it would be nice to have some company. I hate eating alone, don't you?"

"It doesn't bother me," he said and then, realising he was being unnecessarily rude to the wife of an old friend, he gave her an apologetic smile. "You must miss Gerry. How long has it been now?"

"Almost three years and, yes, I do. It's the little things, you know?" She gave a sad smile. "I used to give out to him about leaving the toilet seat up, not putting the top back on the toothpaste, not hanging up his coat when he got in or not cleaning his shoes on the doormat and walking dirt all over the house. Now I don't have to worry about any of that. My house is always clean and tidy and so, so empty and lonely."

Kieran looked away. This was a little more sharing than he was comfortable with, but he was touched by her words nevertheless. Perhaps he'd been too hasty in judging her. "I suppose I didn't have that problem. I had three noisy children to distract me when Maggie died."

"Yes. Children do make it easier. My son, Gavin, and his wife are in Melbourne now and I have a wonderful little grandson. We chat on Skype and I'm going out there in the spring but, I have to admit I'd prefer it if they were here."

"I suppose I'm lucky that I still have Sinéad and Max."

"Now, that's not what I meant at all." She looked at him, obviously distressed. "You lost your poor daughter; you must be heartbroken."

"I am," he admitted. "The kids say that I should get out more but I can't be bothered."

"In your position I'd find it difficult to get out of bed," she retorted.

"Some days I do."

"Do things in your own time." Her smile was sympathetic. "Everyone expects me to be over Gerry, but though I've developed a new routine it doesn't mean I've got used to living alone or that I've forgotten him."

Kieran thought of his former colleague. He had been a fit and active man and it had been a shock when he died suddenly of a heart attack. "He was the last person I'd have expected to die so young — he seemed so healthy. I smoke, drink and don't take enough exercise. It doesn't make sense, does it?"

"He suffered badly with his nerves," she confided. "And there was a history of heart disease in his family."

A waitress came to clear the table. "Can I get you anything else?" she asked.

"Will you have a drink?" Kieran said, amazing himself that he wanted to prolong the chat.

"A cup of tea would be nice." She smiled. "If you're sure you don't want to be left to read your newspaper in peace."

"I wasn't really reading it," he admitted. "Two teas, please," he told the waitress. When she was gone he decided it was time to come clean. "I'm really sorry, but I can't remember your name."

She threw back her head and laughed. "It's Beth and there's no need to apologise. I wouldn't have remembered yours either, but for your daughters. When I saw them on *The Late Late Show* I made the connection. I was at Sheila's memorial service. You seemed overwhelmed."

He nodded. She really had the kindest eyes. "I remember, thanks. It was very nice of you to come."

The waitress brought their tea and Beth poured. "How is Sinéad? It must be very hard for her to carry on in the business without her sister."

"Yes," he said, feeling guilty. When was the last time he'd even asked Sinéad about the business?

"You were close?"

He sighed. "Very. Sheila was the organiser, the glue that kept us together. She's left a huge hole in our lives."

"It must be even harder for Sinéad, losing her twin like that."

"Yes," he mumbled, his guilt mounting.

Obviously sensing his discomfort, Beth changed the subject. She told him about her plans to visit her son, but confided she'd never flown before and was terrified at the prospect.

"Why not take a trip to London or even just down to Cork first, break yourself in gently?" he suggested. "Get a friend to go with you and the time will fly," he grinned. "Sorry, pun not intended."

She laughed. "I'll think about it."

"So, have you never been abroad?" he asked, incredulous.

"Oh, yes, but always on the ferry. We had some wonderful holidays in Britain and Europe. I miss them. I haven't been away since Gerry died."

"Haven't you any sisters or friends you could go away with?" he said, surprised. She was good company and he imagined she'd have no problem finding someone to go on holiday with.

"No sisters, but some good friends, though none that I would really want to spend all day, every day, with. I like some quiet time too, you know what I mean?" She threw back her head and laughed. "Would you listen to me? I said I was lonely. I'm a mass of contradictions."

"No, I understand what you mean. I like quiet time too and there aren't many people that you can be silent with."

She smiled into his eyes. "That's it exactly."

He stared at her for a moment, mesmerised. "More tea?"

She glanced at her watch. "Oh, no, goodness I must run. I'm in work in an hour."

"What do you do?" he asked curiously.

"I just have a part-time job in my local library, but I enjoy it."

"Plenty of silence there." He smiled and stood to help her into her coat.

"Indeed!" She chuckled. "Thank you for the tea and the company, Kieran. I enjoyed it."

"Me too," he said and surprisingly it was true.

"You're welcome to come over for some lunch on Sunday if you're at a loose end," she said almost shyly.

"Sounds good," he said, and it did.

She gave him the address and they exchanged numbers and, after a quick kiss on his cheek, she was gone. Kieran absently touched his face knowing it was probably covered with red lipstick. But he didn't care. And he was still smiling.

CHAPTER
SIX

"Okay, Sinéad, I'll look forward to seeing you then. Take care." Philip banged down the phone with a scowl. He'd had just about enough of his sister-in-law. He thought he'd got through to her, then he noticed the last time they met that the suspicious look was back in her eyes and on the phone her voice was like ice. But he was determined to keep close to Sheila's family. He could just imagine the gossip if there was any suggestion of a rift.

At least they'd agreed to the party. Sheila and Sinéad had always celebrated their birthday together and it would look odd if they just ignored the day. He thought of the bash he'd thrown them last year in Lilli's. It had been a great night, full of family, friends and of course some important contacts, too. You were never off duty in the world of politics, and Sheila understood that.

But Sinéad was moody and unpredictable. He was probably nuts letting her loose in public. He had been determined that Christmas would be like every other year, but perhaps he should rethink that. It was only October. Better to just concentrate on the birthday in five weeks and see how that went first. Although they had agreed for it to go ahead, none of his inlaws were keen on the idea. Was he crazy to do this? What would Sheila say? Even now he found himself thinking that on an almost daily basis. He hadn't realised how much he depended on her.

She remembered everyone's name and even their kids' names. She could remind him who had a sick partner or had been recently bereaved and as a result he could make the right sympathetic noises. It was incredible how much that meant to people. Thankfully, they made allowances for him since she'd gone; he had all the sympathy in the world — a widower at just thirty-three. But people forgot, life moved on and he would have to move with it or he would lose everything that he'd worked so hard for. His thoughts returned to Sinéad. He never knew from one day to the next how she would be with him. There had to be some way to get her back on side. What would Sheila tell him to do?

He remembered her laughing at his nervousness the first time she took him home to meet her family. "Just don't be the car salesman, Philip. Be yourself."

That was it. That was where he'd been going wrong. Jumping to his feet, he hurried out of his office. "I'll be back in a couple of hours, Cathy," he told his assistant as he breezed past her desk and down the stairs onto the street. His driver looked up from his newspaper in surprise. "Blackrock, please, Barry. I need to see my sister-in-law."

"No problem, boss."

Sinéad was alone in the shop filling boxes when Philip got there. He put his finger on the buzzer and kept it there. She looked up, her eyes widening in surprise. He glared at her and, scowling, she got to her feet, dusted off her hands on the back of her jeans and came to let him in.

"I'm not deaf, Philip. What are you doing here? I told you on the phone that I don't want to invite anyone to your party."

She turned away, but he took her arm and swung her back to face him. "Not good enough, Sinéad."

She shook him off, her eyes angry. "What the hell do you think you're doing?"

"I could ask you the same question. You've been treating me like shit lately and I don't deserve it. You're not the only one grieving, Sinéad. You're not the only one who misses Sheila."

"Sure," she said folding her arms, her mouth twisting into a wry smile.

"Don't mock me. I loved — love," he corrected himself, "Sheila and I hope and pray she'll walk back through the door. In the meantime, I'm just trying to get by, okay? Just because I'm not a drunken, broken mess doesn't mean that I don't care. I'm sorry you think it's a bloody sin to laugh and smile but, tough, we all deal with things in our own way. I miss Sheila every day, Sinéad, every fucking day."

She stared at him, obviously startled, and then she crumpled, sobbing. "I'm sorry, Philip. I'm so sorry. Please forgive me."

He folded his arms around her and patted her back. "It's okay."

"I know I'm not handling this very well, I know that everyone thinks I'm wallowing in self-pity, but I just miss her so much, Philip."

"I know."

She pulled back and looked up at him, her eyes red and puffy. "She wouldn't kill herself, Philip. She wouldn't do that to me — or to you," she added hurriedly. "You can't believe she did."

He leaned back against the counter and massaged the bridge of his nose. "People do all sorts of things if they think they have no other choice."

"What do you mean, no other choice?"

He cursed inwardly. Why the hell had he said that? "I'm just saying that sometimes, when people are upset or depressed, they do things on impulse that they wouldn't do when they're thinking rationally. But you're right, that's bullshit, Sheila was very rational. It had to be an accident. You know that she liked to walk when she was stressed and she always loved Sandycove."

"I suppose."

"What?" Philip asked, seeing the doubt in her eyes. He had finally got through to her and he wasn't going to leave until he was sure that she believed him.

"It'll sound silly."

"Try me."

She sighed. "I feel I would know in my gut if she was dead, and I don't."

He stared at her, lost for words for a moment, then pulled himself together. "Sweetheart, I hope you're right." For the first time he looked around and noticed the bare shelves. "What's going on?"

"We're — I'm — closing."

"What?" Philip straightened and looked down at her. "Why on earth would you do that?"

"The truth is, Philip, I've let things go and business is very bad. Max has come up with a plan to dig me out and part of that plan is to close the shop."

Philip felt a flash of anger at this bombshell. Sheila had come home daily with reports of yet more orders pouring in. She had even been contemplating opening a shop in the centre of Dublin. He struggled to hide his feelings. "But where will you work from?" he asked when what he really wanted to say was, How the hell did you manage to fuck up all of Sheila's hard work?

"We're looking at a few options," she said, fidgeting with her hair. "There's a lot of empty office space around these days, so it shouldn't be a problem finding somewhere suitable and cheap."

Be polite, Philip, don't lose the ground you've made, Philip. Count to a fucking hundred, Philip. "Is there anything I can do to help?"

She smiled, looking relieved. "I think Max has it all under control, but thanks."

"Well, the offer's there if you run into any problems. And about this birthday dinner, Sinéad, if you want me to cancel it, I will. It was a lousy idea."

"No, no, really, it's fine! I want people to remember her and talk about her."

He searched her eyes. "So, are we good?"

66

"We're good," she said and threw her arms around his neck.

"Great." He hugged her and kissed her cheek. "I feel so much better now that we've talked, Sinéad."

"Me too," she said still tearful.

He hugged her again. "I'd better get back to work. Talk soon."

Before the car had even pulled away from the kerb, he'd pulled out his mobile and dialled a number.

"I was going to tell you, Philip," Max said, sounding weary as they sat at the bar in Buswell's hotel, "I've just been busy trying to sort out this mess."

Philip nodded to a member of cabinet who'd just walked through the door with a detective. "And have you?"

"I'm getting there. Mainly by calling the retailers who'd cancelled orders telling them that my sister basically lost the plot after Sheila disappeared and offering them more attractive terms if they give her another six months' trial. I told the bigger accounts that we were in the process of hiring a very talented new designer to work alongside Sinéad."

"Oh, well done!"

Max looked at him, his expression grim. "That's a small fib but I have a couple of agencies working on it."

"You're taking a bit of a chance, aren't you?" Philip muttered and, catching the barman's eye, ordered another round.

"Yeah but, worst-case scenario, we get someone young and enthusiastic just out of college. On the up side, Sinéad got quite a shock when she realised how bad things were. I think she'll get things back on track." Max looked at him. "What brought you out to the shop?"

"I thought it was time Sinéad and I had a chat. It went well, we cleared the air and she's even given the birthday dinner her blessing."

Max looked surprised at the news. "Well, I'm glad to hear it. I must get her to invite a couple of retailers. It's a perfect opportunity to mend some fences."

"Indeed. Have you found new premises for Sinéad yet?"

"No, Sinéad said she'd look after that herself."

Philip frowned. Sinéad had said her brother was taking care of it. What was she playing at? "Well, I hope it all works out. I'd love to see her get back to her old self."

"Me too."

Philip glanced at his watch. "I have to go, Max. Thanks for meeting me. Let me know if there's anything I can do to help."

"Will do." Max stood and shook his hand. "And thanks for being so patient with Sinéad. I know it hasn't been easy."

"No problem." Philip patted his shoulder and left feeling a lot better. With both Sinéad and Max in his corner, his future felt a lot more secure.

Sinéad sat in the café sipping an Americano and waiting for Ellen and Rory to close up. She was feeling better after the chat with Philip. Dylan was right. She'd obsessed far too much about what might have happened to Sheila, but no more. She was going to make a go of her business. She opened her pad and looked through the sketches she'd done this morning. They were fine but they were missing something. Sinéad always knew when a hat was going to work just from the drawing. She would be able to see it in her mind's eye, imagine it on a catwalk or in a shop window. She didn't get any of those feelings looking at these sketches. They were staid, safe, possibly even boring. Had she lost the gift? The thought caused a flutter of panic in her stomach.

"Sorry for keeping you waiting, sweetie." Ellen appeared at her side with another coffee for Sinéad and tea for herself.

Rory turned off some of the lights and joined them, setting a plate of biscuits on the table and settling back with his espresso. "What a day."

"Don't complain," Ellen warned him. "The takings are better than they have been in weeks."

"I know," he yawned. "We really should consider opening in the evenings even if just over Christmas and New Year."

"Yes, we could offer a short menu and maybe do that 'bring your own wine' business and charge for corkage." Ellen looked at Sinéad. "At the moment you just have to do anything you can to get customers through the door. Every penny counts."

"Which brings me very neatly to the reason why I wanted to talk to you guys." Sinéad looked nervously at them.

Rory perked up. "Go on, then, we're all ears."

She leaned forward on the table and looked from one to the other. "Well, you know I'm selling the shop."

"We can't afford to buy it and expand, Sinéad. If only we could," Ellen warned.

"It would be great, but the cost of knocking the wall down is beyond us at the moment," Rory agreed.

"No, that's not what I'm suggesting. I wondered how you'd feel about having a tenant."

Rory frowned. "I don't understand."

Sinéad nodded at the ceiling. "Your place upstairs is just like mine, right?"

"No. When we first moved in we planned to put tables in upstairs so we made it one big room."

She beamed. "Even better. Guys, I need a studio and I hate the idea of leaving Blackrock. Well, the truth is I'd miss you. So I wondered —"

"Yes, yes, yes." Ellen clapped her hands in delight. "Oh, my God, why didn't we think of this before?"

Rory grinned. "I have no idea. Sinéad, we would love to have you."

"Thank you!" She reached out both her hands to take theirs and gave a sigh of relief. "Max has been pushing me to find somewhere but I didn't want to move out of the village and I knew that you guys could probably do with the cash. I'll be the perfect tenant and I'll pay you a fair rental. Get in touch with a couple of agents and find out what the going rate is."

Ellen rolled her eyes at this. "Don't be ridiculous, you're like family, and we only ever use upstairs for storage."

"No, we're going to do this properly or not at all," Sinéad insisted. "This is a business proposition."

Rory smiled. "Okay, Ms Fields, you have a deal. How are you managing to get out of the lease next door so easily?"

She grinned. "My brother, the wheeler-dealer, is subletting it."

"Please tell me it's not to another restaurant or coffee bar," Ellen begged.

"Of course not, as if I'd let him do that," Sinéad retorted. "No, it's a launderette and dry-cleaning firm."

Ellen smiled at Rory. "That will be handy."

"Very. I must make them a cake to welcome them."

"Oh, good idea, sweetheart." Ellen squeezed his hand.

"This is such a relief, you have no idea," Sinéad said with feeling.

"I was dreading you leaving," Ellen admitted.

Sinéad felt tears well. "You amaze me. I've been impossible to live with since . . . well these last few months, but that's all going to change."

"You are going to be just fine." Ellen jumped to her feet. "Come on, to hell with the coffee, let's go to the pub. We've got some celebrating to do."

CHAPTER
SEVEN

Krystie felt a little emotional as the plane flew along the coast and began its descent into Dublin. It had been a tearful goodbye at the apartment and she was glad she hadn't let Sandy accompany her to the airport: it would have been far too hard on them both. She'd promised to Skype her friend as soon as she had Internet access and after a tight hug she'd jumped into the yellow taxi that would take her to the bus station and waved at her flatmates as the tears coursed down her cheeks. She had picked up the phone a number of times to call her folks and let them know she was coming home but she still couldn't bring herself to admit that her dreams had come to nothing. In the end she had phoned her good friend, Sharon, instead who had immediately invited her to stay for a few days. Krystie jumped at the offer. It was only putting off the inevitable, but it would give her a chance to take stock and to catch up with Sharon.

"Wow, it really *is* green." The American woman beside her leaned across to get a better look.

"Yeah, it is," Krystie couldn't suppress a proud smile as the plane cruised along the coast and then turned and began its descent into Dublin airport.

Once in the terminal she weaved her way through passengers down the long corridors towards Immigration and joined the queue at Security. As she neared the kiosk she heard the Garda's broad Dublin accent and started to giggle.

He held his hand out for her passport, eyeing her suspiciously as she stepped forward. "Is something funny?"

"Sorry, it's just I haven't been home for a while and it's good to hear the accent," she explained.

He looked up from her passport. "You're from Dublin? How the hell did you end up with a name like Krystle?"

She cringed. "Awful isn't it? Me ma was mad about *Dynasty*. My brother is Blake and my sisters are Fallon and Alexis, but she calls herself Alex."

"You drew the short straw, then," he said sympathetically.

"It's not too bad. I call myself Krystie."

"Ah, now, there's a grand Dublin name! *Fáilte abhaile, a chara.*"

She laughed. "*Go raibh maith agat.*"

"Oh, was that Gaelic?" her neighbour from the plane journey asked, wide-eyed and clearly impressed.

"Yeah." Krystie smiled. "He said welcome home, my friend, and I said thanks."

"Are you fluent?"

"Sure! We only ever speak Irish at home," she lied, glibly.

"That is *so* cool. Everyone should preserve their heritage the way you guys do."

Krystie felt a pang of guilt at deceiving the woman. "Thanks. Lovely to meet you. Have a great holiday," she said, and hurried on to collect her bags.

When she finally emerged into the arrivals hall, she looked around and grinned in delight at the sight of Sharon McCarthy jumping up and down and waving frantically. She rushed forward to hug her old friend. "Hey! It's so great to see you."

"You too, Krystie. I can't believe you're here." Sharon was beaming but her eyes were bright with tears.

"Stop that, you silly cow," Krystie said affectionately, but there was a lump in her throat too.

"Well, that's charming, that is!" Sharon laughed.

"Are you sure you don't mind putting me up?" Krystie asked as they pushed the trolley out to the car park.

"Are you kidding? I've been really looking forward to it."

"I'm so sorry about you and Marty," Krystie said. Sharon had been married only a couple of years but a few months ago her husband had announced out of the blue that it had been a mistake and he was leaving.

"I suppose I should be grateful that he left now instead of waiting until we had kids."

"Yeah," Krystie said, thinking this all sounded just *too* familiar. "He's still a bastard, though."

Sharon threw back her head and laughed. "Oh, I'm glad you're home. We're going to have a grand time." They reached the car and stashed Krystie's bags in the boot.

"I'm afraid I can't afford to go out partying," Krystie warned her friend. "I'm broke."

"Aren't we all?" Sharon said cheerfully.

"And I need to stay out of the city. If word gets back to Ma that I'm home and haven't been in touch I'm in serious trouble."

"But why haven't you told them, Krystie? They'll be thrilled that you're home."

"I know that, but I was talking to Alex last week and my folks are seriously struggling to manage at the moment. Dad's hours have been reduced and Blake's still living at home and he's on the dole. The last thing they need right now is another mouth to feed. But I knew Ma would be hurt if she knew I was in Ireland and staying somewhere else."

"You'll have to tell them some time."

"I will once I get a job and can pay my way," Krystie assured her, "but for the moment I'm going to lie low."

"There's not much chance of you meeting anyone you know where I live."

"Exactly where *do* you live now?" Krystie asked.

Sharon grinned. "Greystones."

Krystie gawped at her. "Greystones in Wicklow? But that's feckin' miles away!"

"It doesn't take long on the motorway."

"Still, you have to let me pay for the petrol. I thought you'd still be living in Ballymun."

"No, I needed to get as far away from Marty and his family as possible. And, though I wanted to buy a place of my own, I didn't want to spend a fortune, either."

"What about your job?" Krystie asked. Sharon had worked as a beauty therapist not far from where she'd lived.

"I'm freelance now. I work in the local hotel health spas. It's great. Variable hours, I get to meet more people and it pays better too."

"Good, I'm glad, you deserve it." Krystie could strangle Marty for all he'd put Sharon through. He'd been damn lucky she'd agreed to marry him in the first place: she was far too good for him, and then he was stupid enough to let her go. She knew that, for all the bravado, Sharon didn't think so right now, but she really was better off without him.

"I warn you, I don't live in a palace."

Krystie thought of the draughty apartment in New York with paper-thin walls and grinned. "Have you got heating?"

"Of course I have!"

"Then it's a palace to me." Krystie laughed.

"I'm sorry things didn't work out in New York for you," Sharon said.

"Oh, well, that's life, eh?" Not the type to dwell on things she couldn't change, Krystie was already thinking of the future.

"What's the plan, Krystie? Are you going to settle down in Dublin?"

"No idea, I'll have to play it by ear."

"You know, I may be living in the next county, but the train station is only five minutes from the house. You're welcome to stay with me if you can't face living with your folks."

Krystie was sorely tempted. Moving back in with her parents seemed a huge step backwards, and a humiliating one — her little sister was going to love it. But it wouldn't be fair to take advantage of Sharon's kindness. "No, really, I'll be grand. I just need a few days to get sorted and then I'll go and see them and make the big announcement."

"Your mother will be so happy to have you home."

"And Fallon will be delighted to see me back with my tail between my legs."

"Feck her. Why does she have to know anything? Can't you pretend you're here for some other reason?"

"Er, I think once I'm living with the folks and working in a burger joint it might give the game away. Oh, look, I had it coming," Krystie admitted. "I pretended to be doing a lot better than I was but now they'll know the truth: I'm a failure."

"Rubbish. You've supported yourself all these years and had quite an adventure. That's not exactly failing. Anyway, forget about it for now and let's concentrate on having some fun."

Krystie smiled. "Yeah, you're right. I've missed you, Sharon. I'm looking forward to catching up. It's been ages since I've seen you."

"My wedding day," Sharon said.

"Oh, God, so it was." Krystie said feeling awful. How could she have forgotten? "But now that you're free and single again it's only a matter of time before a gorgeous, rich man comes along and sweeps you off your feet."

"Gorgeous and rich? Yeah, I keep tripping over guys like that. No, I'd settle for a nice, straightforward guy that I could cuddle and watch telly with in the evening," Sharon assured her with a sad smile. "Just a good man that I could depend on."

"Agreed. But it wouldn't hurt if he was gorgeous and rich too."

Sharon grinned. "Ha, no, that wouldn't hurt at all."

Twenty minutes later they drove into the pretty little seaside town and Krystie lowered the window to breathe in the salty sea air.

"What are you doing? It's freezing," Sharon complained.

"After New York this is mild," Krystie assured her. The sky was grey but it was a dry day with only a light breeze. "It's years since I've been here. Ma used to bring us out on the train when we were kids."

"We came a few times but more often we got off in Bray. We loved the promenade, the bumper cars and the amusement arcades."

"Oh, we would have loved that but Ma was terrified of taking us there. Her da was a gambler and she wouldn't let us near a slot machine. She was sure it was genetic."

"It's a fool's game," Sharon agreed, turning the car into a laneway. "We're home!"

Krystie looked around at the horseshoe of pretty little chalets painted in pastel shades of blue, green and pink. "Seriously?"

"Seriously. Having second thoughts about staying with me?"

"Are you crazy? I love it." Krystie smiled as her eyes roamed round the tiny gardens with white picket fences and, despite the season, the hanging baskets swaying by each hall door.

"Me too," Sharon said. "It will look even better in December. We all club together for fairy lights and string them across the road between the telegraph poles and we put up a Christmas tree on the green."

The "green" was a tiny patch of grass in the centre of the horseshoe and Krystie could imagine how pretty it would look at night with the lights twinkling.

"And this is my place." She parked outside a chalet on the far side of the green. It was painted pink and the hall door was a rich shade of plum.

"Oh, Sharon, it's gorgeous."

"You haven't seen inside yet," Sharon warned. "It's pretty basic."

"You don't say 'basic', you say 'contemporary', darling," Krystie told her in her posh accent.

Sharon laughed. "Come on, I'll show you round and make a cuppa and we'll get the bags later."

"Fine by me. I have the important one right here." Krystie held up the duty-free bag.

The hall door opened into the sitting room and Sharon threw her coat on the sofa and gave her the grand tour.

"My bedroom." She threw open the first door on the right. It was a small square room decorated in muted pinks and plums and it was pretty and warm and inviting.

Krystie smiled. "I'd say the men love this."

"They might if they ever got to see it," Sharon said dryly, "but currently this is a man-free zone, and that's

79

the way I like it." She opened the second door to reveal a small but immaculate blue and white bathroom. "The bathroom. The shower is a bit unpredictable so always check with your hand before you get in."

"Will do." Krystie saluted.

"And this is your room." She opened the third door to reveal a bedroom much like her own but done out in different shades of blue.

"It's gorgeous, Sharon, thanks so much for inviting me."

"You're welcome." Sharon hugged her. "It's great to have you here." She led the way through a small archway to a kitchenette. "And this is where I open the takeaways and store the microwave meals."

Krystie laughed. "Still a lousy cook, then?"

"I'm the only person I know who can burn a boiled egg. You know, I probably miss Marty for his cooking more than anything."

"Well, I'll cook for you. That's one thing I got quite good at. Laura, one of my flatmates, was from an Italian family and she taught me how to make some really gorgeous and cheap pasta sauces. And Sandy's mother gave us the most amazing cookbook with loads of easy recipes for meals under five dollars."

"In that case, missus, you can come and stay any time you like. Coffee?"

"Got any cream?"

"Is the Pope a Catholic?"

"Then let's make them Irish coffees, or French, or Mexican." Krystie took a bottle of whiskey, a bottle of brandy and lastly a bottle of Tequila from the bag.

80

"It's only lunchtime," Sharon said, laughing.

"Oh, nearly forgot lunch. *Ta-da!*" Krystie produced a box of chocolates.

"Oh, go on, then, why not? How the hell did you manage to bring in that amount of booze?"

"I befriended this very nice Mormon lady who gave me her allowance."

"You always could sweet-talk your way in and out of anything."

"Not always," Krystie said, remembering Phyllis's grim expression when she fired her.

"Okay, you go grab your bags and I'll put the coffee on."

Krystie went out to the car and paused again to breathe in the tangy sea air and admire the pretty little nook that Sharon called home, feeling suddenly happy and optimistic. The breeze picked up, making her shiver, and, after taking her luggage from the car, she hurried back inside.

CHAPTER
EIGHT

The next few days were devoted to an orgy of sleeping, strolling along the beach, lazy pub lunches and long evenings curled up on Sharon's sofa catching up on all the gossip. Krystie couldn't remember the last time she'd felt so relaxed. Sharon had such a comfortable little home and it was a bonus to find that she also had wi-fi. Krystie had enjoyed a long chat on Skype with Sandy the previous night and had been able to introduce her American best friend to her Irish one.

"You have to come and visit," Sharon had said, taking an instant liking to the girl.

Krystie loved the idea of showing Sandy around Dublin and was delighted that the two girls liked each other. She yawned and stretched like a contented cat as Sharon bustled around the place getting ready for work.

"I hate leaving you alone. What are you going to do all day?" Sharon drained her mug of coffee and put it in the sink.

"Don't worry about me, I'll be fine."

"Come with me," Sharon urged. "I'm working in Stillorgan today. I could drop you off in Blackrock on my way. You could do some window shopping and then we could meet up for lunch."

"Are there are any fashion shops in Blackrock?"

"Of course." Sharon laughed. "You've been away too long."

Krystie hopped to her feet. "Cool. I'll go get dressed."

An hour later Sharon dropped Krystie at the entrance to the shopping centre. "If you go downstairs, there's an exit that will bring you out right in the centre of town. I'll call you when I'm finished for the morning and we can decide where to eat."

"Great. Is there a bank around? I need to get some euros."

"Yeah, there's one on the main street. Don't go wild." Sharon laughed and, with a wave, she was gone.

"The chance would be a fine thing," Krystie said aloud, thinking of her dwindling savings.

She went into the centre and was pleased to see there was a supermarket. She would come back later and get the ingredients to make Sharon some nice dinners — it was the least she could do. Krystie loved Sharon's little house and the friendly community it was in. She had already met some of the neighbours, who were mainly retired, single or separated, and they seemed like a nice bunch.

"We have the odd get-together," Sharon had told her, "though mainly in the summer when we get the barbies out."

"Any eligible men?" Krystie had asked with a wink.

"I'm not looking and I'm not interested," was the retort.

"Ah, now, you know that it's important to get back on the horse, Sharon."

Her friend laughed. "Back in the saddle?"

"Exactly."

"Nah, I think I'll keep my feet firmly on the ground for the time being."

Krystie had noticed her eyes grow sad and given her a quick hug. Bloody Marty had a lot to answer for. She'd never understand men. She thought of Jacob and quickly dismissed him from her mind. Sharon was right: being part of a couple wasn't all it was cracked up to be. The most important thing on her agenda right now was finding work, preferably doing something she liked. If she was desperate, she could always stick up an ad in the local shops and do alterations from her ma's house. The thought depressed her and she decided that it would be her very last resort.

She wandered through the shopping centre combing the boutiques to check out the style. The fashion in New York was very different from Ireland, but, then, New York was different from everywhere. She'd noticed already that, while the Irish dressed formally for office jobs, the only other time they really dressed up was for special occasions such as weddings. She seemed to be surrounded by people wearing tracksuits — a designer's nightmare. She'd never understood the attraction. Even as a child she had been drawn to pretty colours and fabrics and hats. How she'd always loved her hats. She remembered a red beret she'd worn every day for months when she was about twelve, convinced it made her look French and cool. After all, everything French was cool!

Smiling at the memory, she went downstairs and out onto the main street. After she'd exchanged her dollars for euros, she rambled down the street, her eyes lighting up when she spotted a wedding boutique. She paused to look at the window display before going in. There were two dresses on mannequins, one a rather fussy piece with ruffles and flounces, the other a simple satin shift dress that was stunning in its simplicity, though it would take a woman with a great figure to carry it off. There were four beautifully ornate headpieces that a veil could be attached to but, in Krystie's opinion, they would look even better without them.

She went into the shop and was immediately approached by a smiling lady who didn't seem at all put off by her torn jeans, patchwork jacket and corduroy flat cap.

"Can I help you?"

Krystie feigned embarrassment. "I'm jumping the gun a bit. We've only just got engaged and haven't bought a ring yet, never mind set a date."

"It's never too early to start looking," the woman laughed. "Have you any particular style in mind? It's clear that you have your own look. I love your jacket. Do you mind me asking where you bought it?"

"I made it," Krystie told her.

"You're pulling my leg."

Krystie grinned. "Nope."

"Well, why on earth would you spend a fortune on a gown from a place like this when you could obviously do just as good a job yourself?" the woman whispered.

Krystie blushed at the compliment. "Okay, I admit it, I was just looking for ideas."

"Great, then let's get started. I'm Paula, by the way."

They whiled away a couple of hours examining and discussing the gowns, and it wasn't long before Krystie admitted that she wasn't engaged but just couldn't help coming in to look at the gowns. Paula wasn't in the least bothered, but suggested she try on a few so that her boss wouldn't get suspicious. The assistant was just helping her out of a very flamboyant and expensive dress when Krystie's mobile rang.

She glanced at her watch and was stunned to see it was almost one o'clock. "That will be my friend. I'm supposed to be meeting her for lunch."

"Go and enjoy and come back any time, Krystie."

"You've been great, Paula, thanks a million."

"Not at all. I've enjoyed it."

Krystie quickly dialled Sharon back and they arranged to meet in a pub just a few doors away. She was about to walk out of the door when her eye was caught again by the delicate headpieces. "Paula, where did you get these? I love them."

"Aren't they beautiful? They're from a shop just down the road."

"Oh, fantastic, I'll call in after lunch."

"I'm afraid that —"

But Krystie didn't hear her and was hurrying towards the pub where Sharon was waiting.

"I've had a fantastic morning," she said once they were settled with their soup and sandwiches. She was positively high after the experience. "I was talking to a shop assistant in a wedding boutique and I learned more than if I'd read a dozen Irish fashion magazines."

"Was she able to point you towards any jobs?"

Krystie stared at her. She was a right twit. She hadn't even thought to ask. She'd been enjoying herself so much she'd forgotten that finding work was supposed to be her priority. "It never occurred to me to ask," she admitted. "Maybe I'll go back and talk to Paula again after lunch. She was really nice and loved my jacket."

"It is fabulous. You turned several heads when you walked into this place, and it wasn't just the guys," Sharon laughed. "I think you were right to come home, Krystie. New York's a bloody big place and, no offence, but you were just another little nobody out of college. But it's different here. Dublin's a small town and everyone knows everyone."

"But I've no contacts in the industry here, either," Krystie pointed out.

"I bet you do, only you don't know it. You need to look up some of the people you were at college with. You've only just stepped off the plane, Krystie, and times are as tough here as in the US, so don't expect a job to be just handed to you on a plate. You need to put in some time and effort. Have you any idea the number of hotels I had to walk into all smiley and charming before I got a break?"

"You're right, Sharon, you are so right," Krystie said glad of her friend's good sense. She was happy that she hadn't stayed at the house lazing around. Not only would she go back to the wedding boutique, but she'd check out that millinery too. If she was lucky, she might be able to wangle an interview. She was glad she'd taken the trouble to update her CV before she came home and had some nicely bound copies back at the house. And then there was Phyllis's glowing reference, which would surely impress.

"I'm always right. Are you happy enough to hang around here and wait for me, or do you want me to give you the keys and you can head home? I won't be finished before six," Sharon warned.

"I'll take the DART and have dinner ready."

Sharon's eyes lit up. "Yum. What's on the menu?"

"Wait and see," Krystie teased.

"No problem. It has to be better than anything in the freezer."

"I guarantee it."

Sharon frowned. "Am I supposed to leave you alone with sharp knives and a hot cooker?"

"It's fine," Krystie assured her with a smile. "I always get warning signals when a fit is coming on, you know that."

Sharon checked her watch. "Okay, then. I must run. I've a pedicure in ten."

"Ugh." Krystie shuddered. "I don't know how you do that job."

"I love it," Sharon laughed. "If you want me to be miserable, make me sew! Seeya."

Krystie went back out onto the street and set off in search of the hat shop. She walked the length of the street but could find nothing. She had been watching both sides of the road but crossed over anyway and went back up through the town. No hats. There was one vacant store that was all closed up but, as it was called Green Fields, she figured it had probably been a grocer's. There was a coffee shop next door and she pushed open the door and went up to the counter.

"What can I get you today?" A woman with a friendly smile came to serve her.

"Oh, nothing, thanks. I was just wondering if you knew where the hat shop is."

"Oh, dear, I'm afraid it's closed down. It was next door."

"It's gone?" Krystie said, gobsmacked. "But that's crazy. I just saw some of their pieces up in the wedding boutique and they're amazing."

"I couldn't agree more, but don't lose heart. The shop is closed, but the business isn't. If you want I can take your number and get the owner to call you."

"I'm not sure there's much point. I'm looking for a job but I guess if the shop's shut down then they're probably not hiring."

The woman eyed her shrewdly. "What sort of a job?"

"I'm a designer but I'd settle for making other people's designs; I need a job."

"Can you wait a few minutes and then we can talk?"

"Sure," Krystie said, surprised.

The woman smiled and held out her hand. "I'm Ellen, by the way. Why don't you take a seat and I'll get us some tea? Or would you prefer coffee?"

"Krystie. A cup of tea would be great." She took a seat at the nearest table, curious as to why Ellen wanted to talk to her.

"Rory, you need to take over for a while."

A tall handsome man came out of the kitchen. "Why, where are you skiving off to?"

"I need to have a little chat with this lady." Ellen nodded over to Krystie.

She smiled at the man and gave a little wave.

"She's a designer."

"Oh!" Rory's eyes widened as he waved back. "Take all the time you need, I'll cope."

Ellen carried two mugs of tea to the table. "Can I tempt you with a pastry?"

"No, thanks, I just had lunch."

"Are you sure? Perhaps a small slice of cheesecake?" She stopped and smiled. "Sorry, Krystie, I'm waffling, aren't I? The fact is the shop belongs to one of my greatest friends and, though she's shut down the shop, she really does need help, although —"

"What kind of help?" Krystie asked before she could go off on another tangent.

"I think it would be better if she told you that herself. Why don't you give me your CV? I'll pass it on."

"Damn, sorry, I don't have it with me."

Ellen's eyes narrowed. "You came looking for a job without a résumé?"

"I wasn't out job hunting, just window shopping," Krystie explained. "Paula in the wedding boutique told me that the headpieces were from a nearby shop so I thought I'd drop by on the off-chance they needed someone."

"Are you a milliner?"

"No, but I have made some pieces for myself and I'm a quick learner and a good designer."

"You don't hide your light under a bushel, do you?" Ellen looked at her, amused.

Krystie laughed, feeling embarrassed. "I've been working in Manhattan for a few years and, trust me, being modest over there gets you nowhere fast."

"Nice jacket. Did you buy that in New York?"

"No, I made it," Krystie said and was delighted when Ellen's eyebrows disappeared under her fringe.

Ellen looked at her for a moment, her eyes thoughtful. "Tell you what. Drop your CV in tomorrow and I'll pass it on."

"Thanks, Ellen." Krystie beamed at her and practically skipped back to the shopping centre to buy Sharon's dinner.

"Incredible," Sharon exclaimed.

"I know! I'm going to go back first thing. It's too good a chance to miss. I know Ellen is only a friend of the designer but I got the impression she's a good one."

"No." Sharon pointed at the pasta with her fork. "I'm talking about this sauce, it's amazing."

Krystie grinned. "It's one of Laura's mom's special recipes."

Sharon clinked her glass of wine against hers. "Then here's to Laura's mom and to you, Krystie. I hope something comes of this. You deserve a break. Do you know anything at all about this designer?"

"Not a thing, only that she's damn good. The pieces in the wedding boutique were exquisite. Still, business can't be that great if she's closed her shop."

"Perhaps she's just moving premises."

"I don't think so, but she's looking for an assistant, so she must have some regular customers."

"Wear the blue beret tomorrow. It makes your eyes look huge and goes well with the jacket."

"Good idea. Oh, and I know just what to wear underneath!"

She hopped up and went into the room to fetch the soft wool pinafore in different shades of blue and brought it out to the kitchen to show Sharon. "What do you think?"

Sharon's eyes widened. "I think it's incredible that a design house hasn't snapped you up. That's fabulous."

Krystie grinned, delighted. "I've never made it as far as getting to show anyone my portfolio; it's bloody impossible to get through the door of these places."

"But not here, I'm sure. Trust me, Krystie, if you wear that outfit this woman would want to be blind not to hire you."

"Thanks." Krystie frowned. "Hair straight and slicked back or curly?"

"Slicked for sure. You'll look as if you've stepped off a catwalk."

CHAPTER
NINE

Sheila was on her usual morning walk in Central Park, her eyes alert for images to capture. These days, despite fingerless gloves and a Styrofoam cup of hot coffee, her hands were too cold for sketching and she was grateful for the snazzy digital camera that Karl had presented her with. She would take dozens of photos each day and then later pick one to paint. She found herself drawn to portraits, an area totally new to her. Perhaps it was her own experiences lately that attracted her to haggard faces, creased brows and worried eyes that told stories words couldn't. This morning she was transfixed by two little girls playing in the leaves. She was pretty sure, going by the similarities and competitiveness, that they were sisters. She was reminded of the days before Mum died when she and Sinéad were young and carefree.

Afraid that she might appear to be some sort of pervert, she circled around the mother and took a position that made it look as if she were photographing the sun rising over the russet and golden treetops, but, thanks to the excellent zoom on the camera, she was able to capture the little girls' expressions. One actually did remind her of Sinéad, but, then, there were daily reminders of her sister. Not that it meant she forgave her but you couldn't switch off love, not just like that. She wasn't sure there would ever come a day when that would be possible.

As the mother called the girls and they continued on their way to school, Sheila headed home, made a pot of coffee and sat down to study her morning's work. She finally settled on a shot she'd taken when the younger girl had fallen and looked up at her sister for help, her eyes full of tears. Sheila printed it off and took it and the coffee into the studio and set to work.

Once the decision was taken Sinéad couldn't believe how fast things were moving but, then, that was Max for you. He didn't believe in wasting time. The space over Café Crème was large and airy and bright and she felt a thrill of excitement at the thought of working there.

She was on her knees opening boxes when Ellen and Rory staggered in with another.

"That's the last one," Rory said, breathlessly.

Sinéad turned and smiled at them. "Brilliant. Thanks, guys, you've been great."

Rory wiped the sweat from his brow and looked at his watch. "Time for a quick cuppa before we open."

"So, what do you think of your new home?" Ellen asked, sitting down at the work table in front of the window.

"I love it."

"You're easily pleased, darling," Ellen drawled, glancing around at the shelving that lined one wall, and

94

the mannequin heads and hat stands scattered about the room. Apart from the table, the only other furniture was a couple of chairs, a trolley with lots of compartments where Sinéad would keep the tools of her trade, and Sheila's old desk and filing cabinet, which they'd put against the wall at the other end of the room. Rory had erected a rail in the corner and Sinéad had hung a heavy, red-velvet curtain on it to create an ad hoc changing room in case any of her clients wanted to try on a headpiece with their outfit. A full-length mirror was on the wall next to it and another large mirror hung above the mantelpiece of the old building where Sinéad had already arranged mannequin heads with her best pieces.

Sinéad plonked herself in a chair and spun around, smiling. "It's great. Really."

"As long as you're happy, sweetie."

Rory returned with their coffees. "Here you go."

Sinéad cradled hers and glanced over at Ellen. "Tell me more about Krystie." She felt nervous at the thought of carrying out an interview and even more so at the thought of working with someone other than her twin.

"She seemed very enthusiastic. She's been working in New York these last few years."

"So why did she come home?" Sinéad frowned. If the girl was doing well she wouldn't have come home unless there were personal reasons.

"I didn't ask for any details. Look, there's no harm in talking to her," she added when Sinéad was silent. "You

95

don't even have to bring her up here. Meet her in the café."

"Yes, I think I'd prefer that. It would be more informal," Sinéad agreed.

"I hope she wears the jacket. It was just gorgeous, wasn't it, Rory?"

"Very nice."

"She has style, Sinéad," Ellen told her, "and I liked her."

"Come on, wife, it's opening time." Rory scrunched his cup into a ball and tossed it into the bin.

Ellen stood up. "Righto. I'll buzz you when she arrives."

"*If* she arrives," Sinéad said.

Ellen grinned. "Darling, I wouldn't be at all surprised if she's standing outside waiting for us to open. She is seriously keen and that's exactly what you need."

Sinéad twirled in her chair as the couple disappeared downstairs, and felt the butterflies in her tummy again. She thought of Dylan's words: "You're the boss." Yes, she was. And, if she was to rescue the business, she needed help; and, if Krystie Kelliher saved her having to do countless interviews, then so much the better. She gave a wry smile and wondered what Sheila would make of her wild little sister now shrinking from strangers. The intercom buzzed and she picked up the receiver. "Yeah?"

"She's here," Ellen said, sounding like an excited child.

96

"Wow, she *is* eager. I'll be right down." Sinéad went to the mirror to check her appearance. She sighed at the sight that greeted her. She was wearing the minimum amount of makeup and, though her black jeans and polo-neck were brightened by a colourful scarf tied round her hips, it was a far cry from the flamboyant clothes she'd worn and loved before Sheila went missing. Her entire world seemed to have split into before and after Sheila. She combed her fingers through her hair. She really needed to get that colour changed. She looked like Morticia Addams. Pinning on a smile, Sinéad took a deep breath, pulled herself up to her full five foot seven and went downstairs.

Ellen beamed at her and nodded at the girl sitting in a booth by the window. Not that she had to. Sinéad would have been able to pick her out no problem. The girl was probably around her own age but she was a kaleidoscope of colour and, when she looked up and smiled as Sinéad approached, her eyes were sparkling and her expression animated. She looked vaguely familiar. "Krystie?"

"Yes!" She stood up and held out her hand.

"I'm Sinéad Fields. Thanks for dropping in. More coffee?"

"No, thanks." The girl stared at her, frowning as Sinéad took the seat opposite and then her lips lifted in a delighted smile. "Oh, my God, of course. How dumb of me for not recognising your name. You and Sheila were a couple of years ahead of me in college."

"Oh, really?" Sinéad said, feeling sick.

"Yeah, small world, isn't it? How's Sheila? Are you running the business together?"

"We were but —"

"Oh, of course, you're closing the shop. Sorry about that, but I suppose these are tough times. But I'm sure it's just temporary. I saw some of your gorgeous pieces in the wedding boutique up the road. That's why I came looking for you." She put a hand up to touch her beret and smiled. "Hats have always been my first love."

"Mine too." Sinéad decided to stick to talking about the job. There was time enough to tell Krystie about Sheila if she decided to hire her. "So, tell me about yourself and what you've been doing since college."

The girl handed over her portfolio, references and CV and chatted away about her experiences in Manhattan. As Sinéad leafed through the designs she got butterflies in her stomach. She hadn't felt this excited since the day the actress had walked into the shop. "These are good," she said, realising that Krystie had stopped talking and was biting anxiously on her bottom lip.

The girl beamed. "Thanks."

"Yet you ended up working in an alterations firm." Sinéad frowned. "I don't understand."

"I was a bit naïve, I suppose," Krystie admitted. "I went to Manhattan expecting to have my choice of jobs, but I couldn't even get in the door of any of the big design houses. I finally got a job with a smaller company specialising in children's clothes. Not really my thing, but I figured it would at least get me on the

98

first rung of the ladder. My boss said I had to start at the bottom, it didn't matter what my qualifications were, that it was the only way to really understand the business."

"It's a fair point," Sinéad said, wishing she'd been given that advice, but she'd just done what she loved to do and left the business end of things to Sheila. It hadn't cost her a thought at the time. It was only now she realised the size of the burden she'd left her twin to carry.

"Yeah, I agree, only he taught me nothing and worked my butt off. I did everything and anything he asked, for a pittance, and then, just like that —" Krystie clicked her fingers — "he retired to Florida and I was out of a job."

"That was tough," Sinéad sympathised.

"Tell me about it. I should really have come home then, but I suppose I kept hoping someone would 'discover' me. Nuts, huh?"

"Not at all." Sinéad looked at her curiously. It was obvious that the girl knew nothing about their success. "We slaved from the moment we left college and didn't make enough to even pay the rent for the shop. Dad did that. We did build up some regular and well-established clients but it was hard work and then —" she smiled at Krystie — "we got our big break."

As she told the story of the famous actress stumbling on their shop by chance she watched Krystie's eyes grow round with wonder, but then why wouldn't they? It was like something straight out of a fairytale.

"So is that why you're moving? Are you moving to London? Oh, my God, you're not headed for Manhattan, are you?" Krystie's eyes shone with excitement.

Sinéad gave a rueful laugh. "No, just upstairs."

"Here?" Krystie shook her head. "I don't get it."

"It's a very long story. Things don't always work out the way that you expect."

"Huh, don't I know it."

Sinéad smiled. "But the good news is that the number of retailers we supplied did increase, so I do need another milliner. There's too much work for me to handle alone. I closed the shop because it was a distraction from the important work," Sinéad fibbed. "I will continue to deal direct, but clients will have to call for an appointment first."

"Cool. That'll make you seem even more exclusive. The snobby lot love that sort of thing."

Sinéad burst out laughing. "You're right. Tell me, did you make everything you're wearing?"

"Nah, I got the boots in a second-hand store in Manhattan and my undies are from Wal-Mart." Krystie grinned.

Sinéad took in the warm tones of the dress, the flamboyant jacket and vivid blue beret perched on the girl's dark hair. None of it should have worked — there was too much going on — but, somehow, it did. Sinéad's eyes returned to the beret. "May I?"

"Sure." Krystie took it off and handed it over.

"It's good." Sinéad turned it round and round in her hands, noting the exquisite tiny stitching and the slightly unusual shape that allowed it to sit more

comfortably on a full head of hair. "Clever."
face lit up at the praise, making Sinéad smile t

"I have to be honest, berets and caps and hea
are all I've tried my hand at, but I'm a quick l
and I'll work hard."

Sinéad gave her back the hat and decided t
her gut, though her brother would no doub'
was nuts. "Why don't we give it a go for a ι
and see how we get on?"

Krystie stared. "Are you serious? Don't you
Sheila to interview me, too?"

Sinéad braced herself. This was the hard part and iι
wasn't getting any easier. So much for time healing.
"Sheila is . . ." She still couldn't bring herself to say the
word dead. "She disappeared last March. Look —" she
made a show of looking at her watch — "I'm sorry, I
have another appointment. When could you start?"

Krystie was staring at her, stunned. "Er, Monday?"

"Great."

"But there's something I should tell you first."

Sinéad frowned. She should have known the girl was
too good to be true. "Yes?"

"I suffer from epilepsy."

"Oh, I'm sorry." Whatever she'd been expecting, it
wasn't this. The poor girl, how dreadful. She really
didn't know what to say.

Krystie waved away the sympathy with a smile.
"Really, it's no big deal. I'm lucky. I have a mild form
of the condition. I rarely get seizures but I thought you
should know."

preciate that." Sinéad relaxed a little. "I'm
know very little about it. You'll have to educate

ell, if I have an attack and I'm holding scissors,
good idea to take them away from me," Krystie
with a grin. "As I said, though, I rarely get them,
d when I do it's over in minutes and I recover very
uickly."

Sinéad was surprised and relieved. "I thought it was much more traumatic than that."

"It varies from one person to the next but often it's more frightening for anyone witnessing a fit. An epileptic doesn't remember anything afterwards. It can be pretty embarrassing if it happens in public or with strangers. That's only happened to me once, though."

Sinéad digested all this and then remembered something she'd heard about seizures. "Don't I have to put something in your mouth?"

Krystie laughed. "No. I believe that's what they did years ago in case you swallowed your tongue, but that's actually not even possible, though you can bite it, and it hurts! If a fit goes on for more than five minutes or if I seem to be having difficulty breathing, then you would need to call an ambulance, but that's only happened to me twice in my life. If you like I can bring you in a leaflet all about it on Monday," she offered.

"Oh, yes please," Sinéad said though she was relieved that it wasn't as scary as she had imagined. "Does it stop you doing anything?"

"Not much. Scuba diving is out but I hate water, anyway, so that's not a problem."

Sinéad shivered. "I hate the water, too."

"And I have to be clear of fits for a year before I can drive, but I don't like driving. I much prefer public transport. It's an opportunity to look at clothes." She smiled.

Sinéad laughed. "That's true, I must take the bus more often. Thank you for telling me about the epilepsy, Krystie. You didn't have to."

"It wouldn't be fair not to prepare you, just in case."

"Well, I appreciate that." Sinéad smiled and stood up. "I'll have my brother call you. He's an accountant and he takes care of the business end of things. He'll fill you in on the package. I hope that you find the terms acceptable."

"I'm sure they'll be fine."

Sinéad shook her hand. "Nice to meet you, Krystie."

"You too, Sinéad. Thank you so much for this opportunity and I'm sorry about Sheila —"

"Thanks," Sinéad cut in immediately. She wasn't ready to discuss that and she didn't want to break down in front of her new employee. "See you Monday." She smiled and fled back upstairs before the girl could ask any more questions.

Krystie sat in stunned silence. She'd got a job? That must be the fastest and easiest interview in history. And not just any job, but a job designing and making hats. At least she *thought* she would be designing. She frowned as she went back over the conversation. Sinéad hadn't actually said that but, hell, what difference did it make? She was going to be trained as a milliner by one of the best and get paid for it. This was very much a win-win situation. She had been relieved that Sinéad had reacted so well when she told her about the epilepsy. It had put other would-be employers off. The interview couldn't have gone better. The only cloud on the horizon was this mystery surrounding Sheila. Perhaps she would get the full story on the Internet . . .

"Can I get you more coffee?"

She looked up to see Ellen standing over her. Here was someone who would know. "Please, Ellen." She smiled. "And could I have a word when you get a moment? It's about Sheila."

Ellen stared at her for a moment and then nodded. "Sure. Give me a sec."

As she waited, Krystie's thoughts returned to her job. Wait till she told Sharon and Sandy. She groaned, realising that Sandy would be happy for her but upset that it would mean she wasn't returning to Manhattan. She definitely had to get her friend to visit Ireland, and soon. Her thoughts turned to Ma and Da. They would be over the moon at the news.

Ellen arrived back with two mugs. "So did you two come to an agreement?"

Krystie grinned. "Yes, it looks that way. We didn't talk money or anything but, to be honest, I'd happily work for her for nothing."

Ellen laughed. "I won't pass that on. Congratulations."

"Thanks." Krystie searched her face. "What happened to Sheila?"

"What did she tell you?" Ellen's expression was guarded.

"She said Sheila disappeared, that's all. I'm not being nosy, honest. It's just that I knew them — well, from a distance. We went to the same college but they were a couple of years ahead. Everyone knew there was something special about Sinéad. She had the 'it' factor. Sheila was different but," she added hurriedly, "she was great, too."

"She has real talent in running the business. They were sisters, best friends and they also made a great team. Sinéad is completely lost without Sheila." Ellen sighed. "It was only weeks after the BAFTAs — oh, do you know about that?"

"About the actress buying one of her headpieces and wearing it to the ceremony? Yes, Sinéad told me, unbelievable."

"It was an exciting time but crazy, too. They were inundated with media people wanting to interview and photograph them and they also had to deal with a huge increase in enquiries coming in from retailers, and not just in Ireland, either. They were both working all hours. Philip, Sheila's husband, was heading off to Brussels. Sheila usually travelled with him but she was exhausted. Not only did she have work to contend with, but her aunt had just moved into a nursing home. Sheila was spending a lot of time settling her in, putting her house on the market and clearing out her belongings. The day after Philip flew out, Max got a visit from the police. Sheila's car had been found on the coast road in Sandycove. Her bag and phone were on the passenger seat and the keys were in the ignition. A guy out walking his dog thought it was odd and, when he saw it still there on his way back, he called the Gardaí."

"Was she into swimming?" Krystie knew there was a famous spot around there for serious swimmers.

Ellen held her gaze. "Not at all and, anyway, no clothes or towel were found."

"Are you saying that she killed herself?" Krystie stared at her in disbelief.

Ellen shrugged. "We'll never know for sure what happened. They didn't find her body but, though there were many reported sightings and the police followed them up, they led nowhere. The investigation into the case was closed down a month ago. Sinéad took that very hard. It was tough for her dad and Max, her brother, too, of course, but Sinéad just couldn't accept it at all. She stays up till all hours checking missing-person sites and phoning up the Gardaí asking them to check a new theory she's come up with. She can think of little else."

"I'm not surprised. I'd be the same. And it just doesn't make sense that Sheila would take her own life, does it? She had so much to live for." Krystie's heart went out to Sinéad. No wonder she seemed so changed. How did anyone carry on after going through something like that? "Did Sheila have children?"

"No kids but she was married to the politician, Philip Healy, you know him, right? He's a TD, a member of the Dáil?"

"Never heard of him, but then I've been away a long time."

Ellen nodded and continued. "He was devoted to her and seems to be coping by just working all hours. It's hard to know how Max is. He's a more private sort of person. But the three of them were very close. And Kieran, their father, well, he's a mess. He went on sick leave for a while and then retired a year early. He just couldn't face going back to work, though he held a senior position in the council."

Krystie considered the situation for a moment. "So Sheila's why Sinéad is closing the shop?"

"Indirectly. Max thought it would be easier for her to concentrate on designing if she didn't have the shop to worry about."

"I hope he's right. She's so talented and sometimes work is the only way to get through tough times."

"That sounds like the voice of experience," Ellen said, her eyes curious.

"My problems are nothing in comparison to what Sinéad has been through."

Ellen smiled. "We all try to help but she needs someone around to talk hats with and remind her of how much she loves what she does. I think you are going to be good for her."

"I hope so," Krystie said solemnly. Although she had come here today in hope of just finding work, she now felt that perhaps she'd stumbled on something much bigger than a job.

CHAPTER
TEN

Max couldn't believe it when Sinéad told him that she had found a designer. Already? Really? And the girl had just walked in off the street? It sounded very dodgy. He just knew that Sinéad had probably just offered the girl a job without even checking her credentials but, when he heard that she'd gone to the same college as his sisters and was the same age as him, he felt a little happier.

He would make his own mind up, though, when she got here. He checked his watch again. *If* she got here, he corrected. She was late. That didn't bode well. What kind of person was late for an interview with a prospective employer? With that the door of Starbucks flew open and a girl in a rather colourful outfit stood in the entrance, her eyes searching the room. He stood up and raised an arm and, with a wide smile, she bounced towards him, her hand held out. "Max?"

"Yes." He took her hand and looked into the bluest eyes he'd ever seen. "You must be Krystle."

"Call me Krystie, please. Sorry I'm late. I was in Brown Thomas ogling hats and lost track of time." She pulled a face.

"Let's hope you don't lose track of time on the way to work," he said, curtly. "Coffee?"

"Latte, please." She smiled, not seeming to notice his annoyance.

Another featherbrain, if a bloody sexy one, he thought as he stood at the counter. He wondered, would she and Sinéad sit talking about hats all day instead of making the bloody things? He'd better make it clear that this was a probationary arrangement. He glanced around to see her chatting on her phone, her back to the wall, one slim pink-clad leg over the other. As he watched, she laughed and he found himself smiling at the sound and the way her face lit up. She was so vibrant, so alive.

"One latte, sir."

He paid for the coffee and carried it back to the table. She had finished the call and was looking up at him expectantly. She'd taken off her beret and her hair was a shining mass of dark curls. He could almost visualise them on the pillow.

"I've read the contract you emailed me and I'm happy to sign it," she said without preamble.

He watched, mesmerised, as she dipped a finger into the coffee and then sucked the foam from it. She grinned like a naughty schoolgirl.

"It's the best bit, right?" she said and licked her lips.

Max dragged his eyes away from her mouth and pulled out his copy of the contract. "Let's go through this, anyway."

She listened, nodding occasionally, as he took her through the document, although he got the distinct

109

impression that she would have agreed to anything just to get this job. "Have you any questions?"

"No, sounds fine."

He looked at her. "You really want this, don't you?"

She met his eyes and nodded. "I can't wait to start."

"Okay, then. There will be six months' probation and then Sinéad will reassess the situation."

"That's fine."

He looked at her. "Any other questions?"

"No, but I would just like to say I'm sorry about Sheila. I remember her. Your sisters were always being held up as examples, Sinéad for her innovation and Sheila for her hard work."

He smiled. "That sounds about right."

"It must have been such a terrible time for you, for all of you."

"It hasn't been easy," he admitted. "I've tried to do my best for Dad and Sinéad, but I'm not sure half the time if I'm doing or saying the right thing." Where the hell had that come from? He'd only just met this girl. He switched back into business mode. "The thing is, Krystie, I need to know that Sinéad can rely on you."

"Oh, she can," Krystie exclaimed, leaning forward. "It's an absolute honour to get to work with her. I can't believe my luck. Anything that I can do to make things easier, you only have to ask."

Max drank in her lovely eyes and red lips, wishing he could take her up on that offer. He cleared his throat. "Just do what you're told and don't ask her about Sheila."

110

"My lips are sealed." She pulled an imaginary zip across her mouth.

Max stared, wondering what it would be like to kiss it.

"Anything else?"

He looked at her. "Sorry? Oh, no, I don't think so. Welcome aboard."

Krystie stared out across Dublin Bay as the DART hurtled back along the track towards Greystones, and thought about her encounter with Max Fields. He was very different from his sisters in every way. Tall and broad-shouldered, he had hair that was strawberry blond and cut quite short, though an unruly lock was inclined to fall across his eyes, which were pale blue and curious. The sort of eyes that missed nothing. He had been beautifully though very formally dressed, but, then, he was an accountant for one of the city's largest firms and obviously stinking rich. According to Sharon, he was a mover and shaker, considered a catch with women running after him, but no one had managed to snare him yet. She could see the attraction in a detached way, but he didn't do it for her. She went for emotional, creative, moody men. Max was too cool and conservative for her liking, although there was definitely something about those pale-blue eyes that was arresting.

She leaped to her feet as the train pulled into her station and, jumping off, she walked briskly towards Sharon's house, saying hello and waving to a couple of the neighbours she had been introduced to. She was glad that Sharon was surrounded by such a nice bunch after what she had been through. She couldn't have moved to a better spot. Thanks to the new friends she'd made and her job, Sharon seemed to be taking things in her stride, but she was obviously nervous of getting involved with another man. Krystie could relate to that. It would be a long time before she let another man close enough to hurt her again, either.

After letting herself in, she closed the door on the cold evening air, switched on the fire in the living room and went straight through to the kitchen. Sharon would be home in an hour and she wanted to have a nice dinner ready for her. If it wasn't for her friend, she wouldn't have this amazing job. She still couldn't quite believe it. She would start work on Monday, and with Sinéad Fields. She had travelled to Manhattan in search of her fortune and ended up finding it in a suburb of Dublin. It was comical. It was also bloody fantastic.

The meal was almost ready when Sharon came through the front door smiling. "Yay, it's Friday and my first appointment isn't till eleven tomorrow. Something smells good." She took off her jacket, kicked off her boots and padded into the kitchen, setting a bottle of Prosecco on the counter next to Krystie. "I thought we should celebrate." She leaned over to inspect the contents of the pan.

"Lovely!" Krystie smiled gratefully. "I'm making risotto, so it's a good job you brought wine. The remainder of the bottle that was in the fridge is in here."

"So how did it go with Max Fields?" Sharon rooted in the drawer for the corkscrew, opened the wine and poured some into two glasses. She hoisted herself up onto the edge of the worktop. "Is he as gorgeous as they say?"

Krystie stirred thoughtfully. "He's a bit stuffy but I like him. I'd imagine he would need to know someone very well before he let his guard down." Although he had momentarily, she realised, when he had talked about his family. "He's got great hair and, as for his suit and the shoes —" she shook her head — "I doubt he got much change from a grand."

Sharon's eyes twinkled. "Excellent. A job and rich-boyfriend material — you're onto a winner."

"Unfortunately, he's not my type," Krystie laughed, mentally comparing Max's fair complexion with Jacob's sultry, Latin good looks. She stretched up to get two plates from the cupboard. "I hope you're hungry: I think I've made enough for three."

"Famished. Let's eat inside. It's too cold to sit out here." Sharon took the wine and glasses through while Krystie plated the food. "I'm going to miss you when you leave, especially your cooking."

"Nice to know I'm appreciated." Krystie followed her in and set the plates down on the small coffee table.

"Have you told your folks your good news yet?" Sharon asked.

"No, I'll call them after I've eaten. It's such a relief that I'll be able to pay my way."

"Are you going to admit you've been home for a couple of weeks?"

"Yeah, I thought I could tell a white lie, say I'd come home for the interview and didn't let them know because I didn't want to get their hopes up."

"Good thinking. You know you really don't have to move in with them, Krystie. It would make more sense to live here given you're going to be working a ten-minute train ride away. Think of the hassle it's going to be commuting from Ballymun every day."

Sharon was right: living here would make more sense, and moving back in with your parents after so many years just didn't feel right. "It would be great, but are you sure you wouldn't prefer to have the place back to yourself?"

"No, it's great to have company and —" Sharon grinned — "a chef."

"Then I'd love to stay, thanks."

Sharon squealed and hugged her. "Brilliant!"

"But I'd better go home for Christmas," she added. Christmas was a big family occasion in the Kelliher household.

"Do what I do: just join them for the day. If I had the guts I wouldn't even do that. My family are all completely mad. There's a lot to be said for spending the silly season with strangers."

Krystie laughed. "There is, but I haven't been home for Christmas in a couple of years and I kind of like all that traditional stuff and the home cooking. If it wasn't for Fallon it would be great. She could start a row in heaven."

Sharon took a sip of wine. "I haven't had the chance to ask you: are you happy about the job or are you just taking it for the money?"

"Are you kidding? I'm thrilled. Sinéad Fields is a brilliant designer and it will be fantastic to work with her."

"It won't be long before you're in the fashion magazines: 'Milliner Krystie Kelliher out on the town'."

Krystie laughed. "Sounds good to me."

"Imagine, someone wearing one of your hats could win the Best-Dressed Lady at the Galway Races or the Dublin Horse Show," Sharon said, wide-eyed.

"I know. This is really a great opportunity for me, Sharon. It's a small operation but it has the potential to be huge."

"It probably would be already if Sheila hadn't died."

"Yes," Krystie agreed.

"I remember seeing the two of them on TV," Sharon continued. "They looked gorgeous and seemed so nice. Everyone was thrilled and proud of their success. It was the kind of story that gives people a lift; a dream come true. And then the dream turned into a tragedy. It was the first thing on the news for days, there was a huge search. It was dreadful that they never found her body. I always think that must be very hard on a family."

"Yes, very hard. So did everyone assume she'd killed herself?"

"It seemed the only real possibility, but why on earth would she?" Sharon asked.

"No idea. You would think she would be on a complete high and enjoying every second of their success."

"Maybe she *was* on a high." Sharon reached for the wine and topped up their glasses.

"Drugs?" Krystie laughed at the thought. "I find that hard to believe. Sheila was very mature for her age and quite conservative. The two couldn't be more different. Mind you, Sinéad's changed so dramatically. She looks more like her sister now than ever before —" Krystie stopped.

Sharon immediately put down her glass and put a hand on her arm. "Are you okay?"

"Yeah, fine. I just had this weird *déjà vu* moment." Krystie shook her head.

"So are you really starting on Monday?"

"I start training on Monday. I have a lot to learn but I can't wait."

"I'm delighted for you," Sharon said and, getting to her feet, carried the empty plates outside. "I'm going to have a nice long soak in the bath with my wine and my book for company. Why don't you call your folks?"

"I will. It's great now that I have some good news to give them."

Krystie smiled when she heard her father's voice. "Hi, Da, it's me."

"Krystie?"

Her smile broadened at the obvious delight in his voice. "Yeah."

"Hello, sweetheart, how are you? Keeping all right?"

"I'm fine, Da, how are you?"

"Grand. I've been looking at the weather reports in New York. Bloody cold."

"Yes, but —"

"Hang on, I'll get your mother. Peg! Peg, it's Krystie," he roared. "You mind yourself, sweetheart."

"Da —" But he was already gone. Moments later Krystie heard some fumbling and then her mother's voice. "Krystie. Is everything okay? It's been ages since we've heard from you. I was worried."

Krystie cringed at the reproach in her mother's voice. "I'm fine, Ma, honestly. I've never felt better. Sorry I haven't been in touch but I've been pretty busy."

"A quick call to let us know that you're okay wouldn't take that much time."

"No, you're right, I'm sorry. But I have some news, Ma." Krystie took a deep breath. "I'm in Dublin."

"Ah, that's great news. Have you just landed? I'll get your da to collect you."

"No, I've been home a few days. I'm in Greystones with Sharon."

There was a pregnant pause on the other end of the line. "I don't understand."

Krystie crossed her fingers. "I had a job interview and I didn't want to get your hopes up, Ma, but, well, I got it."

"You got a job? Here in Dublin?"

Krystie grinned. "Yep."

"Oh, my God, that's wonderful news. You're home for good. Larry? Larry, she's home!"

Krystie held the phone away from her ear and laughed. "I suppose that depends on whether the job works out but, yeah, looks like I might well be."

"So tell me all about it."

Krystie wasn't surprised that there was another shriek when she said she was going to be working alongside Sinéad Fields.

"It was so sad about her poor sister," her ma said after she'd calmed down. "Are you taking her place?"

Krystie shivered at the thought. "I wouldn't say that. I imagine I'll just be Sinéad's assistant until I've learned the ropes."

"I'm delighted, love. But why are you all the way out in Greystones when there's a room here for you?"

"I'm going to be working in Blackrock, so it makes a lot more sense for me to live over here."

There was a short silence and then a resigned sigh. "Well, if that's what you want, but, if you change your mind, you only have to say."

"I know. Thanks, Ma."

"I'm so glad you'll be here for Christmas. It hasn't been the same without you these last couple of years. We'll have a grand time. We're all going to Alexis for tea on Christmas Eve and then to Midnight Mass from there and then everyone will be here on the day."

Alex was a pet and the best big sister ever, and Krystie got on well with her husband, Sam, but she still didn't fancy spending two days with the family fending off queries about Jacob and the reason she had come home. "Oh, Ma, that's weeks away yet! I'll definitely be there on the day, but I'm not sure about Christmas Eve. Sinéad wants us to get as much done as possible before Christmas because in January we'll be busy putting together a spring collection."

"I suppose you have to show willing in a new job," her mother agreed, "and at least you're home. Your father and I worried about you when you were in New York."

"There was no need, Ma." She smiled.

"When you're a parent you never stop worrying, trust me."

"So I shouldn't have kids, is that what you're saying, Ma?" Krystie teased, trying to lighten the mood.

"Oh, no, love. It will be the happiest day when your father and I see you settled down with a good man to look after you and, well, if you're blessed with children we would go to our graves content."

"Jeez, Ma, you're only in your sixties. What's with this doom and gloom? And you can forget about me settling down for a while: I've got more important things on my mind."

"Money won't keep you warm at night," her mother insisted.

"Nah, but I'll be able to afford a decent electric blanket," Krystie retorted, laughing.

"What about that lad you're dating? What does he think of you coming home? He's not with you, is he?"

Krystie's heart sank at the hope in her mother's voice. "Jacob and I split up, Ma."

"I'm sorry, darling. You seemed to be getting on grand."

"I thought so too but, let's say, the more he got to know me, the more he realised I wasn't the woman for him."

"Then it's his loss. You can find yourself a good Irish man."

Krystie smiled at the wonderfully typical answer of a loving mother. "I'd better go, Ma. I'll drop over on Sunday and say hello."

"Come for lunch. I'll do roast pork with the crackling, just the way you like it."

Krystie grinned. She couldn't bring herself to tell her mother that it was Fallon who loved pork. "Sounds gorgeous."

"Welcome home, Krystie."

"Thanks, Ma. Goodnight." Krystie hung up, feeling happier. Now that she'd heard their voices and had admitted she was in town she couldn't wait to see her folks. And she wouldn't let Fallon get under her skin and she'd try to stop her getting under anyone else's too. They would have a great family Christmas, she would make sure of it.

CHAPTER
ELEVEN

Sheila woke in the early hours and glanced at the clock. Sinéad would be awake soon. It was the twenty-eighth of November and their twenty-ninth birthday. It would also be the first birthday that they hadn't been in contact. She picked up her phone and stared at it. She could call. She could end all this but her anger and hurt stopped her dialling the number. She huddled under the covers and stared into the darkness. There was no comfort in knowing that this would be a hard day for her twin and, despite everything, Sheila knew it would be a hard day for her too. She decided not to tell Karl it was her birthday. He would want to celebrate and that was the very last thing she wanted. She turned on her side and stared at the clock, tucking her hands firmly under the pillow. She should have realised she would feel emotional today, it was completely normal. But she would get through it, and so would Sinéad.

Sinéad woke from a rather raunchy dream involving Hugh Jackman and then realised what day it was and her good mood promptly vanished. She was twenty-nine today. She glanced at the alarm clock. It was seven forty-five. Any year they had been apart on their birthday, Sheila had always phoned at eight. She put her hand out and checked that her mobile was on, the volume was turned up and the battery was fully charged, and then snuggled down under the covers with it on the pillow beside her. Philip had thrown a party for the two of them the last three years. It had been as much about PR for both him and them as it had been about a birthday celebration. She and Sheila would have already agreed on outfits that complemented each other's and put a lot of time and effort into the headpieces they would wear with them. On the day, they always lunched together and had then gone on to the hair salon. Seven fifty-five. Maybe . . .

"Morning, Birthday Girl!" Dylan walked in with a large mug of coffee. He set it down in front of the clock and bent to give her a long, lingering kiss.

Sinéad broke away with a tight smile. "Coffee. Lovely, thanks." She sat up and reached for the mug, her gaze fixed on the clock.

"Are you okay?" He sat on the edge of the bed and studied her face.

"Sure." Seven fifty-nine.

"Tonight will be fine, Sinéad. You'll be fine." He turned her face to his. "I know that you miss Sheila, but it will get easier."

One minute past eight. "Just leave it, Dylan, please?" She choked back her tears.

"Sure. Happy birthday." He stood up, put a small parcel on the table beside the clock and walked out of the room.

"Dylan!" she called after him just as the front door slammed. She reached for the package and glanced at the clock beyond it. Six minutes past eight. She wiped her eyes with the heel of her hand and unwrapped the gift. She opened the red velvet box and smiled at the delicate net of silver and turquoise stones. She took it out and, scrambling out of bed, went to the dressing table and held it against her neck, admiring its simple beauty. Unlike other years, she hadn't bought a new dress for the party, but she had made a hair appointment. She'd had enough of being a brunette; she needed a lift. She walked to the wardrobe and flicking past the black outfits she'd been living in for the last few months, she started to examine her more colourful options. She drew a fitted, navy, silk cocktail dress with lace sleeves. It was low-cut, barely covering her shoulders, and would show off the necklace beautifully. She hung it on the wardrobe door and, picking up her phone, she typed a text to Dylan: "It's beautiful, thank you and I'm sorry. xx."

As she dressed in a white shirt, short plaid skirt and black opaque tights, Dylan responded: "I'm glad you like it. See you this evening, xx."

She smiled, happy that at least that was resolved, finished getting ready for work and hurried out to her yellow Mini. She had wanted to sell it but Dylan and Max had laughed at her. "But it just doesn't seem right driving something so bright and cheerful, not now."

"It's only a bloody car," Dylan had said.

"At least wait until January and trade it in then," Max said, as always thinking about the best return on investment. She heeded him but used his advice only when she had to. They could laugh, but that was the way she felt.

When she got to the café, it was already quite busy and she had to queue along with the other workers getting their morning fix of caffeine.

"Good morning and happy birthday!" Ellen stretched across the counter to hug Sinéad, and then stepped back, her eyes dark with concern. "How are you doing?"

Sinéad nodded. "I'm okay. I'll have a vanilla Americano to celebrate."

Ellen grinned. "On the house, and you'd better make it two." She nodded towards the ceiling.

"Does she sleep here?" Sinéad laughed. Krystie was in before her nearly every morning, no matter how early she arrived.

"Don't knock it. Dedicated people are hard to find. Is she any good, that's what's important?"

"Oh, yeah. She has a very special gift. She absorbs information like a sponge, it's fantastic. Her biggest problem is that she's a perfectionist and takes too long on one piece."

"But she'll get faster as she gets used to the work, and she's so easy to get on with."

"She's great," Sinéad agreed.

"And so pretty. I assume she'll be sporting one of your pieces tonight."

Sinéad frowned. "I haven't invited her."

Ellen looked surprised. "Oh, Sinéad, why not?"

"She's only just started and, well, I don't want people to think I've replaced Sheila." Sinéad felt the tears well up and dug her nails into her palms. She couldn't cry here.

Ellen was around the counter in an instant. "Rory, take over," she called over her shoulder as she steered Sinéad towards the door that led upstairs. "You're not replacing her, you're just introducing your new assistant to your friends and prospective clients. Oh, sweetie, I'm sorry, I didn't mean to make you cry."

Krystie brushed the tears from her cheeks. "No, you're right, Krystie should come along tonight. I'll ask her."

Ellen patted her shoulder. "Good girl. You go on up, I'll bring the coffee."

Sinéad stopped on the landing and checked her eye makeup and hair in the mirror of her compact before going into the studio. Krystie was working on a piece of pink felt and was surrounded by feathers, lace and gauze, so completely immersed in her work that she never even noticed Sinéad walk in. "That looks interesting," she said, making Krystie jump. "Oops, sorry."

The girl laughed. "That's okay. I was just in a world of my own."

Sinéad tossed her bag in a corner and perched on the table beside her. "So, what do you think? I know it's early days, but do you think you could get to like the hat business or would you prefer, in the long term, to work in general fashion?"

Krystie looked up, her eyes shining. "Oh, hats, definitely! They say so much about a woman. They *do* so much for a woman, inside and out. In a nice dress or coat she might feel good but when she wears a hat it gives her confidence and says to the world, 'Here I am.'"

Sinéad smiled at the passion in the girl's voice. "What a wonderful way to put it. Look, Krystie, I know it's very short notice but are you doing anything tonight?"

"No, why?"

"It's my . . . our birthday. Philip, Sheila's husband, always threw a party for us and he decided to give a more low-key affair tonight rather than ignore the day altogether."

"That's nice." Krystie said, looking uncertain. "I'd say happy birthday, but it doesn't seem right. It must be kind of weird for you."

"It is. Anyway we, Sheila and I, always used it as an opportunity to show off a couple of new headpieces, and so I wondered, if you've nothing better to do, would you like to come along?"

"I'd love to! If you're sure I won't be intruding."

"No, of course not. This will be a good opportunity to introduce you. Most of the women who'll be there are customers and, anyway, Philip's idea of low-key is sixty people or more. I don't suppose you have a dress you could wear that you made yourself?"

Krystie thought for a moment and then grinned. "As it happens, I do."

"Great. What's it like?"

"It's satin and an aubergine colour. It's fitted to the waist and then it flares out to just above the knee with a net overskirt of the same colour. It's long-sleeved and has a cowl neck so it looks quite prim, but the back goes into a deep V to the waist."

"That sounds amazing," Sinéad said, wondering yet again how this girl hadn't been snapped up by one of the big fashion houses.

"But what headpiece could I wear?" Krystie glanced around the room at the mannequin heads and glass cases that sported Sinéad's creations.

"You could always make something."

Krystie looked at her, panic-stricken. "For tonight?"

Sinéad laughed. "Relax. Close your eyes. Imagine you're standing in front of a full-length mirror wearing the dress. Your makeup is perfect and you have your jewellery on. Now, think. What way is your hair done and what can you add to make that image just perfect?"

Obediently, Krystie closed her eyes and after a few seconds her lips started to turn up in a slow smile.

"Good," Sinéad said, getting a kick from her reaction. She'd never seen herself as a teacher but she was really enjoying the experience. Krystie was such an eager student, so hungry to learn. It was funny, they would probably have never met but for their love of design. They came from different worlds. She and Sheila had gone to one of the best schools in the city, whereas Krystie had gone to the local national school, taken a job and though she had achieved the same degree, Krystie had done it at night while she and Sheila studied full time and got pocket money from their father.

Had she received an application from Krystie in the post, Sinéad realised she'd probably have discarded it based on her address and education before she even looked at her work experience. The thought made her feel a bit ashamed of herself. She'd always seen herself as classless, nothing like some of the prima donnas of clients she and Sheila had had to contend with at times. Still, maybe she was no better than they were. When she'd met Krystie she'd vaguely remembered her from her college days. Even then her clothes had been edgy and fun and, most importantly, eye-catching. Her style had become even funkier now but classy, too, a look that wasn't easy to create.

Sinéad had worried that Krystie would turn up her nose at designing the more traditional hats, but she seemed happy to try her hand at anything. The biggest problem was getting her to take a proper lunch break and work shorter hours.

Krystie opened her eyes. "I need to keep it simple, right?"

Sinéad nodded, smiling. "Exactly."

"Then I've got an idea but I need a decent hairdresser."

"Not a problem. There's a salon around the corner we use." She faltered and then forced herself to continue. "I've an appointment later. I'll call and see if they can take you, too. Now, tell me your plan and what I can do to help."

"You don't have to do that," Krystie protested.

"Damn right I do. If your photo ends up in the papers the Fields name will be judged on that headpiece."

Krystie's eyes widened in alarm. "Maybe I should stay home."

"You will not," Sinéad laughed. "Get together the bits and pieces that you need and I'll call the salon."

Krystie's expression cleared and her concentration returned. Sinéad could almost see her mind working.

"Tell them I need a hairpiece, a long braid."

"What if they don't have anything to match your colour?" Sinéad asked.

Krystie shrugged. "They can change my colour, I don't mind. I do it all the time."

"Me too," Sinéad laughed. "This is going to be fun!"

The rest of the morning flew by and Sinéad couldn't believe how great it felt to be so engrossed in work that she was able to forget everything and everyone else. And, though the atmosphere was relaxed and they laughed and joked as they worked, Krystie's level of concentration and attention to detail never wavered. Sinéad was on her way out of the door for her hair appointment when Krystie called her back.

"Thanks for inviting me along tonight, Sinéad."

She smiled at the girl. "No, thank you. I thought today was going to be really tough, but you've helped me forget."

Rory was coming out of the storeroom as she flew down the stairs. "Happy birthday, darling!"

"Thank you, Rory. Are you guys still on for tonight?"

"But of course. As if we would miss it. Are you okay, sweetheart?" he asked, his eyes soft with concern.

"I'm fine." She gave him a quick hug. "I must go. Will you do me a favour, Rory? Remind Krystie that she's due in the hairdresser's at three."

"Will do."

129

"Thanks, darling." She blew him a kiss and hurried off.

Adele met her eyes in the mirror. "Well, what's it to be?"

"Blonde," Sinéad said emphatically.

The hairdresser's eyes lit up. "Really?"

"Yes, and straight. I'm going to clip it back on one side with this." She opened up the small hat box and carefully lifted out the headpiece.

"That's so pretty."

"It was one of Sheila's. It goes with my outfit and, well, I thought it would be nice to wear something of hers tonight."

Adele squeezed her shoulder. "It's a lovely idea. Okay, let me get the colour chart and we'll get started."

She was just blow-drying Sinéad's silken ash-blonde hair into a bob when Krystie raced in the door. She paused at the desk. "Hi, I'm Krystie Kelliher. I've an appointment."

"Of course." The receptionist smiled, took her jacket and led her to a seat.

"Well, what do you think?" Sinéad asked

Krystie turned her head and stared at her.

"Don't you like it?" she prompted, when the girl still said nothing. Sinéad turned back to the mirror. "Is it too pale?"

"No," Krystie said, "you look gorgeous! Sorry, it's just that you look so different, I didn't recognise you."

"It suits you, Sinéad," Adele agreed. "Now shall I put in the clip or will you be able to manage it yourself later?"

"I'll do it." Sinéad stood up and took off the protective gown. "Thanks so much, Adele." She turned back to Krystie, who was still watching her. "Are you okay?"

"Sure. Want to see the finished product?" Krystie asked.

"Absolutely."

Krystie took out her hat box and lifted the lid to show off her handiwork.

Sinéad smiled, marvelling at its delicacy. "Great work, Krystie, really great."

The girl flushed with pleasure. "Thanks."

"I have to run." She patted Krystie's shoulder. "You are going to knock 'em dead!"

She drove home feeling happier than she had when she had woken up this morning; she'd actually enjoyed today — so far. Krystie was a natural designer and her love of her work showed in every careful stitch. She was a different person once she became lost in the creative process — they were quite alike. Sheila had never been as absorbed, always thinking about the business and the figures rather than the simple enjoyment of creating something beautiful. Sinéad turned her thoughts back to Krystie, determined to maintain her good mood. Her braid would look spectacular, Sinéad was sure of it. She just hoped Krystie's dress lived up to it. So far she had only seen Krystie in casual clothes and couldn't imagine her wearing a demure cocktail dress, though her description had sounded beautiful. And, knowing Krystie, whether it was to Sinéad's taste or not, it would definitely be eye-catching, which was the most important thing.

She'd led the girl to believe the evening would be casual, though it would be anything but. Philip didn't know how to do "low-key". Still, better Krystie remain in ignorance till this evening. Once she got over the initial shock, Sinéad was confident that she'd take to it like a duck to water.

CHAPTER
TWELVE

Krystie and Adele agreed on a sixties-style look but the heavy fringe would be tinged with a deep pink to give it a more funky look. The plait Adele had found was a good match to her own hair colour and it would take very close scrutiny to tell it wasn't real. As Adele got to work, Krystie painstakingly sewed the headpiece into the braid so that the beads and gems in the aubergine ribbon ran in a perfectly straight line down the centre.

"If you ever get fed up making hats, you can have a job here," Adele said, admiring her work. "It's going to look sensational and every time you turn your head it will catch the light. Tell me about the dress."

Krystie was glad to. Chatting distracted her from her nervousness. From listening to Adele and the staff talking, tonight was a much bigger deal than Sinéad had led her to believe and it would be the first time she would be introduced as a Fields designer wearing her first official creation. It was a very simple piece but damn effective, and she was proud of it. She had enjoyed every moment of her job so far. The hardest part of her day was going home. But then she and Sharon would usually curl up at opposite ends of the sofa and chat or she would Skype Sandy and catch up with her. She felt more comfortable in Greystones now that she was employed and could pay her way. Also, Sharon had the house to herself again for a lot of the time and, when she worked evenings, Krystie got some space and privacy too. It was the perfect arrangement.

Other than going to the local pub with Sharon, she'd had no social life since she'd come back to Dublin, but it didn't bother her. She was happy with her new life and perfectly content to simply put her feet up at the end of the day.

Adele came over to check her colour. "You're ready. Come on over to the basin. Do you want me to get Nuala to do your nails while I'm doing your hair? We have a good choice of varnish. I'm sure you'd find something to go with your dress."

"Really? That would be cool, thanks."

An hour later, with the girls' shouts of good luck following her, Krystie hurried out of the salon and was walking towards the train station when she spotted a taxi. To hell with the expense, she wasn't going to take any chances on her hairdo getting messed up, and she couldn't afford any delays, anyway. It was almost six.

Back at the house she quickly dug out her dress — thankfully wrinkle-free — and shoes. After a delicate wash, taking care not to splash her hair, Krystie applied very pale foundation, outlined her blue eyes with black kohl, dusted the lids with a silvery shadow and added three layers of mascara. She rummaged through her makeup bag until she found the perfect lipstick, a pale frosty pink.

She had just stepped into the silver stiletto sandals and was twisting and turning in front of the bathroom mirror when Sharon arrived home. "In here," she called.

"Holy shit!" Sharon stood in the doorway, wide-eyed. "You look amazing. And your hair!"

Krystie turned around so that Sharon could get a look at her handiwork. "You like?"

"I like." Sharon came closer. "Who did this for you?"

"I did."

"Wow, well done you." She walked around Krystie, taking in every detail. "It's as if the jewels are a part of your hair and the ribbon is perfect with the dress. Brilliant. The silver eyeshadow works so well with your sandals and the gems in your hair; you're like Cinderella! Bag?"

Krystie led the way back into her bedroom and held up a shiny silver clutch bag.

"Perfect." Sharon grinned.

There was the sound of a horn outside. "That will be my taxi."

"What are you wearing over it?" Sharon asked.

Krystie sighed. "I've nothing suitable so I'm going like this."

"Are you mad? It's freezing out there. Oh, wait!" Her eyes lit. "I've got just the thing."

"Really, don't worry, I must go." Krystie opened the door and waved to the taxi driver just as Sharon reappeared carrying a white fur wrap. "What do you think? It's fake and cheap but you can take it off as soon as you get in the door."

"It's just right, Sharon, thank you."

Sharon carefully lifted the braid as Krystie wrapped it around her. "Is my back covered?" she asked.

"Yeah, and the guys will be gagging for you once you take it off."

"To hell with the guys. Once Sinéad and her customers are happy I'll be over the moon." She pressed her cheek to Sharon's. "Thanks, hon, you're the best."

"Have fun, Cinders!"

"Bloody hell," Krystie breathed when the taxi pulled up outside Sinéad's apartment block and had to buzz the intercom and give her name before the barrier went up.

"You won't find anyone on the dole in this place, love," the driver laughed.

"Do you think they'll let a girl from a council estate into a place like this?" she asked with a nervous giggle and stepped out of the car.

He looked her up and down. "The way you look, love, you'd get into Buckingham Palace."

"Ha, you sure know how to get a good tip!" She handed over the cash and walked towards the entrance, where a porter was already opening the door.

Jeez, she was beginning to feel like a bloody celebrity. He pressed the button for the elevator — lift, she reminded herself — and then the button for the fourth floor. "Apartment 4B," he said with a polite smile before withdrawing.

As it glided silently up, Krystie studied her reflection in the mirrored walls. She was happy with the final result. Sharon's wrap might be from a chain store but it didn't look it. With her thick, glossy, dark fringe feathered with pink framing her dramatically made-up eyes and the rich colour of her dress, she looked positively festive. The lift doors opened and she stepped out, crossed the hall to apartment 4B and rang the bell. The door was opened almost immediately by Max, looking handsome in a dark suit. She fidgeted nervously as he stood staring at her making no move to let her in. "Max, hi. I don't know if you remember me. Krystie?"

His blue gaze raked her very slowly from head to toe. "Oh, I remember," he murmured.

She took off her wrap. "I'm doing a spot of advertising." She spun slowly around and heard his intake of breath.

"That's quite a dress."

She felt herself blush, realising it was her bare back that had caused his reaction.

"She meant her hair." Sinéad joined them, laughing. "Turn around again, Krystie."

She did, conscious of Max's eyes burning into her.

"Truly beautiful," he said when she turned back to face him, and, when she saw his expression, it was clear that he wasn't talking about her hair or the dress.

"I think my brother is too overcome by the whole package to pay much attention to your lovely handiwork, Krystie, but, in his defence, you do look stunning." Sinéad turned Krystie around again. "I'm guessing *you* worked the piece into the braid, not Adele."

Krystie smiled. "Yeah, how did you guess?"

"You have an attention to detail that is quite spectacular."

"Thank you," Krystie said, her heart fit to burst at the compliment.

"I'll be honest. When you were mixing in the silver stones with the purple beads I really didn't think it would work, but you've used so few that they do their job of attracting the eye without being overpowering." Sinéad shook her head, looking almost envious. "As for that dress, are you quite sure that you want to be a milliner?"

"Oh, yes," Krystie laughed. "I love it, really I do."

"Good, glad to hear it."

Sinéad turned her head and it was only then that Krystie noticed her headpiece. It was like a loving hand cupping the side of her head and covered one ear, but it was made of peacock feathers and beads. It scooped Sinéad's hair back, leaving her lovely neck bare and drawing attention to the stunning necklace that glistened against her creamy skin and dipped into her cleavage. "You look fabulous and that headpiece is a work of art."

Sinéad put a hand up to caress the feathers. "Isn't it? Sheila made it." Her voice wavered but then she smiled and took Krystie's arm. "Come, let me introduce you to the others."

She drew Krystie into a living room twice the size of Sharon's. It was furnished with leather chairs, a sofa, a large desk with a chair either side and a floor-to-ceiling bookcase.

138

"This apartment is awesome, Sinéad," Krystie said.

"We picked it up for a song," her boss said with a grin. "It belonged to a B-list celeb that got into trouble with the taxman and had to leave Ireland in a hurry."

She led Krystie to the window, where two men stood talking. "Krystie, this is my dad, Kieran, and my partner, Dylan."

Krystie watched Dylan put his arm on the small of Sinéad's back and give her a warm smile before turning his attention to greet her. God, he was gorgeous and unnervingly like Jacob. No, she was not going to think about him, not tonight. "Hi."

"Nice to meet you." Dylan shook her hand.

"Hello," Kieran said with a nod and an absent smile. He was like an older version of Max but shorter, or perhaps that was just the slump to his shoulders. Krystie sighed. She'd have to remember to tread carefully tonight. Despite the cheerful atmosphere, it was clear this was a family in mourning.

"Champagne?" Max was back at her side and handing her a glass.

"Thank you," Krystie said, conscious of his hand brushing hers. She looked up to find him watching with those piercing eyes and shivered. She took a sip from the heavy crystal glass and tried to look as if she drank champagne every day of the week.

"Show them, Krystie," Sinéad urged.

She did as she was told and stood patiently as Sinéad explained to her dad and Dylan the work that had gone into the piece.

When she turned around again Kieran smiled. "I don't know anything about this sort of thing but you look smashing." He glanced over at his daughter, his eyes suspiciously bright. "You both do."

Sinéad slipped her arm through his and kissed his cheek. "Thanks, Dad."

The doorbell rang. "That will be Philip," Dylan said and went to let him in.

"So, you're settling in all right, Krystie?" Max asked.

"Fine, thanks. I'm really enjoying it, and Sinéad is being very patient with me."

Sinéad grinned. "I'm just lulling you into a false sense of security. I'll be a tyrant when the orders start rolling in."

"No problem," Krystie said happily.

"Evening, all."

She looked around to see a beaming, well-dressed man approaching. So this was Sheila's husband.

He made a beeline for her, his hand outstretched. "You must be Krystie." He took her hand and then covered it with his other. "Philip Healy, delighted to meet you."

"And you," she said while really thinking how false he seemed. She watched him hug Sinéad and noticed that she didn't seem that comfortable with her brother-in-law either. The men, however, chatted easily enough. Only Kieran looked as if he'd prefer to be anywhere else but here. Her heart went out to him. He was obviously going through a very tough time. She glanced back at Sinéad, noticing that, though she was smiling, her eyes were sad — and who could blame her?

140

"We should be going." Philip smiled at Sinéad. "You can't be late for your own birthday party."

"Philip, you promised low-key." Sinéad gave him a reproachful look.

"And it is, I promise, but I'm sorry." He shrugged, suddenly looking vulnerable. "I couldn't ignore the day."

"None of us could." Kieran put a hand on his shoulder and raised the other in a toast. "To Sheila. We miss you, darling."

Feeling very uncomfortable, as if she was invading their privacy, Krystie silently joined them in the sad toast. Sometimes life sucked.

Philip hustled them outside to the waiting limo and they were whisked the short distance from Mount Merrion to the Four Seasons hotel. He explained on the way that, though they had a private room for dinner, they would have drinks in the bar first. He smiled at the girls. "And hopefully get these lovely ladies into the social pages."

It seemed unlikely to Krystie that there would be photographers hanging around hotel bars just in case someone important wandered in, but she was amazed when they arrived that a camera flashed as soon as Philip opened the door. "Smile, girls," he said and held out his hand to Sinéad. Krystie saw a flicker of panic cross her face, but Dylan whispered something in her ear. Sinéad nodded and, taking Philip's hand, stepped out of the car and smiled for the two photographers,

"Your turn," Max said to Krystie with a reassuring smile.

Philip posed with the two of them while Max, Dylan and Kieran stood in the background looking on. At first Krystie felt awkward, and then she remembered that this was the break that she had dreamed of for years and, letting her wrap slip down, she looked back at Max as if she were asking him something. Immediately there was a rapid clicking of camera shutters.

Max smiled down at her and touched her cheek. "Smart as well as beautiful. I think I could fall for you, Krystie Kelliher."

She stared into his eyes, mesmerised. "That would be a really bad idea," she murmured, but smiled to take the sting out of her words.

"Enough," Sinéad muttered, "let's go."

Krystie tore her gaze from Max, waved at the photographers and hurried after Sinéad.

CHAPTER
THIRTEEN

Krystie stopped and stared in the doorway of the crowded lounge. "Is everyone here going to the dinner?" she asked Max.

"Who knows?" He grinned and, taking her hand, led her through the crowd, pausing every so often to say hello and to introduce Krystie as Sinéad's new designer. Finally, they found Dylan and Kieran sipping yet more champagne. Philip stood in a group of people a short distance away, Sinéad at his side. Krystie accepted the glass that Max offered her, but she was more interested in drinking in the gowns on the women around her than anything else. It was disappointing that she and Sinéad were the only ones wearing headpieces. Sinéad saw her and immediately came over, looking tense.

"Come on, Krystie, time to work. There are lots of rich women here we need to show off that braid to. Besides, if you're with me it might stop them asking me how I'm bloody feeling. Such a stupid question. How the hell do they think I'm feeling?"

"Sure, sorry, I didn't think." Krystie was alarmed to see tears in Sinéad's eyes. She looked around to tell Max, but he was talking to a very pretty woman who was gazing adoringly up at him. Krystie turned quickly away before he spotted her watching them.

"We'll take a wander around the room and then Philip promises we'll be going in to dinner," Sinéad told Dylan and her dad.

"Why don't we go to the bar and get a pint, Kieran?" Dylan suggested.

"Now you're talking," Kieran muttered.

Sinéad led Krystie back towards Philip's group and immediately he drew Krystie forward. "People, allow me to introduce Krystie Kelliher, Sinéad's new protégée."

Krystie shook hands with each of them. Smiling, she made a point of turning her head, a few times, earning a nod of approval from Sinéad.

"I love your hair," one woman said. Her own was pulled into a severe knot on the top of her head. "It must have taken hours to do. I just don't have the time."

"It didn't take long at all," Krystie told her. "The braid is a hairpiece."

"And she made the jewelled ribbon herself," Sinéad chimed in.

"Wow, that's amazing. I've bought a couple of fancier grips to try and make my hair look better but they never look this good. You should stock them."

"We're closing the shop due to the increasing orders from retailers but you will still be able to come to our wonderful new studio next door. Krystie is creating a whole new range of simple pieces like the ribbon that she's wearing, and they should be available in all the main department stores early next year."

I am? They will? Krystie was very impressed at Sinéad's exaggerated spiel, but the women seemed impressed. She quickly smiled and nodded. "Yes, they'll be easy to fit and more casual-looking, but fun." She shot Sinéad a grateful look as she realised that she'd said the range would be Krystie's. A waiter tried to top up her glass but she shook her head and put her glass on his tray. She was drinking it far too quickly and on an empty stomach. She wanted to remain sober and enjoy every moment of her first outing as a designer.

The group had broken into male and female and more women joined them full of compliments at Sinéad and Krystie's headpieces. Krystie felt a thrill of excitement. Who knew when she was struggling to gather together the fare to fly home that she would be employed and the centre of attention just a few weeks later? It was surreal.

A member of staff came and whispered something in Sinéad's ear. "Dinner's ready," she announced and they all started to move towards the dining room. Dylan materialised out of nowhere and snaked an arm around Sinéad's waist, pulling her tight to his side. Krystie watched them. She really wished he didn't remind her so much of Jacob. From behind they looked so similar. Dylan moved like a man comfortable in his own skin, had the same slender build and dark, close-cropped hair. Had Jacob ever looked at her the way Dylan looked at Sinéad? She didn't think so. Strange, she was so sure that if her moment of fame came he would be with her to share it. She was pulled back to the present by a hand on her bare back.

"Come sit with me and I'll protect you from the madness."

She looked up to see Max and smiled gratefully. She could never be called the shy type but she did feel a bit intimidated tonight. She'd wager that every other woman here was kitted out head to toe in designer gear. She was grateful that, though her sandals were second-hand, they were a respected upmarket American brand. She hid her bag under her seat. At least her dress couldn't be judged by its label and it looked as good as, if not better than, most of the gowns on the women around the three tables. Her eyes were drawn to Sinéad. Despite the muted colour of her dress, she stood out, her bare neck as flawless as the beautiful necklace around it. Her blonde hair made her look younger and much prettier, despite the anxiety in her eyes.

They were about to take their seats when Max took her hand. "Wait, I want to show you something." He led her between the tables to the display of photos at the other end of the room. Though Sinéad was in many of the shots, this was really a shrine to Sheila, her beloved twin. There were photos from childhood right up to a still from their TV appearance. One photo caught Krystie's attention. It was of the sisters when they were about ten. One had her head thrown back laughing while the other stared solemnly into the camera. "Which is which?" she asked Max.

146

He chuckled. "Oh, that's Sheila wearing her mammy face." He pointed at the more sober-looking child.

She looked up at him. "What do you mean?"

"Our mother died twenty years ago when the girls were nine and I was seven," he explained. "Sheila was the bossy sort and apparently tried to take over. Sinéad says now that it was as if she wanted everything to be exactly the same as when Mum was alive. I suppose it was her way of coping with the loss while Dad went to pieces and Sinéad cried all the time."

She stared at him, lost for words. They'd lost their mother and sister? "What about you?" she said eventually.

"Once I was fed I was happy," he said with a grin.

Krystie didn't buy that but didn't push it. This was heavy stuff and she barely knew the guy.

"My aunt, Mum's sister, moved in to look after us," he continued, "but she wasn't used to dealing with kids. She didn't really know what to make of us."

"Is she here tonight?"

He shook his head. "She's in a home, premature dementia."

"I'm sorry."

"Me too. She might have been better able to deal with Sinéad and Dad than I am. Still, Sinéad has perked up a lot since you arrived on the scene." He smiled at her. "Perhaps you're our good-luck charm."

"What happened to your mother?" she asked as they moved on to look at a group of photos that were obviously taken when the shop had opened.

"She drowned."

She stopped and stared at him.

"It was an accident," he added hurriedly. "We used to take a mobile home down in Kilmucridge for the summer. Dad would come down for the weekends. Once we were asleep, Mum would go for a swim — she loved swimming. One night she didn't come home. Her body was washed up a few miles down the coast a couple of days later."

"Jeez, you guys haven't had it easy, have you?" Krystie said, shocked.

Max shrugged but his eyes were sad. They were moving on to the next montage of photos when waiters emerged from the kitchens with the starters. "Come on, let's eat."

But she barely heard him, her eyes riveted to a photo of the twins sporting knitted hats pulled low over their eyes.

"What?" Max frowned.

"Oh, it's just that in this one they're impossible to tell apart," Krystie murmured, her eyes still locked on the photo.

"I often couldn't tell them apart when we were kids until they spoke. It was much easier when they got older as they had very different styles, but they could still fool people when they wanted."

Philip stood and tapped his fork against a glass for attention and Krystie allowed Max to lead her back to their table.

"Friends, I won't make a big speech but I just wanted to say thank you for being here tonight to join us in celebrating Sinéad's birthday and taking the opportunity to remember and honour Sheila."

He paused and looked down, and Krystie couldn't help feeling that it was all for effect. She looked around the room but everyone seemed captivated and you could have heard a pin drop.

"It has been a terrible time for our family and we wouldn't have got through it without each other or without good friends. So please join me in toasting Sinéad —" he raised his glass — "and Sheila, wherever she may be."

Everyone stood and echoed the toast. Sinéad remained in her seat with her head bowed.

Wherever she may be. Krystie thought of a woman staring at a window display in Manhattan, and she stared at her boss. She could see Dylan murmuring into her ear but Sinéad was staring into the middle distance with a blank expression.

"Don't you like the seafood?" Max asked.

She picked up her knife and fork. "Yes, lovely."

He frowned. "You're very quiet. Is there something wrong?"

"I just feel a bit uncomfortable. This is a dinner for friends and family. I really shouldn't be here."

He laughed. "Friends? Are you kidding? These aren't friends: they're business contacts. Philip has either invited them because politically they can be of use or they're potential clients for Sinéad."

"That sounds very cynical. Don't you like him?" Krystie asked as she made a half-hearted attempt to

149

eat. Somehow her earlier hunger seemed to have deserted her.

"Sure I do. I'm just saying this is more business than pleasure."

"Do you think Sheila was happily married?"

He gave her a sharp look. "Why do you ask?"

"No reason, just curious."

"Yes, I think she and Philip were very close."

Krystie smiled, but in her head she was back in Manhattan in front of a store window staring into the sad eyes of a woman. A woman she was now convinced was Sheila Fields.

CHAPTER
FOURTEEN

"Well, I know what my excuse is. What's yours?"

Krystie looked around and gulped when she saw Kieran Fields leaning against the wall, smoking a cigarette. "Too much expensive champagne," she lied, smiling. "I'm only used to cheap plonk." In reality the shock of her realisation had driven her outside, despite the cold, to get some fresh air and try to think. Meeting Sinéad and Sheila's father was the last thing she'd expected or needed.

"It's far from champagne that lot were reared on." He smiled at her. "Are you settling into the job okay?"

"Yes, thanks. I love it."

He smiled again. "That comes across. It's good for Sinéad to have someone working with her again. She's not used to being on her own, needs company." He stubbed out his cigarette and tossed it into the grass. "I suppose I'd better get back in there. Coming?"

She followed him inside and took her place next to Max just as the main course was being served.

"I thought you'd got fed up and gone home, not that I'd blame you," Max remarked.

"No, of course not." She smiled at him. "I got talking to your dad."

Max raised his eyebrows. "Then you really are a lucky charm. The man has barely opened his mouth since Sheila's death."

Krystie took a quick look around. The other people at their table were engrossed in conversation. "You're the only one who ever uses the word 'death' when we talk about Sheila. Why is that?"

"Because I'm the only one willing to face facts," he said, sounding resigned and fed up. "I loved my sister, Krystie, but she's dead and gone and we just have to get on with it. Dad and Sinéad won't accept that. Despite the fact that every lead has ended in a cul-de-sac, they still hope, and it's destroying them."

This was it. This was her opportunity. And who better to talk to than Max? She could tell him what she had seen that day in Manhattan and then he could decide what to do. She'd just opened her mouth when the woman on his other side put a hand on his arm.

"Max, we must set up a meeting soon. I really need your advice. Perhaps over lunch some day?"

Krystie sighed both at the interruption and the woman's rather obvious come-on. It seemed Sharon was right: Max was certainly popular with the ladies. She pushed her food round the plate and glanced over at Sinéad. She was smiling and nodding at a woman chattering away to her and Dylan while Kieran sat in silence sipping his pint. As for Philip, he seemed in great form altogether. Shouldn't tonight be as hard for him as it was for Sinéad? Exactly how happily married had Sheila and he been? Was he the reason she'd left? But how could she do it to the rest of her family?

152

Krystie knew she was far from being a perfect daughter, but she couldn't imagine being that heartless. Her eyes returned to Kieran. God, he looked so miserable and broken. No, she definitely couldn't do that to her dad.

Everything Krystie had heard about Sheila had been positive. She'd mothered them, cared for them and basically been the centre of the family. They would be thrilled to hear there was a possibility that she was alive — but was it up to Krystie to tell them? She sighed heavily.

"Hey, what was that for?" Max whispered in her ear. "Aren't you enjoying yourself? You should be. Everyone's watching you. You're the most beautiful woman in the room."

She shivered at the desire in his eyes. "I'm fine, just feeling a bit overawed. I've never been in a room so crammed with rich people."

"You're just as good as them — no, better."

Out of the corner of her eye Krystie saw Sinéad hurrying out of the door. "Excuse me. I just want to check in with your sister and see who she wants me to chat up after dinner."

He smiled in approval. "Good girl. I think you two are going to make quite a team."

Krystie was surprised to find the ladies' room empty. She reapplied her lipstick, tucked a few hairs back into place and was about to leave when she heard sniffling coming from the disabled toilet cubicle at the other end of the room. She hunkered down and recognised Sinéad's high heels. She knocked gently. "Sinéad?" The sobbing stopped abruptly. "It's Krystie. Are you okay?"

After a moment the door opened and Sinéad pulled her inside. "Lock the bloody door. I can't let anyone see me like this." She sat down on the lid of the toilet, grabbed a handful of loo roll and started to dab at her eyes. "Am I a mess?"

"Don't worry, I'll fix your makeup before we go back in," Krystie said. "Take a minute. It's only natural that you're finding this tough. To be honest, I think it was very brave of you to agree to it at all."

Sinéad sighed. "Oh, Philip can be bloody persuasive and I haven't been particularly nice to him lately, so I felt I should."

"Why haven't you been nice to him?" Krystie asked.

"I suppose I just find it hard watching him carry on as normal. Still, we all deal with grief differently."

"Yeah," Krystie said, unconvinced. Something about Philip just didn't ring true.

"The only problem is I'm not sure I can deal with it." Sinéad's tears started to flow again. "It's great working with you, Krystie, I'm enjoying it so much and you are so talented —"

"But I'm not Sheila," Krystie finished for her.

Sinéad dropped her head into her arms and sobbed like a baby. Krystie crouched down and put her arms around her. "Oh, to hell with it, I can't handle this any more. Sinéad, there's something I have to tell you. I think Sheila is alive; in fact, I'm almost sure of it."

"Tell them." Sinéad sat huddled on a chair looking pale and shaken despite the repaired makeup.

154

Krystie looked nervously as Max, Kieran, Philip and Dylan looked at her expectantly. They were gathered in a small office area off reception.

"What's going on?" Philip demanded, his usual pleasant expression creased in annoyance. "We can't just disappear on our guests like this."

"At this stage I doubt they would notice," Dylan drawled. "Most of them are plastered."

Max put a hand on Krystie's shoulder. "What is it?"

"It's about Sheila. I . . . I think I saw her in New York a few weeks ago."

Max pulled his hand away abruptly, his eyes widening with incredulity and anger. "What the hell are you playing at?"

"This really isn't funny," Dylan said, glaring at her and putting a protective arm around Sinéad's shoulders.

"I'm not making it up," Krystie protested. How could he think that?

"Stop it, both of you. Tell us." Kieran grasped her hand, his eyes full of hope.

Krystie repeated her story word for word as she had told Sinéad, how the penny had dropped when she saw that photo of Sinéad and Sheila. She was as certain as she could be that the woman she had seen staring into the hat shop was Sheila.

"Sheila wasn't blonde," Max said.

"If she didn't want to be recognised, of course she'd dye it," Sinéad said, staring into space.

"But you didn't hear her voice?" Max persisted.

"No," Krystie said. "I spoke to her but she seemed alarmed and hurried off."

"It's her," Sinéad said.

"Thank God." Kieran crossed himself, his eyes bright with tears.

"Dad, she caught a glimpse of a woman with blonde hair who looks like Sinéad, that's all," Max protested.

"She was looking into the window of a hat shop," Sinéad reminded her brother.

Dylan squeezed her shoulder. "Don't go getting your hopes up, sweetheart."

"It's her," she insisted.

"Even if it is, you may as well try to find a needle in a haystack."

"If she's alive, I'll find her," Sinéad assured him.

Max drove towards his father's house. He found it hard to believe Dad had been as chatty as Krystie had said. He sat in the passenger seat, lost in thought, responding to anything Max said with just a nod or a grunt. Krystie was silent, too. He glanced at her in the rear-view mirror. Her head was resting against the window, her eyes closed. Stupid, dumb, infuriating and bloody gorgeous, sexy woman. It had been such a good evening before she went and ruined it. He didn't know which he wanted to do more, strangle her or make love to her. And that dress! Every time she'd turned to look around or leaned forward to talk to someone across the table he'd get an exciting glimpse of the creamy skin of her back, and it had been exquisite torture resisting the temptation to touch her. He had risked it briefly a couple of times and she hadn't objected, but he knew if he touched that soft, velvet skin again he would want to continue his exploration.

"You missed the turn."

His father's first full sentence since he'd got into the car snapped him out of his daydream. "Shit." He pulled into the kerb, waited for a car to pass and then made a U-turn.

On the doorstep, Kieran turned to give him a hard stare. "Don't you dare give that girl a hard time."

"I won't, Dad."

His father nodded and went inside.

"Night, Dad," Max said to the closed door, and walked back out to the car. He glared when he saw Krystie still slumped in the back seat. He yanked the door open and was horrified when she cried out and started to fall. He caught her in his arms. "Shit, sorry, Krystie."

She blinked. "What happened? Did we crash?"

"No. I just dropped Dad off. I didn't realise you were sleeping. I'm so sorry. I thought you might want to join me in the front."

She straightened and looked at him, her lovely eyes full of remorse. "Are you sure you want me?"

He held her gaze. If only she knew how much. "I'm sure."

She waited until they were back on the road before speaking again. "I had to say something. How could I not?"

"Yeah, well, I just wish you'd told me and not Sinéad. She's fragile enough as it is."

"But that's exactly why I told her. So she wouldn't be sad any more," she said, twisting round in the seat, her skirt riding up.

Max dragged his eyes away from her long slender legs and forced himself to concentrate on the road. "You think it makes her feel better thinking that her sister, her twin, might have walked away from her life leaving us in limbo, worrying, hoping, grieving? Have you any idea what the days after she disappeared were like? We went through hell. One minute there would be hope and then it would be gone, and, each time we began to accept that she was gone, we would be given more hope. It got to the point where I wanted them to find her body, and then was eaten up with guilt for wishing her dead. But it's not knowing, Krystie, it makes you crazy. And time drags — it's like living in a time warp, a nightmare and you get to the point where you can't allow yourself to hope any more. At least that's the way it was for me. If I do, then it means I have to grieve all over again, and I can't, I just can't." He tightened his grip on the steering wheel as he struggled with the emotions she'd brought to the surface.

"I'm sorry. I'm so sorry."

He looked across at her and saw huge silent tears rolling down her cheeks. It was impossible to stay angry with this girl. "It's okay. Look, I feel damn sober, but I'm probably over the limit and really shouldn't be driving. Do you mind if we go back to my place and I'll phone a taxi to take you home?"

158

"Just drop me anywhere here, it's fine," she mumbled.

"I am not dropping you on the side of the road at two in the morning."

"I'm sorry, Max, really I am. I didn't plan on blurting it out like that. I knew I had to tell one of you but I wasn't sure who, so I was going to talk it through with Sharon tomorrow."

He looked at her. "Sharon?"

"My housemate, my best friend. But then Sinéad went to pieces in the loo and it just came out. Jeez!"

"What?" he said as he stopped the car outside his apartment block and pressed the remote to open the gates.

"Do they let nobodies like me into places like this?"

He parked and turned to look at her. "You are not and never will be a 'nobody'."

In the lift to the penthouse suite he smiled at her obvious discomfort and the blush at the compliment he'd paid her. Despite life in New York and her smart mouth, there was still a delectable innocence about her.

His hand shook slightly as he put the key in the lock and he wasn't sure whether it was because of the emotional evening or Krystie's proximity. God, the effect this girl had on him was ridiculous. Get a grip, Max. "Make yourself at home." He flicked on the lights and pulled off his tie as he went through to the kitchen. He phoned the local cab firm but, lowering his voice, told them there was no rush. Taking a bottle of wine from the fridge, he grabbed two glasses and returned to find her studying the abstract hanging above the fireplace. Max put the wine and glasses down and, after switching on the gas fire with the remote, came to stand beside her. "What do you think?" he murmured, making her jump.

"Oh! I didn't hear you come in. I was too busy trying to figure out what I was looking at. It's random but . . . interesting."

He smiled at her. "Liar. You hate it."

"You're right. I hate it." She grinned and went to sit down on the cream leather sofa.

"I hate it too. I bought it as an investment." He poured the wine, handed her a glass before sitting beside her.

"How much did you pay for it?" She took a sip and turned towards him, crossing her legs.

He tore his gaze away from them and looked at her. "Two grand."

She spluttered out the wine. "You're kidding, right? Tell me you're kidding."

He laughed. "I'm assured it will be worth ten times that in a few years. I hung it there to see if it would grow on me but I think it's time to move it into the spare room."

She looked at her glass and then back at him, her eyes teasing. "Shouldn't we be drinking coffee?"

"After everything that's happened tonight I need a drink, and, as that's down to you, the least you can do is keep me company."

Her smile disappeared. "What do you think Sinéad will do?"

"I'm hoping she'll leave Philip to follow it up but she's not known for her patience."

"He's a cool customer, Philip, isn't he? You were angry with me. Your dad and Sinéad were all emotional and Dylan looked like he wanted to thump me, but Philip . . ." She shrugged. "Nothing."

"You need a poker face in politics," Max said. His brother-in-law had been silent until Sinéad had said she was going to find Sheila, at which point he'd told her that he would hire a private investigator in New York. It was true he had seemed to take the news very calmly, but perhaps he simply didn't believe Krystie or was afraid to hope, poor bastard. "Oh, Krystie, I wish you'd told me first." He reached out his hand and tucked a wisp of her hair behind her ear and let his hand trail down the curve of her cheek to her neck. God, he wanted her.

"Me too." She met his eyes. "But would you have done anything?"

"Of course I'd do something. What do you take me for?" He took his hand away, annoyed.

"What?" she challenged him.

"Are you always so confrontational?" he countered. My God, she had to be the most complicated woman he'd ever met. She irritated him, amused him and fascinated him, and right now he really wanted to kiss that mouth. "If you convinced me that it was really Sheila I would contact the police."

She looked at him, her beautiful blue eyes reproachful. "So you doubt me."

"It's nothing personal, Krystie, but you only saw her for moments so, yes, I think you were probably mistaken. And think about it: if it *was* her, what does that mean?"

"I don't understand."

"Her car was left by a pier with all her things inside. It looked like suicide or some sort of attack or abduction, and then she turns up in New York, not a bother on her, window shopping? There's only one conclusion I can come to: that she wanted us to think that she was dead."

Krystie stared at him. "But why?"

He held up his hands. "You tell me. It would be a cruel thing to do, wouldn't it?"

"Yes," she said, looking guilty again.

"You don't know Sheila, Krystie, *really* know her. We've been through so much as a family and she was the one who got us through it and out the other side. She would never do anything to hurt us; it's just not in her makeup. Quite apart from the fact that there is no logical reason in the world why she *would* do it. There were no family rows, no worries. Sheila was happy."

"But if she was happy why would she take her own life? Or do you think someone killed her and tried to make it look like suicide?"

"I don't know, Krystie. I just know that if she left she took nothing with her. No clothes, no cards, no passport. How could she have got into the USA without a passport?"

She dropped her head into her hands, distracting him with another look at her delicious bare back. "I'm

162

going mad. I must be. I was so sure it was her. I was *so* sure. I'm sorry."

"Hey." He put a hand on her shoulder. "Don't beat yourself up, you meant well. I'll talk to Philip tomorrow and we'll come up with a plan of action."

"But if she didn't have her passport —"

"It doesn't matter, Krystie. Dad and Sinéad won't rest until we follow this up."

Her eyes filled with tears. "I've really fucked up, haven't I? You must wish you'd never laid eyes on me."

"I wish for many things, Krystie, but that isn't one of them," he said and, tilting her chin, he bent his head and kissed her lightly on the lips. When she didn't pull away he pulled her close and kissed her again. She tasted even sweeter than he'd imagined and when he ran his thumb down her spine she shivered, put her arms round his neck and buried her fingers in his hair. He deepened the kiss and she melted against him, returning his kisses with a hunger that matched his own. Max moved his lips down her neck to her bare shoulder and slid his hand inside the back of her dress. She trembled under his fingers as he caressed the base of her spine with one hand and ran the other up the inside of one silken thigh.

A buzzer rang loudly and Krystie jumped. "What the hell was that?"

"The damn taxi," he muttered. He was about to suggest he send it away, but Krystie was already on her feet straightening her clothes, her cheeks flushed, whether from embarrassment, wine or passion he

163

wasn't sure. "Saved by the bell," he joked, standing up and taking her hand.

She smiled and kissed his cheek. "Thanks for the wine, Max, and again, I'm sorry."

"Stop apologising. What's done is done. And if nothing else you've made Dad and Sinéad very happy."

She sighed. "I hope it stays that way."

"Amen."

CHAPTER
FIFTEEN

Sheila had been working hard all morning and was feeling quite pleased with herself. She had never felt so creative or happy or fulfilled. Yes, of course she missed home, and sometimes Sinéad's absence from her life was like a physical pain, but her heart would harden. She would adjust and the happiness she felt from doing what she loved best and being here in Manhattan with Karl made up for all she had lost. Well, it would — given time.

She was contemplating braving the icy temperature and going for a walk before making dinner when the phone rang. Assuming it was Karl, she hurried to where she had left it on the kitchen counter and froze when she saw the number. What the hell? They had agreed no contact unless it was something very important, a matter of life or death. Her stomach churned as she picked up the phone with trembling fingers. "Hello?"

Sheila was sitting in the window seat, her knees drawn up to her chin and her arms clutched around them when Karl got home from work. He walked in and turned on the light, starting when he saw her. "Jeez, you gave me a fright, I thought you were out. What are you doing sitting in the dark?" He crossed the room and dropped a kiss on the top of her head.

She looked up at him. "They know, Karl."

He sank down beside her. "The family? They can't possibly."

"They do. I don't know where this leaves me. I'm not sure what to do."

"Calm down." He took her shaking hands in his. "Tell me what's happened."

She told him about the phone call. "Can you believe the coincidence? Not only the fact that in a city with more than eight million people I bump into a girl who knows me, but she ends up working for Sinéad. What are the chances? It's laughable but I feel more like crying."

"She *thinks* she saw you, so they don't 'know' anything for sure. Don't assume the worst."

"You don't know Sinéad. She will get right on this and before you know it there will be photos of me on the Internet and posters plastered all over town. It's only a matter of time before one of your friends or someone from the building makes the connection."

He snorted. "Sweetheart, this is New York. How many people do you think even notice those posters, let alone read them?"

"Perhaps I should just go back and face the music, get it over with."

"There's no reason to make any snap decisions. Come on, let's go out. We can talk about it over dinner."

"Oh, I don't know —"

166

He stood up and pulled her to her feet. "I won't let you turn into a hermit. Now go put some clean clothes on, woman, I'm starving."

Sheila humoured him and dropped the subject, but all she could think about was what was happening back home right now. She knew how each of her family would be reacting. Dad would be emotional, hopeful. Max would be sceptical. Philip would be panicking and Sinéad would want to take immediate action; she was probably booking her ticket to JFK right now. Yes, her sister was the biggest threat to disrupting her new life. She would be like a dog with a bone, just as Sheila would be if the situations were reversed.

Kieran sat down on the edge of the grave. "Incredible, isn't it, Maggie? I'll be honest with you, I'm afraid to believe it."

He threw an apologetic glance at the headstone. "But Sheila never suffered with her nerves. Even when she was doing her exams and Sinéad was in a panic, Sheila just got on with it. Perhaps she just had too much on her plate. I know I depended on her too much but, trust me, she liked being in control. She liked organising us all. I don't believe Philip would have ever got elected without her."

He glanced at his watch and quickly finished tidying the grave. Beth would be waiting. "Now don't go thinking that this means anything, Maggie. It's just nice to have some company my own age and, yes, female company. You know better than anyone that I always preferred it. It's no more than companionship and

167

there's no doubt she's a bloody good cook." He chuckled and, getting to his feet, dusted off his hands. "Right, Maggie, I'll see you next week and, please God, I'll have some good news." He hurried out of the graveyard, passed the pub and headed for Beth's house.

He had been very tempted to take Beth to Philip's party. It would be nice to go out as a couple. But he hadn't told Max or Sinéad about her, so just showing up with a strange woman on his arm would have come as a right shock. Also he knew that he wouldn't be in the best form on their birthday. God, was he glad now that he hadn't taken her with him with the bombshell that Krystie had dropped.

Maybe it was wishful thinking, but he was inclined to believe that Sheila was alive. Although, if she was, why had she left her car on the end of a pier, left her bag, her phone . . .? The only logical answer was that she wanted them to think she was dead. Why? It had to be something serious, something traumatic, to drive her to take such a step, and that worried him. He'd racked his brains, trying to figure what could be so unbearable that it would drive Sheila to walk away from her life, from Sinéad, her beloved sister and best friend. What was so bad that she couldn't even confide in her twin? His thoughts immediately turned to Philip, as they had over the last few days. Sinéad had been suspicious of him from day one and perhaps they should have trusted her instincts. Had he done something to make Sheila run? The thought filled him with fury and by the time he reached Beth's house his fists were clenched as he wondered what he could or should do.

"You're not looking too happy."

Beth stood, arms crossed, looking at him. He hadn't even noticed her open the door. He tossed his head, smiling. "Sorry, in a world of my own. How are you today?" He stepped inside and hung his coat on the hook by the door.

"I've had a busy morning," she said, bustling into the kitchen. "I got stuck into clearing out the spare room."

He followed her into the warm, bright kitchen. "Something smells good."

"Bacon and cabbage," she said, going to the cooker.

"Lovely. So why the clear-out? Are you expecting visitors?"

"No, it's where I kept all of Gerry's things, and I decided last night that it was high time I went through them. There are plenty of good suits and jackets that the charity shop will be glad of and it's not as if I'm ever going to read all his books or use his fishing gear." She chuckled as she started to carve the meat.

"Would your son not want any of it?"

"No. Gavin took everything he wanted. He's the one who's been nagging me to get rid of it all."

"To be honest, I couldn't bring myself to do it at all," Kieran admitted. "Maggie's sister took care of it."

"And your children didn't mind?" Beth asked.

"Ah, no. Sure, they were only kids at the time and she kept all the important stuff: jewellery, letters, mementos, that sort of thing."

"You were lucky to have her."

"I was. Bridie was a good woman. As hard as nails, mind you, and not great at showing affection, but a heart of gold underneath."

"Did she never marry?"

He shook his head. "No. She lived over in America for years. I think she might have been involved with someone there and, when it didn't work out, she came home."

"And then she lost her sister. That's very sad."

Kieran felt the usual pangs of guilt he always did when he thought of Bridie. "She's in a nursing home now, suffers from dementia. Most of the time she doesn't recognise any of us."

"God love you, Kieran, you've had more than your fair share of troubles." Beth served up the food onto two plates and carried them to the table. "There's beer in the fridge if you fancy one," she said, fetching parsley sauce and mustard.

"Will you join me?" he asked, going to the fridge.

"No, just some water for me, ta."

As he tucked into his meal — she really was a great cook — Beth told him about the call she'd got from her son last night and how she was thinking of turning part of the garden into a vegetable patch. He liked that she didn't expect anything more than a nod or a yes or a no. Her warm voice that always seemed to hold a smile washed over him and he relaxed with her in a way that he couldn't with his own family. She seemed to have no expectations and made no demands. He had been afraid that she'd start suggesting they go out to a movie or for a drink, but she seemed quite content for him to just drop in to see her every so often and when he was leaving and kissed her cheek she never asked if or when she would see him again. All in all, being around Beth was easy.

He let her chatter on and waited until she'd made coffee and sat down again before he spoke. "I told you about the dinner that Philip, my-son-in-law, was giving, didn't I?" he said.

"Oh, yes, how did it go? I imagine it must have been very emotional for you and for poor Sinéad too — her first birthday without her twin."

"Yes. But, well, we got a bit of a shock too."

"Oh? Why, what happened?" she asked, her face creased in concern.

He hesitated. He barely knew this woman, which was part of the attraction of talking to her. She didn't know any of his family and he could be frank with her. But Philip was a public figure and Sheila's disappearance had been big news. Could he trust Beth to keep his confidence?

"Maybe if it's a family matter you'd better keep it that way," she said.

He obviously looked as uneasy as he felt. She was a very perceptive woman. He decided to tell her. If Krystie was right and Philip was going to reopen the search for Sheila, it would be all out in the open soon, anyway. "I need to talk to someone or I'll go mad and I'd be glad of your opinion, Beth."

"I'll be happy to throw in my tuppence-worth if it will help. And I promise, Kieran, anything you tell me won't go any further."

171

"I appreciate that." He took a drink of coffee before he began his story. "Sinéad hired this new girl to work for her. She's just moved back here from New York. I only met her at the party, but we had a chat and I took to her." He smiled at Beth. "You know the way it is with some people, you just take an instant like or dislike to them?"

"I do."

He did a double take at the twinkle in her eye. "Yes, well . . ." He cleared his throat. "She seems quite bright and is doing well and it's obvious that Sinéad really likes her."

"It will be great for her to have some company."

He nodded. "Anyway, the dinner was finished and, the next thing I know, Dylan, Sinéad's fella, is telling me that she needs a word with us outside. I thought that the night had just been too much for her. I wasn't sure it was a great idea to begin with, to be honest, but it seemed important to Philip." He grimaced at the thought. "I suppose it would have been wrong to just let the day pass. Anyway, out I go and there's all the family in this little room off reception and Sinéad sitting there, looking like she's seen a ghost. Then she says that Krystie has something to tell us." He sighed. "The fact is the girl claims she saw Sheila in Manhattan a few weeks back."

Beth's coffee cup clattered into the saucer. "I don't understand. How could that be?" She looked as bewildered as he felt.

"I don't know. If the lass is right, and Sheila is still alive, well, what happened to her? If she was out shopping alone then she obviously wasn't abducted or, if she was, she'd got free. But if that was the case she'd call us, not go shopping. I go over it again and again and I can't make sense of it. The only thing I did wonder was, had she been diagnosed with something fatal and she didn't want to give anyone the trouble of looking after her?"

"So instead she pretended to take her own life?" Beth raised her eyebrows in disbelief.

"I know. It doesn't make sense to me either."

"Maybe she had some sort of breakdown."

"A breakdown that would cause her to pretend she's dead?"

Beth's eyes lit up. "Maybe she was planning to do it and then realised she couldn't and just ran away instead."

"But why wouldn't she come and talk to one of us?"

"She wouldn't have been thinking rationally, Kieran."

"That sounds possible but what could have upset her that much? She was such a sensible and well-adjusted girl."

"There'll be a good reason, there has to be. We just have to figure it out. I don't know about you but I need a drink." She fetched them two brandies and took a sip. "Sheila loved her family and you were very close, you say."

"Yes, honestly, that's the truth; she was kindness itself. She put everyone before herself."

"So, if Krystie is right, when you find Sheila you can help put right whatever upset her. That's good news, isn't it?"

Beth's voice was gentle and kind and Kieran blessed the day he'd bumped into her. He nodded and smiled slowly. "You're right, it is. But I'm still left wondering what would make her go."

Beth stared into her drink. It was a long time before she spoke again. "I can only think that I would do it if it were the lesser of two evils."

"What could be worse than running away from everyone who loves you and leaving them not knowing if you were alive or dead?" Kieran took a gulp of brandy and winced as it burned its way down his throat.

Beth sighed. "Because she was angry, upset, worried or —"

Kieran looked up and caught the look of alarm on her face. "Or what? Please, Beth."

She raised troubled eyes to meet his. "Or she was afraid."

CHAPTER
SIXTEEN

Krystie stood staring out of the kitchen window, eating cornflakes and hoping that Max wouldn't drop by today. She still felt mortified when she thought about the night in his apartment. If he hadn't done the decent thing and put her in a taxi, she knew that she would have ended up in his bed.

Sharon had woken up when she got home that night and grinned knowingly when Krystie walked in looking flushed, her chin red and her once perfect braid askew.

"Oh my God, no need to ask what you've been up to! Max?"

"Yeah." Krystie had gone straight into her room and closed the door while she stripped and put on pyjamas.

"Tell me," Sharon demanded, following her into the bathroom and watching impatiently as she took off her makeup and brushed her teeth.

"It was just a cuddle on the couch, that's all," Krystie tried to make little of it.

"You look perfectly sober to me. Hang on a sec. What couch, where?"

Krystie sighed. "I went back to his place."

"Oh, my God, I don't believe it. What happened to him not being your type?"

"He isn't, it just happened. I drank too much wine," Krystie insisted.

"Yeah, sure. So —" Sharon grinned — "is he a good kisser? He must be: he's had lots of practice."

Krystie frowned. She didn't like to think of Max kissing other women. Oh, this was ridiculous, what was wrong with her?

"Well?"

"Yeah, he was good," she admitted, as she remembered the feelings Max had aroused in her.

The next time Max had dropped by the studio she had been relieved that he made no reference to their romp on his sofa, but his eyes had bored into her making her shiver. She didn't know what she would do or say the next time they were alone but, thankfully, the task of trying to find Sheila was uppermost in everyone's thoughts, and when he did stop by it was usually to talk to his sister or whisk her off to a meeting with Philip.

Sinéad was behaving as if she'd been pumped full of adrenaline and when she was in the studio she spent all of her time teaching Krystie the intricacies of millinery. They regularly ended up sitting cross-legged on the floor surrounded by the various materials, Sinéad showing her how to stretch and bend sinamay — the material used for the base of most hats — or how to paint on stiffener once she was happy with the shape, and drumming into her the importance of leaving it until it was completely dry to ensure a quality finish. She showed her how to use the hat block to cut out shapes, and set Krystie tasks to make the different hat shapes starting off with a simple percher, then a fan, a pillbox and lastly a knitted hat, reminding Krystie of that fateful photo.

She spent her time on Skype telling Sandy about the steep learning curve she was on but said nothing of Sheila. She had blurted out her suspicions and now she planned to let the family do what they wanted with the information and concentrate on her work. She didn't even tell Sharon in the end. Anyway, her friend was a lot more interested in what was happening with Max.

"Morning." The lady herself appeared in the archway, rubbing her eyes. "Oh, it is so cold!"

"Yeah, but it's a nice day. Go inside, the heater's on in there, and I'll put on the kettle."

"Thanks," Sharon said, and went to huddle up on the end of the sofa nearest the radiator. "You looked as if you were in a world of your own when I came in. Dreaming of Max?"

Krystie shook her head in amusement. "No, I was thinking about my family actually, and trying to decide what to buy them for Christmas."

The kettle clicked and she made two mugs of tea and carried them through.

"Ooh, thanks." Sharon held the mug in both her hands to warm them, and took a sip. "Keep it simple, wine, chocolate or perfume."

"Yeah, I think you're right, though I'm going to make Ma a hat."

"Great idea, she'll love that. Are you going over there for Sunday lunch today?"

177

"Yeah." Krystie was amazed at how quickly she'd fallen into the old routine. Ma had always put on a big spread on Sundays. "Everyone should be there."

"A practice run for Christmas Day, huh?" Sharon grinned. "Has Fallon been behaving herself?"

"She has. She can't think of anything to slag me about. Ma keeps going on and on about my brilliant job and has the newspaper photo of me and Sinéad pinned up on the kitchen noticeboard."

"That was a great photo. Pity there wasn't one of you with the delicious Max, though."

"I'm delighted there wasn't. I don't want people thinking I'm his latest squeeze."

"True," Sharon agreed. "You should be famous in your own right."

"Famous?" Krystie threw back her head and laughed. "I make hats, Sharon."

"No, you're an ace designer who makes hats. Stick with that family and you'll go places, mark my words."

Krystie thought about her friend's words on the bus ride over to Ballymun. She would have laughed at Sharon a couple of weeks ago but she'd seen for herself the night of the birthday party that the Fields family and Philip Healy were definitely minor celebrities. A politician, a successful designer and a suave, rich bachelor, and the added tragedy of Sheila's disappearance, ensured that. For the first time she could see why Philip might take advantage of it. Their photo had appeared in three newspapers and, while politicians usually got a rough time, there was a lot of sympathy for Philip, which might not be there if he wasn't still so close to his wife's family. Again, the word "calculating" came to mind.

Her dad opened the door and took her in his arms to hug her. "Howaya, sweetheart?"

Krystie smiled. She'd been home over a month but her da still lit up like a Christmas tree when she came through the door, and she enjoyed her visits and catching up on the news. She kissed his cheek. "Hi, Da."

He rolled his eyes. "Glad to see you. I'm sitting like an eejit listening to your brother's new girlfriend natter my ear off and Blake's sitting there drooling."

She laughed. "He'll never change, will he? Is this one as bad as the others?"

"She's a decent enough girl but, God love her, a breeze could go in one ear and out the other."

"In that case I'll go and give Ma a hand in the kitchen."

"Ah, your mother's got everything under control. I'm the one that needs help," he complained.

"Alexis and Fallon will be here soon, won't they?"

"Fallon will but she's already had a go at the poor girl and now they hardly talk to each other, and Alexis isn't coming — she has a tummy bug."

"Ah, that's a pity. Okay, let me say hi to Ma and then I'll come and rescue you." She opened the kitchen door as her mother was basting the roast potatoes. "Smells good."

Her mother looked around and smiled. "Hello, love, how are you?"

"Mad busy but I'm enjoying every second."

179

"You wouldn't believe the number of times I've been stopped by neighbours who saw your photo; they're all raving about it."

"Aw, that's nice."

"Whoever thought I'd be the mother of a celebrity?" Peg shook her head in wonder.

"That's a bit of an exaggeration now, Ma," Krystie laughed. "Apart from that night I've hardly been outside the door since I came home, and Sinéad doesn't go out much, either. Max —" she stumbled on his name — "he's the only one who lives the high life."

"He's always in the paper."

"I can't understand Irish newspapers. Why would they want to photograph an accountant?"

"Because he's rich, single and always has a gorgeous girl on his arm. Let me think. Who's the latest?" Peg screwed up her face. "Her name's on the tip of my tongue. Oh, yes, Natalie McHugh, the fashion model."

Krystie itched to ask more but she didn't trust herself. She could already feel her cheeks growing hot. Natalie must be an ex, she decided, otherwise Max would have brought her to the birthday party. And he never would have come on to her the way he had if he was dating someone, would he?

"What do you think of Blake's new girl?" she asked, deciding it was safer to change the subject.

Peg smiled. "Ah, Leah is a nice enough lass but not for him. I think we're going to have to send him on one of those dating shows. He just hasn't a clue what he's at and the poor lad always ends up getting his heart broken."

180

"Don't we all?"

"Are you missing Jacob, love?"

"No, I am not," she retorted and then caught her mother's knowing look. "Okay, I admit he really hurt me, but now that I've got this job I don't have time to think of him and it's nice having Sharon to come home to every evening, I missed her."

"Poor girl, how's *she* doing?"

"Great. She's so strong and positive but not interested in guys at all."

"Is it any wonder? He couldn't wait to get her down that aisle and then the fecker walks out before their second anniversary. It's a wonder her father didn't go after him with a shotgun." The doorbell rang. "That will be Fallon. Go and let her in, will you, love?"

Krystie opened the door and smiled broadly. "Hi, Fallon, howaway, Pat."

He gave her a shy smile. "Hey, Krystie."

How someone so nice and quiet and kind had ended up with her little sister she would never understand.

Fallon's smile was as false as her suntan. "Hiya. Everything okay, Krystie? You don't look the best."

"Never better," Krystie assured her and turned the wattage up on her smile. "It's great being home."

"I meant to ask, Krystie, why *did* you come home?"

"I missed you," Krystie said sweetly and, turning on her heel, headed for the living room.

Her father looked up, relief in his eyes. "Ah, there you are, sweetheart. Leila, this is Krystie."

"Dad, it's Leah." Blake scowled.

"Of course it is. Sorry." He smiled at the girl. "How the hell am I supposed to remember? I can't keep track with all the girls he's brought home," he said to Krystie out of the side of his mouth.

"Nice to meet you, Leah." Krystie smiled at the young girl with the black-tipped blonde tresses and bulging blue eyes.

"Hi! Blake says you're a designer. We're in the same business. I'm a model."

"Really? That's great." Krystie tried to hide her surprise. Leah had nice skin and a pretty smile but she didn't have the cheekbones or height usually associated with the job.

"She's a hand model," Blake said proudly.

"I do mainly adverts for rings and washing-up liquid," she said holding out her hands.

"Lovely," Krystie said, obediently admiring them.

"Things are really taking off for Leah," Blake said proudly. "She's hoping to give up her day job soon."

"Yeah, I work in a meat-processing plant and of course I wear gloves, but I really shouldn't be doing work like that."

"You should have your hands insured," Da said. "Who was it, Ginger Rogers or Ava Gardner who had their legs insured for millions?"

"I must check that out," Leah said seriously.

Krystie met her dad's twinkling eyes and suppressed a grin.

"Dinner!" her mother called and, relieved, Krystie led the way out to the kitchen determined to take the chair next to her da and avoid bitchy comments from

182

Fallon and long discussions about hands with Leah. Of course she ended up with the two of them opposite with Pat, who'd hardly opened his mouth since he walked in. Ma was beside her and her father and brother at opposite ends of the table. As they passed the serving dishes around the table Fallon smiled over at her. "You must be finding Dublin very dull after Manhattan, Krystie."

"Not at all, I'm enjoying it."

Her father nodded at the photo on the noticeboard above her head. "Dull? She's only just home and she's in the newspapers."

Leah looked around and gave an excited squeal. "OMG, that is *so* cool. That guy in the background, is that Max Fields?"

Krystie peered up at the photo. She hadn't noticed but Max was indeed in the background of the photo and he was looking straight at her. She swallowed hard. "Yes, he's my boss's brother."

Leah's eyes widened. "He is seriously sexy."

"Hey, you're not supposed to be drooling over other fellas when your boyfriend's beside you," Blake complained.

"I love it when you're jealous." Leah blew him a kiss. "But you don't have to worry about me running away with Max Fields. It's obviously your sister he's interested in. Look at the way he's looking at her."

"You're imagining it," Krystie laughed.

"You are," Fallon agreed. "Why would he be even interested in Krystie when he's dating a stunner like Natalie McHugh? No offence," she added with a smile.

Krystie made her smile even sweeter. "None taken."

"A man like that wants more than a brainless bimbo on his arm," her father said. "I'm sure if Krystie wanted him she could have him. She's got the brains and the beauty."

"Thanks, Da." She smiled at him as Fallon stabbed her fork into a carrot. "How's your job going, Fallon?" she asked, determined not to let her sister get under her skin. Fallon worked as a receptionist in a beauty salon.

"Fine, but I fancy a change. I might open my own place."

One look at Pat's expression made it clear that this was the first he'd heard of it.

"That would be bloody stupid," her father retorted. "Why would you start a new business in the middle of a recession? And, anyway, what do you know about running a hair salon?"

She glared at him. "I hold that salon together."

"Ah, yes, you make the coffee, buy the magazines and sweep the floor. Perfect qualifications for starting a business," he jeered.

Krystie felt sorry for Fallon. While Da was right, there was no need to be quite so cruel about it. "It is a dodgy time to start a business but if you're interested in a change why not apply to one of the salon chains? There's probably more chance of promotion."

"I've thought of that too," Fallon said, her eyes on her dinner.

"You have a very cushy number there. You'd be mad to leave," Pat grumbled.

184

"Oh, for God's sake, I said I was just thinking about it, okay?"

The conversation turned to more mundane and less controversial matters, but soon Leah was back talking to Krystie about fashion and the photo and what other personalities had been there. Krystie had more important memories of that night but she obligingly told Leah about some of the VIPs she'd met and as soon as they'd finished lunch she rose to leave.

"I've a load of washing and ironing to do," she said when her mother protested, "and there's never a chance during the week."

"You take care of yourself. I don't want you getting sick because you pushed yourself too hard."

Fallon turned to Leah. "She's an epileptic."

Krystie stiffened, annoyed. Okay, her health was no secret, but it was up to her if she wanted to tell people. Fallon had no right to announce it like that. She could see from her parents' expressions that they weren't too impressed, either.

"I'm sorry, Krystie, I didn't know."

"There's nothing to be sorry about," she reassured the girl. "I have a very mild version of the condition and I've only had a handful of fits in the last ten years. Anyway, nice to meet you, Leah. Good luck with the modelling."

"Thanks, Krystie. Good luck with the hats and —" she grinned — "with Max."

Krystie laughed and went out into the hall, followed by her mother.

"Don't mind Fallon. She forgets to put her brain in gear before opening her mouth."

"I don't, Ma." Krystie smiled and hugged her mother. "Thanks for a gorgeous dinner. I'll phone you during the week."

CHAPTER
SEVENTEEN

"So, Philip, where are we at?" Max asked, watching his brother-in-law finish his dinner with obvious relish. However the man was feeling, it certainly wasn't interfering with his appetite.

Philip swallowed a mouthful of jalfrezi chicken before replying. "I've set the wheels in motion, talked to a couple of people, and they're going to put me in touch with a private investigator."

"Why can't we get things moving ourselves?" Sinéad asked, spreading her rice out on the plate and drawing a design in it with her fork.

"We could put up her details on the missing-persons sites in America, or just New York," Max said.

Philip looked at each of them in turn, his eyes solemn. "That's really not a good idea. This is a delicate matter and it's best to do it privately and quietly."

"Why?" Sinéad said, clearly irritated by his softly-softly approach.

"Because if we do as you suggest journalists will doorstep each of us day and night wondering why we're reopening the investigation. The tabloids will no doubt come up with all their own mind-boggling and nauseating theories and, frankly, I think that's the last thing any of us need, especially your dad."

That was true, Max realised. When word got out that there had been a suspected sighting of Sheila in Manhattan the press would go after it and he'd prefer to find out the reason why she'd left before he read it in a newspaper. While there was no such thing as bad publicity there was no knowing how this would play out. "Philip's right, Sinéad. The quieter we can keep this the better. It's a family matter, not something we want splashed all over the tabloids."

She twisted the strands of hair framing her face and bit her lip. "I just want to find her."

"We all do," Philip said. "But bear one thing in mind, Sinéad. If Krystie is right, then at least we know one thing for sure. She is safe and well."

Max saw her expression soften and thought of Krystie's observation, that Philip was a cool customer. Maybe, but Max thought "careful and cautious" described him better. "It's a nice thought. I have no idea why she would have put us through all of this, but I don't really care. What's important is that she's okay. Right, Sinéad?"

She sighed. "Yes, but I'm still going to give her hell for putting us through this."

Philip's smile was sympathetic. "I think that's perfectly understandable."

"Won't you be angry with her?" she asked.

Max watched him curiously. He seemed thrown by the question.

"I hadn't really thought that far ahead," he said eventually.

Sinéad was silent for a moment and then looked up at him, smiling. "I've got an idea that might help us track her down. Rather than just give your investigator a photo of her, I thought you could take a photo of me dressed up the way she was when Krystie saw her."

"That's a great idea, Sinéad," Max said, impressed at her ingenuity.

"If Krystie can remember, then, yes, that would be great," Philip agreed.

"She will," Sinéad assured him. "I'll talk to her in the morning."

He smiled. "Great. Now, before I let you go I just wanted a word about Christmas . . ."

Max sighed. This was bound to set Sinéad off again but as it was only a couple of weeks away now they needed to make some arrangements. He tried to make eye contact with her but she'd gone back to doodling in her rice.

"You're welcome as always to come along to the drinks party on Christmas Eve, but if you don't want to I completely understand. I would like to keep up the tradition of Christmas Day, I really would. Please come. I thought we could eat later than usual, just the family."

Sinéad looked up. "And Bridie?"

He seemed slightly confused by the question. "Of course, she must come too. Sheila would be disgusted with me if I left her out."

Max felt despondency wash over him at the thought of spending the day looking at his aunt sitting in a chair either staring vacantly into space or getting into a panic over an imagined wrong. The last time he'd seen her she had been convinced he was trying to cheat her in some way. While he knew that it was just the damn disease, it had still hurt. He'd been her favourite and now he was not only a stranger to her but an enemy too.

He wished yet again that he could piss off for the holidays, only this time it was Krystie he imagined on the sunbed beside him, not Natalie.

"That sounds fine, Philip." Sinéad smiled at her brother-in-law and then she looked back at Max. "Should we tell Bridie what's going on, do you think?"

"There's no point. She probably doesn't even know who Sheila is any more."

They sat in silence for a moment lost in their own individual thoughts. Bridie might have been a tough character but she had been all they'd got.

"How's your dad doing?" Philip asked. "I left a couple of messages on the answering machine but he never got back to me."

"I don't think he even checks it," Sinéad said.

"Yeah, he's fine," Max said, though the last time *he'd* seen his father the man had been more preoccupied than ever. He glanced at his watch. "Well, if there's nothing else, I have some papers to read through for an early-morning meeting."

Sinéad stood, too. "I'll get that photo to you as soon as possible, Philip."

He kissed her on both cheeks. "Great."

"Thanks for dinner," Max said, "and for taking charge of the whole Christmas business. I wasn't too sure how that would work out and, to be honest, I wasn't looking forward to it."

"I'm still not. Oh, nothing personal, Philip," Sinéad added hurriedly. "It will just seem weird without Sheila and with Bridie going steadily downhill. Is there anything I can do to help?"

"It would be great if you could supply dessert."

"No problem at all."

"You don't cook," Max said, frowning, as they walked to the door.

"No, but my landlord does." Sinéad grinned and put on her coat.

"I'll organise the wine," Max told Philip, although he knew the man's garage would be heaving with bottles from the many constituents trying to curry favour with their local politician.

They said goodnight and Max walked his sister to her car. "Happy with that?"

"I suppose so. We're going to find her, I know we are."

"Krystie could have been mistaken."

Sinéad shook her head and smiled. "She's not."

He sighed, thinking how upset she was going to be if nothing came of their search and wondered if that meant the business would go downhill again.

"I don't know what I'm going to say to her," Sinéad said, interrupting his thoughts.

"To Sheila?"

She nodded. "I miss her so much, I love her so much but at the same time I want to kill her."

"Put it out of your mind for now. It could take months, maybe years to find her, or we may end up back where we started, with a complete mystery on our hands."

She shook her head, her eyes distraught. "I'll go out of my mind, Max."

"No, you won't, Sinéad. It doesn't matter what happens. It's time you put your life first and stopped living in the past. Even if we find Sheila, it's unlikely she's going to want to come home."

Sinéad turned to stare at him. "Why not?"

"Why would she? She must have had her reasons for leaving and for staying away. She made a decision to start a new life and you need to do the same. Concentrate on your work that you love so much — that will distract you. I know it's not the same without Sheila, but you're the one that created the piece the actress wore to the BAFTAs. You are damn good at what you do, Sinéad. There's no reason why you can't make it internationally. I can see your hats in the best stores in London, Paris, Rome, Berlin —"

She slapped a hand to her mouth and then laughed. "That's it! Yes! Don't you just love Leonard Cohen?"

He frowned. "What?"

"You just reminded me of his song: 'First We Take Manhattan'!"

"I'm struggling to make a connection," her brother said.

192

"Okay, let me explain. You're right about Sheila. It is going to be like looking for a needle in a haystack. But if my hats went on sale in Manhattan, in somewhere like Saks or Bloomingdale's, she wouldn't be able to resist coming to see them."

Saks? Bloomingdale's? Max was about to say she was dreaming but, if she was going to use the business to try to get to Sheila, it could only be good for the books. "Getting your hats into one of those shops won't be easy," he warned, afraid that she was building herself up for another fall.

"No, not easy, but remember, I've photos of an award-winning Hollywood actress wearing my headpiece."

He grinned. "So you do. But how can you be sure that Sheila would even know that your hats were on sale in Manhattan?"

"I can't, Max, but at least I'll feel like I'm doing something. I know that Philip is probably right about keeping the whole thing private but, to be honest, he's just too sensible and slow for me. If anything happened to me and Dylan reacted so calmly I wouldn't be a bit impressed."

"If you disappeared, Dylan would probably throw a party! I don't know how he's put up with you for this long."

"Damn cheek." She poked him between the ribs with her car key. "He's lucky to have me!"

He looked down and smiled at the mischievous twinkle in her eyes. This was the sister who had seemed to disappear along with Sheila. He hoped she was back for good. "Night, Sinéad."

She reached up to hug him. "Goodnight, Max."

He stood and watched her drive off before climbing into his own car. The more that he thought about it, the more he realised this could only be a win-win situation. If Sinéad was working her butt off bringing her range up to scratch, it would keep her mind occupied and stop her pestering Philip about the investigation. It would also bring the business back on track and keep her motivated. He still wasn't convinced that they would find Sheila, but he would do whatever he could to keep the sister he still had, and he was convinced that her salvation lay in the business. When she was making hats, creating, she was a different person.

They would need a publicist to launch the new range and they had to make a fuss about introducing Krystie to the public. Her CV might not be that impressive but her work spoke for itself; there was no questioning her talent. And she would be sensational on TV and radio. She was beautiful and funny and her husky voice and quirky Dublin/New York accent was damn sexy.

On impulse he pressed a button on the hands-free phone, but all he got was her voicemail. He thought quickly as he listened to the message, and then cleared his throat at the beep.

"Hi Krystie, it's Max. I'm looking for a favour. I want to get Sinéad something special for Christmas but I'm completely out of ideas. Will you help me? Please? Look forward to hearing from you. Bye."

There, that sounded okay. He wasn't asking her out on a date, although he planned to buy her lunch or, better still, dinner. Then what he'd like to do was take her back to his apartment to finish what they'd started, but it was too soon for that. She'd been friendly but distant since that night but he knew he hadn't imagined her responses. Of course, none of it would have happened if it hadn't been such an emotional evening. She wouldn't have ended up in his apartment if she hadn't been overcome with guilt at upsetting his family. But he didn't want her to date him because she felt beholden to him or worried at offending her boss. Max wanted her to date him because she was as attracted to him as he was to her, and she wasn't quite there yet. In the meantime, he needed to clear the decks. He pressed the remote and swung the car into his parking spot. Glancing up at the window of his apartment, he sighed when he saw the light was on. She was here.

It had been easy to put off this moment, as Natalie had been on a cruise, but when he received her text today saying she was back and had a present for him his heart sank. He had told Security to let her in, half hoping that she'd get the message when he was vague about what time he'd be home. But, he should have realised, it would never occur to Natalie that any man wouldn't want her. She was supremely confident in her beauty and her sex appeal. She didn't love him and would have no problem at all in replacing him, but at the moment she wanted him. She saw herself as an actress, not a model — though that was where she had earned her money and made her name — and wanted to be taken more seriously. She seemed to think dating a well-known accountant rather than a footballer would help and Max had been happy to oblige. She was sexy, independent and fun, exactly what he liked in a girlfriend.

Until he'd met Krystie. From the moment she'd breezed in the door of Starbucks she'd wormed her way into his consciousness and when she'd arrived at his sister's apartment wearing that dress she'd taken his breath away. She was so incredibly beautiful and soft and kind and funny and caring. He wanted her. And not in the way he'd ever wanted a woman before. This was serious. And he was willing to take it slowly and wait until she felt the same way. He knew she would. There was no doubting the chemistry between them. He also needed to get rid of Natalie. He stepped out of the car and strode towards the door. Time to face the music.

"You bastard! No one dumps me." Natalie's beautiful eyes flashed, angry and incredulous.

"Don't be like that, sweetheart. We've had fun, haven't we?"

She pulled the duvet up over the wispy, black negligée — his present — and glared at him. "You're a shit."

"I'm sorry," he said with a helpless shrug, and walked to the window.

"So who is she?"

"Who?" He pretended innocence but Natalie wasn't stupid.

"My replacement," she spat at him, dressing.

"There is none," he said honestly and added "yet" in his head.

She stormed around the bedroom and bathroom, gathering up the few bits and pieces that she'd left there, and didn't speak again until she was about to walk out of the door. "You'll regret this."

He felt bad when he saw that she seemed close to tears and had to steel himself not to take her in his arms. Instead, he kissed her cheek and sent her away with a gentle lie. "I probably will."

Only moments after the door closed behind her his mobile rang. He pulled it out of his breast pocket and smiled when he saw Krystie's name flashing at him. Had she called a few minutes earlier it could have been really awkward. He took the timing as a good omen. "Krystie, thanks for getting back to me."

"Hi, Max."

He closed his eyes, relishing the sound of her voice. "So, are you going to help me out?"

"I'd like to, Max, but we are so busy at the moment. I really can't afford to take time off."

He was prepared for that one. He grinned as she played right into his hands. "That's why God invented late-night shopping."

"Oh. Right."

She didn't sound happy. His confidence wavered but he pushed on. "I could pick you up from the studio tomorrow evening if that suits and we could head into town from there."

"Er, I thought the idea was to surprise Sinéad. Isn't it going to give the game away if you pick me up?"

He smiled at the laughter in her voice and the American twang to her accent. It would strike him as false and pretentious in anyone else, but not Krystie. God, he had it bad.

"Hello?"

"Sorry, I was thinking. Yeah, you're right. How about you take the train into town and I'll meet you outside Trinity College?"

"Okay, but I'm not sure what time —" she started.

"No problem, it's a five-minute walk from my office."

"I'll text you when I'm on the train. By the way, what are we shopping for exactly?"

He laughed. "No idea. Why do you think I'm taking you along?"

She groaned. "Great!"

"See you tomorrow, Krystie, and thanks."

"Seeya, Max."

He ended the call, smiling broadly. Now, the Max Fields charm offensive kicks into action, he thought.

He collapsed into an armchair. Who was he kidding? Any other girl he'd brought home would have told him to send the taxi away that night and probably have ended up in his bed, but not Krystie. He shouldn't have been such a gentleman, but he knew he couldn't be anything but with Krystie. She was different and he didn't want to manipulate or trick her into bed. He wanted her to come to him willingly or not at all. Max hardly knew her but he couldn't stop thinking about her. It wasn't about a quick roll in the hay. He wanted much more than that. He wanted the whole damn package.

CHAPTER
EIGHTEEN

The Met was just opening when Sheila arrived. The security man recognised her and nodded and she lowered her head and hurried past. She came here most days now, early in the morning while the tourists were still gorging themselves on the breakfast buffet. She would be long gone by the time they started to arrive. Feeling anxious today, she made straight for Gallery 822 and the *Water Lilies* painting by Claude Monet. As always, when she first saw it she gasped, and then felt the tension leave her body. She stood, allowing its beauty to envelop her and peace and serenity to descend. While she was immersed in the detail, the brushwork and the simplicity of the masterpiece, she was able to block out the horror of what she had done to her family.

She had lived in this wondrous cocoon that Karl had created for her until that phone call. Then the scales had fallen from her eyes and the cruelty of her actions struck her like a knife through the heart. No longer did she see things from her point of view but from Sinéad's. It was as if she had been consumed by her sister and now existed only to relive the hurt and the pain and the anguish that Sinéad must have gone through, that

Sheila had caused. There was none of the sense of justice she'd felt as the plane had climbed out over Dublin and she'd looked down on her hometown without a shred of guilt or regret. Only the thought of coming face to face with her twin had brought her to her senses, and now she felt nothing but a deep sense of shame and remorse.

Karl tried to reassure her, saying repeatedly that she'd done the right thing. He said it was time to put herself first, that this feeling would pass, she was just in shock. But she'd tuned him out, was barely aware of him. He was an unwanted presence in her private world of misery and nothing he said or did helped. But nor could she face doing the one thing that *would* help: going home. A lethargy descended on her and she felt weary and miserable spending all of her time in bed or here in the Metropolitan Museum of Art.

Some people went to a church to find peace but Sheila's sanctuary was the Met. Sometimes she wandered aimlessly from room to room but other times she would remain transfixed in front of one piece and was brought out of her trance only by the sound of tours arriving. Nothing really gave her comfort or solace, but Monet came close. She found it impossible to stand in front of a canvas by the man she'd worshipped since childhood and not be distracted for a few precious moments.

A cough snapped her out of her trance and she spun around to see a man studying a painting nearby. He seemed unaware of her, lost in the work, but she still tugged her woollen hat down lower over her eyes and hurried from the room. It was almost ten thirty and the gallery was already coming to life. Time to go home.

She emerged onto the street, her head down, hands plunged deep into her thick winter coat, oblivious of everything and everyone. What dream world had she been living in? How had she ever thought that she could just walk away? She had obviously been in shock when she'd come up with this crazy plan. Now she was wide awake and horrified at her actions. It just wasn't possible to move on before she resolved things with her family.

She thought of the studio Karl had created for her and the body of work she had built up. Her reinvention had all been part of the madness. Why had he done it? Had he realised it was therapy? She sighed, realising it was more than likely true. He was a clever man.

And it had worked then, so maybe it would work now. Sheila quickened her pace. She would paint and paint and paint and maybe, just maybe, the answer would come to her. Maybe she would figure out what to do next. Maybe she would figure out a way to heal her sister's damaged heart.

Karl's face lit up when he came home to find her in overalls. Heedless of his beautiful suit, he hugged her and kissed the top of her head. She was glad for his silent support. There were no words left to say. She allowed her body to relax against his for a moment and, when she finally stepped back and looked up at him, she was surprised to see tears in his eyes. She touched his cheek and he covered her hand with his before turning it and kissing her palm. How glad she was that she had come looking for him. She'd put little thought into it. She just knew that she had to leave Dublin and it seemed fitting to come looking for Karl. He had been so happy to see her, welcomed her into his home and provided the safe haven she so badly needed at the time.

She swallowed back her tears and smiled at him before turning back to her work, and a few moments later heard the gentle click as he left the room.

As she worked, she found her mind wandering back to her childhood and the Christmas before her mother died. While Sinéad made decorations with her mother, Sheila would kneel on a chair at the kitchen table and make lopsided mince pies and Christmas cake from her grandmother's private recipe book. Though her efforts might not have been pretty when she was eight, they were still edible and the family scoffed the lot.

"You're so practical, just like your Aunty Bridie," she remembered her mother saying, sounding disappointed.

Mum had always been happy at Christmas. She loved the carols and the festive colours and their excitement as they wrote their Santa letters. She would fill the house with deep-green holly and pretty red poinsettias and there was always a scent of mulled wine, mince pies or plum pudding in the air. Sheila was happy in the warm kitchen with her mother, preparing for the big day. She had one clear memory of helping to make the stuffing for the turkey and her mother singing along to the radio. To this day the smell of thyme and

Bing Crosby singing "White Christmas" always reminded her of that moment. Christmas had lost its sparkle when Mum died and Bridie was ruling the roost, but once Sheila was old enough she'd reinstated all the old traditions and had done every year since.

Her dad's only job had been to collect the Christmas tree, trim it and put it up. Of course, he always ended up on the floor in a tangled mess of lights with Max crawling happily around him, clapping in delight when they lit up, only to wail when a fuse blew.

Dad had always been useless around the house. How relieved he must have been when Bridie had offered to move in and look after them all. Sheila remembered, as a very obstinate ten-year-old, how resentful she'd felt at this woman coming into their home. They were doing just fine, they didn't need help. She could do everything her mother had. But Maggie hadn't been the most conventional of mothers and had a slapdash approach to housework and cooking, and so Sheila quickly came to appreciate the benefits of having her aunt around. You could always rely on her. Bridie was always waiting at the school gate and the aroma of a casserole in the oven or freshly baked bread would greet them when they got in the front door.

Bridie didn't "experiment" the way Mum had. She believed in plain, healthy eating and shepherd's pie and Irish stew featured regularly on the menu. She was strict, insisting they change out of their uniforms and do their homework the instant they came home. They were also expected to keep their rooms tidy and help with the housework. It was a discipline that they had never known but one that Sheila embraced. But Sinéad had hated it and rebelled. Bridie was so very different from her beloved mother. She would go crying to Daddy, but he knew better than to take on Bridie and instead would bring home sweets to placate her. Max, a happy child, had accepted Bridie's arrival just as he accepted everything. Once his life went along smoothly, he wasn't too bothered who looked after him.

With Bridie in control, Dad had his life back. He played golf on Saturdays and he occasionally went for a pint. Bridie went to a ladies' club on Mondays and to bingo on Wednesdays, but, while she was always back before ten, they would be asleep when Dad got home.

Though Bridie had been brilliant when it came to running a household, she'd never been one to kiss or cuddle or sit on the floor and play with them. Sheila and Max had taken that in their stride, but it was hard for Sinéad. She had always been a tactile child and sensitive. Just like Mum.

Sheila stopped and stared out across the Manhattan skyline, the brush dropping from her fingers. "Just like Mum," she breathed.

She stumbled from the studio and blindly made her way to the window seat. She pulled her knees up to her chin and stared out, unseeing, rocking as the enormity of what she'd done to her sister hit her like a freight train. Her moans and sobs were like that of an animal and her shoulders and ribs ached as all the pain and guilt and fear gushed from her. She never even heard Karl come in and he had to repeat himself a few times before she heard him.

204

"Sheila! Sheila, what is it?" Karl was at her side, his arms around her.

But, though she opened her mouth and tried to speak, nothing came out.

Sheila became aware of voices, Karl and another, male, deep, musical. She had no idea how much time had passed, but she was lying on the large sofa in the living room. The small lamp was on and firelight created shadows on the walls. Karl had removed her overalls, dressed her in pyjamas and tucked a rug around her. It was like having the chickenpox all over again. She wondered if he planned to feed her hot broths and read her a comic as Mum had when she was little. The thought made her giggle and then the giggle turned to hysterical laughter and then she was sobbing again. The voices went silent and then Karl was crouched beside her. "Donna?"

His anxious expression made her sob harder and he held her until she'd calmed down again.

"Why don't you give us a moment alone, Karl?"

She looked up into the gloom and groaned when she saw the man standing there.

He raised an eyebrow and grinned. "Good to see you too, Donna."

"I was worried," Karl said when she turned questioning eyes on him. He squeezed her hand and stood up.

She watched him leave and then looked back up at her visitor. "Why are you here, Zach? I'm not your patient." The man was an old friend of Karl's and he

205

and Sheila had hit it off straightaway when Karl introduced them. She liked him, she liked him a lot, but, then, what was there not to like? Not only was he handsome and funny, there was something very warm and caring about him. If ever a man was in the right job it was Zach Taylor.

"Karl's worried about you." He pulled up a footstool next to her and lowered his large frame onto it, his knees almost level with his chin. "He thought that I might be able to help."

She smirked. "You're the one who is going to need a doctor if you sit like that for long."

He grimaced. "You could be right but stop changing the subject. I'm here to talk about you. What's wrong, Donna? You can talk to me. We're friends, aren't we?"

She nodded, tears welling up again at the compassion in his dark eyes.

"I could arrange for you to see a counsellor if that would be easier."

She wiped her eyes with a knuckle. "I don't want to talk to some stranger about my problems."

"Then talk to a friend."

She looked up at him, blinking away her tears. "You?"

"Well, I'm here now." He smiled. "And I hope I'm a friend."

"Friends share their problems," she pointed out. "It isn't one way."

He nodded thoughtfully. "So if I were to tell you some of my problems it would be okay?"

She couldn't help smiling. "I suppose it would."

"Okay, but you're right, I need to get off this goddamn stool."

As he stood up Karl put his head round the door. "I was heading to the gym, Donna, but if you'd prefer me not to —"

"Go, I'll be fine," she reassured him.

"I'll look after her," Zach promised.

Karl came over to give her a quick hug. "See you later. Thanks, Zach."

"So?" Sheila looked at him expectantly when they were alone.

He raised his eyebrows. "Me first, huh?"

She nodded.

"Okay, then." He stretched out on the floor and leaned his head against the sofa.

"I can't see your face now," Sheila complained. But he was so close she could reach out and touch the thick black hair tinged with grey. She was taken aback at how much she wanted to.

"That's the idea," he muttered. "You're not the only one who finds it hard to open up."

She moved her cushion to the edge of the sofa and lay on her side so she could at least see his profile. "Go on, then, I'm listening."

He shrugged. "I honestly don't have any other than patient-related ones. My life is simple and uncomplicated."

She studied him in silence for a moment. "Will you tell me about your wife?" Karl had told her the little he knew, but, although Sheila had spent many evenings in his company, Zach had never mentioned her.

He let out a long sigh before speaking. "Nancy was beautiful and clever and funny and I looked at her every day and wondered, how the hell did I get to be so lucky? We met at med school and we studied together and slept together — and I mean slept, the hours were gruelling. We were pretty much inseparable. As soon as we qualified we got married and moved into this tiny apartment in an ancient building that was practically falling down around us." He chuckled. "It was such a dive but we were happy."

Sheila sighed, envious of a young couple so much in love that they didn't care where they lived once they were together. "Go on," she prompted.

"We both got residency in the ER of the same hospital, which we were delighted about, but our shifts often overlapped and we saw more of each other at work than at home. We were tired all the time." He shook his head. "I fell asleep everywhere. On the underground, over dinner, it was exhausting. It's pure luck that I didn't kill a patient, but I sure made plenty of mistakes. Nancy had a tougher time. She suffered from anaemia and if she hadn't eaten or had her period she sometimes fainted. One night she was finishing her shift and I was just starting. She was so pale and tired I wanted her to get some coffee and have something to eat before she went home, but she just wanted to sleep. And so I kissed her goodnight." He paused. "That was the last time that I saw her alive."

Sheila gasped and put a hand on his shoulder. "I'm so sorry."

"She'd walked out in front of a car. The first I knew about it was when the ambulance arrived. I was on duty and went to meet it, but suddenly everyone was pushing me back and I knew from their faces it was her. I didn't trust anyone else to treat her, I wanted to do it. I wanted to look after her, to make it better, but then I realised that no one was rushing and some of the team were crying and I knew it was too late. She was already gone."

Seeing his cheeks were wet, Sheila swung her legs round, slid down on the floor beside him and took his hand.

He looked down at it in surprise and then turned his head to look at her. "This is not how it's supposed to work. I'm supposed to be helping you."

She smiled. "No, you're supposed to be behaving like a friend and you are. I'm sorry I asked about Nancy. I didn't mean to upset you."

He wiped his face with his hand. "It's just a natural reaction to reliving the moment and, trust me, I don't need you to make me do that. It's a regular occurrence."

"How long has it been?" she asked. He was a lot older than she was and he'd said it happened shortly after they qualified.

"Fifteen years."

"Fifteen and you're still single?" she blurted out.

He turned his head, grinning. "Yeah, I couldn't find anyone else crazy enough to take me on."

She stared into his eyes and became acutely conscious of the feel of her hand in his.

"Your turn," he said.

"Okay, but I think I need some wine." She pulled her hand from his and scrambled to her feet.

"Can you join me or are you on duty?"

"It's my day off. Wine would be nice."

She padded out to the kitchen and returned with a bottle of red and two glasses. She poured the wine, handed him a glass and sat down on the floor again, but this time she rested her back against the armchair so she was sitting at right angles to him and wouldn't be tempted to hold his hand or touch his hair but could look into his eyes. They were lovely eyes. "Sorry Karl dragged you over here. There really was no need."

He looked at her, amused. "I'm here now, I have wine and we had a deal. It's your turn."

Sheila shook her head as she thought of the length and complexity of her story. "How many days do you have?" she joked.

He held her gaze. "As many as you need."

"I don't even know where to begin."

His eyes were shrewd. "I think you probably do but you're not sure yet whether you're ready to talk about it. You've been keeping secrets for a long time and it's a hard habit to break."

She tried to hide her shock at the baldness of his statement and its accuracy. She felt exposed and suddenly she didn't want him here.

"You know what? I love walking in the park in the cold. There aren't many people about and it's easier to think."

210

She was thrown by the change of topic. "I like that, too."

"So how about we continue this conversation in the morning as we walk? That way you won't have to look at me."

She met his eyes and then shook her head smiling. This guy was dangerous.

"Oh, come on. At the very least you get some exercise and if you're good I'll take you to my favourite deli. Deal?"

She looked at the challenge in his eyes and after only a moment's hesitation nodded. "Deal. So what do we do now?"

He shrugged. "Got any good movies?"

CHAPTER
NINETEEN

Sheila's eyes flew open. What the hell had she been thinking of? What had she done? She swallowed back the wave of panic threatening to engulf her. There was no need for it, she reassured herself. It wasn't as if she had done anything illegal — had she? And Zach was a good man. She couldn't imagine him betraying her trust. Somehow, none of these thoughts made her feel any better. She glanced over at the alarm clock. It was eight fifteen. Karl would already have left for work and Zach would be calling for her at nine. Time she got up and took a shower.

As the punishingly hot water flooded down over her body, she closed her eyes and turned her face up into the stream. Why was she worrying so much? She didn't have to tell him everything. She didn't have to tell him *anything*. All she had to do was leave him feeling that he could go back to Karl and reassure him that she was fine. Yes, that was it, simple. And she could pull it off. She could fool him. Hell, she was an expert. She'd been fooling people for years. She massaged shampoo fiercely into her scalp, then turned the water to cool and gasped at the change in temperature. She tolerated it for a minute and then jumped out feeling refreshed and in control. Everything would be fine.

Zach stared at her when she emerged from the lift. She looked down at herself. "What?"

"Er, nothing, just I thought we were going for a walk in the park, not a trek up the Andes."

Sheila flushed under her Barbour hunting hat and scarf. The only parts of her body on show were her eyes and nose. "I feel the cold," she said, self-conscious under his scrutiny.

"No kidding?" His eyes twinkled. He was looking even more handsome than usual in a padded black jacket worn over a blue turtleneck sweater and jeans and a black beanie pulled down low on his forehead, making his eyes seem even darker than usual.

"I'm not used to New York winters," she pointed out as they emerged onto the street and she pulled on her gloves.

"Who is? I thought Boston was cold until I got here."

They crossed the street so they could be warmed by the winter sunshine.

"You're from Boston? I thought you were a New Yorker."

"With this accent?" He laughed. "And you? Did you always live in Dublin?"

She nodded. "Yeah, very boring."

"I don't think so. If you've got all you need, why would you leave it?"

She said nothing and they walked on in silence, but when he went to turn up Park Avenue she put a hand on his arm to stop him. "Let's avoid the shoppers and take seventh."

"Sure." He tucked her hand through his arm and held it there as they crossed the road.

Sheila was glad he didn't release it when they reached the other side. "Have you brothers or sisters?"

"Are you trying to distract me?" He shot her an amused look.

She lowered her eyes from his shrewd ones. "I was just interested."

"I have two brothers and I'll happily tell you all about them, but right now we're supposed to be talking about you."

She didn't reply and he didn't push her, and they walked on arm in arm in silence. It was cold but the most beautiful morning, and Sheila started to feel the tension leave her body. It was good to have company on her morning walk, especially such attractive company. As they approached the park he paused by a street vendor. "Coffee?"

She shook her head. "Not on an empty stomach."

"You haven't had breakfast?"

"I woke late."

He shook his head, sighed and turned her round. "Okay, breakfast first and then a walk," he said, and propelled her towards Broadway.

She stopped. "I'm really not hungry —"

"You're going to eat," he said and dragged her on.

In the diner she made for a booth at the back of the room and sat with her elbows on the table and her hands covering most of her face, surreptitiously checking out the other diners as he ordered for them both.

"Even you can't be cold in here," Zach said, removing his coat and hat.

"I'm always cold." She shrank down further in the seat.

"So you're planning to eat breakfast like that? Are you wanted by the CIA or something?" he joked.

Reluctantly, she opened her coat and unwound the scarf. "Happy now?"

He looked pointedly at her hat.

"Oh, no, bad-hair day," she said with a brittle smile, her nerves shot as she resumed her examination of their fellow diners. Before she even realised what he was doing he'd pulled off her hat and dropped it on the table between them.

"Looks good to me." His smile faded when he saw her horrified expression. "What is it, what's wrong?"

"I can't do this." She stood up, jammed the hat back on her head and headed for the door.

Zach shouted an apology to the waiter and ran after her. "Donna, hold up!" He followed her outside and spun her to face him, sighing when he saw the tears in her eyes. "What is it?"

"You'll freeze," she pointed out.

He put on his coat and hat and, taking her arm, he guided her back in the direction of Central Park, stopping at a stall to buy two large cups of chicken soup. "The cure for everything," he joked as he handed one to her.

"In Ireland it's tea. Everything can be sorted out over a cup of tea."

"I'm sorry. I didn't mean to upset you," he said as they entered the park and turned left to walk up the west drive.

"I'm sorry, too."

"What are you so frightened of?" he asked.

"Meeting someone I know or who knows me," she blurted out, then stopped, shocked by her honesty.

"Why?"

She smiled. Zach didn't waste his words; she liked that. She felt more comfortable now that they were walking again. "I came to New York to start over," she said. "I don't want any complications."

"You're married."

It was a statement rather than a question. Sheila hesitated. She didn't feel married, but technically she was still Philip's wife. "Yes," she said.

"You're a grown woman, Donna. If you don't want to be married any more then, however hard it is for everyone concerned, you don't have to be. Have you children?"

"Of course not. You think I would have left if I did?" How could he think that of her? That said, was what she had done to her family any better?

He shrugged. "People do all sorts of things that are completely out of character when they feel trapped."

"What makes you think I felt trapped?" she said curiously.

He stopped and looked down at her. "You may not be very forthcoming, Donna, but your eyes say quite a lot." He tucked a wisp of hair that had escaped back under her hat. "Am I wrong?"

She gazed into his eyes, almost wishing that he could read her mind, that he could take away the pain and free her from the guilt that consumed her. "It's more complicated than that," she said finally. "And, by the way, my name is Sheila, not Donna."

He smiled. "Sheila. That's a lovely name, I like it. You know, there's almost always a solution. It's just a matter of finding it."

"I found the solution, I'm here."

"But you're not happy."

"I was until . . ." She shook her head. "I could go back and try and sort things with my family, but I'm afraid."

"There's a good chance talking to them might help. It certainly can't do any harm. You're already hurting."

It sounded simple but she wasn't convinced it would be that easy. She started walking again and he fell into step beside her.

"What does Karl think?"

She smiled. "Karl thinks life is too short to worry about what other people think, especially ones who hurt you. He thinks that I need to be myself and that isn't possible in Dublin."

"Is he right?"

She thought for a moment and then sighed. "Maybe. I have a habit of taking care of people and putting their needs before mine."

Zach looked at her. "So why did you leave?"

She held his gaze. "I found out some stuff that turned my world on its head and I just —" she shrugged — "ran."

"Aah." He nodded. "So, who hurt you?"

"What difference does it make?" She shivered.

He stopped, put up his hand to hail a cab and took her hand. "You must be starving. Come on."

"Where are we going?"

"Somewhere you won't have to worry about being recognised."

Minutes later they were in a taxi on their way to Zach's apartment.

"Don't you ever actually work?" she asked.

He laughed. "Now and again."

"There are better ways to spend your spare time than counselling one seriously messed-up woman."

He looked straight into her eyes. "Is that what I'm doing? And I thought I was spending time with a friend."

She smiled, feeling a warm glow inside at his words and the look in his eyes. No, Sheila, she told herself, life is complicated enough. Anyway, he was just being kind. It was obvious that he was still madly in love with his wife. He wouldn't be single fifteen years on otherwise.

The taxi pulled up outside an old building and they took the elevator to the ninth floor. Zach threw open the door. "Please, make yourself at home." He led the way into a long, open-plan room, tossed his coat and hat across a chair and went to open the fridge.

Sheila looked around in surprise. The room was full of colour and warmth with books on almost every

218

surface and a small, old-fashioned, upright piano in the far corner. "This is not at all what I was expecting," she said pulling off her hat and unravelling the scarf from around her neck.

"Yeah, it's a far cry from Karl's pad, huh?" He laughed as he took out a range of vegetables and started to chop. "It's certainly not as tidy!"

"I love it," she assured him. "This couldn't be the place that you lived in when you qualified?"

"No, that was in Boston. I moved here after Nancy died but I've only lived in this building five years."

She wandered down to the piano, lifted the lid and played the first few notes of "Fur Elise".

"You play?"

"It's been years," she admitted. "There never seemed time."

"You must always make time for music, it's the law."

She laughed and came back to join him. "Can I help?"

"Nah, I'm just going to throw a stir-fry together." He looked up. "You like stir-fry, right?"

"Sounds great." Her stomach rumbled as she sat up on a stool at the breakfast bar.

"I'm guessing you're a good cook," he said.

"I'm not bad."

He heated a wok, added oil and garlic and then scraped the vegetables into the smoking pan.

"You'll have to make me Irish stew some time."

"Sure." She grinned, liking the idea of cooking for him. What was it about this man that made her feel so relaxed, so comfortable?

219

He doused the pan with sauces and rice wine and then added noodles. "Plates are above your head and there's wine in the fridge if you fancy some."

She reached up and took down two plates. "I think I'll stick with water." He served up the food and she sniffed appreciatively. "This smells amazing. Thank you, Zach."

"Hey, it's just a few vegetables."

"I wasn't just talking about lunch." She looked up at him. "I've felt better last night and today with you than I have in a while. In fact I've hardly said a word in days." Sheila shook her head and sighed. "Poor Karl. I'm sure he's regretting asking me to move in with him."

"Rubbish, the man adores you."

"This is delicious," Sheila said, pointing the fork at her plate. "Did you take lessons?"

He looked at her, his eyes twinkling with amusement. "Relax, Sheila, I'm not going to get heavy or question you."

She looked up at him feeling torn. "I didn't mean —"

"Eat. If you want to talk, great. If you don't, that's okay, too."

God, this man was just perfect. "You know what? I think I would like that glass of wine."

He looked up and grinned. "Yeah?"

She smiled and nodded. "Yeah."

The rest of the lunch passed without further reference to tears or secrets, although that night in bed Sheila

220

couldn't remember much of what they had actually talked about. All that stayed with her was how comfortable she had felt in his company. And how, when they had been sitting on the sofa finishing off the wine, she had reached out a hand in gratitude and he had held on to it, stroking it almost absently with his thumb as they talked. She had found it hard to concentrate. The simple feel of his touch on her skin was distracting. He had seemed oblivious, but when it was time to part he became conscious of her hand in his and seemed almost surprised to see it there. His eyes met hers and for a moment she'd seen something there, but it was gone before she could define it. She sighed at the memory and, turning on her side, closed her eyes and slept through the night for the first time in days.

CHAPTER
TWENTY

"What do you think?"

Krystie walked around Sinéad, turning her one way and then the other. "Something's not right."

"I thought you were sure these were the sort of clothes she was wearing." Sinéad looked at her in exasperation.

"I was, I am! Sorry, I don't know why but it's just not quite right," Krystie said, feeling anxious and confused. Jeez, was Max right? Had she got this completely wrong? She felt physically ill at the thought.

Sinéad tossed the coat and hat on her chair. "I'm going for a coffee."

Krystie stared after her as she stomped down the stairs. She understood and shared Sinéad's frustration, but there was no point in doing this unless they got it right. She sat down at the table and started to sketch the image of the woman she'd seen that day in Manhattan. There was something about the eyes that wasn't right. She reached for one of the photo albums that Sinéad had brought in and started to leaf through it again. She stopped at the series of photos taken the morning of Sheila's wedding. There was one of her in a towel, laughing and pushing the person holding the

222

camera out of the bathroom. Krystie was staring at it mesmerised when Sinéad returned.

She put the coffee on the table and began to gather up the albums. "Let's just take the damn photo, Krystie, and be done with it."

"Hang on, I have an idea." Krystie went to her bag and pulled out a packet of wipes. "Sit down. I'm going to take off your eye makeup."

"What?" Sinéad stared at her as Krystie gently pressed her into a chair.

"Humour me, please?"

Sinéad shrugged and closed her eyes and Krystie carefully wiped away her eyeshadow and eyeliner leaving just the mascara. "Okay. Open your eyes."

Sinéad did and Krystie felt a flicker of excitement at the difference. "Now put the coat and hat on again."

"Sheila would never go out without makeup," Sinéad grumbled, shuffling into the coat.

"Sheila would never pretend she was dead, either." Krystie clamped a hand over her mouth. "Shit, I'm sorry."

Sinéad's eyes met hers in the mirror. "It's a fair point." She tucked her hair under the hat.

Still red-faced and determined to think before she spoke in future, Krystie moved around in front of Sinéad, freed a few blonde wisps to frame her face, straightened the hat from the jaunty angle Sinéad had it at and tugged it down lower on her head.

"Yuck, that's dreadful." Sinéad looked in disgust at her reflection.

Krystie moved a few steps away and stared at her. "Turn and look at me and don't smile." Sinéad did as she was told. "That's it!" Krystie cried, her stomach doing a somersault.

Sinéad turned back to look at herself, her eyes incredulous. "Really?"

"Really."

"Get the camera."

"What are you doing for Christmas?" Kieran asked as Beth set the sandwiches on the table. He carried over the two bowls of piping-hot broth and took his seat opposite her.

"I told you." She looked up at him in surprise. "After Mass I will call in on a few friends and then have a nice bit of dinner in front of the soaps."

He blew on his soup before trying it. "This is delicious. What would you say to coming along to Philip's with me?"

She put down her spoon and stared at him. "I'd feel I was intruding and I don't think your family would be too impressed."

"You wouldn't be intruding and, as for Max and Sinéad, I've had to put up with plenty of their partners over the years." He glanced up and saw that she was blushing.

"There's a difference between partners and friends, Kieran," she said, sounding almost shy. "You wouldn't want to give them the wrong impression."

"What impression would that be?" he asked. "That I enjoy your company? That I find myself thinking about

224

you all the time? That I've been happier these last couple of months than I have in a long time?"

"Oh, Kieran!" She looked at him, startled. "I've enjoyed them too."

He took her hand. "I know I'm a grumpy old sod."

"You're not. You're sad, and why wouldn't you be? I hope Sheila comes back to you, sweetheart, I really do."

"Once I know that she's okay it's not important where she is." He smiled into her eyes. "So, will you come?"

"Have you told them anything about me at all?" she asked.

"No." He went back to eating his soup. "Not because I'm ashamed or embarrassed, nothing like that. There's just been so much upheaval and upset lately that I didn't want to add to it and I suppose I've enjoyed having you to myself."

"Do you know, I don't think I've ever been as comfortable with anyone as I am with you?" Beth said.

"Apart from Gerry," he said, pushing aside his empty bowl and helping himself to a sandwich.

She paused for a moment and then said, "Including Gerry."

Kieran looked up at her in surprise.

"He was a good man," she said, "a good husband and father. I don't think that we ever had a cross word but . . ."

"But?" he asked trying to read her expression.

"But nothing, really. I suppose it's just the way I am with you has made me realise that we were never really close."

Kieran shifted uncomfortably. He still found Beth's openness unnerving. "I'm not sure that I understand."

"Everyone was very sympathetic when Gerry died. He was so young, they said. How awful it was that I was left alone, they said. I must be so lonely. And I was," she said. "It's strange after more than thirty years of marriage to cook for one, to iron for one, to go on a day's shopping trip and come home and the house is the same way I left it. That all takes getting used to."

"I can imagine," Kieran said. Even though he had lived alone for years now, Max and the twins had their own keys and were in and out on a regular basis, especially Sheila. He'd caught her on more than one occasion checking the contents of the fridge and freezer. She often arrived with food saying, "I cooked too much lasagne last night, Dad, so I thought it would save you cooking," or some such excuse. He'd been more than happy to go along with the pretence. He'd never been much of a cook and he didn't see the point in it when there were so many things you could buy and just pop in the microwave.

"But it's only since you've been visiting me, Kieran, I've realised that Gerry and I never talked, not really," Beth continued. "He'd complain about the weather or the traffic or the bills. I'd tell him about any gossip from the neighbours, if Gavin had been in touch, what he had to say, but we never talked about us, you know? I didn't even know that much about his job. It was so strange at the funeral. So many people he worked with talked to me about him and it may as well have been a different man; it wasn't the Gerry I knew at all."

"I think all men are a bit like that. At the end of a long day you want to leave the office behind and relax. When you've been together a long time you don't need to talk."

"Maybe." Her eyes searched his. "So we only get on so well because we're just getting to know each other, is that it?"

He smiled. "That's it."

"Then I'd better make the most of it because I'm having a lovely time."

"Me too. You're great company, Beth, and such a good friend and above all . . ."

"Yes?"

He winked at her. "You're a bloody marvellous cook."

"Cheeky fecker!" she said, laughing.

"Seriously, though, Beth, I've been very low since Sheila disappeared and I didn't think I would ever come out the other side."

"I think that's because you have some hope now, Kieran," she said matter-of-factly.

"That helps, no argument, but I started feeling better before I got that news, Beth. I started feeling better because of you."

"Oh, Kieran." Her eyes filled up.

"So, woman, will you spend Christmas Day with me or not?"

She beamed at him. "I'd love to."

Max stood outside Trinity College and smiled as he saw a familiar figure weave her way through the crowds towards him. He waved and she smiled and waved back, making his heart skip a beat. What was it about her that was so irresistible? He couldn't remember ever being so obsessed with a woman; he seemed to think of little else. She was wearing a green leather jacket over a black polo-neck top and tight red jeans, a vivid multicoloured beret and a red scarf. She was like a sexy Santa elf and was making heads turn, but she seemed completely oblivious of the admiring glances.

"Sorry, have you been waiting long?" she said, slightly breathless when she reached him.

"I just got here. Shall we head into Brown Thomas?"

"Depends on what you want to buy." She fell into step beside him.

"She likes big earrings," he offered.

"I thought you wanted something special," Krystie protested. "What does she do for fun?"

"No idea." He frowned. It had been a long time since he had seen Sinéad do anything other than sit around looking miserable.

"What did she do before Sheila went missing?"

He thought about it for a moment and then smiled. "She loved music. She couldn't function without it. Wherever she was, her music was with her."

"I've never heard her play music," Krystie said in surprise. "What kind of music does she like?"

He sighed. "Oh, wow, everything and anything."

She stopped and closed her eyes briefly. "Can we go somewhere quiet?"

Max stared at her in stunned delight. "Great idea. We can go and have a bite to eat at Dobbins. I'll phone —"

"No . . . you don't understand." Her eyelids fluttered. "I need help."

Realising that she was about to pass out he put an arm around her waist and half carried her to his offices around the corner.

"Mr Fields! I thought you were gone for the evening." The cleaner, who was pushing a large vacuum cleaner back and forth across the carpet, looked up in surprise as he practically dragged Krystie down the hall of his offices.

"I forgot I had one more appointment. Would you do something for me, Sylvie? Would you nip down to the canteen and get me a sandwich or roll, nothing fancy. Oh, and a bottle of water?" He pulled a twenty out of his pocket and handed it over.

"Of course, Mr Fields." She beamed at him in delight. He never accepted change so she was always happy to run his errands. He kicked the door closed behind him and lowered Krystie onto the small sofa in the corner of his office. She was looking slightly dazed. "Krystie, are you okay?"

She didn't respond. He scanned her face. Her eyes were glazed. She was obviously conscious but completely unaware of him. He gently moved her into a lying position, eased off her boots, whispering as he did, telling her she was safe, that everything was okay. He opened her jacket and, lifting her head, unwound the scarf. Suddenly, she drew her legs up and clenched her fists like a prizefighter, stiff, eyes still staring. He sat down on the floor beside her, bracing himself. "It's okay, Krystie. Everything is going to be fine. I've got you."

She remained like that for a minute or so and then she started to jerk. He lay alongside her to prevent her falling off and hurting herself.

"Mr Fields, what are you doing?"

He looked up to see Sylvie in the doorway looking horrified and realised how this must look. "She's having an epileptic fit, Sylvie." His words were just out when her movements started to become less frenetic and she started to gasp for breath.

"Oh, the poor girl. Is there anything I can do? Will I call a doctor?"

"Just wait for a moment with me until she starts to come out of it. Then it would be best if you disappeared. She's going to be embarrassed enough that *I've* seen her like this."

Krystie slumped back on the sofa, groaning, her eyes closed. Max pulled out a handkerchief and wiped the drool from the corner of her mouth. "It's over, Krystie. It's all over." He looked up and smiled at Sylvie's worried face. "She'll be fine now."

She nodded and smiled. "You're a good man, Mr Fields. I will leave you but I will be on the next floor if you need me."

When she was gone, he smoothed Krystie's hair back from her face and wiped the smudged mascara from under her eyes. God, she was so beautiful. She moaned again and he stroked her hand. "You're safe, Krystie. You're safe, darling."

Her eyes flickered open and she looked around, her expression confused, frightened. She became aware of him, stared at him, but didn't speak.

He smiled what he hoped was a reassuring smile. "You had a seizure, Krystie. I brought you to my office. Would you like some water?" She didn't answer and after a moment sat up. He opened the bottle of water that Sylvie had left on his desk and handed it to her. She looked at it blankly and then took it and drank. Some of the water spilled down her chin and he handed her his handkerchief.

"Thanks." She dried herself. "Sorry about that. Was it bad?" She looked around her and ran her hand along the leather couch.

"You have nothing to apologise for. It was very low-key. Good of you to wean me in gently. What's the last thing that you remember?"

She shook her head slowly.

"Are you hungry?" He picked up the sandwich Sylvie had left. "Ham and cheese?"

She shook her head again and he shut up to give her a chance to gather her wits.

"What happened?" she asked finally, looking pale and tired.

He sat down next to her. "You were fine one minute, and then you went into a sort of daze. We're in my office. I just got you here when you seized up. It was all over quite quickly. Rest a moment and then I'll take you home."

"No, it's fine."

"We're not going shopping, Krystie," he told her.

She frowned and then nodded. "Oh, yes, for Sinéad. Just give me a moment and we'll get started."

She rested her head back against the sofa and closed her eyes and after a few minutes he thought perhaps she was asleep. "I really think it would be better if I took you home."

She opened her eyes. "I'm not an invalid," she protested.

"I know that but, to be honest, the shopping trip was just an excuse to spend some time with you."

Her lips twitched. "Why didn't you just ask me out?"

"Would you have said yes?" he asked.

"Probably not," she admitted.

It wasn't what he wanted to hear but he had expected it: she had been distant since the night of the party. He adopted a mournful expression. "My confidence is shattered."

She raised a weak smile. "I doubt that."

"Come on, let's find a quiet café and you can tell me why you're rejecting me."

CHAPTER
TWENTY-ONE

It was only ten when Max dropped her home. She was grateful because, though she had recovered very quickly, she was tired. He had taken her to a small Italian restaurant round the corner where he was obviously well known. The place seemed full to her, but when they saw Max a table for two magically appeared in a quiet alcove. Once they'd ordered he dived straight in and asked her all about epilepsy.

"So that was a tonic-clonic seizure, right?"

She'd looked at him, surprised. "How do you know that?"

"When Sinéad told me you had epilepsy I read up on it online. I wanted to be sure that we knew exactly what to do and how to help if you had an attack." He grinned. "I'm a bit anal like that."

And then it was: When had she been diagnosed? Were the seizures all the same? Had they got better or worse over time? At first she had felt uncomfortable with this inquisition, wondering if he was asking these questions because he was afraid she'd be an insurance risk, or stab his sister with scissors, but as she talked she could see that, not only was he genuinely interested, he wasn't spooked, either. He didn't offer her wine with the meal and as soon as they had finished eating he called for the bill and told her that he was driving her home. Normally, she would be irritated at being bossed around, but she did feel tired and was grateful for his consideration. And he'd been delighted with the idea she'd come up with for Sinéad's Christmas present.

When they got to Greystones he came in to meet Sharon, charming her completely, but left again after a few minutes, insisting that Krystie needed rest. She walked him out to the car. "Thanks for looking after me, Max."

"I'm glad I was there. Now I know the signs I'll be better prepared in future and I can tell Sinéad what to watch out for." He bent his head to kiss her and then stopped, looking down at her, his eyes widening in mock horror. "Oops, I forgot. I'm not allowed to do that, am I?"

"No, you're not," Krystie agreed, and pulled his mouth back down to hers. She shouldn't have, of course she shouldn't. It was a really bad idea to encourage Max at all. It would end in disaster. But as he drove away she stood looking after him, smiling, her fingers touching her lips.

Sharon was waiting when she went back inside. "I sense a change in this relationship. Tell me all." She hit the mute button on the TV and looked at her expectantly.

"It's not what you think," Krystie said, but she couldn't wipe the smile off her face. "I had a fit."

234

"Oh, my God. Are you okay?" Sharon was immediately all concern.

"Fine. I was more embarrassed than anything else but he was cool."

"He *seems* cool." Sharon smiled. "I don't understand why you don't fancy him. He's gorgeous and it's obvious he fancies you."

"Is it?" Krystie grinned.

"It is." Sharon sighed. "A knight in shining armour *and* in a fancy car. I'd be quite happy to let him take care of me."

Krystie looked at her wistful expression and hugged her. "Your knight's out there somewhere."

Sharon hugged her back. "Go to bed, you look tired. I'll bring you some hot chocolate and a hot-water bottle."

"You are the bestest friend a girl could have, know that?"

Sharon laughed. "You better believe it."

When she was settled in bed with her hot drink, Krystie felt warm inside as well as out. Max had been so wonderful this evening. He had taken control, kept calm, looked after her and, though she felt embarrassed that he'd witnessed her having a fit, he'd soon made her feel completely at ease. Although she still couldn't remember the actual seizure — she never could — she remembered how gentle and reassuring he'd been beforehand. On impulse she picked up her phone and sent him a text: "Thank you for being so great tonight, Max."

She hesitated for a moment then added an "x" and pressed send.

A moment later his reply came back making her laugh: "You should be asleep!! Neil Young concert booked. Sinéad will be thrilled. Tnx for the idea. xx ☺"

She typed back: "Great!"

His reply was instant: "Sleep! x."

And, smiling, she switched off the phone and settled down for the night.

Krystie was brushing her hair the next morning when her phone beeped. She smiled when she saw it was from Max: "Hope you had a good night. See you later. x."

She frowned, wondering what that meant. He must be just dropping by to see Sinéad. Looking at her watch, she realised that she needed to hurry. Her boss had announced that they had a lot to talk about and could she be in for eight thirty. Perhaps Max was joining them. She put on a cream polo-neck over jeans, added a suede belt and tugged on her cowboy boots. After pulling her plaid cap down low over one eye she shrugged into her leather jacket, grabbed her bag and legged it for the train.

She only just made it to the station in time to slip between the doors of the last carriage. Since she'd woken she'd been thinking about the fit and wondering what had brought it on. She got them so rarely that when she did she tried to evaluate what had triggered it and make damn sure to avoid it in the future. Max had been wonderful, but he was still her boss to an extent and she needed to show both him and Sinéad that she was a good bet and a safe one, and that they could rely on her. She would phone her old GP this morning and arrange an appointment as soon as possible. He would organise a brain scan and possibly change her medication, though in her heart she knew that it wasn't necessary. She was pretty sure that the combination of working long hours, not eating regularly and drinking more than usual was the reason. That and the fact that she was completely hyper about her new job and seriously stressed about the mystery surrounding Sheila and the part she'd played in it. It would be a bloody miracle if she hadn't had an attack. She had to calm down and take care of herself. Now that she had the job of her dreams she couldn't and wouldn't risk losing it.

"Someone is very quiet today," Ellen remarked as Krystie stood in the queue at the counter lost in thought. "Everything okay?"

"Fine," Krystie said brightly, feeling her cheeks grow hot. She was glad the other woman was too busy at the coffee machine to notice. "Make it a weak one, Ellen."

"Weak? Now you really have me worried."

"I've decided it's time to get healthy. I might even go jogging with you and Rory."

"Seriously?" Ellen turned to look at her.

Krystie rolled her eyes dramatically. "Duh! In your dreams. I'm right on the beach and I keep promising myself that I'll go for early-morning walks, but the bed is just too comfortable."

"Get a dog," Rory said, coming out of the kitchen with two plates of bacon and eggs.

"God, that looks good," Krystie said, her mouth watering.

"Sit down and I'll make you some."

She checked her watch. "No time. I've a meeting in ten minutes and, anyway, I've already had a bowl of porridge."

Ellen brought her coffee. "You really are on a health kick."

"Don't tell anyone but I actually love the stuff." Krystie grinned. "Later!"

"Morning, Sinéad, cold out there, isn't — Oh my God." Krystie pulled up short and stared around her. The floor was littered with designs and Sinéad sat cross-legged in the middle of them with her sketch pad, music blaring. She dropped her bag and bent down to pick up the pages nearest to her and then moved slowly around the room picking up one page after another, studying them in silence.

Sinéad, who hadn't opened her mouth, watched her and waited, chewing anxiously on her pencil. Krystie went to turn down the music before facing her boss. "These are amazing."

"Really? Don't just say that because I pay your wages," Sinéad warned.

"I mean it, Sinéad," Krystie said, fervently. "They're giving me goosebumps. They're jumping off the page. I can visualise them; I can almost feel them in my hands."

Sinéad's face lit up with a mixture of excitement and relief. "Are they good enough for New Yorkers?"

"They're good enough for royalty!"

Sinéad laughed. "Oh, there's a thought. But right now I'm focusing on Manhattan."

"Seriously?" Krystie's eyes widened.

Sinéad stood up, stretched and then sat down in her chair. "Yeah, I've decided to lure my sister out of hiding."

Krystie sat down opposite. "I'm listening." Her eyes flickered between her boss and the designs as Sinéad explained her plan.

"So, what do you think?"

"I think you're right. I doubt she'd be able to resist checking you out. She would be so proud."

"I hope that's true. But there's something missing."

Krystie looked at the sketches and back at Sinéad. "What?"

"You. I need you to create some designs of your own."

She gaped at Sinéad. "But I've still so much to learn!"

"About millinery, yes, but not about design, and that's what's important here. I have much more chance of getting into the big stores if I can present them with two contrasting styles. Do you think you can do it?"

"Yes, yes, I think I can. Thank you." Krystie leaned forward and flung her arms around Sinéad.

"Don't thank me. I'm using everything and everyone at my disposal to find Sheila."

"That's fine too. I'd love to be able to help."

Sinéad smiled. "Thanks, but I hope you're ready for a lot of hard work and long hours."

"No problem," Krystie said, promising herself she would get a lot more early nights. She was on the point of telling Sinéad about her seizure but realised that she would have to say she was with Max when it happened. She'd better talk to him about it first so they got their stories straight.

"Then let's get started."

It was amazing how Sinéad's smile changed her from being an attractive woman to a stunning one, Krystie thought. She looked at the sketches and thought that they weren't just the work of a talented person but a passionate one.

"Tell me," Sinéad said, "where or how do you design best?"

"I usually just go window shopping and then when I think I have some ideas I sit down somewhere with my pad and pencil." Krystie looked back at all Sinéad's designs. "When did you do all these?"

"I've been up since five listening to Leonard Cohen."

"You did all of this in one morning?"

"It doesn't usually work like that but I suppose it's been so long since I designed anything, once I started I couldn't stop. I tell you what. Let's get to work on a couple of them and then you can take off early and head into town and see if you get any ideas."

They worked steadily all morning and, when Sinéad went out for lunch, Krystie rang her GP to make an appointment.

"We have a cancellation at six. Could you come in then?" the receptionist asked.

Krystie hesitated. She didn't want to let Sinéad down, but it was more important for both of them for her to get a check-up. "Yes, I'll be there, thanks."

She was about to call Max when she heard someone coming up the stairs and the man himself appeared. "Hey!" She smiled at him. "I was going to ring you."

"I like the sound of that," he grinned. "Were you offering to take me out to lunch?"

"No, my boss is a slave driver, she doesn't allow me out."

He frowned. "You make sure to eat and take a break. You need to take better care of yourself, Krystie, and you certainly shouldn't be overdoing it after last night."

"I've been thinking along the same lines and I've made a doctor's appointment for this evening."

"Are you worried?" He took his sister's chair and pulled it closer.

"No, it's standard procedure to have a scan done after a seizure," she assured him, touched by the concern in his eyes. "I've been really dumb these last few weeks. I brought the attack on myself but I've learned my lesson. I'll be sensible from now on. Anyway, I won't have time to misbehave. Sinéad told me about her plan. I'm so excited."

"I'm not sure there *is* a plan, is there? Sinéad has started to design but I don't think she's figured out how she's going to get these big New York fashion stores to actually take a look at them."

"I have some ideas about that," Krystie said, anxious to help.

"Great, as long as it's not too stressful: that wouldn't be good for your health."

She opened her mouth to deny it but he was way ahead of her.

"Don't tell me I'm wrong. I told you, I've read up on it."

"I'll be careful," she promised, smiling.

"I think we need to make a few changes around here to make this place safer." He spun around in the chair and scanned the room with a critical eye.

Krystie wasn't sure she liked the sound of that. Sometimes people focused too much on the illness and forgot that it was only a tiny part of her life. Still, no doubt he had to think of the insurance implications.

"Really, there's no need," she tried to reassure him.

"Do you always know when you're about to have a seizure?"

"Sometimes I think I'm going to have one and don't but, yeah, I get some strange feelings when it starts, so I have time to get somewhere safe."

"Good. We'll install a panic button and link it to the café and you can press it if you're alone and think you're in trouble. A safety gate at the top of the stairs too, I think."

"Oh, for crying out loud! Why not just put me in a play pen just to be on the safe side?" She laughed.

He raised an eyebrow. "Do you think Rory and Ellen would prefer to find their tenant in a heap at the bottom of the stairs with a hat pin sticking out of her

242

jugular?" She had to laugh. He rolled his chair closer and took her hand. "Look, Krystie, I'm not trying to make an issue of this or turn you into some kind of invalid. I just think once everyone knows the drill then we can all relax and get on with life. Does that make sense?"

She nodded, touched by his thoughtfulness. "Yeah."

"Great. We'll talk to Sinéad when she gets back."

"There's just one little detail that you're forgetting. How do we explain to your sister why you were with me last night when I had the attack?"

He smirked. "We'll just have to tell her that we were on a date."

"But if we went on one date don't you think she'd expect us to go on more?" she said, disturbingly aware that he had moved even closer.

He reached out and ran a finger very gently down the curve of her cheek. "I think she might."

He leaned in to kiss her and, despite all the promises Krystie had made herself, she found herself turning her mouth up to his and sliding her arms around his neck.

CHAPTER
TWENTY-TWO

Sinéad sat with her back against the sofa, a pad resting against her knees, the radio belting out hits from the eighties in the background. She was working round the clock on her plans to take her designs to New York, determined that she would make it happen. She didn't feel as angry at Sheila any more, either. She knew in her gut that her sister was alive, although she had given up saying so. She was fed up being told not to get her hopes up. But she couldn't stop wondering what had made her leave and in such a way. Her thoughts as always came back to Philip, but she still couldn't make sense of it.

"You're up early." Dylan walked in and, wincing, lowered the volume on the radio.

She looked up and smiled. "Yeah, I can't seem to switch off." She was going though a list of celebrities, columnists and fashionistas in New York that Krystie thought they should send hats to. It was a costly business and she wanted to make sure that they got their money's worth.

He sat down next to her and leaned in for a kiss. "I am delighted to see you happy, Sinéad, but do you think you could take this evening off?"

244

She looked up at him. "Why?"

"Because tomorrow is Christmas Eve and we'll spend most of the next few days with our families. It would be nice to have one evening with just the two of us."

She kissed him and smiled. "Sounds good. What did you have in mind?"

"Meet me in town after work. We'll have some dinner and if you're good I might even take you dancing."

Sinéad couldn't help thinking that a late night was the last thing she needed. She had to come up with the best collection ever in order to draw out her sister and intended to work until lunchtime the next day, when she and Dylan would go to his parents' home for the annual exchange of gifts. But she had hardly seen him in the last couple of weeks and he had been pretty cool about it, so she owed him one night out. "Ellen and Rory are having a party after they close at six so I'll have to show my face, but I could be in town for eight."

"Wonderful." He kissed her again and slipped his hand inside her pyjamas, his eyes twinkling. "We don't really have to go dancing, do we?"

She shivered as his fingers moved down across her stomach. "No," she murmured. "No dancing."

Arriving into work a little later than planned Sinéad smiled when she saw Ellen dressed in her Mrs Claus outfit. "Any chance of a strong Americano? You can tell Santa I've been a very good girl."

Ellen raised an eyebrow. "That's not what the elves tell me. You're coming along later, right?"

245

"Of course I am, along with the lovebirds." Sinéad grinned. She still couldn't believe that Max and Krystie were dating.

"Are they really an item now?" Ellen asked.

"It's looking that way."

"I'm delighted. They make a nice couple."

"Yeah, they do," Sinéad agreed.

"Oh, don't forget to pick up your desserts before you go tomorrow."

Sinéad gasped. "Oh, crikey, I'm glad you reminded me. I am so focused on work at the moment, Christmas is sort of passing me by."

"There will be plenty of Christmases. I think that you've got your priorities right. I hope it works, Sinéad." Ellen smiled. She and Rory were the only ones outside of the family whom Sinéad had told about Krystie spotting Sheila in Manhattan and her plan to find her sister.

"You are one lovely Mrs Santa." Sinéad hugged her. "See you later."

Krystie was already bent over a hat when she arrived. "This is what I like to see, the staff hard at work."

"Morning! I'm afraid the staff is working on her ma's Christmas present," Krystie admitted.

"I think given the hours you put in I can let you away with that, just this once." Sinéad put down her coffee, took off her coat and hat and came to join her at the table. "Oh, Krystie . . ."

"What?" The girl looked up at her. "Is it awful?"

"Oh, please, you know it's not," Sinéad laughed.

Krystie grinned but then looked back at the hat in her hands and sighed. "But something's missing."

Sinéad sat down and took the hat from her. "Tell me about your mother. Is she going to wear this or just keep it and stare at it because her darling daughter made it?"

Krystie laughed. "No, she'll wear it. She loves hats, and they suit her too. But, yes, it will mean a lot to her that I made it. I thought that this would be a good Sunday hat but it's too fancy with the trim and too plain and boring without it."

Sinéad stared intently at it. The hat was based loosely on the cloche style in a rich but understated moss green. The trim was cream with a floral motif in the same shade of green. "Her eyes are green?"

"Hazel."

"Hmm." Sinéad chewed her lip. "What if you made the trim a plain velvet or silk band in the same colour, but perhaps a shade darker or lighter?"

"Oh, yes, that would work. You are so good at this," Krystie said with a wistful sigh.

Sinéad laughed. "I'd better be, I've been doing it a long time. Don't doubt yourself, Krystie, you're a natural and you're a human sponge. I can't seem to teach you fast enough."

The girl shrugged. "I'm enjoying every second."

"It shows. Now, do you mind if we forget about Ma for the moment and do some work that will actually bring in some money?"

Krystie grinned and put the hat on a mannequin head. "Yes, boss."

They chatted amicably as they worked on finishing off a wedding order, the radio belting out Christmas songs in the background. "Fairytale of New York" by the Pogues came on and Sinéad sat back in her chair and sighed.

Krystie looked up. "You okay?"

"Yeah, just that's one of Sheila's all-time favourites."

"Funny."

Sinéad looked at her.

"Oh, I don't mean funny ha-ha," Krystie said quickly. "I mean funny strange now that she's probably *in* New York."

Sinéad smiled. Krystie had doubted herself when Dylan and Max had quizzed her, but since she'd seen Sinéad dressed in the same clothes and without makeup she was adamant that it was definitely Sheila she had seen.

"I'm sure she's fine," Krystie said, "and hopefully you'll get to see her very soon."

"I think it might be a little more complicated than that." Sinéad decided to change the subject. "You're going along to Ellen and Rory's party later, right?"

Krystie laughed. "I'd be afraid not to. Ellen threatened all sorts if I didn't show up. I'm looking forward to it."

"So what other plans have you for Christmas, Krystie?"

The girl flushed. "Max has asked me to go along to Philip's party tomorrow evening, but I'm not sure. I hardly know the man. Then Christmas Day I'll spend with my family."

"Philip would be thrilled to have you there," Sinéad assured her.

"I don't know." Krystie looked dubious. "I'm not sure I'd fit in with all those political types."

"It won't be just politicians, and Max will be there to look after you."

"Aren't you going?"

"I hadn't planned to, but now that we've launched Operation Manhattan I suppose I should circulate more."

"You really should. The more reviews and photos of celebrities that you can send out with the hats the better, and you should make a point of inviting all the key fashion writers to every event. The reason I got nowhere in New York is because I didn't know anyone. Contacts are everything."

Sinéad smiled at her. "So perhaps we should do some advertising again at Philip's drinks party tomorrow. It'll be full of important people."

"People from the fashion business?"

Sinéad frowned. "No, but it's not too late to change that. I'll call him."

"But we don't have time to make anything special," Krystie pointed out.

Sinéad hopped up and reached up to take a large hat box down. "Don't worry. There's always my little treasure trove."

Krystie stood up to get a good look. "Oh, wow, this is, like, every little girl's dream dress-up box!"

Sinéad laughed, lifting out hairbands studded with stones, feather clips and beads and flowers of all colours and sizes. She found a beaded skullcap and twirled it round. "How the hell did this end up in here?"

"It's beautiful."

"Why don't you take the box home with you and you can decide what works with whatever outfit you're wearing?"

"Can I?" Krystie looked as if all her birthdays had come together.

"Sure." Sinéad laughed. "I look forward to seeing what you come up with."

By the time Max had arrived for Rory and Ellen's party they had put the final touches to the pieces needed for three weddings on New Year's Eve and were on a high.

"Are you two planning to join the fun downstairs?" he asked.

Sinéad glanced at the clock and saw that it was six thirty. "I had no idea it was so late. You go on, Krystie, I'll finish up here."

"Are you sure?"

"Yeah, I'll be down in a few minutes."

As they left Sinéad went in search of labels. Where had the damn things got to? With a sigh of frustration she started to pull apart the drawers of the desk and eventually located them in the bottom one. They had obviously slipped down the back. She was about to close the drawer when her eyes fell on the leather pouch of her passport. She'd been wondering where it was. She really should take it home and put it somewhere safe. Come to think of it, she knew it expired this year. She'd have to organise a new one because, if Philip didn't get things moving soon, she was going to New York herself. She flicked it open to check the expiry date and then stared at it in confusion. This was her old passport. How the hell did *that* get in there? She threw it on the desk and started to pull the drawers apart but she couldn't find the up-to-date passport — Oh, my God!

She hurried downstairs as the pieces of the puzzle fell into place. Smiling vaguely and greeting the local businesspeople, she searched the café for her brother and finally spotted him leaning on the counter chatting to Rory and Krystie. She pushed her way through the crowd and touched his arm.

He turned his head and smiled. "I was just asking Rory if he fancied joining us on Christmas Day. I'm a bit nervous about Philip cooking a turkey."

"Yeah, me too." She laughed. "Can I have a word? Sorry, Krystie, I'll bring him straight back."

"What's so important that it couldn't wait till tomorrow?" Max asked, reluctantly following her up to the studio.

"This." She shoved the passport into his hand.

"It's your passport, so what?"

"Take a closer look."

He opened it and shrugged. "It's your old passport. What's your point?"

She looked at him. "It's my old passport but it's in the new cover, the one that Sheila bought me last Christmas."

He frowned. "I don't follow."

"She switched them, Max. She took my passport. She travelled to the US under the name Sinéad Fields, not Sheila Healy."

He hesitated. "But the police told us they checked the flights and, regardless of the name being different, you're identical twins, Sinéad."

"We don't look alike in our passport photos and anyway all she'd need is a wig or a hat and she'd get through passport control without a second glance. She's alive, Max, and very probably in New York."

He stared at the document in his hand. "If you're right it should be easily verified, but we still won't know where she is exactly."

"We're a step closer."

He nodded and smiled. "Yes, we are. My God, wait till we tell Dad. This is the best Christmas present you could give him. We need to call the police."

"But Philip didn't want to involve them, remember?" Sinéad sank into a chair with a sigh of frustration.

"I think this changes things, don't you?"

"Let's go and talk to him."

Max stared at her as if she were mad. "Now?"

"Why not? Tomorrow is Christmas Eve, Max. If we don't act quickly you can bet nothing will happen before the New Year. But in America Christmas is a one-day event. If Philip talked to the private investigator tonight we could get things moving."

He sighed. "Right. I'll go and talk to him and call you later."

She jumped to her feet. "Not a chance. I'm coming with you."

"Okay, okay. Let's go."

CHAPTER
TWENTY-THREE

Philip opened the door and looked none too pleased to see them, but within seconds his customary smile was in place. He looked over his shoulder.

"Sorry for dropping in unannounced, Philip." Sinéad brushed her cheek against his. "We're not interrupting anything, are we?"

"No, no, of course not."

She started to head towards the kitchen but he blocked her way and steered her towards the living room. "I've just been catching up on some paperwork. Let's go in here. Confidentiality and all that, you understand."

Sinéad locked eyes with her brother and saw that he didn't believe the man either. There was a woman in the kitchen, she'd take a bloody bet on it. The bastard!

"Can I get you a drink?" He smiled at her. "It is Christmas, after all."

"No, thanks," she said.

"We won't keep you from your —" Max hesitated just a second — "work. But we thought you would want to know the latest development."

"Development?" Philip said, his eyes sharp.

"Sheila took my passport," Sinéad told him.

He looked at her for a moment and then shook his head. "I don't understand."

"She took my current passport out of the cover and replaced it with the old one. She obviously got out of the country under my name."

"So, Philip, I think this changes how we proceed, don't you?" Max said.

"Yes, in that we can find out for sure if she used the passport and where she flew to," he agreed. "But then we still need to track her movements from then on."

"But, once the police establish that Sheila did fly to JFK, surely they'll reopen her case," Sinéad said, feeling impatient and frustrated. What the hell was wrong with the man? He must have found another woman and didn't want Sheila back, she was convinced of it. Oh my God, had Sheila found out there was another woman and was that why she left? Well, to hell with him. If he wouldn't find her, Sinéad would.

"I'm sure they will, Sinéad. It's great news and I will get right on it first thing in the morning."

Max pinned him with his eyes. "We thought you could make a call this evening. After all, it's only lunchtime in New York."

"Yes, of course, I forgot that. I'll get right on it and let you know as soon as I have any news." Philip steered them towards the door.

"Okay if I use your loo?" Sinéad asked and was out of the door before he could reply. She hurried down the hall and stuck her head into the kitchen, but the room was deserted except for the table strewn with files. So he *was* telling the truth, she thought, feeling guilty, and

254

then she spotted the two mugs amid all the papers. She heard the men coming into the hall and dashed into the loo before she was caught.

"There was someone else there," she insisted as Max drove them back towards Blackrock.

"Maybe, but does it matter? Finding Sheila is what's important, and we're a step nearer to that, thanks to you, Sinéad." He patted her hand.

"I always believed Krystie but it's great to have concrete proof to back her up."

"Maybe the four of us could go out for dinner to celebrate. Is Dylan coming to the café or do you want to call him and we could pick him up on the way?"

"Shit!" Sinéad groaned looking at her watch. "I was supposed to meet him thirty minutes ago in the city centre."

Max pulled in and waited for an opportunity to do a U-turn. "Phone him and tell him you'll be there in ten."

"It's odd he didn't call me," Sinéad murmured as she waited for Dylan to pick up.

"Yes?"

She sighed at the cold clipped response. "Dylan, I'm sorry. Something came up. Max is driving me in to town now. I'll be with you in ten minutes."

"Don't bother. I left."

"I'm really sorry, darling." She sighed and rolled her eyes at Max. "Where will I meet you?"

"I don't want to meet you, Sinéad."

"Oh, come on, Dylan —"

"I'll see you later. Maybe," he added.

Sinéad stared in disbelief at her phone. "He hung up on me."

"Not surprised. It must have been bloody hard to get a table two days before Christmas. You're spending too much time at the studio, Sinéad. He's going to get fed up with you if you're not careful," Max warned.

Sinéad smiled, thinking of their morning romp. Somehow she didn't think it would be a problem. Dylan was annoyed and she didn't blame him, but he would calm down. "It will be fine."

"So do you want to go home or come back to the party?"

"The party of course. We have something to celebrate!"

Krystie's heart lifted when she saw Max walk back into the café and make a beeline for her. No, stop it, she told herself. You're just reacting like this because he was kind to you. But gratitude was no substitute for love and she couldn't lead him on, she mustn't.

She'd enjoyed these last couple of weeks. They had spent a lot of time together but had only kissed and cuddled. She was actually a bit disappointed that he hadn't pushed for more and began to wonder about the girlfriend her mother and sister had told her about; was she still on the scene? Both Sinéad and Max were in great form on their return and when Rory turned up the music they all danced and sang along to all the corny Christmas songs. After a few glasses of wine Sinéad slipped away, slightly tipsy, saying she wanted to get home to Dylan. Not long after, Max pulled Krystie close.

"Let's get out of here," he murmured.

She was surprised at the urgency in his voice. "Why? Is there something wrong, Max?"

"No, I just want to be alone with you."

Krystie knew that she should probably say no, but her instincts told her she could trust this man although her instincts had also told her that Jacob was the love of her life. Despite the conflicting emotions raging inside, she found herself nodding and, after brief goodbyes to Rory and Ellen, she let him lead her out into the cold night air. He stopped by the car and, holding her shoulders, bent and kissed her, hard, and then stared into her eyes. "Come home with me, Krystie. We don't have to do anything. I don't expect anything, I just —"

She put a finger to his lips. "Let's go."

On the way to his apartment, Max stopped to pick up food and within the hour they were sitting in his kitchen eating, drinking wine and chatting as if they had known each other for years. They lapsed into companionable silence and then she looked up to find him watching her. She shivered under the intensity of his gaze, the unmistakable desire in his eyes.

"I want you."

She almost choked on the forkful of duck she was eating.

"That wasn't quite the response I was expecting. Sorry." He handed her a glass of water. "You know, if you get to know me better you might discover that I'm not so bad."

She looked at him in surprise. "I don't think you're bad at all, Max, quite the opposite."

He pulled a face. "I sense a 'but' coming."

She looked into those blue piercing eyes that seemed to read her every thought and she made a decision. "There's no 'but', Max, other than I want the last spring roll."

He sighed. "You are a cruel and heartless woman."

"But I share." She smiled and held the roll to his lips, watching as he ate it from her fingers and licked them.

"I should put you in a taxi and send you home. You are nothing but trouble."

She held his gaze. "You should."

"More wine?"

"Yes, please."

She felt disappointed when, yet again, he did put her in a taxi a couple of hours later. They had moved back in to sit on that wonderful sofa and kissed and cuddled in the light and warmth of the fire.

"I want you," he'd said again, "but you have work in the morning and need to get some sleep."

He'd paid the driver and kissed her goodnight and, as the car pulled out into the road, she'd turned to see him standing staring after her, his white shirt gleaming in the darkness. She wanted him, too, but she was touched that he wasn't rushing her into anything.

The house was silent and in darkness when she got in, and, creeping past Sharon's bedroom door, she dropped her bag and coat and went into the bathroom to brush her teeth. She looked at the woman staring back at her in the mirror, not sure that she recognised her. Why was she grinning like a bloody idiot, and how could her eyes be shining when she felt so tired? She collected a glass of water from the kitchen, turned out the lights and went to bed, but, even though she felt exhausted and had to be up again in less than six hours, she couldn't sleep. Her thoughts flickered back and forth between two men, two sets of eyes. Jacob's black as night and Max's the palest blue. Jacob was her type. Max wasn't. He really wasn't. So why had she agreed to date him? And why had she felt disappointed when he'd sent her home? She wondered, if he and Jacob were side by side, which one she'd be drawn to. The man whom she had loved for years but who'd run out on her, or the man she really liked who wasn't put off by her health problem? She rolled over and pounded the pillow. "Forget men, think hats," she muttered and closed her eyes.

When Sinéad, Krystie and Max arrived at the club where Philip was hosting his drinks party, it was already full, and there was a pianist in the corner playing show tunes. Sinéad checked her phone. No message from Dylan. Typical. Silence was how he always punished her. She hadn't heard him come in last night, it must have been late, and he was still sleeping — or pretending to be — when she'd left for work this morning, so she knew he was mad at her. But she couldn't believe when she arrived home at lunchtime that he'd already left with all the presents for his family. Of course, she could have grovelled but she had apologised on the phone last night. What the hell more did he want?

She slipped the phone back into her bag and painted on a smile as Philip approached.

"Who needs Christmas decorations? The room lit up the moment you two walked in. I'm so glad you could come." He kissed Sinéad. "Where's Dylan?"

"He has an evening wedding. He might be along later." It was a credible lie. Dylan's main income came from doing wedding photographs. She moved closer and lowered her voice. "Any news at all?"

"I've passed on the information. Oh, sorry, must run, Sinéad." He gave her a brief hug and moved forward to meet his new guests.

"Crikey!" Krystie's eyes widened as she watched Philip shake hands with the Taoiseach and his wife. "He really does know all the important people, doesn't he?"

"He's like a bee moving from flower to flower," Sinéad observed, frowning.

"Pressing the flesh." Max grinned and beckoned the waiter, carrying a tray of mulled wine. "You should be doing the same."

"That's the plan." She took the glass, wrapped her fingers around it and scanned the room. "The woman in the purple dress is a customer, Krystie, and a good supporter. When you've put some pieces together I'll invite her and a few others in for a private viewing."

"Jeez, suddenly I feel bloody nervous."

"No need to; she'll love you," Sinéad assured her.

"They all will," her brother said with an adoring look.

"Max, isn't there some banker you want to go and talk to?" Sinéad rolled her eyes, but he was right: Krystie was looking very sexy in black leather trousers and red silk top. She'd pulled her hair back into a ponytail and wore a delicate black velvet percher low over one eye.

He grinned and kissed Krystie briefly on the lips. "Just wave when you've had enough."

Sinéad worked the room introducing Krystie and was delighted when she spotted two fashion writers at the bar. She explained who they were and then took Krystie over to make the introductions. From time to time she surreptitiously checked her phone but the silence continued. By the time Max came back to claim Krystie, they had talked to all the most valuable people there, and Sinéad was more than ready to leave.

"We're going to grab a bite. Want to come?" he asked, his eyes saying, Don't you dare say yes.

She shook her head. As if she needed to watch the two of them making eyes at each other across the dinner table. "No, I'm tired. What time are we picking up Bridie tomorrow?" She didn't want to visit the nursing home where her aunt lived, but sometimes Bridie became agitated in the car, so Max couldn't collect her alone.

"Three. I'll pick you up at half-two."

"Fine." Sinéad wished Krystie a merry Christmas, hugged them both goodnight and then went to find Philip. He was in serious conversation with a beautifully dressed young man at the bar and didn't even notice her until she put a hand on his arm, making him jump. "Sorry for interrupting. I just wanted to say goodnight."

He hugged her. "Goodnight, Sinéad. Thanks for coming."

"It was fun and a good opportunity to introduce Krystie to a few people."

He nodded sagely. "She seems like a nice girl."

"She is, and very talented." Sinéad nodded back thinking it was rather odd that he hadn't introduced her to the other man. "Okay, well, have a good evening. See you tomorrow, Philip."

In the taxi she wondered about her brother-in-law and his strange behaviour but, as she neared home, her thoughts turned back to Dylan. She wasn't in the mood for a row but she felt there was one brewing. Silent, reproachful smouldering over a long period followed by a volcanic eruption — that was the way Dylan operated. She climbed out of the car, paid the driver and braced herself.

When she opened the front door to the apartment, though, the place was in darkness. She didn't know whether to be pleased, annoyed or worried. She switched on the lights and pulled the blinds, deciding that a warm bath and a glass of wine were called for. In the kitchen there was a note propped up on the table. She eyed it warily as she poured Merlot into a large glass and took it through to the bathroom. She turned

262

on the taps, added some oils and went back into the bedroom to undress. She carefully took out the pins holding her cap in place, set it on the hat stand on her dressing table and then stepped out of her gown. She caught sight of herself in the mirror. She had worn her sexiest underwear and stockings, thinking that she and Dylan would be making up and he would be the one undressing her. Feeling miserable, she switched on the iPod, flicked through her playlists looking for something to suit her mood and opted for the sultry, sad songs of Melody Gardot. After stripping off her lingerie, she walked naked to the bathroom, flung them in disgust into the laundry basket and turned off the taps. She lit some candles, took a mouthful of wine and then went back out to the kitchen for the note. She slid beneath the foam before she unfolded it. Despite the temperature of the water, she shivered as she read.

You probably won't even notice I'm missing but, just in case, I thought I should let you know that I've gone to spend Christmas with Jackie. I need a break from playing second fiddle to a ghost and I think you need to think about what you want. I know that I want a partner and a lover, not a lodger. I hope you have a good Christmas. I'll see you in the New Year.
D

Sinéad read the words again and again and then, stretching out her hand, let the note drift to the floor. In all the time they had been together, despite their ups

263

and downs, Dylan had never walked out. And to Jackie's! His sister lived in Edinburgh and, while Dylan got on okay with her, they were by no means close. He must have gone straight to the airport from his parents' house. She needed to think about what she wanted, he said. She laid back her head and closed her eyes. What did she want? "Answers" was the only word that came to mind. She wanted to know where Sheila was and why. By parking her car at the end of that pier and leaving the country under a different identity, Sheila had clearly wanted them to believe that she was dead. But why?

She thought that Dylan understood, but Max had been right: he'd run out of patience, and where did that leave them? For the moment she was here in their lovely, lonely apartment and he was on his way to spend Christmas in his sister's tiny spare room. It was comical, really, only she felt closer to tears than laughter. Why hadn't he talked to her, shouted at her instead of this? But, in her heart, she knew that he had been telling her for months; she just hadn't been listening.

She got out of the bath and, wrapping a towel round her, went out to the desk in the lounge. She rooted through papers and files until she found what she was looking for. The folder of prints of the photos he took when he went out on his rambles. The photos he'd prefer to be taking rather than the wedding and family photos that were his bread and butter. She fetched her wine and, after putting on a robe, curled up on the bed and opened the folder. There were many black-and-white shots. Dylan loved the gritty reality of monochrome, where colour didn't distract the eye from the subject. There were many seascapes from various points along the Dublin and Wicklow coast. A nice shot of two elderly women paddling on Dollymount beach. Another of kids learning to windsurf in Malahide. A man sitting on a platform in a train station engrossed in a crossword and gloriously oblivious of the harassed commuters rushing past. A woman struggling along the street with a heavy bag of groceries in one hand, and a toddler tugging on the other. Sinéad felt a sense of pride as she admired his ability to spot and capture that special something most people missed.

She smiled as she flicked through them and then gasped when she was confronted with a photo of herself. It was a shot of her sitting in her father's garden staring into the middle distance. There was nothing particularly unusual about the photo. It was one that anyone might snap of family. But it was the angle that Dylan had taken it from that made it different. It was a profile shot, but from very slightly behind her. Sinéad barely recognised herself. She was sitting forward, her shoulders hunched, her legs clamped together, tucked tight under the seat, her arms crossed, her expression — what you could see of it — blank. She didn't look like a woman but more like a frightened animal braced for an attack.

Tears filled her eyes and she moaned softly at the next image, which was infinitely worse. In it she was asleep on the sofa, her pyjamas grubby and crumpled, her hair a tangled mess and her cheeks smudged with mascara. Again, her arms were hugged tightly around her. She stared in shock at the mess she had been and knew in her heart that this was an image that Dylan could have taken any night in the last few months. She was also quite sure that there was a wine bottle just out of shot, probably empty. She flicked on through more of the same and then looked at some of his most recent shots taken at various points along the coastline. They were all dark shots, taken in dull, dismal weather, an air of bleak hopelessness about them that she knew reflected his mood.

He had talked to her, tried to help her. He had been understanding and patient. And he had planned this special evening and she had forgotten about it, forgotten about him. Why hadn't she followed him over to his parents' house today? That might have stopped him taking this step. His note had said, "I'll see you in the New Year." Was he seriously planning to stay away for at least a week? The idea of spending the entire holidays without him now seemed unbearable.

She went to take a sip of wine and then, wrinkling her nose in disgust, took it out to the kitchen and tossed it down the sink. She switched on the coffee machine and, as she waited for it to heat, she wondered what she should do. She was tempted to phone but she knew that he would be in no mood for talking to her. It took a lot to anger Dylan but, when he did blow, he wasn't easily placated. She would send him an email, she decided, write him a letter. There was hope. He hadn't said it was over: he'd said he needed time to think. She just had to figure out what she could say to persuade him to give her another chance.

CHAPTER
TWENTY-FOUR

Kieran woke on Christmas morning feeling happier than he would have thought possible a few weeks ago. He'd hoped Krystie was right and Sheila was alive, but when Sinéad had told him that her passport was missing he was sure of it. Yes, he was still worried about why Sheila had left, but thinking she'd run away was infinitely better than imagining her at the bottom of the ocean.

He felt hopeful and was actually looking forward to spending the day, a proper Christmas day, with his family and Beth, lovely, lovely Beth. He still couldn't believe that she was in his life. It was only her warmth and kindness that made him realise how very lonely he had been all these years. He cringed now, ashamed at the way he'd judged her that first day in the pub. He'd been so bloody full of himself, thinking that she was after him when she had simply treated him the way she treated everyone, with compassion. A man would be lucky to have her on his arm and, on the few occasions they had gone out together he had seen her get many an appreciative glance. He was amazed at how it irked him but at the same time made him feel proud that it was him she chose to be with. Today he would introduce her to the family. He couldn't see it being a problem. They might be surprised but he thought they'd be happy for him. Bridie, God love her, probably wouldn't know what was going on, and, as for Philip, well, he didn't care what he thought. His good mood faded a little at the thought of his son-in-law. He didn't really want to spend Christmas Day with him.

He looked at the clock and realised the morning was almost gone. It was time he got his act together. Max had been surprised at his refusal of a lift and seemed almost worried at the thought of him driving. His own bloody fault, of course. If you behaved like an invalid, people started to treat you as one. Well, those days were over. He would collect Beth and drive them to Sheila's house — he would always think of it as hers, not Philip's — and then he could leave when they'd had enough and enjoy the remainder of the evening with Beth.

After he'd showered and shaved he put on a suit, a snow-white shirt and a bright, colourful tie Sinéad had bought him, but he'd never worn. Kieran grinned at his reflection and barely recognised himself. How rarely he'd smiled these last few months.

Thirty minutes later he stood on her doorstep feeling as nervous as if he were on a first date.

The door was thrown open and Beth stood before him resplendent in a vibrant print dress in different shades of red.

"Well, don't *you* look very grand! Come in."

"It's just as well I went mad and put on a suit when I have to escort such a gorgeous woman." He stepped into the hall and hugged her. "Happy Christmas, Beth."

268

"And a very happy Christmas to you, too, Kieran." She pulled back and smiled at him, her eyes shining. "Have we time for a cup of tea?"

"We do of course," he said, going and settling down on the sofa. He loved the warm cosiness of this room and Beth had a pretty little Christmas tree in the corner and cards hung along the edge of the fireplace. It was a home, whereas his house was just that: a house. "Did you hear from your son?"

She appeared with a tray. "First thing." She set out the cups and saucers of her best china and a plate of mince pies. "That Skype is great, isn't it? I was able to see the little ones open my presents; it was wonderful." She ran a finger under her eyes.

"It's not easy being without your family at this time of year," he said, feeling sorry for her.

"Gavin would love me to move to Melbourne but I don't think it's for me. I can't imagine living anywhere other than Ireland."

"Neither can I, but I wouldn't mind moving house," he admitted, surprising himself. He had given no thought to selling up, but he supposed spending time here made him realise how soulless and empty the place was now. Though it was full of memories, he took no comfort from them. He wanted to stop living in the past. He wanted to stop just existing.

He searched in his pockets. "Oh, shit, don't tell me I forgot." And then he found what he was looking for in his inside breast pocket. He handed her the gift and smiled. "Happy Christmas, Beth."

"Oh, Kieran." She took the long slim box in her hands and stared at it.

"If you don't like it we can always go back to the shop and you can pick something else. I was never very good at choosing presents and I'm a bit out of practice —"

"Will you shush!" she said opening the box and taking out the chunky gold bracelet.

He watched her anxiously. He'd been taking careful note of the jewellery she wore this last week and he'd finally gone into the jeweller's in the nearby shopping centre and picked out something he thought she'd like. "Well?" he said when she just sat staring at it in silence.

"It's beautiful, Kieran. Will you put it on for me?"

He rummaged for his glasses and fumbled with the catch.

"Why do they make these bloody things so small? Ah, there we go."

She stretched out her arm to admire it. "Thank you so much, I couldn't pick nicer."

He smiled, relieved. It had been a long time since he'd bought jewellery for a woman. "I'm glad you like it."

"I have something for you, too. It isn't much," she said shyly and bent down to get a beautifully wrapped gift from beneath the tree.

He grinned, delighted. "It's the thought that counts." He tore the paper off and smiled when he saw it was the box set of the *Godfather* series. He'd told her soon after they met how much he loved those movies. He looked up at her. "You remembered?"

She shrugged and smiled. "I thought you could enjoy them at your leisure."

"Maybe we could watch them together."

"That sounds nice."

He leaned over to kiss her cheek but she turned her head slightly and he caught the corner of her mouth. He drew back in surprise and looked into her eyes. She held his gaze and needing no further encouragement Kieran put an arm around her and kissed her again and was surprised and delighted when she put her arms around his neck and kissed him back.

Finally, she pulled away from him, looking flushed and a little embarrassed. "I think we had better go."

He didn't laugh, but stared at her intently. "You're right, but do you think it's something you might like to continue later?"

"I think I might," she said, and smiled.

The nurse came into the Reception, her expression frosty. "I don't think we've met before. You're here to take Bridie out for the day, yes?"

Max watched the disapproving look on the woman's face as Sinéad went forward to meet her, bloody judgemental cow.

"Yes, I'm Bridie's niece, Sinéad, and this is my brother, Max. We haven't been here often. My sister, Sheila, was always closest to her."

"Oh, yes, of course." The woman flushed in embarrassment. "Well, Bridie is quite calm today but there's no knowing how she'll react when she sees you. If she gets upset it may be better if she stays here."

"Is that likely?" Max asked. Was she talking about the same woman? Bridie hadn't been remotely aggressive or hysterical last year. Absent was the word he'd have used to describe her. "She raised us, she knows us well," he told the nurse.

The woman's eyes were pitying. "I'm afraid there's no guarantee of that any more. She might recognise you today and not at all tomorrow. I'll take you to her and let's just see how it goes."

Sinéad shot him a frightened look as they followed her down the hall, and he patted her shoulder.

He was glad at least to find the place wasn't half as depressing as he'd remembered. Christmas music was being piped through the building, but not too loudly; decorations and holly hung from the ceilings; and the aromas of the Christmas dinner being prepared were causing his stomach to rumble.

The nurse stopped at a door, knocked and went in. "Your family are here, Bridie," she said, her voice bright and cheerful.

Max relaxed a little when he saw his aunt. She looked fit and well and it was hard to believe there was a thing wrong with her. He crouched down beside her chair, overcome with guilt that he hadn't seen more of her. This woman had been like a mother to him. He took her hand and kissed it. "Hiya, Aunty, happy Christmas."

She smiled broadly at him. "Maxie!"

He looked up in delighted surprise at the nurse, who just shrugged and smiled.

272

Sinéad pulled over a chair and sat on her other side. "Happy Christmas, Bridie."

"Hello, Maggie. I thought you'd be up to your eyes getting the dinner ready, or are you waiting for me to do all the work?" Bridie laughed.

Sinéad looked at Max and he looked at the nurse. What were they supposed to do? Go along with her or say something? The nurse shook her head slightly and stepped in to save the day.

"I love turkey and stuffing, do you, Bridie?"

"Oh, yes." Bridie's face lit up like a child's, but then she scowled at Sinéad. "You didn't put sage in the stuffing, did you, Maggie? You know I can't stand the stuff."

"No sage," Sinéad promised.

Max straightened and held his arm out to Bridie. "We'd better go before Dad and Philip eat everything."

Bridie stared up at him. "Philip? Who's he?"

"Sheila's husband."

She stood up slowly. "Ah, poor Sheila."

So she remembered what had happened to Sheila. Max looked at Sinéad. She looked as surprised as he was.

"Is it very cold out?" the nurse asked. "I think your blue coat would be the warmest."

"Oh yes, I like the blue one," Bridie said, immediately distracted.

The nurse looked at Sinéad. "Why don't you help Bridie get ready? Max, if you come with me I'll give you your aunt's medication."

He turned to her in the corridor. "She seems okay apart from thinking Sinéad is our mother, her sister."

"It's quite common for people with advanced dementia to confuse people from their past and present, or they may watch a movie and afterwards think it's true. They might look in the mirror and think the reflection is a stranger. It's different for everyone and it can change from day to day. Just go along with it and soothe her if she gets frustrated or angry. Distraction works, too. People with dementia have a short attention span. Whatever you do, don't correct her, don't try to explain — oh, and don't leave her alone for long."

Max nodded, feeling overwhelmed by the responsibility.

She patted his arm. "Don't worry. Most of the time Bridie is quiet and she loves her food and the TV, but it's best not to put on anything upsetting."

"So, *Sound of Music* rather than James Bond," he said.

She laughed. "That's the idea. And, if she takes a dislike to someone, just keep them out of her sight."

"Okay." Max took a deep breath and nodded.

"I'm just preparing you for the worst-case scenarios. Bridie seems in very good form today. I'm sure she will be fine and you will have a nice time."

Max chatted to his aunt as they went outside and helped her into the back of the car. Sinéad scrambled in the other side and strapped the seatbelt around her before putting on her own.

"You didn't put sage in the stuffing, did you, Maggie?"

"No, Bridie. I made it just the way you like it."

"Are we going to Sheila's?"

Max met Sinéad's eyes in the mirror and gave her a reassuring smile. "We are, Aunty. Would you like me to drive along the coast road?"

"Oh, yes, Maxie, but I don't think we should stop today. It's too cold for a paddle."

"It is," Sinéad said.

"My handbag, where's my handbag?" Bridie's voice rose.

"It's right here," Sinéad assured her.

"You didn't put sage in the stuffing, did you? I hate that bloody stuff."

Sinéad sighed. "No sage, I promise."

Philip was glad he had put Christmas dinner back a couple of hours. Quite apart from cleaning up after the drinks reception this morning and the last of the food preparation to be done, he needed time to gear himself up for the Fields family, and it would mean a shorter time in their company, which could only be a good thing. He would also be able to hide out in the kitchen from time to time. He didn't have to worry too much about Sinéad seeking him out there: she was no domestic goddess.

He sighed as he thought of Sheila bustling around last year, serving up a magnificent meal despite the fact that she'd spent the morning looking after his guests. And she'd tidied everything up while he'd taken chocolates to some of his older constituents, who were living alone. He'd known it would be hard without her, but he had no idea that he would miss her this much. He had tried to make the house look the way she had last year, but it still wasn't the same. Nothing was the same without her soothing, calming, smiling presence.

He lifted the turkey out of the oven and left it to rest on the carving dish before taking a gulp of his wine. He should probably drink some water. Getting pissed today of all days really wasn't an option: God knows what he might say. He took another gulp, anyway, before attending to the gravy, and he had just put the potatoes on to roast when the doorbell rang. He paused in front of the hall mirror, smoothed his hair, took a deep breath and went to open the door. Sinéad stood there looking ill at ease, and he put on his brightest smile and held his arms out. "Welcome, Sinéad. Happy Christmas."

"Happy Christmas, Philip." She glanced over her shoulder at where Max was coaxing Bridie out of the car. "You need to know that Bridie's gone downhill since you saw her last. At the moment she thinks that I'm my mother, is preoccupied with stuffing and thinks everyone is trying to nick her handbag. Apparently, we must just ignore it and try to distract her if she gets anxious."

"Got it," he said as Max approached, linking arms with a very apprehensive-looking Bridie. It was strange. She hadn't changed that much physically but the indomitable spirit that the family had once depended on had slipped away gradually. Just over a year it had

276

become clear that she could no longer live alone and the nursing home was the only option. Kieran had the space to take her in but never offered. Only Sheila had been riddled with guilt over it, but she'd have had to give up work and Philip had put his foot down about that. It would have been a ridiculous and illogical sacrifice.

He watched now as Bridie stood looking up at the house with a bewildered expression. He came forward to take her hand and smiled. "Hello, Bridie. Happy Christmas."

"Daddy!" Her face lit up and she threw her arms around him.

He held her, patting her back as an incredulous Sinéad rolled her eyes. He looked over Bridie's head at his brother-in-law. "Merry Christmas, Max."

"Merry Christmas, Philip. Thank you for having us."

"Do you have a Christmas tree?" Bridie asked.

"Of course I do." Philip led her into the living room and she stood in front of it, her eyes round in wonder, like a child's.

"Can we open the presents?"

"When Kieran gets here."

Bridie's smile was replaced by a glare and she looked around at Sinéad. "You've asked that man here?"

Sinéad shrugged. "Just for a little while, Bridie. It is Christmas."

"You're a fool. How many more times are you going to let him break your heart?"

Philip touched her arm. "Bridie, I'm not sure the turkey is cooked through. Will you take a look?"

She shook her head and laughed. "Are you trying to poison us? Come on, Maggie, let's check this bird."

Sinéad obediently followed her out of the room.

"What has she got against Kieran?" Philip asked.

"No idea." Max lowered his long frame into an armchair. "The nurse said she's mixing up people from the past and the present. Just nod and smile, Philip."

"Poor woman," Philip said, although it occurred to him that Bridie's presence might actually make the day easier. It would be impossible for Sinéad to get into any intense discussions about Sheila with her aunt like this. "I'm surprised your dad's not here yet. Do you think we should call him?"

Max glanced at his watch and frowned. "Let's give it a few more minutes."

"Why didn't he come with you?"

"He insisted on driving, no idea why." Max shrugged.

"I suppose it's a good sign. He's grown very dependent on you and Sinéad."

"True."

"A drink?" Philip offered.

"A tonic with just a hint of gin," Max said.

"You and Krystie seem to be getting on well." Philip made the drink and handed it to Max.

"Yes, we are," Max said, his cheeks going red. "She's great."

"I haven't had much of an opportunity to really talk to her, but she seems nice and she and Sinéad seem to get along well."

"They do."

Philip smiled. "I'm happy for Sinéad. Oh, I'd better go and rescue her. God knows what your aunty's up to."

When he went into the kitchen, though, Bridie was standing at the hob, stirring the gravy, looking serene. Sinéad stood just close enough to step in if needed. "Good job, Bridie. Come back inside. I think you've earned a small sherry."

She looked up at him in disgust. "Sherry? When have you ever seen me drink that stuff? Give me a gin and tonic and make it a large one."

Philip was startled to hear her sound just like her old self and burst out laughing. "Yes, ma'am, coming right up. Will I make it two?" he asked Sinéad.

"Why not?" She grinned.

He followed them out into the hall. "Did you remember dessert?"

"Oh, yes, it's in the car. I'll go get it."

The doorbell rang. "That will be your dad," Philip said and did a double take when Sinéad flung open the door and Kieran stood there with his arm around a woman.

CHAPTER
TWENTY-FIVE

"This is wonderful stuffing, Philip. You must give me the recipe," Beth said, smiling.

"No sage," Bridie muttered without looking up.

Sinéad hadn't said much since they'd sat down. She looked up to find her father watching her. She couldn't tell if she saw defiance in his eyes or a plea for understanding. She looked back down at her plate. She felt annoyed with him. He had barely opened his mouth to her for months and here he was all dressed up, full of chat and with a bloody girlfriend in tow. The nerve of the man. Max kept shooting her warning looks, and it was only that and the risk of upsetting Bridie that made her keep her mouth shut.

"Isn't it better to see him like this than the way he was?" Max hissed at her as they made their way into the dining room. He was probably right, but she still couldn't help feeling angry. All the time he'd been playing the grieving father he'd been cosying up to a widow.

He had never brought a woman to meet them before, though she knew there had been a few over the years. She had initially looked at Beth and wondered, had her father lost his mind. The woman had terrible taste, wore far too much makeup and talked a bit too much for her liking. But, as they sat over dinner, Sinéad realised that Beth was a genuine sort with an infectious laugh, and it was impossible not to like her.

Philip was more than happy with the uninvited guest. In seconds he'd set another place at the table and fetched an extra chair before disappearing into the kitchen to get the starters. Beth had quickly tripped after him with offers of help and when she'd returned she'd taken the seat next to Bridie and chatted away to her, taking all of her aunt's peculiarities in her stride.

Sinéad let the conversation drift around her and sipped her drink. Though Dylan wouldn't even have been here — they always spent Christmas Day with their respective families — she missed him. He hadn't responded to her email and after waiting for ages for him to call this morning she had weakened and sent him a text saying "Happy Christmas". After about ten minutes she got an equally terse response. She couldn't believe it. She had poured her heart out in that letter. How could he be so hard?

The meal turned out to be surprisingly successful and Sinéad had to admit it would have been a very sad and miserable event if it hadn't been for Beth. She kept the conversation going, pulled crackers, insisted they wear the silly party hats and even told a few dirty jokes. Sinéad was surprised when Bridie had a moment of complete lucidity and told them about a man she'd once worked for who told filthy jokes and felt her up in the lift. Sinéad had never been close to Bridie but the wine was making her feel sentimental, and she tried to coax her aunt to continue, but within seconds the fog returned and Bridie had retreated back into her own little world.

Looking upset, Max excused himself, and Sinéad had to wipe away some tears of her own. Her dad squeezed her hand and Beth and Philip carried on the conversation, giving them time to recover.

"How did you two meet?" Sinéad asked her father when they finally got a moment alone. Beth was helping Philip clear up, Bridie was dozing in an armchair and Max had disappeared, she presumed to call Krystie.

"We just bumped into each other in the pub. Her husband used to work for me," he hurried on when she raised her eyebrows. "He died a couple of years ago."

"Are you serious about her, Dad?" His face told her he was, but she waited for him to answer, not quite sure how she felt.

He hesitated for a moment and then looked her straight in the eye. "Yes."

"Why now, after all these years alone?" Sinéad asked.

He gave a shrug and smiled. "Because I hadn't met Beth I suppose."

It was almost an hour later before Sinéad had the chance to talk to Beth. Bridie was engrossed in *Mary Poppins*, her dad had gone outside for a smoke, and Max had gone with him, and Philip was making coffee. He was spending quite a lot of time in the kitchen, she'd noticed, but that suited her just fine.

"Dad says you're a widow. I'm sorry. Christmas must be a difficult time for you."

"I'm getting used to being alone." Beth frowned and shook her head. "No, that's not true. I suppose I've just stopped feeling sorry for myself. I have some good friends and I make more of an effort to see them regularly. I work part-time at the local library, too. Keeping busy gives me less time to dwell on the past and I find the house too empty, so I get out as much as possible."

"And now you've met Dad."

Beth smiled. "Yes. I invited him for a meal for Gerry's sake, to be honest. He had a lot of time for your father, and Kieran just seemed very low and so thin!"

"Yes, he has lost weight although . . ." Sinéad realised that her father had filled out again and was looking much fitter. She looked at Beth. "You've been feeding him up."

"Yes, and it's been a pleasure. I like my food, as you can see," Beth chuckled and patted her tummy. "But I hate eating alone and somehow it's easier to talk over a meal."

"I'm glad he's been talking to someone," Sinéad said, hearing the bitterness in her voice.

"Isn't it always the way? Talking to a stranger that you can't hurt is so much easier."

Sinéad looked at her, wondering if Beth knew that her dad was serious about her. "But you're not strangers any more, are you?"

The woman blushed like a teenager. "No, I suppose not."

"I'm glad," Sinéad said, not altogether sincerely. Her brother's and father's love lives made her feel more miserable as she thought of Dylan in Scotland, remote from her in every way.

"Where's my handbag?" Bridie jerked awake and immediately started to scramble around in a panic.

"Right here," Sinéad said, going over to place her aunt's hand on the bag tucked in beside her.

Bridie smiled and touched her face. "You're a good girl, Sheila. I'm sorry."

Sinéad knelt at her feet and smiled. "You have nothing to be sorry for, Aunty."

"I thought it was for the best."

Sinéad looked up at her, worried at how agitated Bridie was becoming. "What do you mean, Aunty? What are you sorry for?"

"Where's my handbag?" Bridie looked cross. "I'm not stupid, Missy. You leave my bag alone, do you hear me?"

"Are you in or out?" Blake looked at Krystie.

She suppressed a yawn and looked at her hand. Three kings, ha, how appropriate! But she couldn't concentrate on poker. All she could think about was Max and last night.

"Krystie?" Fallon frowned impatiently and took another swig from her can of lager.

"I've nothing." Krystie threw down her hand, stood up and went to put on the kettle.

284

"Are you feeling okay?" Her mother looked at her over the rim of her glasses.

"Fine, Ma, but I think I'll take my tea up to bed."

"You're not feeling sick, are you, love?" her mother asked, coming to stand beside her.

"No, honestly, Ma, just tired. I've been working pretty long hours."

"And you had a late night last night, didn't you? Go on to bed, then, Krystie."

Krystie took her mug, kissed her da and, waving to the others, said goodnight.

Her mother walked out into the hall with her. "It's wonderful to have you home, love, and thanks again for my hat."

"Are you sure that you like it?" Krystie asked. "I can alter it."

"You will do no such thing, it's perfect as it is. I adore it." Her mother smiled. "I had no idea you were so talented, Krystie. Your dad and I are very proud of you."

Krystie gave her a tight hug. "Thanks, Ma, that means a lot to me."

Up in her little bedroom, Krystie pulled the covers up to her chin and looked around at the pale-pink wallpaper with the tiny rosebuds and the white wardrobes and dressing table. Nothing had changed since she had left nearly seven years ago. It was strangely comforting and she snuggled down and thought about Max.

Last night he hadn't put her into a taxi. When they'd finished dinner he'd looked her straight in the eye and asked her to come home with him and she'd just nodded. In fact she couldn't remember saying another word until he had gently and very slowly removed all of her clothes. He'd dragged his eyes away from her body, looked into her eyes once more and asked her if she was sure she wanted to go ahead, and she had said yes.

She felt both excited and nervous. Though there had been boyfriends in the past, they hadn't lasted long, and Jacob was the only man who'd ever made love to her. She felt so close to Max now that she really wanted this to be a special experience. She felt guilty about the way she'd compared him to Jacob at the start. Jacob had always come out on top.

She smiled and stretched. That hadn't been the case last night. Max had been wonderful and it had been the most incredible night of her life.

She'd woken up early and smiled as she became conscious of the possessive hand on her hip. She turned slightly and examined his features. His fair lashes brushed his cheeks and his strong features were softened in sleep. She looked at his lips and shivered as she remembered how wonderful they had felt against her skin and how special Max had made her feel. She couldn't help comparing him to her ex. Though Jacob had been incredibly passionate, he'd also been selfish and thought more about his own pleasure than hers. But Max, my God, he had worshipped her body. It had felt as if all he cared about was making her happy — and he had, again and again. As she stared at him in wonderment his eyes flickered open and when he saw her staring at him his mouth had curved into a slow, sexy smile.

"Happy Christmas, beautiful," he'd said, and reached for her.

She had made several attempts to leave but they were half-hearted and, finally she just gave herself up to the joy of being adored, worshipped. "This has to be the best Christmas present ever," she'd said after he'd taken her once more to dizzying heights and she lay sated in his arms.

"Oh, your present, I forgot." He hopped out of bed and walked over to the dressing table.

She propped herself up on one arm and admired the view. When he turned around and saw her watching him he grinned. "Is everything okay, Ms Kelliher?"

"Oh everything is very okay," she assured him.

He climbed back in beside her and handed her an envelope. She looked at it and then at him. "Go on, open it," he urged.

She did, and she frowned as she flicked through the documents, and then her eyes widened as she tried to figure out what she was looking at. "A return ticket to New York? Are you trying to tell me something?"

He grinned. "It works both ways."

She shook her head. "I don't get it."

"Well, I know you miss your friend, Sandy, so I thought you might like to go see her or invite her over here. The tickets are open and valid for six months so you don't have to decide right now —"

He didn't get to finish, as Krystie threw her arms around him and kissed him.

He kissed her back, moulding her body to his, but she pulled away to look in his eyes. "That's so thoughtful, Max, but I can't take it."

"Why not?" He frowned.

"It's too much, we've only just met."

"I feel as if I've known you for ever."

His eyes held hers and Krystie touched his cheek and kissed him. "I do too."

"And look at it this way: it cost a lot less than that bloody painting you loved so much."

She laughed. "You really were out of your mind when you bought that." She looked at the ticket and back at him, shaking her head. "I don't know what to say."

"Say 'Thanks, Max' and give me a big sloppy kiss."

"Thank you, Max," she murmured and, winding her arms round his neck, kissed him. "My present for you seems incredibly stingy now," she complained.

His eyes and hands roamed over her. "I've got my present right here."

She laughed and stretched out of the bed, shivering as he ran a hand over her butt. She rummaged in her bag for the small package.

He opened it and took out the frame and stared at it and then at her. "Where did you get this?"

"Sinéad found some old photos in Sheila's desk. This was one of them but it was all crumpled and torn. I thought it was gorgeous so I dug around for the negative and asked Dylan if he would develop and frame it."

288

She watched him anxiously as he stared at the photo of his four-year-old self, in his mother's arms. His head was thrown back laughing and she was looking at him in total adoration.

"She was very beautiful," Krystie said.

"She was," he agreed.

She looked at the sadness in his eyes and sighed. "Shit, this wasn't supposed to make you sad. I've screwed up again."

He had taken her hand and kissed her palm and then held it to his chest. "You haven't screwed up at all, Krystie. It's a very thoughtful gift and I will treasure it always. I remember the photo but I thought it had been lost. It's wonderful to have it back. I'll keep it on my desk."

He'd leaned over and kissed her very tenderly on the lips. "Now I wonder how I can show my gratitude," he'd said and pushed her gently back down on the pillow.

CHAPTER
TWENTY-SIX

Between meetings Max sent texts and during them he found himself surreptitiously checking for replies, grinning like an idiot when he saw a message from her. They'd been behaving like a couple of lovesick kids since Christmas Eve; he couldn't remember ever feeling this way before. Krystie was like no woman he'd ever met. His mind wandered back to that first night, as it so often did. The very last word to describe it was sex. When he had eased her dress from her shoulders and she hadn't resisted but had stood before him, her eyes staring into his, he had felt like a fumbling schoolboy on his first date. His hands had actually been trembling as he'd run them hesitantly over her body. But her body had been so beautiful and inviting and when they'd kissed it had been the sweetest, most gentle kiss he had ever experienced, and he had lost himself in her.

And, as if he were not besotted enough with her, she gave him the most precious and thoughtful gift he'd ever received. It amused him how thrilled but uncomfortable she'd been about the amount he'd spent on the New York tickets. Natalie had often dragged him into shoe shops, chosen a pair of designer heels and matching bag and then given him a brief peck when he'd picked up the tab, as of course she had expected him to.

Krystie was different in every way. He talked to her the way he'd talked to no one else, especially about Sheila. And she listened, really listened. And he loved to hear about her past, too — something he hadn't given a damn about with her predecessors. The more he learned about Krystie, the more he loved her and wanted to protect her. She'd told him about her ex, a guy who sounded like a complete shit. It annoyed him that he had been her first real lover. Well, if he was honest, he hated the thought of any man having touched her but, as they were the same age and given his track record, he could hardly complain. But he felt a ridiculous jealousy at the thought of Jacob or his fumbling predecessors having even seen her lovely body. Not only had the women he usually dated had many previous lovers, he knew some of them, but he had never felt this possessive. But how did *she* feel? He couldn't help wondering if she still held a candle for Jacob. He couldn't imagine Krystie staying with a man that long unless she'd loved him, and they had been on the point of moving in together when the asshole had jilted her. He would just have to make her forget him, Max decided, grateful that the guy lived in New York and not Dublin.

The phone rang and his heart jumped, but when Max looked at the display he was disappointed to see it wasn't Krystie, just his father.

"Hi, Dad."

"Oh, good. I'm glad I got hold of you, Max."

"What's wrong?" he asked, when he heard his father's muted tone.

"It's Bridie. She passed away this morning."

Max sat with Sinéad and his father in the office with the nursing home manager, the doctor and the nurse who had found Bridie.

"She woke up in great form, very alert, and ate a good breakfast. And when I came back with her medication she was gone."

"It was a massive heart attack," the doctor told them, "very quick. She really wouldn't have suffered that much at all."

They were brought in to see Bridie and Max was surprised when he felt a lump in his throat. He had seen little of his aunt in recent years. He led such a busy life that the odd phone call had been the most he could manage, but Bridie hadn't been the sensitive sort and didn't seem bothered or upset by the lack of contact. He'd always got the impression that she was quite enjoying her freedom. But it didn't take from the fact that she had been the one who'd bandaged him up when he'd fallen and helped him when he'd struggled with his Irish homework. She was the one who had nursed him through all his childhood illnesses, done his laundry and kept the larder and fridge well stocked. But where had he been when she was going through her crisis and still aware enough to realise that she was losing her mind? It must have been very frightening.

Sinéad sat silently by the bed while Dad stood with his arm around her shoulders.

"We need to make funeral arrangements, let people know," Max said, but at a loss as to where to begin. He didn't know who her closest friends were, whom she would want them to contact or what kind of ceremony she would like. "Do you know what she'd want, Dad?"

"She was never one for a big fuss. I think she'd prefer something simple."

"We should check her diary. She wrote down everything in that — at least, she used to." Sinéad dabbed her eyes with a tissue.

"Oh, the red leather one? I remember that." Max felt relieved as he recalled the thick hardback notebook that Bridie had noted everything in, from addresses to birthdays to recipes. He opened the drawers and wardrobe but there was no sign of it or, indeed, any personal belongings. Even the handbag that she had clutched on to so tightly held only a handkerchief, a purse with some loose change and a plastic wallet of old photos. "There's nothing here at all."

Sinéad frowned as she joined him in the search of their aunt's room. "There has to be more stuff than this. Maybe they keep patients' personal things in lockers."

"That's probably it. I'll go and ask." He paused by the bed and then bent to press his lips against his aunt's cold forehead. "Rest, Aunty. Thanks for everything."

The nursing home manager was an efficient sort but with kind eyes. She waved him to a chair and rang the kitchen to bring coffee. "Your aunt was very anxious when she first arrived," she explained when he asked about Bridie's belongings. "She was convinced that she was going to be robbed and wanted to keep everything personal where she could see it. It's not that unusual. Displacement is hard and frightening for everyone and especially for someone suffering from dementia. I'm sorry I never met her in the whole of her health. I could see glimpses of her personality from time to time and I imagine she was quite a strong woman."

Max wondered if this was the patter that every relative received but, as he thought of Bridie's occasional lucid moments on Christmas Day, perhaps not. "She was never demonstrative but she showed her love in other ways; you could always depend on her." He swallowed hard again taken by surprise at the grief he felt. "She never let me down but I let her down, I never visited."

"Some people can't cope with seeing their loved ones ill." She shrugged.

"Some people don't have a choice and have to get on with it whether they like it or not," he replied.

"There's no point in torturing yourself. Your sister, Sheila, was wonderful with Bridie. She could always get through to her and calm her down. In the end she took all of your aunt's private papers and jewellery. It was the only answer. Bridie wasn't sleeping, convinced someone would steal her things."

"But they weren't with Sheila's stuff," Sinéad said when he told her. She looked pale and weary. It had been a long day. They had been to the undertaker's, where Kieran had insisted on the best of everything. They'd phoned distant relatives and the few people he could remember her being close to and then paid a visit to her church to talk to the priest. Happily, he had known her well and suggested they leave the funeral for a couple of days to allow word of her death to spread. Through him they learned that Bridie had been quite active in the community and particularly the local primary school.

"We knew so little about her life since she moved out," Sinéad marvelled.

They had dropped their father at Beth's and Max was driving her to the studio.

"She practically raised us and once we left home we just forgot her."

"That's not true," Max protested. He felt guilty enough. "We saw her just as much as we saw Dad."

"Bullshit. How often did you visit?"

"She wasn't around much *to* visit," he protested. "She lived a full life."

"Doing what?"

"Well, I don't know, do I?" He glared at her. "Do you?"

Sinéad sighed. "Not a clue."

"Strange she never got married," Max said as he turned into Blackrock village. "I wonder, did she think that Dad would ask her?"

"Well, I think it's safe to say, looking at Beth, that Bridie was not his type."

"What do you think of Beth?" Max asked.

"She's okay," she said, though it was clear she wasn't that impressed with how close her father was growing to the woman.

"She's good for him," Max said as he pulled up outside the café.

"Are you coming in to say hello to your beloved?"

"No, I don't have time. Tell her I'll call her later. Will you double-check Sheila's things for Bridie's diary?"

She paused, her hand on the handle of the door. "I told you, Max, it's not there. I'm sure of it. Philip must have them."

"Okay, I'll talk to him."

He met Philip in Buswell's, the hotel across the road from government buildings. When he arrived, his brother-in-law was in a corner of the lobby, working on his laptop, a large pot of coffee on the table in front of him.

"I'm so sorry about Bridie," he said, his face sombre as he clasped both his hands around Max's. "It's hard to take in. Physically, she seemed fine on Christmas Day." He sat back down and poured the coffee. "Wasn't it great that we had that time with her, though? And, given her condition, I suppose it wasn't a bad way to go. She was still quite young, wasn't she?"

"Yes, only sixty-six. Thanks for meeting me, Philip. The reason I wanted to see you is we're trying to track down Bridie's belongings. The nursing home manager said that Sheila had taken them away because Bridie was very anxious about them, convinced they'd be nicked."

Philip chewed on his bottom lip. "I seem to remember something about that. Was there anything in particular you were looking for?"

"Her diary — or perhaps 'journal' is a better description. It's a thick A4 hardback notebook with a dark-red, leather cover. It's old. I can remember her writing in it when she first moved in. But she had her close friends' numbers in there. I'm putting death notices in the newspapers but I wanted to contact them personally if possible."

"Of course." Philip topped up his own cup. "Sheila gave all of Bridie's things to the solicitor for safekeeping. He's the man who took care of the sale of her house and he drew up her will too. Do you have a death certificate yet?"

"No, that's next on my list. I should probably make an appointment to see that solicitor." Max ran a tired hand through his hair.

"Don't worry about your executor duties right now. Concentrate on arranging the funeral for the moment. I'll give him a call if you like?" Philip offered. "I'd like to feel useful in some way, for Sheila's sake."

"That would be great, Philip, if you don't mind?" Max said, a sense of relief washing over him. The thought of sorting out Bridie's estate had been preying on his mind. It seemed wrong that he should be privy to all her private business when he had effectively abandoned her these last few years. Max was pretty sure that Philip had seen more of his aunt than he had.

"No problem at all," Philip assured him. "Send me a copy of the death cert when you get it and I'll pass it on, and in the meantime I'll have him get the diary couriered over to you, or will I get it sent to Sinéad or your dad instead?"

Max thought about it for a moment. Dad seemed to have reverted to his silent introverted self and was probably up at the grave, where he always went when his mood was dark. "Best send it to Sinéad, Philip, and thanks again."

Sheila and Zach were making sandwiches when the phone rang. "Don't you dare put pickle on mine," she warned as she wiped her hands and went to answer it.

"How can you have corned beef without pickle?" he protested, shaking his head.

She laughed and picked up the phone. She listened in silence for the most part. Instinctively, Zach sensed something was wrong and came to stand in front of her, his dark eyes searching hers. She reached for his hand.

"Keep in touch and tell me what's happening, yeah?" she said to the caller. She listened for another couple of minutes before hanging up. She tried to come to grips with it. She hadn't expected it, not for years.

"Sheila, what is it, what's wrong?" Zach asked.

He wiped tears from her cheeks that she hadn't even been conscious of. "My aunt is dead."

"Sweetheart, I am so sorry." He put his arms around her and rocked her gently as she sobbed. "After all you've told me, I feel as if I knew her."

She took out a tissue and wiped her eyes. "You know more about my family than they do," she said with a watery smile. "I've told you things I've never told a soul."

"I'll take that as a compliment."

"That's the way it was meant." Sheila hugged him. "It seems strange to be here when the family are going through this."

"Do you want to go to the funeral?" he asked.

"Yes. No." She sighed. "It would make no difference to Bridie and it would throw everything into chaos if I turned up out of the blue. Right now I have something much more important to do. Right now there's someone else who needs me more."

He looked at her. "Karl?"

She stared up into his eyes feeling completely overwhelmed. "Yes. Karl."

CHAPTER
TWENTY-SEVEN

Sinéad woke with a start. There was another noise, she wasn't imagining it. Had she put on the alarm? She couldn't remember. She looked around for the phone and realised it was sitting on the kitchen table with her sketch pad and laptop. Great, that would make life easier for the burglar, she thought, her heart thumping in her chest. What should she do? Huddle under the duvet and pretend to be asleep or find something to defend herself with and go out there and tackle them? Them? Shit, if there were more than one she didn't have a hope. She glanced around, looking for anything that could be used as a weapon. Apart from her high-heels, the only other thing was the heavy bedside lamp, and, even if she were able to lift that, she doubted she could throw it.

She crept out of bed and went to the wardrobe in search of her oldest shoes — well, there was no point in destroying a perfectly good pair of heels. Then she went into the *en suite* and took a can of deodorant. It was full and she was pretty sure that a spray of that in the eyes would be painful enough. Pulling on heavy pyjamas, she was about to go out and confront the thief when she had an idea on how to attract attention just in case she got into trouble. Her neighbour went berserk at noise and complained incessantly. Selecting a pop channel, Sinéad turned the volume up full on the clock-radio, took a deep breath and threw open the door.

Dylan dropped his mug of coffee and yelped as the hot liquid landed on his crotch. "Holy shit, you scared the hell out of me!"

"I thought you were a burglar!" Sinéad ran to the freezer as he hopped around groaning. "Take off your trousers, quick."

"Those words *should* be music to a man's ears," he said, gingerly taking off his jeans and sitting down.

She came back with a bag of peas wrapped in a cloth. "Well why didn't you tell me you were coming home? I was all ready to attack you."

He gingerly placed the makeshift ice pack over his boxers and winced. He eyed the stilettos and spray she'd dropped on the table. "You were going to attack a burglar with those?"

"It was all I could find."

"Why is the radio blaring?" he asked.

"Oh, shit." She ran to switch it off. "I thought that if I was attacked, grumpy from downstairs would come up to complain about the noise and find my body before it started to smell."

"I just love the way your mind works." He grinned.

Sitting down at the table, she stared at him, not sure what to think. He had been gone for so long with hardly any contact and now he was behaving as if everything was fine. "Are we through?"

He looked at her baffled. "Why on earth would you say that?"

"You never replied to my email or to my texts."

"I did reply to your email."

She looked at him not sure whether to believe him or not.

"Fuck! I promise you I replied and I told you that we were going up to the Highlands for the New Year and that there was no phone coverage up there." He reached for her laptop and went in to check her Internet connection.

"So you never got any of my texts?" Sinéad looked at him.

"Not since the one you sent on Christmas morning."

"Oh."

He looked up at the tone of her voice. "What?"

"Bridie died, Dylan. Dad is having a wake for her tomorrow and the funeral is the following morning."

"Oh, sweetheart, I'm so sorry. Are you okay?"

"I'm not sure how I feel, to be honest."

"I'm glad I got back in time."

She looked at him. "When you didn't respond I assumed it was over between us."

He shook his head and handed her the laptop. "Silly girl. You really need to learn how to reconnect your Internet, Sinéad. Why don't you read the emails you missed while I go and take a cold shower?"

"We have some cream somewhere for burns," she said vaguely, her eye running down the list of seven — no, eight — emails Dylan had sent her.

"I'm fine, back in a minute."

302

She started with the oldest email, the response to her heartfelt letter written on Christmas Eve.

My darling Sinéad, thank you for this letter. I've tried to help you through this awful time but I know that I got it wrong . . . a lot. I felt so frustrated and helpless and I suppose that didn't help. I don't think I said "pull yourself together" at least I hope I didn't, but it was so hard to watch you drinking and sleeping all of the time. I missed you when you moved into the shop but at the same time I thought it might be exactly what you needed. I didn't realise until Max told me how bad things were, how low you were. I was so thrilled when Krystie arrived and you started working again, it was just like old times for a while. But then it was as if you didn't even see me, let alone need me. It was childish of me leaving without talking to you, I'm sorry.
If you want me to come home, Sinéad, say so and I will be on the first available flight.
I love you,
Dylan, xx

The other emails were only a couple of lines long. The first were humorous: "So you don't want me back . . ." etc.

Then an ultimatum. Unless she had any better suggestions he would spend the New Year and Hogmanay in the Highlands and, when she didn't respond to that email, two short frosty notes advising her of his travel arrangements. She was wiping away her tears as he came back into the room in a bathrobe.

"They weren't supposed to make you cry," he joked.

She stood up and buried her face in his neck. "I love you, Dylan. I'm so sorry that I shut you out. You were wonderful and kind and patient and I took it all for granted."

He pulled back, cupped her face and stared into her eyes. "Don't be so hard on yourself. It has been one hell of a difficult year."

She turned her mouth in to the palm of his hand and kissed it. "Even so, I shouldn't have taken it out on you."

"Enough. I'm just glad that we're back on track. I've missed you so much, Sinéad." He kissed her.

She groaned at the wonderful taste of his mouth on hers and pulled him closer, acutely aware of his body through her thin robe.

"I want you," he said, his breathing ragged.

"I want you too," she said.

He pulled her towards the bedroom and started to drag off her pyjamas.

She looked down at his boxers and then smiled at him, her eyes twinkling mischievously. "Do you need me to rub some cream into that scald?"

"Oh, yeah," he said and stretched out on the bed. "I think that's exactly what I need."

Rory rattled off the dishes he'd prepared for this evening. "And if we run short of anything I can always nip back."

"Great." Krystie smiled. He and Ellen had sprung into action when Sinéad had told them about the wake and not only were they providing food for tonight but they'd insisted on coming along to serve it, too.

"How's she doing?" Rory nodded towards the loo on the landing, where Sinéad was getting changed.

"I think she's okay, but it's all come as a bit of a shock. Apparently, Bridie was fine on Christmas Day." Krystie went to the mirror to fix the collar of the charcoal jacket she wore over her black jeans and turtleneck. She added a blue scarf. "Do you know how to get to Kieran's?"

"Yeah, your beloved gave me the directions." Rory grinned at her.

Krystie flushed. "Feck off."

He laughed. "I'm going! See you there."

Sinéad emerged from the bathroom. In the simple but beautifully tailored black dress and black silk flower holding her hair back over one ear, she looked pale and delicate.

"That was Rory," Krystie told her. "He and Ellen are heading over to your dad's now."

"I don't know what I'd do without those two. They're always there when I need them." She shivered. "I wish I didn't have to go to this damn wake, or the funeral for that matter. It's just a body. Bridie's gone."

Krystie knew that Max had been just as surprised when Kieran announced that he wanted the remains brought to the house the evening before the burial.

"I'm sure it won't be too bad," she said, although she wasn't that keen on the evening ahead, either, and she'd never even met Bridie. But she'd be there for Max and, indeed, Sinéad. "I remember going to my granddad's wake. It freaked me out. At one stage there was a guy actually leaning his elbow on the coffin as he joked and drank. I was tempted to go over and punch him."

"You should have," Sinéad retorted.

"Maybe." Krystie grinned. "I was only seven and about the right height to have done some real damage."

Sinéad laughed and glanced at her watch. "Where is Max? He should be here by now."

"He's probably looking for parking. You know what Blackrock's like at rush hour."

"He's taking this quite hard, Krystie. He barely remembers our mum and, although Bridie wasn't the most maternal woman in the world, she was all he really had. He's feeling guilty that he didn't spend more time with her in the last few years. I'm so glad he has you to help him through this, and that I have Dylan too, for that matter."

Krystie looked up in surprise. Dylan had been the elephant in the room all over Christmas and any enquiries resulted in the same clipped response from Sinéad. His sister in Scotland was going through a tough time and he'd gone over to spend the holidays with her. But Krystie was convinced they'd had a row. "He's home?"

Sinéad's face lit up. "Yeah, he got in last night."

"I'm so glad."

"Me too," Sinéad said with obvious feeling. Krystie eyed her curiously and she reddened and added, "I'm relieved he made it in time for the funeral."

Krystie heard Max's distinctive tread on the stairs.

"Hi." He smiled at Sinéad and then came to kiss Krystie. "Hello, you."

His voice was as breezy as ever and he smiled, but now, armed with new information, Krystie was more conscious of the pain in his eyes.

He looked from her to Sinéad. "Ready?"

"As I'll ever be," Sinéad said.

Krystie put her bag over her shoulder, slipped her hand into his and gave him a reassuring smile. "Ready."

She stayed close to him all evening and she knew he appreciated it in the way he took her hand or brushed her hair back from her face. When he walked her out to the taxi, he stopped at the gate and slung his arms loosely around her shoulders.

"You've been great, Krystie," he said with such love in his eyes.

"I did nothing," she protested.

"You were here beside me and it helped."

"I wish I could do more."

He kissed her tenderly. "Not possible. Go get some sleep and I'll see you in the morning."

She hugged him again, got into the taxi and blew him a kiss as it drove away.

She sighed as the cab whisked her home. She ached for Max and wished she could do more to take the sadness from his eyes. She yawned and was glad he'd

307

insisted she go home. It would be another long day tomorrow. Max had wanted her to go in the mourning coach with the family, but she had refused point blank, saying that it would be totally wrong. Reluctantly, he'd let the matter go once she promised to sit with him in the church. She didn't feel comfortable doing that, either, but couldn't refuse him, even if it meant tolerating the whispers of "Who's yer one in the family pew?"

Max had also wanted her with him for the day but Sinéad had soon put him straight.

"We are snowed under with work and you want her to hang around a graveyard and stay for a lunch where she won't even know anyone? Give her and me a break, Max."

And he had agreed and apologised, but Krystie knew he'd be happier if she was with him. It was a wonderful feeling to be needed and she was determined, while she was there, she wouldn't let him down.

She would wear her houndstooth coat for the service in the morning — she wasn't family, so full black would be too much — but she'd team it with black knee-high boots, a black headscarf tied gypsy-style and plain, hoop earrings. It was a relief, really, that it would be for only an hour or so and then she could escape back to the studio. But she still felt as if she was deserting him. Sinéad was right. This was hitting him harder than he was letting on. She could tell by the set of his mouth and the tension in the way he held himself. On impulse she reached for her phone and sent him a text: "How are you doing?"

308

Within seconds he phoned.

"Why aren't you asleep?"

"I was worried about you. Are you okay?"

"A little bit drunk, to be honest, and tired. It's been one hell of a day."

"Tomorrow won't be any easier, Max. Slip away, you need sleep."

"Not until Dad does. I can't leave him. Sinéad bailed out an hour ago."

"Is Beth still there?"

"Yeah."

"Then your dad will be just fine. Go home, Max. Get some rest."

"Thanks for today, Krystie."

"For what? I just stood round feeling useless."

"You were great," he assured her. "Go to sleep, Krystie. See you in the morning."

"Goodnight." She turned off her phone and snuggled under the covers.

Sinéad had felt exhausted when she got home but, despite going straight to bed with Dylan, she couldn't sleep. This evening hadn't been as tough as she'd expected it to be and it was certainly easier when Dylan arrived and remained by her side throughout. She looked over at him sleeping so peacefully next to her, and smiled. It was so good to have him home and to feel so incredibly close. She had told him all about that night in Philip's house when she was convinced there was a woman in the house and that he didn't want to find Sheila at all. Dylan had listened and promised her that, no matter what Philip did or didn't do, he would help her to find Sheila. He had also made a point of keeping Philip away from her this evening, although her brother-in-law didn't seem that anxious to be near her, either.

She had found the wake a surreal experience. Chatting, drinking and even laughing had seemed wrong, given that her aunt was laid out in the next room. But the number of people who'd turned up to pay their respects and exchange anecdotes about Bridie, had been heartening. There were distant relatives, parishioners, neighbours and women from her ladies' club who told stories of fun and high jinks that she would never have associated with her sensible aunt.

She'd spent a long time chatting with two women who had gone to school with Bridie and had known her mum, too. It was wonderful to hear anyone talk about her mother and what she was like as a girl growing up.

"Maggie was the life and soul of the place but Bridie was much quieter and the smartest in the class," Maureen said.

"She wanted to be a teacher," Ann added. "I never understood why she took off for America without at least finishing school."

Sinéad had been astonished at that little nugget of information. She knew that Bridie had only come back to live in Ireland after her father died but she hadn't known that she had gone to America at such a young age. "How did that come about?" she'd asked the women.

Ann looked at Maureen, who answered. "She went over to visit some relation and she never came back."

"But how come my mother didn't go?" Sinéad asked.

"I don't think Bridie got on too well with your grandfather," Ann explained looking a little embarrassed.

Sinéad was surprised at that. The little she remembered of her grandfather, he seemed a kind and friendly man. "I can't believe that I never heard this story before."

"We were all very jealous of her at the time," Maureen remembered, smiling. "It seemed such a glamorous and adventurous thing to do."

"I wonder why she decided to come back to Ireland," Ann mused.

"You're going to have to wonder. It looks like Bridie's taking her secrets to the grave." Maureen raised her glass. "Good luck to her."

Realising that there was no way she was going to sleep yet, Sinéad crept out of bed so as not to disturb Dylan and went into the kitchen. She made some coffee and settled down on the sofa with Bridie's diary. She was surprised at how little she knew about her aunt, and it had been a revelation spending time with people who knew her when she was young. It had helped meeting her current friends, too, and to confirm that, until the dementia had taken hold, Bridie had been living an active and seemingly happy life. But why she had left Ireland or, indeed, returned was a mystery.

Leafing through the notebook made her smile. Bridie, as organised as ever, had it split into different sections. One page was devoted to family birthdays, another to their vaccinations and general health information. Another section had snippets about programmes or books that either she wanted to read or planned to use or recommend. She had another part devoted to basic, domestic matters and detailing policy numbers and bank accounts. Sinéad made a mental note to take a copy of this and pass it on to Max. It might be useful, as he was executor of her will.

She flicked on, stopping in surprise when she came across pages of poetry. She'd never have had Bridie down as a poet and it was sad, poignant verse too, all dedicated to K. Who was K? she wondered. A lover, she assumed. Someone Bridie had known in America? Was K the reason she had come home? Did he break her heart?

She stared at her aunt's neat, careful handwriting and traced her finger around the letter K . . . She stopped. Kieran? Dad? No, of course not! She laughed at her own foolishness. She flicked back to the birthdays and, yes, there was an entry for K but no, it wasn't the same date as Dad's birthday. Relief flooded her. The thought of Bridie and her dad being involved would be just too much to handle.

She yawned, closed the book and went back to bed wondering about K. Perhaps Ann or Maureen would know who he was. He might even turn up at the funeral in the morning and the mystery would be solved.

CHAPTER
TWENTY-EIGHT

Kieran polished his shoes and then scrubbed his hands clean before going to dress in the black suit, white shirt and the new black tie Beth had rushed off to buy him. As he dressed he remembered going through the same sad process when Maggie had died. He'd drifted through that day in a haze. Today was different. He was glad that Bridie had died quickly and without pain. They hadn't always seen eye to eye, and she had been a tough woman, but she'd had a hard and lonely life and yet, despite her own problems, she'd devoted her years to looking after other people.

Once she moved out they hadn't kept in touch much. But they hadn't fallen out, as he knew Sheila had always suspected. They just reminded each other too much of difficult times and it was a relief for them both to move on. That was nearly ten years ago now. He was glad that they seemed to be happy years for her. When they caught up on the various family occasions she seemed softer and more content.

Sheila had been the one who first suspected Bridie was sick. She saw her regularly and began to notice her aunt's increasingly erratic behaviour. She finally told the doctor of her suspicions and somehow persuaded

Bridie to go and see him, and within weeks they had their diagnosis. That was almost three years ago now, but how quickly she had gone downhill. At first, when she still had moments of clarity, she made Sheila promise not to lock her up and they had worked out a system of health visitors and neighbours and family so that she was never alone for long. But then Bridie had taken to wandering, often in a state of undress, and soon couldn't manage to wash or clean herself.

"But I promised," Sheila had said, filled with guilt, when the time came to concede that a nursing home was the only option left.

Kieran had tried to comfort her but she was inconsolable. It had been a blessing in so many ways the day that actress had walked into the shop, bought that fancy hat and worn it to the BAFTAs. It gave Sheila such a lift and she threw herself into making the most of the incredible marketing opportunity.

Everything had been going so well and then she'd disappeared. He couldn't help wondering if there was some link to Bridie that had made her do it but he couldn't figure out what. It was one of the main reasons he hadn't visited his sister-in-law much in the nursing home. He'd found it so frustrating that the secret to Sheila's supposed death could be locked in Bridie's mind, but there was no key.

He heard the front door close as Max arrived. "Just coming," he called to him, knotting his tie and smoothing his hair with his hands before going downstairs.

"You look well, Dad." Max gave him a grim smile, his hair and skin seeming even paler against the black suit.

314

"You too, son. Bridie would be proud of you. Let's have a quick drink." He led the way into the kitchen, took a bottle of Jameson and two tumblers from the cupboard and poured generous measures into them. "To Bridie." He raised his glass.

"Bridie." Max clinked his against it and drank. "The car should be here in a minute. Are we picking up Beth?"

"Yes. She didn't want to come in the car with us but I insisted. She's going to be part of the family soon enough." Max coughed on his whiskey and Kieran clapped him on the back chuckling. "Sorry about that."

His son stared at him. "You're getting married?"

"I know it's a bit sudden, but you can't exactly hang around at our age, and I want to be with her; and, strange as it may seem, she's willing to take on this grumpy old bastard. Does it bother you?"

"Not at all. I'm delighted for you. Beth is great."

"I had hoped that you or your sister might beat me to it."

"Well, you never know, Dad, one of these days . . ."

Kieran lowered his glass and looked at him. "Krystie? Ah, that's great, son."

"It's early days, Dad. We're just getting to know each other," Max warned him, "but I think she's the one; how she feels about me is another matter altogether."

Kieran thought of the way Krystie's eyes had followed Max around the previous evening. "I don't think you've anything to worry about there. She's a lovely girl, son. Your mother would have loved her." The doorbell rang and Kieran sighed and patted his son's shoulder. "Let's go and send Bridie to her rest. If anyone deserves it, she does."

Krystie glanced over at Sinéad. She was kneeling on the floor, bent over a hat block with a Stanley knife, but she had already wrecked two pieces of the pink sinamay textile and there wasn't much left. She was working ridiculously long hours but she was a woman on a mission, she wanted to find her sister. Krystie could understand but, even to her novice's eye, she could see that Sinéad's usual standards had slipped and she was making costly mistakes.

"Shit!"

Krystie looked up to see Sinéad cradling her hand, blood running between her fingers. "Let me see," she said, putting down the pillbox she had been hemming. She knelt down on the floor beside Sinéad and examined the cut. It wasn't huge but it was deep and in the crease of the palm. "I'll get a bandage. Hold your hand up in the air."

Sinéad stared at her. "Why?"

"No idea but that's what Ma always told us to do when we cut ourselves." Krystie grinned and went to fetch the first-aid kit. There were only a few small plasters in it and no bandages. "These are no good. I'd better nip out to the pharmacy."

"There should be something in one of the desk drawers," Sinéad snapped impatiently. "Hurry up, I want to get this base done today."

Krystie started to pull the desk apart. "No chance. That hand will bleed if you try to use it and that's the last of the pink; you can't afford to get blood —" She stopped and stared at the photo that was tossed in among buttons, ribbons and loose sketches.

"What's wrong?"

Krystie turned around, the photo in her hand. "Is this who I think it is?"

"Yeah, I told you all about that," Sinéad said dismissively. "Bandage?"

"Sorry." Krystie rummaged again and came back with another kit and the photo. "You told me an actress; you didn't say it was her! What was she like?"

Sinéad smiled. "Surprisingly shy and really nice and full of praise for the shop."

As Krystie cleaned and bandaged her hand, Sinéad reminisced about her big break. It was the stuff of dreams, the stuff that had filled her head when she left Ireland and the Fields sisters hadn't had to leave their shop; the dream had come to them.

"What?"

She looked up to find Sinéad frowning at her. "Sorry?"

"You're wearing your pissed-off face."

"I didn't know I had one," Krystie smirked.

"You do," Sinéad assured her. "So?"

Her job done Krystie sat back on her heels and picked up the photo again. "I just can't believe you did nothing with this."

"What do you mean?" Sinéad protested. "How do you think we got all of the media attention and the orders from the department stores?"

"That just happened because of the BAFTA awards. Do you have this on your website? Have you used it on social media?" She sighed at Sinéad's blank expression. "Have you put this photo up on Twitter or on Facebook?"

Sinéad wrinkled her nose. "I'm not really into any of that. Even emails are a challenge for me."

"But it's free advertising," Krystie said, unable to believe her ears. She'd checked out the Fields website the night before she'd met Sinéad and it was quite basic and out of date, but she'd assumed that was because, like so many businesses, they had moved on to using social media instead.

"Advertising?" Sinéad looked sceptical. "To some saddos who have nothing better to do with their time? The audience are hardly likely to be the sort to buy designer hats."

Krystie went to correct her but realised that Sinéad was in no mood for it and bit her lip. Her mother would be proud — no, stunned. She held up the photo and studied it. "You know, this really is great and I'm not surprised that she bought that piece. It is gorgeous. How would you feel if I did a little online promotion?" she asked casually.

Sinéad shrugged and reached for her sketch pad. "If you want, but we have more important things to do."

"It's okay, I'll do it in my own time. It's what I do to relax, anyway."

"If you think it's worth a shot." Sinéad shrugged, turned up the volume on the radio and, curling up in her chair, began to sketch.

"Do you have this photo on your laptop?"

"Yeah, it's my screensaver. Help yourself."

Sharon shuffled into the sitting room, yawning. "Krystie, it's after midnight."

"Not in the US. Sorry, did I wake you?" She looked up at her friend.

"No, I needed to get a drink." Sharon went out to the kitchen for some water and came back and sank onto the sofa beside her. "What the hell are you doing?"

"I'm setting Sinéad up on Facebook and Twitter."

"That's not in your job description. Tell Sinéad to get lost. You shouldn't be putting in such long hours, and working on that screen all evening after a day's work isn't exactly good for you, is it?"

"I'm just done. And she didn't ask: I offered. She has this amazing photo and she's done nothing with it." Krystie handed over the print version.

"I vaguely remember this. God, the girl is stunning, isn't she? Look at those eyes and cheekbones. The hat suits her perfectly."

"Which is why I plan to make sure the virtual world sees it."

"And how are you going to manage that?" Sharon asked, looking as sceptical as Sinéad had.

"I'm going to ask the lady herself to help. It turns out she's a regular tweeter, so I've said hi — as Sinéad, not me — and thanks for the business your purchase has brought in and asked her to send on the photo to all of her two hundred and sixty thousand followers." Krystie could barely contain her excitement. She'd been pretty sure that the actress would be on Twitter but she'd been delighted to discover she was an active user *and* responded to tweets from strangers.

Sharon sighed. "Even if she does that, what difference will it make?"

"Duh, are you kidding? You can bet there are zillions of people in the fashion industry following her, she's a trendsetter and if she's wearing Sinéad's hat that means other people will want to."

Sharon frowned. "But that coverage was on every news channel and the photo in newspapers and magazines all over the world and it didn't make Sinéad famous then; why would it work now?"

"Sinéad and Sheila were inundated with queries but they spent so much time doing interviews that they hadn't even started ploughing through them."

"And then Sheila disappeared." Sharon looked at her.

"Exactly. So, I'm going to try and remind the world."

"Good for you, but I wouldn't go getting Sinéad's hopes up."

"No, I won't say a word about it. She's not expecting me to get anywhere, anyway."

"And you won't get anywhere if you're sick so, please, call it a night, yeah?"

Krystie laughed. "Yes, Ma." The words reminded her that she hadn't been in touch with her mother in days. She'd call her first thing.

The next morning after she'd collected her coffee from Ellen and gone up to an empty studio, she phoned home. When her mother finally answered she sounded breathless.

"Hello, sweetheart, how are you?"

"Fine, Ma, but you don't sound so good. Have you been out jogging?"

"I was just upstairs when you phoned," her mother laughed. "How are Sinéad and the family doing?"

"They're okay, I think," Krystie said, though she wasn't sure. Sinéad was preoccupied and not saying much and she'd hardly seen Max since the funeral, as he had attended a conference in County Monaghan the week after and been very busy since he got back. Krystie was working hard, too, and wasn't really up to going out, but she did miss him. He called every day but talking on the phone wasn't the same and she felt that the closeness that had been between them had faded a little.

"They've gone through so much, it's a shame," her mother was saying. "Oh, I saw a nice photo of you in a magazine in the hair salon and Tanya said I could bring it home."

"A photo?" Krystie said frowning. The last occasion she remembered being photographed was at Philip's party on Christmas Eve, nearly a month ago now, and they had already appeared in the magazines and a couple of newspapers' social columns. "Where was it taken?"

"At the funeral."

"That's sick," Krystie muttered. She hadn't seen any photographers about. Someone must have snapped her with a phone. "Is it a picture just of me?"

"No, you're with Sinéad in the churchyard, and then there's another of the brother and his girlfriend."

Krystie frowned. "Girlfriend?"

"Yes, Natalie, the model. Did you not meet her yet?"

"No," she said faintly. "I thought they'd broken up."

Her mother laughed. "It doesn't look that way in the photograph. I'll keep it for you."

"Great, thanks, Ma. I'll see you at the weekend."

When she finally hung up, Krystie sat staring out of the window, stunned. She tried to stay calm. It was a photo, it meant nothing. There was nothing that odd about an ex-girlfriend attending the funeral and offering her sympathies to Max. Only she hadn't surfaced while Krystie was there and Max hadn't mentioned her afterwards, and the way Ma had talked it sounded as if they were up close and personal in the photo.

"Stop jumping to conclusions," she told herself. She would wait until she saw the photo and then, if she had doubts, she'd just ask Max about it, simple as that. And if it was true . . . well, she would worry about that if or when she had to.

CHAPTER
TWENTY-NINE

Sheila glanced over at Karl, practically hidden behind the *New York Times*. He'd hardly opened his mouth in days. She wanted to scream at him, to provoke some sort of reaction, but Zach had said she should give him time and space to process this. And so she just kept out of Karl's way, staying in bed until he had left for work and pretending she was going for a walk or to the gym in the evenings and hiding out in Zach's place.

"Put yourself in his position, Sheila. His world has come down around his ears," Zach had said, but, then, he didn't have to live in this silent, charged atmosphere.

She had been surprised to come downstairs and find Karl here this morning, although it was almost ten o'clock. "Aren't you going in today?"

He muttered something about arrangements to be made. She was about to ask what, but bit her lip. He would tell her when he was ready. She sat and drank coffee, nibbled on a bagel and waited, but eventually he stood up and left without another word. Immediately, she was on the phone to Zach but he was tied up with a patient and told her to come to the apartment for lunch and they could talk then.

"He didn't say what arrangements?" Zach asked as he made them an omelette.

Sheila set two places at the breakfast bar and climbed onto a stool. "No. He barely opened his mouth to me. I wish I'd never told him about that phone call."

Zach turned to look at her. "You know you didn't have a choice."

She rested her chin on her hand and sighed. "I know. I just hate to see him upset."

"Everyone gets hurt sometime. That's life." He divided the omelette onto two plates and carried them to the bar.

"Sounds like a line from a song," she joked, though she didn't feel like laughing. She watched him and his easy, relaxed manner. "I don't think anything or anyone could hurt you."

He chewed thoughtfully, looking straight into her eyes. "I think I've had my fair share."

She thought of Nancy and wished the ground would swallow her up. "I'm sorry. I didn't mean it like that. I'm talking about now. You seem impregnable."

"So I'm devoid of feeling?"

"No, Zach, of course not," she cried.

He chuckled. "You really have to lighten up, Sheila. It was a joke."

She glowered at him. "Hilarious. Is it surprising I've lost my sense of humour after everything that's happened?"

He pulled a face. "Stop waiting for someone to give it back to you. Go find it."

She groaned. "Why don't men ever get that women just want you to listen and empathise? Why must they always try to provide solutions?"

He shrugged. "We can't have babies, so we need to feel useful for something."

Sheila laughed.

"And I've made you laugh." He grinned at her in triumph.

"I don't think you could make Karl laugh. Somehow I don't think he'd see the funny side of anything at the moment." She took a small mouthful of the delicious egg but she had no appetite. Her stomach seemed to be in a constant knot of anxiety.

He put a hand out and caressed her cheek. "I know this is very difficult, for both of you, but there's nothing you can do to change the past, so concentrate on the future. And remember, you're not alone."

She covered his hand with hers. "Thank you. I suppose I am anxious because I can't really do anything until Karl makes a decision."

"That's not true at all, but I'm not going to tell you what to do. You must make your own decisions, Sheila."

He continued to eat his lunch and she felt a flash of irritation. It didn't seem to bother him, one way or the other, what she did. He was so self-contained and calm and removed from her and her problems and she didn't like it. "I need to go." She stood up and gathered up her things.

He looked up. "Aren't you going to finish your lunch?"

"I don't feel very hungry and I have some thinking to do." She searched his eyes, looking for some sign that he cared for her, but just saw the same gentle kindness that was always there. Maybe she was so desperate to find someone to cling to that she had imagined that he had feelings for her. But what about the small caresses and gentle kisses?

He swivelled around on his stool and opened his arms to her and she walked into them and sighed at the feel of his breath on her neck.

He held her tight and, tangling his hand in her hair, gently pulled her head back so he could look in her eyes. "It will be fine, Sheila. You are so much stronger than you realise."

"Please tell me what to do," she whispered.

"Do what makes you happy."

She looked up at him. "What about you?"

"I'll wait for you whatever happens," he said, and kissed her, and she felt the tension leave her body. With that promise she knew she could face anything.

She wandered home, deciding it was time to ignore one piece of advice that Zach had given her. She wasn't going to give Karl any more space. He'd had enough time. This just wasn't healthy. She would make him talk to her and then . . . Well, she hadn't thought any further than that. She just knew that this silence wasn't helping either of them.

When she let herself in she was surprised to find the alarm off. "Karl?"

"In here," he called from the bedroom.

She went in, tugging off her hat and scarf as she went and stopped short when she saw that he was sitting up in bed working on his laptop. "What's going on? Are you sick?"

He opened his mouth to reply but had to turn his head to sneeze.

"That answers that. Poor you." She sat down on the edge of the bed. "Can I get you something?"

He reached for a tissue and blew his nose. "I don't suppose you have some chicken soup in your purse, do ya?"

"No but I can nip down to the deli and get you some." He smiled and she realised that it was the first time in days.

"You're very kind."

"I'll stop by the pharmacy and pick up some cold remedy. In the meantime, forget about work, and rest."

"I'm not working." He spun the laptop to face her and she saw that he had the Irish airline, Aer Lingus, website open.

She stared at it and then looked back at him. "What are you doing?"

He shrugged. "I think it's time I paid a visit."

She clambered up beside him and took his hand. "I don't understand. You could have gone home for the funeral, Karl. Why go now?"

He coughed. "You'll get my cold."

"Karl, tell me!"

He opened the file beside him on the bed and took out a letter. "This came in the mail today."

She took it from him and read it. "Oh, my God."

He laughed, though there were tears in his eyes. "I know. Crazy, isn't it? For whatever reason, she didn't want me in her life, and I came to accept it. And now this."

Sheila put her hand over his. "At least she didn't forget you."

"Too little, too late," he said, his voice hard. "And she still didn't tell me who my father is. She left that little nugget out. But I'm going to Dublin and I'm going to find him." He looked up at her. "Come with me, Sheila."

"Oh, Karl . . ."

"Wouldn't you like some answers, Sheila?"

She stood up and began to pace, wringing her hands, shaking her head. "You were the one who said I never had to go back."

"Perhaps I was wrong. Maybe you need to go back in order to go forward." He sighed. "I don't know, Sheila, but I know it would be easier if you were by my side."

"Karl, that's not fair," she wailed.

"I know it's not. But please come anyway."

She stood looking at him, at a loss what to say or do. "I'll go and get that soup."

How *could* she go back? She tugged her hat on as she stepped out of the lift and headed for the door. She had been full of anger when she left Ireland, but that was largely gone now. She felt nothing but contempt and disgust for her father, but she felt bad now about what she had done to her sister and brother and a little guilty that she hadn't been there in the end for Bridie, although she knew the woman wouldn't have known one way or the other. She felt an urge to talk to Zach again but decided against it. He was right, she had to make this decision.

When she arrived back from the store Karl was full of remorse.

"I'm sorry, I'm being selfish. It's so hard to believe that this is actually happening. I feel excited and sad and nervous and," he sighed, "emotional."

She bent to hug him. "I'm going to work. Eat your soup and I'll check in on you later."

She grabbed an apple and a bottle of water, changed into her overalls and went into the studio. Although it was freezing outside, it was a bright and sunny day and the room was flooded with light. Looking at the canvases that lined the walls, she smiled. They weren't all the stunning works of art that Karl made them out to be, but they were pretty good and she felt proud of them. Some of them brought tears to her eyes as the colours and content were like a diary of her frame of mind since she'd got here; a psychiatrist would have a field day. She had told Zach about them and he had been delighted saying that it was probably more effective than any therapy. He seemed a little hurt that she wouldn't let him see them, but she didn't feel ready and he accepted that, the way he accepted everything. She put some Sinatra on low and hummed along as she prepared her brushes and paints. As she did so, she glanced at the canvas. It was the most colourful piece she'd done yet. She had snapped some photos in Central Park on one of her early-morning walks with Zach and this had been one of the best. It was a shot of a homeless woman sharing her sandwich with her little dog. They were on a bench by the water and the light was spectacular, but it was the laughter in the woman's eyes as the dog licked her face that had captured Sheila's heart, and she felt compelled to paint it. She had done the sky and trees and now she would concentrate on the pond. She studied the print of the photo she'd taped to the noticeboard and marvelled at the many colours in the water alone. How had she been content to make bloody hats for so long? They were so constraining. Where possible, she had worked with feathers and beads, but she couldn't get excited about the shapes and materials in the way Sinéad did. But at moments like this she could understand Sinéad's total absorption and why her sister was always at her most serene when she was working.

The thoughts of her twin brought her predicament back to mind. Could she really go back to Ireland and face them all? Would it help or make things worse? She really wasn't sure. Max would at least listen but she wasn't so sure about her sister. She shivered at the thought of a confrontation with Sinéad. They'd had minor squabbles in the past but they'd never fallen out over anything, not like this. What would she do in her twin's shoes? It would be hard but she couldn't imagine herself turning her back on Sinéad once she'd heard the full story. How she wished she could turn the clock back. She should have confronted her sister before she left instead of just disappearing.

It really wasn't like her to do something so cruel and dramatic. She figured she must have been slightly unbalanced when she came up with the idea of leaving the car by the pier. She felt embarrassed and ashamed, although there was still some small satisfaction in the fact that she had hurt her father; he deserved it.

She worked blues, greens and greys into the canvas with a palette knife to create the reflection of the sky and trees as her mind continued to wander. Quite apart from the reaction of the family if she went back, there would be a public reaction, and it wouldn't be nice. My God, she could even be charged with wasting police time. They might want her to pay for the cost of the search. She doubted Karl had considered that. She paused, wiped her hands on a cloth and took a drink of water. She walked to the window and stared out across the rooftops. She hadn't given any thought at all to the emergency services and friends and neighbours who had spent days searching for her. She had been so upset she hadn't considered the ripple effect of her actions on innocent people. She thought back on the euphoria of those early weeks in New York and was overcome with guilt and shame at her selfishness.

She returned to her canvas and worked at a frenetic pace, pausing only to dash tears away on her sleeve. Her mind was as active as her hands. She couldn't make the same mistakes again. She couldn't just sweep back into Dublin without carefully thinking how her reappearance would affect Sinéad and Max. Philip's feelings, his position and, indeed, his political career needed careful consideration, too. She paused, suddenly overwhelmed. It would be so much easier to ignore everything that was going on in Dublin but she knew that it was only a matter of time now before there was a knock at the door, especially once Karl visited Dublin. She could run but she didn't want to leave Manhattan. And, if she was honest with herself, she didn't want to leave Zach.

CHAPTER
THIRTY

Max was about to go into a meeting when he got a call on the mobile. When he looked at the display he realised it was the solicitor who was handling Bridie's estate. "Hello, Max Fields."

"Mr Fields. Pat Brennan of Doyle and Brennan."

"Good morning."

"I realise that you're a busy man but we really need to deal with your aunt's estate. She was very specific about how she wanted the matter handled, as I told Mr Healy. He did say that you would be in touch as soon as possible."

Max frowned. Philip hadn't said that there was any urgency in sorting out Bridie's estate. On the contrary, he had said that Brennan had told him it was all quite straightforward and Max could drop in after the dust had settled and they would soon have it sorted out.

"I'm very sorry, Mr Brennan, I had no idea. There was obviously a breakdown in communications." He checked his diary. "I could drop by any time before eleven in the morning; does that suit at all?"

"Eight thirty in the morning, Mr Fields? Sorry to hurry you on this, only it is a rather complicated and sensitive matter."

Max digested this in silence. What could be sensitive or complicated about Bridie's small estate? "I'll be there, Mr Brennan and, again, my apologies for the confusion."

He put down the phone and thought about calling Philip but decided against it. For some reason his brother-in-law had deliberately withheld information from him. Why? What possible reason could he have for doing that? How would Bridie's estate impinge on him in any way? He remembered Philip recommending some investments to her at some stage but Max couldn't imagine him trying to cheat the woman, yet it seemed as if Philip had deliberately tried to delay him from finding out the contents of his aunt's will, and he was eager to know why.

He went through the rest of the day distracted. He was going to contact Sinéad and his dad and let them know that he was seeing the solicitor, but what was the point? Better to wait until he knew exactly what Bridie's will contained. He imagined from Brennan's call there was something in it that would surprise them, but he doubted it. A large part of the proceeds from her house had gone into paying for the nursing home. She'd insisted on that arrangement as soon as she was diagnosed although she hadn't expected to go downhill so quickly. As for savings, she couldn't have had that much put by. He smiled. Perhaps she'd left it to an animal-rescue centre. Good for her. It wouldn't bother him and he knew that Sinéad wouldn't mind either.

Max was ten minutes early arriving at the solicitor's office the next morning, but Brennan came out to greet

334

him immediately and ushered him into a meeting room and offered his condolences.

"Your aunt was an impressive woman." The solicitor pulled a file towards him but, rather than opening it, he linked his hands on the cover and paused as if trying to choose his words carefully. All of Max's instincts told him there was something wrong, but he waited patiently for the man to gather his thoughts.

"You probably have some expectation as to your aunt's beneficiaries," Brennan said finally.

"Don't worry. I don't expect any shocks. My aunt discussed everything with me."

"No, Mr Fields, she didn't. She wanted the contents of the will to remain confidential until after her death. She was very keen that you handle matters, but she didn't want to discuss her wishes with you."

"So what was so shocking that she didn't want us to find out? Did she leave everything to the ladies' club?" Max joked, though he was rattled. What had been so important or sensitive that Bridie didn't want them to know? Immediately he had a flashback to the funeral and the discoveries Sinéad had made about their aunt and her opinion that Bridie's return must have been because of a man.

Brennan looked at him. "No. Her entire estate has been left to her son."

"Bridie has a son?" Max gave an incredulous laugh.

"Yes."

"Who is he? Where is he? Why wasn't he here when she needed someone to take care of her?"

"She gave him up for adoption and has never met him."

Max sat in silence, speechless for a moment. "Do you know who he is? Where he is?"

"Yes. I have written to him but haven't received a reply yet."

Max sat in stunned silence as he tried to get his head around this. He supposed he should have guessed, given Bridie's sudden departure to the US. "Will we get to meet him?"

"That will be up to him — and to you, of course. If he makes contact, would you like me to pass on your number?"

"Yes, I'd appreciate that, thank you."

"Your aunt left a letter for you to explain although I don't know the exact contents. She wanted you to read it before you left the office. Perhaps she thought you may have questions." Brennan produced an envelope and handed it to him. "I shall leave you alone to read it. Would you like anything? Coffee?"

"No, thank you."

"I will be in the next room if you want me."

Max stared at his name on the envelope written in Bridie's careful script and with a sigh tore it open.

Dear Max,

I have just been diagnosed with dementia and, as you know, I've been putting my house in order. There are some matters that I feel the family should know about and I wanted to write them down now before my mind gets more confused. Why have I not just told you all? Because I felt entitled to my privacy. I will give you the simple facts and leave it to you to decide, based on the circumstances after my death, what should be passed on to the rest of the family and what is best left unsaid.

Mr Brennan will have told you that you have a cousin. I gave birth to my son in Boston just after my sixteenth birthday. I was raped on my way home from the library. I told no one at the time but I soon realised that I was pregnant and so was forced to tell my parents. To save embarrassment they sent me to live with my uncle and aunt in Boston and the child was given up for adoption.

Bridie was raped? Max stopped reading, stunned at this horrible revelation delivered in such clinical language. How difficult it must have been for Bridie to write this. Was it any wonder the woman had turned into such a cold and hard creature? Was it any wonder she'd remained single? He picked up the letter again.

Please ensure my son gets his birthright, Max. He has tried many times to make contact but I refused to allow the authorities to divulge my name. I couldn't face meeting the result of the crime against me. But he did nothing to deserve that and this is the only way I can atone. I'm sorry if you or the twins are disappointed but you are a clever family and don't need my meagre savings.

I liked Boston, I felt safe there. I suppose I always feared meeting my attacker again and so I begged my parents to let me stay. They agreed of course. There was less chance of my secret being leaked when I was out of the country and they wouldn't have to deal with the shame and embarrassment. Your mother knew of course but she would never have told anyone. Had she survived me I could have relied on her to look after my son and no one would have been any the wiser.

It was much more expensive to travel in those days and so the first time I returned to Ireland was for my father's funeral.

I moved back for good because of your poor mother, she needed me. I'm sorry to tell you, Max, but your father was not a good husband. He had many women and he didn't hide the fact. She loved him very much and it broke her heart but she put up with it. The news that one of his girlfriends was expecting his child finally tipped her over the edge. I'm sorry to be the one to tell you, Max, but your mother's death was not an accident. She walked into the sea that night because she couldn't go on. She left a suicide note but I hid it. I thought it was best for everyone if it looked like an accident.

Again, Max stopped, shocked. His mother had taken her own life? They had always been assured it had been a tragic accident. And she'd done it because of Dad? Feeling his world had been turned on its axis, he had to force himself to read on.

I can't help blaming myself for her death. I should have realised how troubled she was. The only way I could make it up to her was by moving in and looking after her children.

I knew I was no replacement for your mother — I was practically a stranger — but I wasn't convinced your father would look after you properly. I was afraid he would go out with his women and leave you alone at night or, worse, bring them to the house.

Forgive me for burdening you with all of this, Max, but I couldn't go to meet my maker without setting the record straight.

I wish you a long and happy life.

Your loving aunt,

Bridie.

Jesus! Max felt sick. He sat staring blindly at the letter for so long that finally Brennan knocked tentatively on the door and asked if he was okay.

"Fine." Max gave a tight smile and listened as the solicitor told him how things would proceed, but he left at the first opportunity and drove aimlessly as he tried to process all this new information.

He found himself walking Sandymount beach, heedless of the wet sand seeping into his Italian leather shoes. He was stunned and saddened that Bridie had been raped but what upset him more was learning that his mother had committed suicide and she had done so because of Dad. He didn't know how he was going to face the man now that he knew the truth. He groaned as he remembered that he would have to, and this very evening. To celebrate his engagement to Beth, Kieran had arranged a family dinner in a local restaurant. Max felt sick at the thought and wondered, was there any way he could get out of it, but it would be unfair to Beth. He walked on and tried to think rationally. Whatever Bridie's concerns about Dad, he hadn't flaunted women in front of them. It was true he had left much of their care to Bridie, but from what the girls had told him he had done the same with their mother. He just wasn't the hands-on sort of dad. But to mess around with other women and make no attempt to hide it from his mother, that was callous. And what of the baby? Was there a half-brother or -sister somewhere? Did his father keep in touch?

Max wasn't sure he cared. He was too preoccupied thinking of poor Mum. He had an image in his head of the beautiful woman from the photo Krystie had given him, so devastated that she had walked into the waves.

His phone beeped and he took it and saw there was a message from Sinéad asking, was there any news? Oh, yes, he thought, there's news. She of course meant about Sheila. She was frustrated that nothing seemed to be happening, and Philip's repeated response that these things take time only incensed her more. How would she react to all this? Max remembered his aunt's words: he was to decide what should be passed on to the rest of the family and what was best left unsaid. "Thanks a lot, Bridie," he muttered. Should he just tell them about Bridie's son and say nothing about the rest? Did Sinéad really need to know her father was a philanderer and her mother had committed suicide as a result? Probably not, but how could he carry on as normal? How could he propose a toast this evening at his father's engagement dinner when he actually felt like punching him?

Maybe he should confide in Krystie. He'd ask her to have lunch with him and see what she thought he should do. As he looked at his text messages he realised that she hadn't responded to the last couple and hadn't replied to his voice message, either. Concern gripped him. Had she had another attack? He called the studio and Sinéad answered.

"Is Krystie okay?" he said, not wasting time on hello.

"She's fine, why?" Sinéad sounded surprised.

Max sighed, relieved. "Can I talk to her, please?"

There was some conversation and then Sinéad came back on. "She's in the middle of something and says she'll call you later."

"Okay. Thanks, Sinéad."

"See you tonight at the happy couple's dinner," she replied and rang off.

He'd heard the dry note in his sister's voice. She wasn't impressed at Dad's hasty marriage. If only she knew how minor an issue that was. His thoughts returned to Krystie. He had obviously done something to upset her but he had no idea what. He'd hardly seen her these last few days. Perhaps that was it. Maybe she just felt neglected. He turned and headed back to the car. He would stop off at the apartment and change his shoes and socks, and then he would go to Blackrock and make Krystie come to lunch with him if he had to drag her out of there by the hair. There was no time for such petty squabbling. He needed her.

CHAPTER
THIRTY-ONE

Krystie was carefully sewing some feathers into the band of a hat when Max walked in. She was so engrossed in her work that she hadn't heard him come up the stairs and jumped when he spoke.

"Why are you avoiding me?"

"I'm not," she lied. She had thought she would tackle him once she saw that photo, but when her mother had handed her the magazine her heart had clenched at the sight of Natalie in his arms, and she felt too upset to confront him. She knew that she would fall apart and the only thing she had left was her dignity.

The photo wasn't explicit, not at all. It was worse than that. Natalie had her arms around his waist and her head was on his chest while Max had his arms loosely draped over her shoulders and his chin was resting on the top of her head. The intimacy of the embrace spoke volumes of the closeness of the couple and made Krystie sick with jealousy. And the more she looked at it — and she looked at it a lot — the more disappointed and betrayed she felt. How could he hold her, make love to her, talk the way he did and then hold another woman like this? She had been so sure that Max would never hurt her but she'd been wrong.

"If you're not avoiding me, then why aren't you returning my calls or texts?"

"Because I don't want to talk to you," she snapped.

He sighed. "Look, Krystie, I've obviously offended you in some way, though I haven't a clue how, but, whatever it was, I apologise. Now please come to lunch with me. I've had a really lousy morning and I need to talk to you. I want your opinion."

She looked up at him hardly able to believe her ears. "Why don't you call Natalie? I'm sure she'd be glad to give you her opinion," she spat at him.

He shook his head in bewilderment. "Natalie? Why would I call her?"

"Oh, please, don't bullshit me."

His eyes narrowed. "I haven't a clue what this is about, Krystie, but I really don't need it right now. If you have something to say, stop talking in riddles and say it."

"I don't have to say a word," she said, pulling the magazine from her bag and tossing it on the table in front of him.

He picked it up and looked at it, then dropped into Sinéad's chair, closed his eyes and massaged the bridge of his nose. "Her name is Natalie, she was my girlfriend."

"Was? This was taken at Bridie's funeral."

"Yeah, and you can bet the photographer was there at her request. Natalie loves getting her photo into the papers."

"He didn't make you hold her like that!"

Max rolled his eyes. "For crying out loud, Krystie. Bridie's coffin had just been lowered into the grave and

344

Natalie came and hugged me. I wasn't exactly thinking about what way I was holding her."

"How many other of your women came to condole? From what I hear there have been plenty."

His lips twitched. "You're very well informed."

"Hard not to be," she shot back. He thought this was funny? "You seem to live your life in the public eye."

"You didn't strike me as the sort to waste time reading that kind of drivel."

"I don't. My mother spotted it and thought I might be interested because you're Sinéad's brother," she told him in case he thought that she'd been raving about him to her family. She had been tempted a couple of times to tell her mother they were dating. She was very glad she hadn't: Ma would have been furious when she saw the photo.

"I like women. I've dated some beautiful ones, and the newspapers like to take photos of beautiful women." He shrugged. "Natalie was the last and she came to Bridie's funeral. I thought she came along to show some support for old times' sake but perhaps it was because she wanted a photo opportunity."

"When did you break up?"

He held her gaze. "The week before Christmas."

"You were seeing the two of us at the same time?" She felt tears fill her eyes and she swallowed them back. She would not give him the satisfaction of seeing her cry.

"No, Krystie. Natalie hasn't been in the country since we met and as soon as she returned I finished with her."

"When?" she demanded, still not sure if she could believe him.

"The night before you had the seizure and, for the record, I didn't sleep with her. I saw her for less than thirty minutes that night."

"I didn't ask," she muttered.

His face was open, his eyes hadn't left hers. "No but I'd prefer if everything was out in the open. I don't want you hearing stories about me and wondering."

She studied him from under her lashes. "How long were you together?"

He considered the question. "About six months, I think. It wasn't serious."

Krystie scowled at him. "Huh, did she know that?"

He shook his head, looking totally frustrated. "Natalie was dating me because she liked being seen moving in the right circles, because getting into the papers kept her in the public eye and that was good for business."

"And why did *you* date *her*?" He raised his eyebrows, his lips twitching, and she put up her hand. She didn't want to think of him having sex with that woman. "Forget it. I don't want to know. Did you live with her?"

"No way!" He practically shuddered at the thought.

"So you didn't love her?"

"No, Krystie, I didn't and don't love her."

"And now you've got me; I'm the latest on your list," she said, feeling like a fool.

He reached out and grabbed her chair, rolling it closer so that their faces were only inches apart. "You are on no list, Krystie. You walked into my life and I felt as if I'd been hit by a freight train. When you're around

346

I can't concentrate on anything but you, and when you're not all I seem to do is think about you."

She stared at him, wondering whether she could trust him, could believe him. "Please don't mess with me, Max. I'm not going out with you because I want my photo in the paper."

His eyes softened as they stared into hers. "I'm not messing, Krystie. I've never been more serious. I've never met any woman I wanted to live with, Krystie, until I met you. I never met anyone who I wanted to share my life with." He kissed her gently and then pulled her even closer, burying his hands in her hair and deepening the kiss.

She felt herself melt into him. "Oh, Max."

He pulled back and looked into her eyes. "I love you, Krystie."

He caressed her bottom lip with his thumb and she kissed it and smiled into his clear blue eyes, which told her he meant every word. "I love you, too," she said and, feeling as if she might burst with happiness, she pulled his mouth back to hers.

"Oh, God, couldn't you take the day off?" he murmured.

"No she cannot!"

They sprang apart and Krystie smirked when she saw Sinéad standing in the doorway, arms crossed, a wide grin on her face.

Max sat back in the chair, his hand on Krystie's thigh, and gave his sister a lazy smile. "Hey, sis. I just dropped in to take Krystie to lunch."

"From where I'm standing it looked as if she *was* lunch," Sinéad laughed.

Krystie felt her cheeks flush and grinned as she stood up. "I won't be long," she promised.

"She will," Max said and took Krystie's hand.

"Take the afternoon off," Sinéad told Krystie. "You've earned a half-day."

"Are you sure?" Krystie asked. She was on top of her work and in fact, as Sinéad was in such good form, had planned to talk to her about her success in social networking.

"She's sure," Max said, and dragged her out of the door.

"I don't know what to say," Krystie said hours later when Max had told her about his visit to the solicitor. They had gone straight to his apartment from work and made love all afternoon, and now she lay in his arms, her head on his chest, his hand tight in hers as he talked. When he told her about his mother she kissed his tears away, conscious that she was crying too.

"I am so sorry," she said when he finally lapsed into silence. "What are you going to do?"

He turned onto his back and stared up at the ceiling. "No idea, Krystie. I don't even know how I'm going to get through this evening."

"Oh, my God, the engagement dinner." She looked at him horrified. "I completely forgot. Do you want me to phone your dad and tell him you're sick?"

He looked at her with a grim smile. "After the way Sinéad found us earlier I don't think that would be credible, do you?"

She sighed. "I suppose not. You could always get plastered."

"Tempting but only God knows what I'd say then."

"I wish I could do something to help," Krystie said feeling frustrated.

"You can take my mind off it," he said, pulling her against him.

"Gladly," she said, winding her arms around his neck.

It was nearly two hours later that the cab dropped her home, leaving her only an hour to get ready before Max arrived to take her to the dinner. She'd offered to get a taxi and meet him at the restaurant but he'd said no.

"Go in there without you beside me? No way."

She felt sorry for him but was also warmed by his words. They had travelled light years in their relationship in one afternoon and, though they hadn't talked marriage, Krystie was confident it was just a matter of time — they were in love. Everything she'd felt for Jacob seemed to pale by comparison. She had never felt this close to anyone before.

She'd already showered with Max and so she'd only to change and put on some makeup. She pulled out a red wool minidress that she would wear with her knee-high boots, the houndstooth coat and the gorgeous red felt cloche that Sinéad had made her for Christmas.

Krystie had just signed on to her laptop and was sitting staring at her messages when Sharon arrived home looking exhausted. "Hey, you're very late. I was getting worried."

"Stacy never showed up, so I had to look after her clients too."

While Sharon sat down and kicked off her boots Krystie went out to fetch her a glass of wine.

"Aren't you having one?"

"No, Max will be here any minute."

"Ah, yes, I forgot about the engagement dinner. Isn't it wonderful that they found romance again?" Sharon sighed.

"Yeah, great," Krystie said, although she found it hard to feel happy for Kieran after what Max had told her.

"How was your day?" Sharon sat back, wine in hand, tucking her feet underneath her.

"Pretty good." Krystie smiled and realised that it would be easier to carry tonight off if she thought about the afternoon in Max's arms rather than the terrible letter his aunt had left him. She wondered about that. Yes, Bridie had to tell them about her son but why tell them about the rest? Why now? She wasn't sure she bought the line about her going to her maker with a clear conscience.

"You look like the cat that got the cream. You've obviously made it up with Max." Sharon smiled.

"Yes," she said, thinking her face would split if she kept grinning like an idiot. "Everything is fine, more than fine. He loves me, Sharon, really loves me."

Sharon's eyes widened. "Has he proposed?"

Krystie threw back her head and laughed. "Of course not. Jeez, give us a chance! But let's say that we're as close as we could be and —" she looked back down at

350

her laptop — "my day just got even better. Our lovely actress not only got in touch but she sent out a tweet with the photo saying how Sinéad's hat was one of her all-time favourites."

Sharon's eyes widened. "Wow, that's fantastic!"

"*And* she put it on her Facebook page, too."

"Sinéad will be delighted."

"You know, I don't think I'll tell her."

Sharon frowned. "But why not?"

"It still may lead to nothing, so why get her hopes up?"

"Yeah, you're right."

Krystie went over to the window and peeked through the curtains to see if there was any sign of Max. "Oh, Sharon," she said, coming back to join her on the sofa, "I never thought I could be this happy."

Sharon put a hand on her arm, her eyes concerned. "Don't go rushing into things the way I did, Krystie."

"I'm not rushing into anything," Krystie protested.

"Good. I don't want you to be with Max just because he makes you feel safe. He should make you feel much more than that."

"He does," Krystie insisted. A horn honked outside and she gave Sharon a quick hug and stood up. "That will be him now. I'd better run."

Sharon caught her hand and looked into her eyes. "I'm happy for you, really. I just don't want any other man hurting you the way that Jacob did."

Krystie gave her an affectionate smile. "I know that, Shaz. Thank you."

CHAPTER
THIRTY-TWO

Sinéad was on edge. She had been for a while. The overwhelming silence from Philip bothered her and she felt uneasy around Dad. She wasn't quite sure why, but she felt angry with him. She looked into her eyes in the mirror as she prepared for the engagement dinner, and suddenly she knew exactly what was wrong. The reminiscing over old times at the funeral had brought back memories from childhood long forgotten. The circumstances of her mother's death particularly went around and around in her head making her feel uncomfortable and guilty. She escaped from that guilt by thinking of the role her father had played in it and how Bridie had protected him. At the funeral, when she'd seen all the love and support for him, the way he seemed to accept it as his due, that was when she had started to feel angry. She had been just a child, and so her mistakes could to some extent be excused, yet she still carried the burden. Dad seemed to suffer no such doubts or remorse. She loved him and she was glad that Beth had come into his life, but she found it hard to shirk these negative feelings.

Dylan walked in from the *en suite* in a towel and came to stand behind her. "What's wrong, Sinéad?" he said, kissing her neck.

She put a hand up to caress his cheek. "I just don't feel like going out tonight."

"Why?" he asked, wrapping his arms around her waist.

She rested her head back against his shoulder. "I'm just not in the mood for playing the adoring daughter."

"Playing? I've always thought you worshipped your dad."

"I do, but it doesn't mean I don't see his faults."

Dylan frowned. "You've never talked like this before. Are you upset that he's getting married? I know it's sudden but Beth seems great and he's been alone a long time. You can't begrudge him some company."

"I don't. I just don't like the way he's painted himself as a victim, as a sad, tragic figure."

"Has he?" Dylan seemed genuinely mystified. "There's no doubt that he's been a mess since Sheila disappeared."

"Yes, a mess but a selfish one. He's hardly bothered with Max or me. He just went into his shell and stayed there until a woman came along to look after him. He's always had someone to look after him."

"You sound so bitter."

She smiled but her heart felt so heavy. "I do, don't I?"

His eyes searched hers. "Why do I feel you're keeping a mountain of things locked up in there?" He tapped the side of her head.

She shook her head as tears filled her eyes.

"You know that you can tell me anything, Sinéad. I'm on your side, I always will be."

"Will you?" she asked, hoping it was true.

"You know I will. Can I ask you something?"

She nodded nervously.

"Did Bridie beat you?"

She smiled, relieved. "No, Dylan. She had a temper and was intolerant and we got the odd slap across the legs or backside but that's all. It was a hell of a shock at the time, though. Mum had never laid a finger on us. She was a bit of a hippie, I think, certainly very different from my friends' mothers. There were no real rules in our house. We ate what we wanted, stayed out playing until late, went to bed when we felt like it. Sometimes she'd wake us up to see a beautiful moon or because there was a good movie on TV. She was fun," Sinéad hesitated, "well, most of the time."

"What about your dad?"

"I don't remember him ever being that involved with us. He always seemed to be worried, especially about money. It was the only thing I remember them really fighting about."

"Have you ever talked to him about all of this, asked him about your mum?"

She laughed. "No. We don't talk about Mum with Dad, we never have."

"Never?" he asked, surprised

"Never. It was tough on Max. He was so little when she died. He always wanted to hear stories about her

354

but Dad would just change the subject or walk away and Bridie told us not to upset him."

"But that was a ridiculous thing to tell children. You were only nine?"

"Yes and Max had just turned seven. It sounds bad now but we just accepted it the way kids do. And Sheila was great. When we were alone she'd tell Max stories about when he was a baby and how much Mum loved him. I think there was as much fiction as fact in her stories but I didn't contradict her. The stories made Max happy and I enjoyed them too. I didn't want to forget my mother."

He pulled her tight against him and she rested her head on his chest, so glad that he was here, that, despite her weirdness, she hadn't scared him away.

"You are one very screwed-up family," he said, kissing her hair.

"We are," she murmured, closing her eyes.

"If we're going we'd better get a move on, Sinéad." He pulled back and looked at her. "Are we going?"

She sighed, then nodded. She would go for Max's sake. She and Sheila had protected him when he was little and she'd never been able to kick the habit. "Sure, let's go, but keep my glass filled!"

The others were already gathered at the bar in Roly's waiting for them. Sinéad smiled and hugged Krystie and her brother, pressed her cheek to Beth's, congratulating her, and gave her father a quick peck before turning back to the group. "Krystie, you look lovely." She smiled affectionately. Although they hadn't

355

even had time to discuss what they were wearing tonight, Krystie looked gorgeous and chic in the hat she'd made for her and a fabulous minidress almost the same shade as the wine she was drinking.

Krystie winked at her. "We're never off duty, right?"

"Right," Sinéad laughed. Despite her dark mood today she had put some time into doing her hair and makeup and wore a black headpiece to match her little black dress.

"You both look beautiful." Beth beamed at them. "You make me feel very dowdy."

"Rubbish, you never look dowdy." Krystie laughed. "And turquoise really suits you."

"You all look great," Kieran said, looking proud as punch.

Sinéad's eyes were drawn to Max, who was unusually quiet and seemed tense, very different from the man who'd been in the studio earlier. She watched Krystie put her hand on his arm, looking up at him with concerned eyes, and saw him patting it and giving her a reassuring smile. Sinéad tried to catch her brother's eye but his attention seemed to be on Beth, who had never been here before and was studying the menu and asking for recommendations.

"I usually have the bisque to start," Dylan offered.

"And you can't go wrong with the fillet of beef," her father added. "Have you been here before, Krystie?"

"Just once."

Was it Sinéad's imagination or was the girl's smile rather cool? Again, she tried to make eye contact with Max but he had turned to Dylan and they were talking about football. She moved slightly so she stood beside her father rather than facing him. She couldn't look at him, not tonight. She took a gulp of wine and raised her eyes to find Krystie looking at her with sad eyes. She raised a questioning eyebrow and got an embarrassed smile back in return before Krystie stuck her head over Beth's shoulder and pretended interest in the menu.

"I'm glad you like Beth, sweetheart, she's a good woman," her father said quietly.

Sinéad hesitated before nodding her agreement. "She is, Dad, you're lucky."

He put his arm around her and gave her a squeeze. "I've always been lucky. Sure, look at the wonderful family I have."

She was struggling to come up with a reply when Dylan appeared at her side.

"Our table's ready."

She gave him a grateful smile and took his outstretched hand. "This is going to be difficult," she murmured as they followed a waiter to the table. "Have you noticed how quiet Max is?"

"Yeah but I assumed he and Krystie had a tiff."

"On the contrary," Sinéad said. "I think he may well be on the point of popping the question himself." Perhaps that's why Max seemed jumpy, but it didn't explain why Krystie was cool with Dad — they'd hit it off from the first time they'd met. "Sit opposite me, Dylan," she whispered, sitting at the end of the table as the others approached, and then beckoned Krystie to sit beside her.

"No, the happy couple should be in the middle," Max said and held the chair next to Dylan for Beth.

"Oh, thank you very much, young man," she laughed.

Kieran took the seat next to Sinéad. "Isn't this nice?"

"Lovely," Sinéad said with a shiver, and shot Dylan a grateful look when he topped up her glass.

It was a relief that Beth was such a chatty woman, and Sinéad sat back and relaxed as Dylan and Krystie drew her out about her son and his family and her upcoming trip to see them in Australia.

"I can't believe you've never been on a plane," Krystie said.

"And you're starting with a long-haul flight," Dylan chuckled.

"Don't," Beth shuddered. "I'm nervous enough as it is."

"And it won't be her first flight," her dad said.

"It won't?" Beth looked at him.

"No," Kieran said with a delighted smile. "I'm taking you to Paris next weekend."

"What?" She spluttered her wine and dabbed her mouth with her napkin.

"Oh, please," Max said quietly, and Krystie's hand shot out to take his.

Sinéad watched him nod silently and take a drink but she felt her father stiffen.

"Something wrong, son?" he asked.

"No, Dad."

"Because if you've something to say —"

"I've nothing to say," Max said, looking him straight in the eye, "other than congratulations and I hope the two of you will have a long and happy life together."

He raised his glass and the others quickly joined in. Sinéad hesitated a moment but when his eyes met hers in a silent message she smiled at Beth, said congratulations and took a sip of her wine. There was an awkward silence for a moment, and then Krystie jumped in to fill it. "Have you decided when and where to have the ceremony?" she asked, directing the question at Beth.

Sinéad looked at the woman, whose eyes were locked on her father.

"We thought we should wait a while and see if Philip's investigators had any luck," he said quietly.

It was the first time her brother-in-law had been mentioned. Despite the awkwardness they seemed unified in not wanting him around at the moment.

"I wouldn't hold my breath," Sinéad couldn't help saying.

"Sinéad."

She looked up and saw the warning look in Max's eyes. "Sorry, Beth, Dad, that's not a topic for a celebration dinner."

Her dad patted her hand. "I understand, love. We're all anxious for news of your sister."

"I'm sure it won't be long now," Krystie said, leaning forward so she could see Sinéad. "Operation Manhattan will take care of that."

"Operation Manhattan?" Kieran looked from Krystie to Sinéad.

359

Krystie mouthed sorry as she realised she'd put her foot in it.

"I'm putting together a collection and targeting the big Manhattan stores," Sinéad explained. "I thought it might draw Sheila out."

"I think that's unlikely," Kieran said, looking amused.

Max banged down his glass. "Don't laugh at her. At least she's *trying* to do something to find Sheila."

"And what exactly is that supposed to mean, that I'm not?"

"Kieran, I'm sure Max didn't mean that," Beth said, and then turned her eyes on Sinéad. "I think it's a great idea, Sinéad."

Her father sat in silence looking slightly shocked that his fiancée had put him in his place.

Dylan reached for the bottle, but it was empty. "Anyone for more wine?" There was silence.

He cleared his throat. "Er, perhaps not."

After they had put Dad and Beth in a taxi they stood around outside the restaurant, Dylan and Krystie withdrawing a little to give brother and sister a moment alone.

Sinéad looked worriedly at Max. "What's wrong?"

He let out a long sigh. "We need to talk."

She bit her lip and nodded. "Come back to our place."

"Perhaps we should leave it until tomorrow . . ."

"No, Max, please, I won't sleep a wink."

"Okay," he agreed and, hailing a taxi, gestured to the others, "let's go."

360

CHAPTER
THIRTY-THREE

Back in Mount Merrion, Sinéad made coffee and organised drinks, and Max watched on in amusement when Krystie spied a chess set and challenged Dylan to a game. He leaned on the back of her chair as they settled down to play, and exchanged stunned looks with Dylan when she took his bishop after only six moves. Was there anything this girl couldn't do?

"I never knew you played," he said, impressed.

She grinned up at him. "There are a lot of things you don't know about me, darling."

Sinéad handed her brother a mug of coffee and a whiskey. "Let's take it inside."

Krystie gave him a reassuring smile and he nodded and followed his sister.

"So, what's up? I thought I was the loose cannon in the family." Sinéad settled down in her usual spot on the sofa.

He drained his glass and put it on the table before sitting down opposite her, cradling the mug of coffee between his hands. God, this was hard.

"Come on, Max, you're freaking me out here." Her smile wavered.

"I went to see the solicitor this morning about Bridie's estate."

"Oh, I'd forgotten all about that," she admitted.

"She'd left a letter for me." He looked into her eyes. "In it she says that Mum's death wasn't an accident."

"Oh."

He watched her and saw distress and panic in her eyes but no surprise. She knew. She already bloody knew. "What the hell is going on, Sinéad? You knew that?"

She stared back at him before nodding. "Yes." Her voice was barely a whisper.

"Oh Sinéad," he sighed. "Why would you keep something like that to yourself?"

"Bridie warned me not to tell."

He watched as both fear and guilt flashed across her face. He leaned forward on his knees. "Forget about Bridie, she's dead now. Please tell me what you know, Sinéad. She was my mum too."

She looked up at him and he gave her a nod of encouragement.

She started slowly, a tremor in her voice. "I woke up that night. Bridie's snoring usually woke me. Sheila and I were on bunk beds in a room with her and you shared a bed with Mum in the other room — do you remember that?"

He smiled remembering how he'd loved to snuggle in to his mother's warmth and breathe in her scent. "Yes, vaguely."

"Well, I couldn't get back to sleep that night so I thought I'd climb in with you two, but Mum wasn't

362

there. I didn't think too much about it but then I heard a noise and felt a breeze and so I went to have a look. Mum was standing at the door. She said she was going for a swim and that I should go back to sleep, and then she hugged me and left." Sinéad broke off, tears filling her eyes.

Max moved over onto the sofa and put his arm around her. "It's okay, take your time."

"I hated her swimming at night, so I decided to sit up and wait. After about an hour, when there was no sign of her, I got scared and I decided to wake Aunty Bridie." Sinéad dragged her hand across her eyes. "That's when I saw the note on the table."

Oh, Jesus. Max stared at her. "Did you read it?"

Sinéad nodded. "I couldn't make out most of it — her writing was terrible — but basically it was that Dad had broken her heart. That it was hard enough coping with all of his women but she couldn't live with the fact that one of them was having his baby."

"That's pretty much what Bridie's letter says," Max told her, but Sinéad was obviously reliving that night.

"I went and woke Aunty Bridie, showed her the note and told her what had happened. She took the note, told me not to mention it to anyone and said she would talk to me about it later. The important thing, she said, was to find Mum. You were still asleep but Sheila had woken when she heard the commotion. We wanted to go look for Mum too but Bridie made us stay with you and a neighbour came in to keep an eye on us."

Sinéad slid down onto the floor and laid her head back on the sofa. The tears rolled steadily and silently down onto the leather and Max felt his own eyes water. He took her hand and stroked it as she talked.

"We fell asleep and at some stage Bridie came to wake me and took me into the other room. She said that it didn't look like Mum was coming back and I cried and cried. She said that it was very sad but it would make everyone, especially Daddy, even sadder if they knew about the note. She said he might even get into trouble because of it and then he would be taken away from us as well."

"The evil bitch," Max said, filled with impotent fury. "How could she do that to a nine-year-old?"

Sinéad sighed. "I suppose, however misguided, she thought she was doing the right thing."

He stood up and started to pace the floor, pausing in the doorway. Krystie and Dylan seemed immersed in a second chess game. They looked very comfortable together and he felt a twinge of jealousy until Krystie turned and saw him and her face lit up. He smiled and then turned back to his sister. "What about this other woman and the baby?"

She shook her head. "No idea. Any time I asked Bridie, she said I was to put it out of my mind, and she warned that if Dad knew that *we* knew he might go and live with his new family. She made me swear not to tell anyone, not even Sheila." Sinéad sighed. "I don't know if you remember, but she was always telling us not to bother Daddy about anything. She said if we wanted anything we should always come to her."

364

He nodded. Sinéad was right. He remembered hearing those words all through his childhood. "How could she do it?"

"Dad was hardly blameless, Max. He let it happen. God, I think every day for that first year I was afraid that he wouldn't come home to us, that he'd go to live with his new family."

Max dragged a hand through his hair. "I can understand you worrying about that as a child or even a teenager, but why didn't you confront him since?"

"I loved him, I still do, Max, and he didn't leave us, did he? I thought about saying something from time to time but it wouldn't bring Mum back and our relationship would never recover from a conversation like that." She looked up at him. "Will you please stop pacing — you're giving me a headache."

"Sorry." He dropped into an armchair.

She gave him a weary smile. "Me too. As for telling him about Mum's note, I thought it would be very cruel after all that time to tell him, or any of you. I wonder . . ."

He looked up. "What?"

She was frowning. "Why did Bridie decide to tell you now? What was the point?"

He thought about that. The only reason he could think of was that she wanted to die with a clear conscience. "She said that she needed to set the record straight before she died. Perhaps she felt she had let Mum down by covering up Dad's part in her death."

Sinéad looked at him. "Or perhaps she just wanted to get even with Dad."

After they'd waved off Max and Krystie, Sinéad fell into Dylan's arms, and though she felt exhausted, she told him everything.

"Why didn't you tell me before, Sinéad?" he asked when she was finished.

She shook her head. "I haven't spoken about it for twenty years, Dylan, why start now?"

"So if Bridie hadn't died you wouldn't have said anything?" Dylan looked at her, incredulous.

"Probably not."

He leaned in to kiss her. "I don't know whether I feel impressed, shocked or horrified — probably a little of all three."

She frowned. "Why are you impressed?"

"You must be a very strong person to have come through all that and —" his lips twitched — "still remain relatively normal."

She laughed. "I don't know about that."

"You're amazing and I love you."

"I love you too, Dylan," she said, and nestled into the safety and comfort of his embrace.

Krystie put her hand on Max's thigh as the taxi took them back to his apartment in Donnybrook. "Are you okay?"

Max squeezed it and smiled. "I'm fine, just a little distracted." He'd given her a brief outline of what Sinéad had told him and then lapsed into silence as he relived the conversation. "Sorry, tonight can't have been much fun for you."

"There's no need to apologise. Do you think Sinéad will be okay?"

Max sighed. He had a new insight into his sister's moodiness now and felt sick at all she had gone through alone. How hard it must have been for her to keep everything to herself, especially from Sheila. "I hope that finally talking about it helped."

"I'm sure it did."

He lifted her hand and kissed her palm. "Krystie, move in with me."

She looked startled. "Where did that come from?"

"I don't know. I suppose it's been such a hell of a day that it's made me realise how lucky I am. Life is short, Krystie, and I love you and I want you with me."

She looked down, a crease in her brow. "I don't know."

"Don't you love me?" He smiled but he was anxious to hear the reply.

"Of course I do." She rolled her eyes.

"So why are you hesitating?"

"Well, for a start, it's too soon, Max," she said. She leaned over to kiss him and smiled into his eyes. "I want to date you more before we take that step. I'm also working very hard at the moment and I'm afraid that if I lived with you it might kill me."

"I would find it hard to keep my hands off you, but I would never risk your health, Krystie."

She laughed. "Not intentionally, but you know we wouldn't be able to keep our hands off each other. And —" her smile wavered — "there's something else, too."

"I'm listening."

She sighed. "Well, every time I'm in your bedroom, in your bed, I'm going to think of the women that have been there before me."

"There haven't been that many," he protested.

"I believe you but even if it was only Natalie I would still always be thinking about you and her together."

"I see." He chewed his lip. It was a fair point. He'd feel exactly the same. Just the thought of her being with Jacob, a man he'd never even seen, made him feel ridiculously jealous. "There's only one thing for it," he said as the cab pulled up outside his apartment block. "I'll have to put the apartment on the market and we'll get a place of our own."

Her eyes widened as she stared at him. "Seriously?"

He paid the driver and helped her out of the car. "Seriously." He cupped her face in his hands and kissed her. "In the meantime, can you cope if we sleep in the spare bedroom?"

"Sleep?" she grinned.

"Among other things," he laughed.

"In the meantime, Max, I'd be quite happy on the sofa," she murmured pulling his mouth down to hers.

Sheila's stomach churned as the plane dipped and she heard the landing gear go down, and it had nothing to do with travel sickness. She was terrified and the closer they got to Ireland, to Dublin, the greater her terror grew. The thought of facing her brother, Sinéad and even her dad made her feel nauseous.

Karl put his hand over hers. "Are you okay?"

She swallowed. "Not really."

His fingers tightened. "I'll be with you every step of the way."

"How can you be so calm?" she asked, envious of his composure.

"I've waited all my life for this, Sheila. It hasn't worked out quite the way I wanted but at least I will know everything there is to know."

She said nothing, staring out as the lights of Dublin rose up to meet them. Karl was right. However hard this was, at least the final showdown would put an end to all the secrets. She had walked away from her family once and, if she had to do so again, at least she knew Zach would be waiting for her. She smiled at the memory of his last text before they boarded the aircraft: "Go with an open mind, listen to what they have to say and then kick ass! I'll be waiting. x."

Zach always made her laugh and nothing ever seemed so bad, no problem seemed insurmountable with him in her life. She wished he was with her now but knew it would have been insensitive to take him along and complicate an already delicate situation. Tears brimmed in her eyes as she thought of the last time she'd seen Philip, and what a difficult time that was for her. How would she feel when they met again? How would he?

The seatbelt sign came on and the steward told them they would be on the ground in minutes. She reached for Karl's hand and clutched it.

"*Que sera, sera.*" He smiled down at her as they touched down. "Welcome home, Sheila."

CHAPTER
THIRTY-FOUR

On days like today Philip wished he smoked. He had been bouncing from meeting to meeting for three days with little time to eat and, when he eventually fell into bed exhausted at night, he couldn't sleep. His heart thumped in his chest, his stomach was in knots and when he did nod off he seemed to always wake up in a sweat.

He'd told Barry he wouldn't need him the next day, as he had some personal business to take care of. The driver had looked surprised. No wonder, as it was the first day off Philip had taken since Sheila's disappearance.

Once inside, he went straight to the drinks cabinet in the corner of the dining room and poured himself a large whiskey.

"Fuck you, Bridie," he roared and for a moment savoured his words as they echoed around the empty room. He rarely cursed and when he did it was under his breath. He'd learned from watching his fellow politicians make their mistakes and he saw it as a badge of honour that he never raised his voice, swore or drank more than two glasses of wine in public. But he wasn't in public now. He poured another glass and took it through to the living room. Were Sheila here, she'd be insisting he eat. He wasn't used to drinking spirits on an empty stomach. She'd cook him something and let him rant and he would feel better; she was always able to calm him. He let his head fall back against the sofa. What the hell had he been thinking? Why had he ever thought he'd get away with it? He'd worked so hard and, now it was finally paying off, he would probably lose everything. No. Bullshit. He sat up, suddenly alert. He had worked his way up from nothing, he was only thirty-four and, if he had to, he could start again. He would take whatever was coming to him and then worry about the future.

His grim determination not to go down without a fight forced him out of the chair and into the kitchen, where he put on a pot of coffee, made some thick cheese sandwiches and put them into the toaster. Then he went to get his briefcase and brought it into the kitchen. Mindful that constituents sometimes dropped in, he ran up and changed into casual trousers and a heavy-knit pullover. He slicked back his hair, brushed his teeth to get rid of the smell of alcohol and went back downstairs.

At the table he opened his briefcase, took out a pad and pen and, ignoring the department reports and constituents' letters — as he had for four days — he took out the one slim file, the contents of which would dictate his future.

He had talked in confidence to his GP, who in turn had arranged an appointment with a psychiatrist.

That was an experience he wouldn't forget in a hurry. He had gone in, all businesslike, and explained the situation, couched in the language his doctor had suggested. He didn't want or need anything official, not yet. He just wanted to know what to expect. But the woman had been very perceptive and before he knew what was going on he was talking about his feelings. He cut it short there and then and she hadn't seemed surprised, but handed him her card with her mobile number scribbled on it.

"I think you are underestimating what lies ahead of you. If you want to talk about it, just call."

He felt afraid, wondering what she had seen when she looked into his eyes, terrified of what he had unknowingly revealed to her, scared stiff of what he might say if he stayed any longer. He'd grabbed the card and, mumbling his thanks, he'd fled.

The meeting with the senior member of the Garda Siochána had been much easier. Philip had known the policeman long before he had gone into politics and the man had seen and heard it all. Philip presented him with a "hypothetical" situation and was very relieved to hear that special allowances were usually made where a person's mental health was at risk.

What Philip couldn't prepare for or control was the reaction of the Fields family. That was in the lap of the gods.

Sinéad felt she'd only put her head on the pillow when the phone rang, rousing her, but a quick look at the clock showed it was almost eight. Damn, she should be in work. Why hadn't Dylan woken her? But she knew the answer. Despite being exhausted, she'd got little sleep since she'd opened her heart to Max. She found herself going over and over the past, and especially that last night in the mobile home, when her mother had walked out of her life for ever. Rubbing the sleep from her eyes with one hand, she grabbed the phone with the other.

"Hello?" As she answered, she saw the note on the pillow next to her from Dylan: "I called Krystie and told her you wouldn't be in today. Sleep! xxx."

She smiled. She had no intention of taking the full day off, but perhaps the morning.

"Sinéad?"

"Max?"

"Yeah. Listen, I just got a text from Philip. He has some news."

She clutched the phone, fully awake now. "What?"

"He wouldn't discuss it on the phone. He wants us to go over."

"To the house?"

"Yes."

"Okay," she said, wondering why the mystery.

"Want me to pick you up?"

"Yeah, that would be great, Max, thanks."

"See you in about an hour."

She was standing outside the apartment block when Max drove in and he was already pulling back out again as she put on her seatbelt. "What do you think this is about?" she asked, searching her brother's face.

"I have no idea but he obviously didn't want to go into it on the phone or meet us in a public place, so I assume the investigators have found out something."

"It has to be good news, right?"

He gave a wry smile. "Exactly what *is* good news in a situation like this? I suppose it would be if it was confirmed that she's alive."

"He could tell us that on the phone, couldn't he?"

"We'll be there in a few minutes and all will be revealed. Calm down, Sinéad." He patted her hand.

Philip paused before opening the door to smooth back his hair and take a deep breath. He couldn't remember ever feeling so nervous, not on his wedding day, not the day after the elections when the votes were being tallied, not even the first time he walked into government buildings and took his seat in the Dáil. He cleared his throat and grimaced. He'd thought he'd broken that nervous habit. He opened the door and smiled. "Sinéad, Max, thanks for coming."

She looked at him as she stepped into the hall. "Is everything okay?"

"Everything's fine, Sinéad, come through." He walked into the sitting room and gave his wife a reassuring smile before standing to one side.

Sinéad came to a stop beside him and gasped as her sister stood up. "Sheila!"

"Hello, Sinéad." Sheila's smile was nervous.

Sinéad threw herself into her twin's arms and Sheila held her tight, her wet cheek pressed against her sister's.

"Sheila, Sheila, Sheila," Sinéad sobbed into her hair, and then she started to pummel her back with her fists. "I hate you, I hate you."

Sheila winced as the blows got harder but when Philip went to help her she waved him away.

Finally, Max came over and gently pulled them apart. "Welcome home, Sheila," he said as Sinéad dropped onto the sofa and buried her face in her hands.

Sheila let out a sob as her brother hugged her. "It's so good to see you, Max."

He stroked her hair. "And you, Sheila."

She stepped back and pulled out a tissue to wipe away her tears, and Philip caught her eye. "I'll leave you to talk."

She went to him. "Thanks, Philip, for everything."

He hugged her close. God, how he'd missed her. He pulled away and looked into her eyes. "Will you be okay?"

"Yes but . . ." Her eyes searched his. "Are you sure about this? It can wait if you want —"

"No." It had taken Philip days to come to a decision and if he backed down now he was afraid he would chicken out altogether. "They're family, they should know." He touched her cheek and smiled. It was so good to see her again and with her support he knew that he would get through this.

"Shout if you need me," he whispered and, with a wave at the others, he left the room.

Sheila looked over at her sister. She still had her face in her hands and her shoulders shook occasionally, yet she was completely silent. Sheila ached for her; she had caused this pain. Max sat rubbing her back and whispering into her ear. Sheila felt like an outsider. It was strange to be here in the same room with them and yet feel further apart than ever. Would they be able to understand what she no longer really understood herself?

Max was the one to break the silence. "Why did you go, Sheila?"

"There were a couple of reasons," she started. "When I was going through Bridie's papers I found out something about Mum's death . . ." She hesitated.

"It's okay, I know everything," he assured her, and then looked at Sinéad. "At least I think I do."

"I found her suicide note and —" Sheila looked from him to her twin — "your letter."

"What letter?" Max looked at Sinéad. "So, I *don't* know everything?"

"You do," Sinéad assured him. "I'd forgotten the letter. I'd tried a few times to talk to Bridie about everything but she'd just close me down, so I wrote to her. Not that it made any difference. She said it was grown-up stuff and that I must just put it out of my mind. I'm surprised she even kept it."

"Why didn't you tell me what happened? How could you keep it from me all these years?" Sheila demanded, frustrated by Sinéad and angry with Bridie.

Silent tears coursed down Sinéad's cheeks. "I was scared. Bridie said she'd have me packed off to boarding school if I didn't keep my mouth shut."

376

Sheila shook her head, feeling riddled with guilt. "How could she do that to a child? I suppose when I was reading I forgot how young we were when this all happened. I just felt hurt and stupid, as if I was the butt of some cruel joke. You knew all this time what kind of man Dad was, and, not only did you let him get away with it, you fawned all over him. How could you, Sinéad? I can understand you doing it as a child, but five years ago, ten years ago, why didn't you do something? Why didn't you tell me then?"

Sinéad sighed and shook her head. "As we got older and everything was okay and everyone was happy, I just locked it all away and tried to forget."

Sheila looked at her sister feeling sick when she thought of how her father and aunt had behaved. "My God, how they both messed with our heads. I knew you didn't really like Bridie but I thought you were just missing Mum and hated how tough she was by comparison. I did my best to protect you and Max, to be a buffer between you. I spent my time promising Bridie we wouldn't upset Dad, while promising him that I would mind you. He went on and on at me about how sensitive you were, that you were missing Mum the most and that as your sister and twin it was my duty to look after you. He even pressured me into doing the design course because he was worried you would get into trouble if I wasn't around to look after you —"

"Hang on just a second — that is bullshit!" Sinéad protested. "You wanted to do that course as much as I did."

Sheila held her gaze. "No, Sinéad, trust me, I didn't. And let me tell you something else, I hated making fucking hats."

Sinéad shook her head in bewilderment. "That's not true."

"It *is* true and you know it and you've always known it," Sheila said, Zach's words ringing in her ears. She'd come here to say her piece and to get answers, too, and, no matter how hard it was, she had to do that. She continued more gently, though. "Think about it. All the time you and Mum were messing around with material and buttons and bows, what was I doing?"

Sinéad just stared at her, either unable or unwilling to answer.

"You were painting," Max said, running a hand through his hair. "You loved to paint."

Sheila gave her brother a grateful smile.

Sinéad's expression hardened. "I thought you'd grown out of that. You never painted after . . ."

Sheila raised an eyebrow. "After Mum died? You're right. Because then it was, 'Oh, Sheila, Sinéad needs help. Sinéad seems lonely. Sinéad's missing Mum, they always used to do that together.' On and on and on it went, but you know what? I didn't mind. I loved you more than painting and I was always happy when I was with you. But making it my career because you were making it yours? That was damn hard. College bored me witless. I did enjoy the challenge of setting up the business. It wasn't what I would have chosen to do, but how many people get to do something they love for a living? So I was content. Until I found out that not only had Dad driven Mum to kill herself but that my sister knew all about it. I couldn't take that, not on top of . . ." She trailed off.

Max looked at her through narrowed eyes. "On top of what, Sheila? What else? Come on now, no more secrets."

She nodded, stood up and walked to the window. "I never should have married Philip. It was a mistake. He was my friend and I loved him, but I wasn't in love with him and I was pretty sure that he wasn't *in* love with me either." She heard Sinéad's intake of breath but didn't turn round. "It wasn't a problem," she insisted, but how could she explain to them that Philip's easy undemanding company was a rest after living with the madness of the Fields household? "We were happy and we had fun together. It was a good life. And, looking at some couples we knew who were supposedly in love but seemed to fight half the time, it seemed to me that our marriage was built on a much more solid foundation." She turned to face them. "I had no intention of telling you this but Philip insisted. He wanted you to know that he was partly to blame for me leaving." She took a break and a breath before she felt able to carry on. "Just before Bridie went into the home Philip told me that he thought he was gay."

"Jesus!" Sinéad's hand flew to her mouth.

"If I'm completely honest I'd had my suspicions, but I just blocked it out, refused to acknowledge it. Yes, it was a shock, of course it was, but as I had never really been in love in the first place I wasn't heartbroken. Philip was very upset, though. He didn't know how to

379

handle it. He came from such a religious family with very strong views and he knew that he would be completely rejected by them if he came out. And he was sure that he would lose me, too. But after I'd had a chance to think about it I realised that I didn't want a separation. We still loved each other and he assured me there was no one else in his life, and there certainly wasn't anyone in mine. So we agreed we'd stay together unless that changed."

Her brother and sister sat in stunned silence, entranced, and they hadn't heard the worst of it yet. She swallowed back tears as she remembered that traumatic day. "It happened sooner than either of us expected. The day that I was clearing out Bridie's house and found the papers, well, I was devastated." She met Sinéad's eyes. "It was bad enough finding out about poor Mum but I felt so betrayed by you, Sinéad."

"But —"

"I know. It was irrational. But it's the way that I felt. I came home still reeling in shock, longing to talk to Philip about it, and when I walked in he was with another man."

"The bastard, I'll kill him," Max said, his eyes going to the door.

"No," Sheila said hurriedly. "Sorry, that came out wrong. They weren't *doing* anything. They were just in here, having a drink, but I could feel the electricity between them and the tension in the room. They had done nothing but they acted like guilty schoolboys and I knew that Philip had fallen in love. I was glad for him, honestly, I was," she added when she saw the

380

expression of disbelief on her brother's face, "and I could have coped with Philip moving on at any other time. But on top of Bridie's bombshell it was the final straw."

There was silence in the room for a moment, and then Max broke it.

"That's awful, Sheila, and I can completely understand that you were devastated. But, if you wanted nothing more to do with any of us, why not just say good luck, goodbye, I'm off? Why did you let us believe you'd killed yourself? Were you deliberately trying to hurt us?"

She flinched, her eyes filling with tears as she remembered that moment in front of the Monet painting when she had realised the enormity of what she had done. "I didn't want to hurt you, Max. You just got caught in the crossfire. I was angry with Sinéad, though, and I didn't see any reason why I should continue to live her dream. All my life since Mum died I'd put her first and I decided it was time to put me first. But the only one I wanted to punish was Dad, for leaving us to Bridie's tender mercies, for playing with my life and for driving Mum to take her own life. I couldn't stop thinking of the night she drowned. It was like a movie that I kept replaying over and over in my head. It drove me crazy and I wanted Dad to suffer the way Mum had. Pretending to drown myself seemed like a good way to achieve that at the time. I'm sorry. It was a cruel, horrible thing to do. I didn't think it through, consider the consequences. If I had I would never have gone through with it. Philip was furious with me."

Max's eyes widened in realisation. "Philip knew you were still alive? He's been keeping in touch with you, hasn't he?"

Shit, she'd walked herself into that one. Her brother was too bloody smart. She looked steadily into his eyes. "Of course he didn't know, Max. Have you any idea the trouble he'd be in if he withheld information like that from the authorities?"

He fixed her with that piercing gaze and then gave a reluctant nod.

"I came to my senses a few weeks ago and I made contact with him and told him everything and that I was thinking of coming home. So Philip spent the last few days paving the way with the authorities for my reappearance. His office will send out a press release in the morning and we will appear outside the house tomorrow evening before the six o'clock news and make a short statement. It would be great if you were all here too but I'll understand if you don't want that. But you must realise that if they get an inkling that there's a rift in the family, they won't leave any of us alone until they find out what it is."

"So what will your story be?" Sinéad asked.

"That I buckled under the pressure of the business and had a breakdown. I will go into a nursing home in a couple of days and spend some time there under the care of a psychiatrist."

Sinéad looked at her in dismay. "But you're not mad, you don't need treatment — do you?"

"I'm fine, it's just something that was suggested to Philip. Apparently, the press will back off a little if I'm under medical supervision. But I think I'd like to talk it all through with a professional now, to be honest. When I look back I feel shocked and a bit frightened that I did what I did, and I'd like to try to understand it."

Sinéad shivered. "This is surreal."

"What about the police?" Max asked.

"They already know I'm back and I'm going down to the station later to make a statement."

Sinéad frowned. "A statement? Why?"

"I may face charges for wasting the time of the police and emergency services," Sheila explained. "They could even ask me to foot the bill of the search but Philip thinks it's unlikely. Apparently, the courts are sympathetic when dealing with cases like mine."

"And everything is okay between you and Philip?" Max asked.

Sheila smiled. "Yes, everything is absolutely fine."

"I think I may have met his boyfriend," Sinéad murmured.

"Promise me you'll say nothing," Sheila begged her sister. "He says he's going to come out but I think he's rushing into it and I certainly don't see why he needs to make a public statement about his private life. I'm trying to persuade him to hold off for a while."

"I'm amazed that you're still so close after all that's happened," Max marvelled.

"We'll always be close, Max. Philip is a truly wonderful man."

They sat in silence for a moment and Sheila waited, wondering if the worst was over but afraid to hope.

Max looked at her. "You know that Bridie passed away?"

"Yes, Philip told me," she said honestly. They didn't need to know that it was the day the woman died. "I'm not sure how to feel about that now. I didn't realise how much she put you through, Sinéad. Oh, I wish you'd told me."

Sinéad's eyes filled with tears. "Me too."

Nervously, Sheila sat down beside her sister but didn't dare touch her. "I know she screwed us up but I don't think it was out of any kind of malice. She must have been pretty screwed up herself."

Max looked over at her. "There's something else you don't know, Philip doesn't know, even Dad doesn't know yet. I only found out myself yesterday. Bridie has a son."

"I do know, Max. I found lots of paperwork about him in the same box I found Mum's suicide note. It was very sad. There were letters from him that Bridie had never even opened. It was reading about him that really resulted in me going to Manhattan."

Sinéad frowned. "Why?"

"That's where he lives and I suppose I felt I had something in common with him. I had no one and he had no one."

"But that was never true," Sinéad said, reaching for her hand.

Sheila clung to it. "I know that now, Sinéad, but, like I say, I wasn't thinking straight."

Max looked at her. "Was there anything in the papers to indicate who the father was?"

"No."

"Bridie rushed off to the States before taking her exams," Sinéad said excitedly. "She must have been pregnant and was sent off to avoid embarrassment and to get her away from the boyfriend."

"That's exactly what happened," Max confirmed and looked back at Sheila. "Did you have any luck tracing her son?"

She smiled. "It only took three phone calls."

"Oh my God, you've met him?" Sinéad asked. "What's he like?"

Sheila smiled and stood up. "Come and find out for yourself."

CHAPTER
THIRTY-FIVE

"Max, Sinéad, meet your cousin, Karl." Sheila opened the door of the kitchen and stood back. Sinéad felt as if she were dreaming. First Sheila appears out of thin air and now the cousin, that she'd only just discovered she had, was sitting at the kitchen table drinking coffee with Philip. Karl stood up and smiled. A giant of a man, somewhere in his forties she guessed, with blond hair and eyes the same pale blue as her brother's, he was casually but expensively dressed and when he smiled she saw a trace of Bridie in his expression.

"Lovely to finally meet you both," he said but she saw his eyes go past her to her twin as if checking on her. She liked that.

"Lovely to meet you too, K."

"Sorry?"

Sinéad shook her head and smiled. "It's a long story."

"You people have a lot of catching up to do and I should get some work done," Philip said, and stood up. Immediately Sheila went to him.

Sinéad watched as he put his arms around her sister and smiled down with obvious affection.

"Will you be okay?" he asked quietly.

"Fine," she said, and hugged him.

Max put a hand on his shoulder as he went to leave the room. "Thank you for bringing her home to us, Philip."

Philip smiled at him. "I think you really have Karl to thank for that."

Sinéad sat down at the table, her eyes shooting between the sister she thought she'd lost and the cousin she didn't know she had. They drank a gallon of coffee and then opened the wine. And with every minute that passed she felt herself growing closer to her twin. There were still questions, there was still hurt, but only time alone together would sort that out. They would get there eventually. As if reading her thoughts, Sheila turned and smiled into her eyes and Sinéad instinctively reached for her sister's hand. Sheila returned the pressure, her eyes bright with tears.

"I couldn't believe it when I opened the door and Sheila told me who she was," Karl was saying in his low, musical drawl. "I'd given up hope of ever tracking down my family."

"I thought I'd cleared out everything in Bridie's house but when I was doing a final check I found a box at the back of her wardrobe with her other private papers," Sheila said, taking up the story. "She had obviously forgotten that it was there."

"When did you first try to make contact with Bridie?" Max asked Karl.

"When I was about nineteen," Karl said. "It took a couple of years but when the agency finally found her she refused to allow them to give me her address. She didn't want contact of any sort."

Sinéad's heart went out to him. "Rejected twice, that's so sad."

Sheila shook her head in exasperation but her eyes twinkled with amusement. "I see you're as diplomatic as ever. Remember that Bridie was only a child herself when she gave birth. She was probably forced to give him up. Can you imagine the scandal it would have been back then to get pregnant at only fifteen?"

"Sinéad's saying nothing I haven't thought a thousand times myself," Karl said. "I suppose I'll never know the full truth unless I can trace my father."

Sinéad saw Max's expression cloud. "You okay?"

"Yeah, sure. Tell Karl about the diary."

"Oh, right, it went completely out of my mind." Sinéad smiled, realising that this would be the best news she could give Karl. "Your mum had this diary for years where she kept notes on anything and everything. But she also wrote some poetry and it's all dedicated to K — to you, Karl."

"Or my father," Karl pointed out.

"Did Bridie name you?" Max asked.

"Yes."

"And is your birthday May thirteenth?"

Karl stared at him. "Yes, it is."

Max smiled. "She has it written in the diary along with all the other family birthdays."

Sinéad smiled. "You are K."

Sheila reached for Karl's hand. "You see, she did love you."

388

He nodded, his eyes filling up. "Excuse me."

Sinéad sighed as he left the kitchen. "Poor man."

"At least now he has some answers," Max said.

"I wonder if Dad knows who Karl's father was," Sinéad said. "Surely Mum would have told him."

"If she knew," Sinéad pointed out.

"Mum knew," Max said. "Bridie said so in her letter to me but I don't know if either of them told Dad."

"We have a lot of questions for him, don't we?" Sheila said, her mouth settling in a hard line. "I think it's time he told us the truth, all of it."

Back home, Sinéad curled up on the sofa, exhausted. She should have gone into work — she knew Krystie was looking for her, but she couldn't think about hats today. There was so much to get her head around that she felt dizzy. The pieces of the puzzle were slowly dropping into place but she couldn't figure out why Bridie had kept her letter and the suicide note. Did she want them to find out what their father had done once she was dead and gone and could no longer be embarrassed or shamed by the family secret? It had never struck her that there was animosity between the two. Though they certainly weren't close, there seemed to be an understanding, a respect. Had it all been an act?

She thought of the teenage Bridie discovering she was pregnant and being packed off to America, terrified and abandoned. How cruel and hard her grandparents must have been. It was sad that Bridie couldn't bring herself to meet Karl. He was a man any mother would

389

be proud of and her life would have been richer for having him in it.

The door opened and she looked up and smiled as Dylan walked in, his face creased in concern. "Hey."

"I got home as soon as I could," he said, coming to sit beside her without even taking off his coat. "How are you?"

"Shell-shocked, but fine."

He touched her cheek, his eyes full of compassion. "And Sheila?"

"She's probably down at the Garda station now. There are procedures that have to be followed. Philip's holding a press conference tomorrow, where we'll play happy families and say how thrilled we are that she's safe and well and ask for privacy."

"He'll have a hard time getting that," Dylan said.

"Oh, I don't know. He's really taken control of the situation, and he's being so kind to Sheila. I feel lousy when I think of all the bad thoughts I've had about him."

He stroked her thigh. "You're human, Sinéad. How do you feel now about your sister?"

"Better," Sinéad admitted. "I had no idea that Dad and Bridie gave her such a tough time and made her feel totally responsible for me. It's funny, people always think twins are so close and can read each other's mind, but neither of us had a clue what the other was going through." Tears brimmed in her eyes at the thought.

"You'll be closer now than ever before." Dylan hugged her close.

She clung to him. "I hope so."

390

"Does your dad know he's having visitors later?"

"Max told him we were coming over, that we needed to talk. He wanted to make sure that Beth wouldn't be there. He didn't tell him Sheila would be with us."

"It's going to be one hell of a shock to open the door and see her standing there. I hope you don't give him a heart attack."

"I'm not sure she'd care. She's very bitter. We all are."

"Do you want me to drop you over?" he asked. "You're probably going to need a stiff drink or three to get through this showdown."

"No, Max and Sheila are collecting me, but I don't think I need or want alcohol tonight, Dylan, just answers."

"Shit, shit, shit, what do I do now?" Krystie cried, flinging down the phone and staring in frustration at her laptop.

"What's wrong?"

She whirled around to see Ellen in the doorway. "Jeez, you scared the hell out of me."

"Sorry but I come bearing gifts." Ellen put a coffee and an egg-mayonnaise sandwich at her elbow. "We haven't seen you all day, so we figured you'd forgotten to eat."

Krystie looked at her watch and sighed. "I did, thank you."

"So why were you turning the air blue when I walked in?" Ellen asked, sitting up on the table and watching as Krystie unwrapped her sandwich.

"You won't believe it, Ellen, I can't believe it."

"What? Tell me. Oh, my God, you've won the lottery!"

Krystie laughed. "Better than that: Sinéad's just been contacted on Twitter by one of the organisers of New York Fashion Week."

"What? No way. I didn't know she was even *on* Twitter."

"She isn't, really. I set it up. She thinks it's a waste of time, but —" Krystie grinned and turned the screen to face Ellen — "she's wrong."

Ellen read the message. "Oh, wow. No, Krystie, this is too good to be true. It has to be some nutjob playing a cruel joke."

"It's not. I checked out the email address and it's legit."

Ellen threw her arms around her. "Oh, Krystie, well done! Have you told Sinéad?"

"No." Krystie sighed in exasperation. "We work side by side every day and the one time I need to talk to her she's not here and she's not answering her messages."

"Is it that urgent? You'll see her tomorrow, right?"

Krystie rested her chin on her fist. "It may be too late. These people act as if they're doing you a favour by even making contact, and, to an extent, that's true. If she doesn't get back to them soon, they'll move on to the next person on the list. And if she goes for it —"

Ellen looked at her in disbelief. "What do you mean, if?"

"Yeah, well, exactly."

"When is the show?"

Krystie turned terrified eyes on her. "Three weeks."

"Holy shit! Call her again, right now, and tell her it's urgent."

"You're right, I will." Krystie picked up her phone and called her boss. She looked at Ellen. "It's gone straight to her voice-mail."

"Leave a message."

She nodded. "Sinéad, it's Krystie. I know you're busy but I have something really important I need to talk to you about ASAP. Please call. Bye." She hung up and started to prowl the room like a caged animal. "We can't miss this opportunity, Ellen, this is huge."

"Life changing, huh?"

"Yes. Apart from a springboard to finding distribution in Manhattan, if Sheila *is* there and *is* following the fashion scene, she would be sure to hear about it."

"In that case, Krystie, you're going to impersonate your boss."

Krystie stared at her. "I can't do that!"

Ellen crossed her arms. "Sinéad wants to find Sheila more than anything else in the world. If she were here what would she do?"

"Call them," Krystie said, and reached for the phone.

"That's my girl. I'd better get back to work. Let me know how you get on."

After Krystie had talked to the receptionist from hell and been put on hold for twenty minutes she was finally put through to a coordinator, who gave her instructions that she scribbled down furiously.

"Honey, I don't know who you know or how you managed to pull this off but you better make the most of it," the guy said. "This is one hell of an opportunity."

"Believe me, I know. Is there any particular style you think we should go for? We have many designs but at the moment they're aimed at the European market."

"Bring everything you've got and decide when you get here," he advised, "but I believe straw is big this year."

"Thank you so much," Krystie said excitedly and, after putting down the phone, she danced around the room. "Oh, my God, we're going to New York Fashion Week!" She sat down again at her laptop and went on Skype, whooping when she saw that Sandy was online. She put on her headphones and dialled.

"Krystie, hey!" Sandy smiled and waved at her. "I was just thinking about you. I can't believe I'll be in Ireland in six weeks. I'm so excited."

"I might see you before then," Krystie said, although she realised that Sinéad might well go alone. "But I need your help, and Phyllis's, too."

"Phyllis? Are you looking for your job back?"

"No way, I'm a milliner now, Sandy," she said, proud just saying that. "I need you guys to do a little research for me. Sinéad's been invited to take part in New York Fashion Week." She pulled off her headphones as Sandy shrieked.

"OMG! You're kidding me, right?"

Krystie grinned at her. "I'm not, and please don't scream again or you're going to deafen me."

"This is so exciting!"

"It is, but do me a favour. Ask Phyllis if she has any contacts that can give us the lowdown on what to expect. I don't want us going in there looking like novices."

"Oh, I wish I could be there," Sandy wailed.

"Me too, but you know only buyers can get tickets. They're like gold dust."

"I'll talk to Phyllis as soon as I get to work. She'll be thrilled. She always had a soft spot for you."

Krystie laughed. "Yeah, sure, that's why she fired me. Look, I'd better go. I have a lot to do."

"Okay, Irish, get to it, and remember me when you're famous." Sandy waved.

Krystie blew her a kiss. "You bet!"

CHAPTER
THIRTY-SIX

"Max!" Krystie could have cried with relief when she looked up from her sewing to see him standing there. She turned down the radio before standing to embrace him.

"Ask me how my day's been," he murmured into her hair.

She stood back and took in his pale face and weary expression. "What's happened now?"

"Later," he muttered and, sitting down in her chair, he pulled her onto his lap.

Much later, Krystie slipped downstairs and, when she returned with coffee, he was walking out of the bathroom straightening his tie. "Feeling better?" she asked, putting down the cups.

His arms encircled her waist. "Much," he said, and kissed her before settling down in Sinéad's chair and reaching for the coffee.

"I wish you weren't going over to your dad's tonight. You've all been through quite enough shocks today. And wouldn't it be better to hold the press conference before you confront him? Afterwards, he may not agree to take part, and that will seem odd."

"I hadn't thought of that," he admitted. "But Philip had it all organised. If he won't attend we can always say he's ill. It's not like he's going to tell anyone otherwise."

"You know, Max, I like your dad."

He gave a brief laugh, his eyes cold. "Yeah, most women do. Sinéad says it's his big sad eyes — they want to mother him."

"Maybe, but he doesn't behave like a womaniser. Even Beth jokes about him looking like a rabbit caught in headlights the first time she approached him."

"However he may 'appear' to you or Beth, Krystie, I have it in writing from his wife and sister-in-law *exactly* what kind of man he was. Perhaps he has changed but it doesn't absolve him of what he did to my mother."

"No, of course it doesn't." She reached for his hand. "I'm sorry. I'm not trying to upset you."

"I'm sorry, too. I suppose I'm a bit on edge." He glanced at his watch. "I should be making tracks. I want to shower and change before I pick up Sinéad and Sheila."

"Oh, shit, Sinéad! I forgot to tell you."

"What?"

She told him quickly about New York Fashion Week and he shook his head in disbelief before lifting her in his arms and swinging her round.

"You are one bloody incredible woman, Krystie Kelliher, do you know that?" He set her back on her feet and kissed her. "I love you."

She stared into his eyes, warmed by the tenderness she saw there. "And I love you, Max Fields, so very much."

"More than Jacob?" He watched her steadily.

"Who's Jacob?" she said and leaned in to kiss him.

He held her at bay. "That doesn't answer the question."

She sighed. "More than Jacob, Max. More than any man I have ever met. I love *you*, just you."

He kissed her again and groaned. "I wish I didn't have to leave you."

"Could I come with you and stay at the apartment? I'd like to be there when you got home — if you don't mind," she added uncertainly.

He raised an eyebrow. "Mind? I'm the one who wants you to move in, remember?"

She held his gaze. "Really?"

"Really."

"Then I'll tell Sharon tomorrow that I'm moving out at the weekend."

He kissed her long and hard. "You won't regret it, Krystie."

On the way to the apartment, Max called Sinéad on the hands-free phone. "Tell her the news, Krystie. It's exactly the lift that she needs before we confront Dad."

He was right of course, and Krystie grinned delightedly at him as Sinéad shrieked at the other end of the phone.

"I don't know what to say, Krystie," she said, her voice emotional. "This is amazing. How can I ever thank you?"

"You know I'm not sure how any of it works yet, Sinéad," Krystie warned, panicking. "We may only get five minutes on the runway —"

"On a *Manhattan* runway! Don't worry, Krystie, I'll take over now and I'll talk to Sheila about it. You can concentrate on designing."

"I will," Krystie laughed, but after they'd said goodbye she started to wonder where exactly she stood now that Sheila was back.

"You're very quiet," Max remarked.

"I was just thinking about work."

"There's no need to feel threatened by Sheila. She won't be coming back to work with Sinéad."

Krystie stared at him. How did he always seem to know what she was thinking? And then his words sank in. "Sheila's not coming back?"

"No, it turns out she never wanted to be a milliner. She just did it for Sinéad. Now she's doing what she loves most, painting, and she plans to make Manhattan her home."

"Oh, wow," Krystie said, surprised and relieved, too. "I never knew that she wanted to be an artist."

"No," he sighed, "neither did we."

"Are you sure you don't mind me leaving you to look after Karl?" Sheila asked Philip as he leaned against the door watching her get ready.

"Of course not. It will be a pleasure. He's a charming man. And it might do him good to get a break from you lot," he joked. "I can tell him the rest of the family secrets."

"That could take a while." She smiled. Any nervousness she had expected to feel with Philip had disappeared as soon as he'd opened the front door.

There was no doubting that he was happy to see her, despite the fact that her reappearance could cause huge upheaval in his life.

"So how did Max and Sinéad take the news about me?" he asked, trying and failing to sound nonchalant.

"It was a shock of course, but once they realised that I was okay with it and that we are still close friends they were happy."

"Your dad won't be."

"Who cares what he thinks?" she said, going to the walk-in wardrobe and putting on one of her favourite dresses. She came back out to him, smoothing it down over her hips. "Do me up?"

He pulled up the zipper and gave a low whistle. "You look good enough to eat — but are you not a little overdressed for a family punch-up?"

She grinned. "I don't care. I am so fed up wearing drab dreary clothes and trainers."

"Trainers?" Philip looked at her in horror.

"I know." She padded over to the closet and smiled at the rows of beautiful shoes. "You have no idea how much I've missed these." She slipped on a pair of black suede stilettos, walked to the full-length mirror and studied her image, frowning. "Maybe it is a bit much."

"No. Red for battle and height for intimidation. Show your father that you mean business."

She sat down on the bed. "Philip, you need to be careful. You can't let anyone know that you knew where I was all along. It could land you in really big trouble, and it would almost certainly end your career. I almost tripped myself up with Max but I got away with it.

Although I know I could trust him, I think he would be very upset if he thought that you knew I was alive all the time and never said anything."

He sat down beside her. "I hated it, Sheila, every moment of it, and, to be honest, there were times when I hated you for putting me in that position."

She put her hand on his arm. "I'm sorry."

He shook his head. "Don't apologise. I played my part, a big part, in tipping you over the edge and once you were gone I felt I owed it to you to support your decision. I'm just saying it was hard. Especially with Sinéad. You know I never really saw you as identical but after you were gone every time I looked at her . . ." He trailed off.

Sheila put her arms around him and rested her head on his shoulder. "I thought of you a lot. I worried about you."

"Yeah?"

She lifted her head and smiled. "Yeah."

"I'm sorry, Sheila," he said, tears in his eyes. "I never wanted to hurt you."

"I know that but it would have hurt me more in the long run, if you'd tried to live a lie. And it wouldn't have been a problem at all if I hadn't discovered all the family secrets the same day."

"Families, eh?" He sighed.

She looked at him. "Have you told them?"

"No way! Trust me, when I come out my folks will be the last ones to hear the news."

She looked into his eyes. "Are you sure that you're ready to come out?"

"No, but it is the perfect opportunity to make a fresh start."

"But it doesn't have to be a public one," she argued. "If we get an official separation and people see that it is amicable and that we're still good friends they will accept it and draw their own conclusions. It would be all more natural and low-key, wouldn't that be better?"

"It would certainly be easier but it doesn't seem fair to Jonathan."

"If he loves you he will want what's best for you." She held up her hands as he went to reply. "Sorry, it's none of my business. You do what you think is best, Philip, and I will support you."

He smiled. "I'm so happy that you've met someone too, Sheila."

"It's early days but, yes, I really like Zach; I think you will, too."

"I intend to spend dinner questioning Karl to make sure he's good enough for my very best friend."

"I have missed you, Philip." She hugged him.

"Me too, darling, especially your organisational and cooking skills."

"Typical." She stood up and straightened her skirt. "You must come and visit us in New York, both of you."

"We'll come for your first exhibition," he said with a grin.

"Ha! Don't hold your breath. But I can't begin to tell you how much I enjoy it. Once I pick up a brush I completely lose track of time."

"Have you broken the news to Sinéad that you don't plan to move home permanently?"

402

She shook her head. "No, but I think she's guessed."

The doorbell rang and she stiffened.

He looked at her, his eyes full of sympathy. "Are you ready for this?"

She straightened her shoulders and nodded. "Ready."

When they went downstairs Karl was in the hall with Max and she smiled at the similarities between the two men.

"You look ready for combat," her brother said.

"Believe me, I am."

"Give your dad my number, Sheila," Karl said. "I'd like to talk to him as soon as possible. He may be the only one who can shed any light on who my father was."

Sheila watched Max's expression darken as he turned slowly to face Karl. "I haven't told you everything that was in your mother's letter. Let's go and sit down."

Sheila stood, not sure what to do. "Will we wait here?"

Karl put his arm around her. "No, sweetheart, no more secrets," and they all followed Max into the sitting room.

They sat, but Max stood in front of the fireplace, with his hands behind his back and looking very uncomfortable. "I'm sorry, Karl, I really didn't want to tell you this. I'd hoped that after all this time you wouldn't care." He shook his head. "Stupid I know. But I couldn't let you waste your time looking for a boyfriend that never existed."

"Don't drag it out, Max," Sheila said, looking worriedly at Karl's pallor.

"No, please just tell me," Karl agreed quietly.

"Your mother was raped, Karl. She was on her way home one evening and she was raped. And she never even told anyone. She was so embarrassed and ashamed she said nothing. It was only when she realised that she was pregnant she told her parents, our grandparents, and they packed her off to her uncle in Boston."

Sheila put an arm around Karl's shoulders. "I'm so sorry."

"Thank you for telling me, Max. I can't say that possibility hadn't occurred to me. In a way it makes it easier for me to accept why she rejected me."

"She didn't reject you," Sheila said, taking his hand. "She rejected what happened to her and tried to forget it. I'm sure that I would have done the same in her position. You know she was never able to show affection or be comfortable in the company of men. Now I know why."

"But in more recent years she seemed content," Max told him, "and apparently did a lot of work in her community, particularly helping children who'd been bereaved or abused."

"And there was a huge turnout for her funeral," Philip added, "and people had nothing but good things to say."

"That's nice to know. Thank you."

Max looked at his watch. "I'm sorry to drop this bombshell and run, Karl, but we really should be going."

He stood up. "Of course. Good luck to you both. I hope it's not too difficult an evening."

Max put a hand on his shoulder. "I hope I haven't ruined your evening."

"Not at all, Max. Just like Sheila, I came to Dublin for answers."

When they went into the hall, Sheila kissed Philip's cheek. "Look after him for me," she murmured.

"I will. Good luck, Sheila. You too, Max."

Max turned to his brother-in-law and Sheila looked on stunned as her brother gave her husband a quick hug. "Thanks, Philip, for everything."

"What now?" Sinéad said from the back of the car, nervous now they were here. She'd chattered all the way here about the wonderful news from New York and the ideas she had for the collection. She owed Krystie so much, so very much. She couldn't believe what was happening. It was a dream come true. But now they sat in Max's car outside Dad's house and the reality of what they were about to do blotted out everything else.

"Maybe Sinéad, you and I should go in first and tell him what we've discovered and then come and get Sheila," Max said.

"What do you think?" Her sister turned to her, looking as nervous and uncertain as Sinéad felt.

"I think that's a good idea. The shock of seeing you might stop him from taking in anything we're saying. Max can tell him what he discovered today and I can confirm it and then we can tell him that's why you left and come and get you. Okay?"

"Yes, okay, but please don't take too long."

"We won't," Sinéad promised, squeezing her hand.

CHAPTER
THIRTY-SEVEN

Kieran sat staring at his two children, stunned at the coldness in their eyes and the hostility in their voices. His little fragile Sinéad was looking at him as if he were something she'd scraped off the bottom of her shoe. He thought of how, as a little girl, she used to look at him as if he were a god, how she had always been so loving and caring. How could she turn on him like this?

"Dad?"

He looked up into Max's expectant, judgemental eyes. "I can't believe that you would believe that of me. I adored your mother."

"Dad, she left a suicide note and Bridie confirmed everything. I have her letter right here. I'll read it to you if you want."

Kieran waved it away, feeling furious with his sister-in-law. "Stupid woman." He turned his eyes on Sinéad, imagining the scared little girl sitting by the window waiting for her mother to come back. "Why didn't you tell me what happened that night, sweetheart?"

"Bridie wouldn't let me. She thought it would be better if everyone presumed it was an accident."

"Ha, yes, well, that does make sense."

"What about the baby, Dad?" she asked.

"Baby!" He gave a bark of laughter at the ridiculous notion. "There was never any baby. Let me see this note your mother wrote."

He watched them exchange glances and then Sinéad said, "It's in the car."

"I'll get it," Max said.

"I can't believe you've felt like this all these years," he said when he was alone with his daughter. "Why would you even want me in your life if you thought me capable of that?"

She looked at him, her eyes dark with sadness. "I'd already lost one parent. I didn't want to lose the other. But when Sheila disappeared and Bridie died —" She stopped as they heard the front door close.

Kieran dropped his head in his hands. "I don't know what to say, I really don't."

"You could start with hello."

He lifted his head and gasped at the sight of Sheila standing in the doorway. He jumped to his feet and rushed to take her in his arms. "Oh, my darling girl, my darling girl. Oh, thank God you've come back to us." He realised that she was stiff as a board in his embrace but he didn't care. She was alive and she was standing in front of him. He stepped back to study her, not even bothering to wipe the tears from his cheeks. "Let me look at you. Oh, Sheila, you look wonderful. Welcome home, sweetheart, welcome home."

She pulled away and went to sit by her sister while Max sat on the arm of the sofa. "I believe you wanted to see this." She pulled an envelope from her bag, carefully removed a page and handed it to him.

He smiled broadly at her as he took it.

"You think this is funny?" she asked.

"Not at all, darling, but I don't care how angry you are with me. I don't mind if you hate me. You're alive and well and nothing else matters." He looked down at the letter in Maggie's untidy, practically illegible hand. "And how did you come by this?"

"I found it in Bridie's house along with the file about her son."

He nodded and started to read.

"You knew Bridie had had a child?" Max asked.

"I did." He continued to read his wife's desperate words, tears rolling down his cheeks. "Ah, Maggie, God love you."

"Is that all you've got to say?" Sheila said, incredulous. "You drove her to take her own life."

"I did no such thing," he protested, "but I suppose I can understand why you would think so after reading this."

"That and the fact that you don't seem surprised that Mum killed herself," Max said.

Kieran nodded: Max was a smart one. He stood up and walked to the door, feeling very tired and old.

"Where are you going? We're not finished, Dad, not by a long shot," Sheila called after him.

He closed his eyes at the anger in her voice. "I have something I want to show you. I'll be back in a minute." He went slowly upstairs, aware of their whispers. God, it hurt to see them turn against him like this but maybe it was no more than he deserved. He'd handed them over to Bridie and gone on with his life while she'd poured poison into their ears.

In his bedroom he pulled the chair over to the wardrobe, climbed up and felt around on top until he found his old briefcase. He took it down, blew off the dust and, sitting on the chair, opened it and pulled out a portfolio of documents. He hadn't looked at this stuff in years, he wasn't even sure why he'd kept it all. Perhaps he'd subconsciously realised this day would come. He flicked through the papers, selecting just a few to show them. There was no point in overwhelming them with all of it: they were upset enough. He put the pages in order, slid them into a folder and went back downstairs. They lapsed into silence when he walked in, looking up at him expectantly. "These will give you the other side of the story," he said, looking at each of them in turn. "It's not a happy story but it may be slightly easier for you to handle than the one you currently believe." He handed the file to Max. "I'll be in the garden if you want me."

It was bleak and cold outside but Kieran didn't care. The temperature inside had been worse. He lit a cigarette and wondered what Beth would think of him when she knew the full story. He didn't exactly come out of this looking like much of a parent or a man. Had he been a good husband? He wasn't even sure of that any more. Why had he gone along with all the secrecy? Why had he let Bridie rear his family knowing even then that she was a damaged woman? Maggie had been

410

diagnosed with mental illness but was Bridie any better? It sickened him that Sinéad had not only known of her mother's suicide but had been forced to stay silent about it. It was a miracle that she had turned out to be the wonderful young woman that she was today. Perhaps, though, he was as bad as Bridie. He had treated Sheila like an adult, allowing her to shoulder ridiculous responsibility simply because of her generous and sensible nature. It had been because he was terrified by Sinéad's fragility, that she would turn out like her mother and Sheila was so reliable and strong and good with her twin. His thoughts turned back to Bridie. Why had she written that pack of lies to Max? Was the stigma of mental illness still such an issue for her that she wanted to deny it even after her death? Or had she thought there must be some truth in the stories Maggie told? Had she suspected him of adultery? He supposed he would never know now.

It was Sinéad who came looking for him, throwing herself into his arms. "I'm sorry, Dad, I'm so sorry."

He tossed away his cigarette and stroked her hair. "It's okay, sweetheart, you weren't to know." He felt her shiver. "Let's get you back inside before you freeze."

When they walked into the sitting room the papers were strewn across the table and Max and Sheila were bent over them. She looked up, her eyes full of tears. "I'm sorry."

"Me too," Max said. "Why didn't you tell us?"

"Why would I? So you could wonder if you had inherited the madness?"

"What exactly was her illness?" Max pored over the medical notes. "It doesn't say."

"They had no real name for the episodes your mother experienced. It was some sort of personality disorder. She would fluctuate between bouts of depression, paranoia and joy. I'm not sure what they'd call it these days but —" he shrugged — "what difference does it make? It's just a name.

"But once she was taking the medication that suited her she was fine for long stretches and when she was she was such a wonderful mother to you and the loveliest wife a man could ask for. But then some darkness would grip her and she would change just like that." He clicked his fingers. "Sometimes because she hadn't taken her tablets but sometimes for no apparent reason. She'd be consumed with suspicion, watching me, listening when I was on the phone, going through my pockets. She was convinced that I was seeing other women, that I was going to leave her and there were even times that she thought that I was trying to kill her."

"Oh, Dad," Sheila said, her eyes full of sympathy.

"And she'd attempted suicide before?" Sinéad asked.

"She had," he admitted, hating that he had to tell them all this, hating the way Sinéad's voice trembled while Sheila sat as still and pale as a statue.

"Did Bridie know all this?" Max asked, waving a hand at all the doctors' reports and another suicide note he'd just found.

"Of course she did. But sure your grandparents had both her and your mother brainwashed. 'Don't tell anyone, never discuss it. If anyone asks, Maggie is just delicate.' Delicate!" He shook his head in disgust as he thought about how they had made his poor wife feel ashamed, as if her condition was her fault. "Bridie admitted that if she was having a 'turn', they wouldn't let her leave the house and locked her in her room if they had visitors. They were ashamed of her and petrified that people would think there was madness in their precious family."

"That's barbaric," Max exclaimed.

"Aye, it was that, son, but they were very odd people. I never took to them but they loved me. They never thought someone would take Maggie off their hands. It was beyond their wildest dreams that she became a respectable married woman. Bridie was better off in Boston though of course it didn't help, the way she left. Apparently they couldn't wait to get shot of her either, more shame on the family. That pair had a lot to answer for. I could never understand why your mother bothered to keep in touch with them."

"Was Mum okay when you met her?" Sheila asked.

He smiled as he thought of those early days when he'd fallen head over heels in love. "She was fine, sweetheart, but no thanks to them. One of her teachers knew something was wrong. She had a relative with a similar condition. She tried to talk to the parents but of course they would have none of it. God bless the woman, though, she took it upon herself to get Maggie help and once she'd seen a specialist and he had put her on medication she was fine." He chuckled. "When she first told me about the illness I didn't believe it, I couldn't. She was clever and funny and beautiful and saner than most, certainly than the pair of eejits who raised her."

"You must have got a shock the first time she got sick," Sinéad said.

He frowned as he thought back. "Not really. It was a gradual thing and her turns were brief and infrequent." He smiled at them. "She positively bloomed when she was pregnant. It was only really in the last three or four years of her life that it became serious."

Sheila looked at him, her eyes sad. "I wish you'd talked to us about her when we were kids, Dad. When she died you and Bridie never mentioned her. It was as if she hadn't existed."

He felt ashamed, knowing it was true. "I'm sorry but I couldn't talk about her without falling apart and I didn't think it was a good idea for you to witness that. I was a mess. I felt as if someone had ripped my heart out. I suppose I was so caught up in my own grief I didn't think about what you were going through. Selfish."

Sinéad's eyes were bright with tears. "It's nice to know that you loved her so much."

"I loved her more than life itself," he assured her.

"But in later years, Dad, why didn't you tell us about her health then?" Max asked. "You give out about Granny and Granddad keeping secrets but you did it too."

Kieran looked at him, shocked. "I did but not because I was ashamed of her, I just wanted to protect you. I didn't want you wondering if she killed herself. I wanted you to only have good memories of her."

"I don't understand why Bridie would have lied in the letter," Max said. "She could have said nothing and we'd be none the wiser. Why would she set you up like that?"

"I was wondering the same thing when I was out in the garden," Kieran told him. "The only thing I could come up with is that she thought there was no smoke without fire, that there was some truth in what Maggie told her." He looked at each of them in turn. "But on my oath, I was never unfaithful to your mother."

"I believe you," Sinéad said, coming to sit at his feet and resting her head against his knee.

"Thank you, sweetheart," he smiled down at her, glad to see the love in her eyes.

"I do too, Dad, and I have a different theory," Sheila said.

"What if Bridie read Mum's suicide note again recently and believed it to be true?"

Max stared at her. "That would make perfect sense."

"Oh my God, you're right," Sinéad agreed and looked up at him. "Dad?"

He shrugged. "Maybe, but does it matter why she did it? We'll never know for sure and I don't see any point in dwelling on it. What's important to me is that you three believe me. That's all I care about."

"We do," Max said, his eyes roaming over all the documents on the table.

"I'm sorry I let you down," Kieran continued. "If I'd been a better father Bridie wouldn't have had the control over you that she did. I let her keep you away from me and that was wrong. I was weak and selfish."

"Don't, Dad," Sheila begged when he could suppress his tears no longer. "We survived, didn't we? We're together again. Everything's going to be fine now."

He smiled at her through his tears. "You're amazing." He looked at each of his three children. "You're all bloody amazing, do you know that? I'm a lucky man and a very proud one." His eyes came to rest again on Sheila. "I can't believe that I've got you back. I have so many questions. I want to know everything that's happened since you left, everything."

"And I'll tell you," she promised, tearfully, "but can you wait until tomorrow? I don't know about the rest of you but I'm exhausted."

Sheila and Sinéad sent Max home to Krystie and shared a taxi. There was no longer any awkwardness or tension, just the silence of two people who knew each other well and were comfortable together. Sheila leaned her head against the window and stared blindly into the darkness. She had cried so much tonight and yet she knew there would be more tears. She could feel the vibration of Sinéad still shaking from the emotion of the evening and reached for her hand. There were rows and reproaches and recriminations still ahead, of course she knew that, but she also knew with certainty that they would come out the other side.

It was clear that she owed a lot to this girl, Krystie. How strange that she was the one to blow her cover but also the one who would become so pivotal to the family. Sheila couldn't wait to meet her and she prayed that she would love her as much as Sinéad and Max obviously did, and even Dad seemed to have fallen under her spell. Things were working out so much better than she could have hoped. In her mind she had cut her father off and never thought they would talk again, and now she had him back and he was completely redeemed in her eyes, in all of their eyes. Now she could put herself in his place and feel the incredible grief he must have felt at losing the love of his life so young. Because what was very clear tonight was that, despite her mother's moods and the outrageous things she'd accuse him of, he'd stuck with her because he loved her.

She wondered if Zach could ever feel that strongly about her or if Nancy had been the love of his life and was irreplaceable. That thought brought such pain that she moaned softly and Sinéad's grip automatically tightened. She closed her eyes, revelling in the fact that she had her sister back and there would come a day when they would once again share their worries. She relaxed back into the seat, and wondered how Philip and Karl were doing. They were both strong, confident men but both going through a tough time in their lives. For Karl it was a good outcome, she felt. It must hurt to know that he was the result of a rape but a comfort to know that Bridie did care and had never forgotten him.

Philip was a different matter. She knew well that people, family included, thought he was false but he was actually a sensitive soul, just a private person. And that was why she was worried that he suddenly wanted to announce to the world that he was gay and in love. She sensed that this was Jonathan's doing. He was a lot younger and probably wanted, maybe needed, Philip to make the grand gesture that Sheila was convinced was a mistake. She couldn't help smiling. Did she ever think, that night she walked in on him and Jonathan, that she would be worrying about their love life just months later?

But it was all thanks to Karl and Zach. Without them she would never have climbed out of that dark place and discovered the joy of going solo, realised that she could be happy again, happier than ever before.

She turned to Sinéad. "You realise that I'm not coming back."

Sinéad was silent for a moment, and when she spoke it was barely a whisper. "I know."

"It's not because I'm angry or upset with you, Sinéad. I just need to do what I was meant to do: I need to paint."

"I know," Sinéad said again.

Sheila wished she could see her sister's face. "Is it okay? Are we okay?"

Sinéad turned her face and Sheila could see the glisten of tears in her sister's eyes.

"It's okay, Sheila. I'll miss you but I'll be fine. Maybe I needed you to go, to find out I was strong enough to go it alone. But please don't ever walk out of my life again."

"Of course I won't, Sinéad, not now. To be honest I think being apart from you will bring us closer. I will be

418

so much happier doing what I love and —" she couldn't suppress her smile — "I've found a really special man."

"Oh, my God, Sheila, really?"

"I don't know if it will last but he makes me feel so good, Sinéad, and he makes me laugh."

"Laughing's good." Sinéad's smile flashed in the darkness. "Will I meet him when I come to Manhattan?"

"Damn right you will."

CHAPTER
THIRTY-EIGHT

There was a burst of applause as the last model strode down the catwalk. "Get out there, they're calling for you," Krystie hissed at her boss.

Sinéad didn't budge and Krystie thought she might have to smack her the way they did in the movies. "Sinéad, snap out of it, everyone's waiting." Krystie gave her a little push and Sinéad stumbled out of the wings. Immediately a model linked each of her arms and practically frogmarched her to the front of the stage, where Dylan stood whooping and cheering along with the glitterati of New York. Krystie clapped and cheered, tears flooding down her cheeks. Jeez, it didn't get much better than this.

Afterwards she changed her mind as she and Sinéad were congratulated and even hugged by people Krystie had only ever seen before on her TV set. Everyone loved them. Of course, it was false, it was temporary, it was a moment of limelight, and, when they returned to Dublin, life would continue much as before. Sheila had made it clear to them both that this was just a first step on a long road and that they'd have to work hard to win a permanent place on this particular stage and Krystie got that. Her years in Manhattan had taught her it was

420

an unforgiving business. But tonight was an acknowledgement, an appreciation and homage from the fashion world that they were good and it meant so much to her. She met Sinéad's eyes and saw that she was experiencing the same euphoria and they beamed at each other like two little kids.

Karl was throwing the after-show party and, as soon as they walked into the small restaurant he'd hired for the evening, the two of them were thronged, hugged and kissed. Krystie couldn't wipe the smile off her face but, despite the feeling of mild hysteria, she still took a moment to adjust Sinéad's headpiece when it was knocked sideways during an enthusiastic hug. Her boss grinned at her and mouthed thank you. Krystie felt a surge of pure happiness. My God, who would have thought when Phyllis kicked her out on her ass that she would end up here? And, speak of the devil, she smiled as she saw her old boss bearing down on her, arms wide.

"You designed that straw fedora, didn't you?" were the woman's first words when she released her.

Krystie laughed. "Yeah, how did you guess?"

The woman raised her eyebrows. "I had you pegged from day one, lady. Say, 'Thank you for firing me, Phyllis.'"

"Thank you for firing me, Phyllis," she said obediently, "and thanks for all the tips — they were great."

"Oh, please, I only wrote that email because Sandy was on my case, but I knew you didn't need it. Go with your gut, kid, and you'll never go wrong. You've got what it takes and your boss ain't half bad, either."

"That means a hell of a lot coming from you."

"Oh, save that crap for the clients," Phyllis retorted. "I'm happy for you, kid. Now point me toward the bar."

Krystie was watching her depart when she heard her name called again. "Sandy," she cried as her friend pounced on her. "I tried to call you earlier but I couldn't get through."

Sandy grinned. "That's because my cell was switched off. I was at the show with Phyllis."

"Oh, my God, you were there?" Krystie was amazed. It had been hard enough for Sinéad to get tickets for her family but she should have known better than to underestimate Phyllis.

"I'm so proud of you, Irish, you're a friggin' star!"

"That's a slight exaggeration, sweetie: we had twelve minutes and I only designed three of the hats."

Sandy put her hands on her hips and shook her head. "Did you even *hear* that applause? They loved you guys."

Krystie grinned. "They did, didn't they?"

"You've made it," Sandy assured her. "Now to more important matters. Where's Max?"

Krystie scanned the room and smiled as she spotted him. "There."

Sandy turned to check him out. "Oh, yeah, he's cute."

"Come on, I'll introduce you." Krystie led the way through the crowd to Max and made the introductions.

422

"Thank you so much for the ticket to Ireland," Sandy said, hugging him. "I can't wait. I've heard it's awesome."

"We're looking forward to showing you round," Max smiled.

"Krystie, come on, photographs."

She looked around to see Sinéad beckoning her towards the corner of the room, where Dylan and a fashion photographer were setting up. "Back soon." She kissed Max and then went to join her boss. Sheila was beside her, looking proud as punch, and when she saw Krystie she smiled broadly and hugged her. "Well done, Krystie. Tonight was a triumph."

"Thanks, Sheila." Though Sinéad's twin had been completely charming, Krystie had still felt uncomfortable around her. After all, she'd taken her place. But then last night, when they'd had dinner at Karl's and Krystie had seen some of Sheila's paintings there, she'd finally relaxed. It was clear that Sheila had been in the wrong job and was now doing something she adored. She was still going to help them out with the promotion of the business in America, but her days of designing hats were over. She was glad to hand over the reins and Krystie was thrilled to take them.

The three of them had decided to wear black tonight with three identical headpieces, but in different colours trimmed with a black veil. Sheila wore blue, Sinéad green and Krystie was pleased with the red, which looked good against her dark hair, which she had pulled back into a tight ponytail. They posed for the photos amid much laughter, the photographer moving them into different positions and taking shots from different angles.

"This one's a winner," he said and they came to look at the display. It was a shot of Krystie staring straight ahead, a twin either side with their backs to her and their faces turned to stare into the lens. There was no doubt it was a great photo and it showed off the headpieces beautifully. He nodded again, smiling. "This will end up on the cover of a fashion magazine, I feel it in my gut."

They looked at each other in astonishment. "Do you think he means it?" Krystie whispered.

"Karl and Dylan say he's very well respected in the fashion industry," Sinéad said, "but who knows?"

Krystie started to smile as she spotted something over her boss's shoulder. "Tell me, Sheila, is Karl married?"

"No, divorced, why?"

"Because my ex-boss is chatting him up big time."

Sheila turned to take a look and laughed. "He seems to be enjoying it and she's an attractive woman."

"She's a ball breaker but kind with it." Krystie saw Sheila's eyes drift away and when she followed her gaze she spotted Zach pushing his way through the crowd towards them.

"Excuse me." Sheila went to meet him.

"Your sister seems pretty smitten, too," Krystie said to Sinéad.

"Who could blame her? Zach's drop-dead gorgeous, isn't he?"

"Nearly as gorgeous as your brother," Krystie laughed, searching out Max in the crowd. He and

424

Sandy were now chatting with Kieran and Beth. She turned back to her boss. "Are you happy with the way everything went, Sinéad?"

"Am I happy?" Sinéad shook her head in wonder and gestured around at the room full of glamorous people, all there to celebrate the success of her company. "I'm in seventh heaven."

Krystie smiled. "I keep expecting to wake up."

"I know what you mean. Sitting in the studio making hats will seem very dull next week."

"Are you kidding? I can't wait," Krystie exclaimed. "I got some great ideas at the show."

"Me too!" Sinéad admitted. "You know, I think we make a damn good team."

"I can't tell you how grateful I am that you gave me this chance."

"I'm very glad I did, Krystie. We wouldn't be in Manhattan if it wasn't for you." Sinéad held up her glass. "To the future."

"The future." Krystie smiled. "Oh, I should phone home and let them know how it went, Sharon too."

"They'll be fast asleep," Sinéad reminded her. "Text them the good news and tell them you'll phone them tomorrow."

"Good thinking."

Zach went to get them drinks and Sheila watched her sister and Krystie and was relieved that she didn't feel even the slightest trace of jealousy. She was happy for Krystie and she and her twin were probably closer than they had been since they were children. Everything would be just fine if it wasn't for Dad. She looked across the room at him now. This had been the first time they'd met since she'd left Ireland. She'd offered to pick him up at the airport, but he'd refused. Karl had invited him to stay with them but he said he didn't want to be a burden and would prefer to stay in a hotel. And since he'd walked in this evening he had done his damnedest to avoid her, and when they were in the same group he'd ignored her. It was really getting to her and she couldn't understand why he was treating her like this. She knew he was upset over the breakdown of her marriage, but it was hardly her fault that her husband had turned out to be gay. She wanted to talk to Sinéad about it, but how could she bother her twin tonight of all nights?

She saw that Max was momentarily alone and, diving into the crowd, she inched her way to his side.

"Hey," he said, smiling down at her. "Great night, isn't it?"

"Terrific. Max, do you know why Dad is annoyed with me?"

Max sighed. "He's not annoyed, he's confused. You've only yourself to blame, Sheila. You need to stop trying to protect people."

She stared at him. "What does that even mean? What have I done wrong?"

"Nothing. That's the problem. Philip took your advice and he's one hell of an actor. When he gives interviews all he talks about are his campaigns, and then he throws in a line about how much he misses you but that sometimes you have to accept that things just don't work out the way that you want them to. So Dad's convinced that he wants you back and you are the one that won't give the marriage another chance."

"But that's ludicrous."

"Try telling Dad that."

"And Philip isn't acting, Max. He is passionate about his work and we do care about each other and miss each other. I'm delighted he heeded me. You know that if he had made a grand confession it would have ruined his career. He worked hard to get elected, Max — you really have no idea — and he could make a difference. The last thing the country needs is to lose a damn good politician over something so petty."

Max held up a hand. "You're preaching to the converted, Sheila, but you need to tell Dad, and this time without any sugar coating."

He was right. She *had* been overprotective with her father, still feeling guilty for putting him through so much over the last few months. She would have to make it very clear to him that she and Philip would eventually divorce and that she would never return to live in Dublin. She was happy in Manhattan, painting and spending time with Zach. She loved him and was pretty sure he loved her too. He had been single for so long that she knew he wouldn't have entered into another relationship unless he was serious.

"I'll talk to him," she promised Max.

She watched him cross the room to join Karl and Krystie's ex-boss. It was nice to see her cousin enjoying himself. She still sensed a deep sadness in him but she supposed it was bound to take time for him to accept the circumstances of his birth. But, now that he had family in Ireland, he was planning to spend more time there and was even thinking of buying a place there.

Sheila found it hard to feel the anger at Bridie that she had when she first heard Sinéad's story. She had been raped when she was only a child and then sent away at probably the scariest time in her life; was it any wonder that she had turned out the way she did?

And she was so glad that all the things she'd accused Dad of had turned out to be just lies. Sheila had felt like an orphan since the night she'd read her mother's suicide note. Of course, it was heartbreaking to learn of their mother's illness but a relief to know that her misery and death had not been her father's fault.

The family should be closer than ever tonight after the trauma they'd been through together, and Sheila hated that her father was being so cool with her. Max was right. She would have to sort it before he went back to Ireland.

"It's been a good night."

She looked up in surprise to see the man himself beside her. She smiled. "It has." His expression was grim and his tone clipped, but he had made the first move in coming over, and her heart lifted. That wouldn't have been easy for him.

He nodded towards Sinéad and Krystie, still surrounded by well-wishers. "No regrets?"

She knew he meant a hell of a lot more than her change of career and she turned to look him straight in the eye. "None at all, Dad."

He sighed. "Look, sweetheart, I know that it's been a tough time but there's not much chance of you and Philip sorting things out if you're not even in the same country."

"There is nothing to sort out," she said gently. "Our marriage is over. Philip is gay."

"He wasn't gay when he married you," he retorted. "I'm not excusing the man, what he did was wrong. But try to forgive him, sweetheart. If you saw him and heard the way he talks about you then you would realise that he still loves you."

"I know that and I love him, too, but only as a very good friend. That's all we ever were, Dad, I can admit that now. I was never in love with him and he was trying to live the life his parents expected of him. And the only reason he's saying all those nice things is because I persuaded him to."

He frowned. "I don't understand."

"I didn't want him to come out publicly. I didn't want people judging him and whispering about him cheating on his poor innocent wife. None of that's true, but that's what people would think. His parents would denounce him, as would many of the more conservative among his supporters, and that would be so unfair. Philip is a good man and he cares; he cares so much. So I begged him not to make any grand gestures but to just let life take its course. He's basically a very honest person, so that doesn't come easy, believe me. But the more that we talked about it the more he realised that he wouldn't be able to achieve any of his goals or deliver on his campaign promises if he lost his seat, and so he agreed to handle things my way."

Her father said nothing for a moment and then nodded towards the other side of the room. "Is that the truth, or is he the real reason you left Philip?"

Sheila looked over and saw that it was Zach he was glaring at. She hadn't flaunted their relationship but she hadn't hidden it, either, thinking that Dad would have accepted that her marriage was over. In hindsight she had been naive. Too much had happened in a very short space of time, far too much to take in. She could have handled things better.

"Zach has nothing to do with my marriage failing, Dad, honestly. Whether I met him or not, my marriage would still be over. Tell me, do you remember what you said the night I came back, Dad?"

"What?" he said, his voice gruff.

"You said you didn't care about anything. All that was important was that I was alive."

"I should have known you'd throw that back in my face."

She smiled and kissed his cheek. "Dad, I'm alive and I'm happy. Happier than I have been in a very long time. And Philip is, too, and I'm glad for him. I'm very fond of Zach and I know you will be, too, once you get to know him, but I'm not about to rush into anything. We're still getting to know each other."

"I'm glad that you still have at least some sense," he retorted.

"It's a good night, Dad. We're all together — and just look at Sinéad, she's glowing!"

430